GRUMBLE'S STAR

~

BLAIR MacKENZIE BLAKE

CONTENTS

"Secrets there are none, but that buried
in the shadow of man's soul."

- Liber Mysteriorum Quintus

CHAPTER I
SPOTSYLVANIA

"Head's pretty far down a rabbit hole, I reckon – just a yonder away from this declivity," a square-set fellow with a raspy southern accent said while pointing an ivory-knobbed cane towards a stand of oaks shrouded in drifts of mist. "If it's that woolly black thing you're chasing after. The dickens nearabout spilled tureens of pigeon soup on my darling Isabella's serving platter in its haste, dash it all," he uttered while tapping the fancy walking-stick on the sodden ground to punctuate his vexation.

"Sorry, it bolted," I said.

"Did it ever."

Wearing a dark green frockcoat with trim that matched his mulberry scarf, the man limped towards me while rolling a minie ball with the thumb of his other hand. Spitting a missile of tobacco juice from the quid tucked in a cheek, his ruddy complexion was all but obscured by bristling grey muttonchops. As a light sprinkle of rain pattered on his felt topper, he paused on the muddy path that twisted through the wildflowers and fixed a steely gaze on me.

"Pardon my asking, but you wouldn't be a shirker, would you? Looking for the rest of that no-account Company Q, seeing how you showed up for the melee without a musketoon as well as without hand-stitched fabric. You could have at least put on some butternut browns to maintain the illusion."

While taking a tentative step down the incline in his colt skin shoes, hazy sunbeams poked through patches of clouds, glinting on the enamel hunting charms that adorned his bistre vest. Nodding my approval of these masculine frills, I squeezed past him and clambered up the grassy slope towards the indistinct clump of trees.

"Got something against the clash of sabers?" I heard him ask before expelling more chew.

When I entered a small clearing in the patch of woods, I saw that dozens of onlookers had gathered at the opposite edge of the tree line to watch the spectacle from the hilly vantage point. Some were seated on paisley quilts with opened wicker baskets.

Ladies in bustled skirts held glistening parasols while nibbling picnic fare from scalloped china. With their rosy cheeks framed by lace bonnets, many appeared doll-like in the forest's amber glints. Standing alongside them were stylishly attired men with heavy sets of side-whiskers, some of who chomped on soggy cigars in the fine drizzle mist while fiddling with their silk cravats.

Taken by the dreamlike quality of the scene, I almost forgot about finding Golliwog.

"There's that bouncing mop," a southern gentleman said while playing dominoes. "Will someone give the inky gallnipper a sliver of boiled ham?"

As the shaggy Puli hurried towards me, panting from chasing the rabbit, she nipped the heel of a stoutly built figure as he peered into luxury opera glasses.

"They're opening the ball!" he shouted excitedly with his eyes still pressed to the glasses. "Let 'er rip, farbs and all. This ain't no punkin' chuckin', my fellow Virginians."

"Going to rattle the salt cellars," said another. "And I was just about to use the necessary."

As the buzzing strokes of snare drums echoed in the distance, a couple of women stepped forward in billowy crinoline hoops. Anticipating what was about to happen, they clapped softly with elbow-length, ivory crochet gloves.

"Take a Kodak of 'em peacockin' about," a lady with a husky voice said while untying a ribbon from a finger sandwich.

Curious to see their view, I carried the dog to where some of the others had assembled and looked down at the grass field in the small valley below. As if right on cue, the light shower let up and wisps of fog dissipated in the bleak sunlight.

A star shell burst overhead, drawing cheers from those watching. The hoisting of colorful flags and sound of thunderous drum commands followed the brightly burning flare. With this signal, hundreds of entrenched Confederate soldiers stood up in the uniforms of their infantry regiments and advanced in tight ranks. At the same instant, an equal number of Federal troops tromped from the dense tree line on the opposite side of the open plain. With the peal of bugles, the formations approached each other with ear-piercing shrieks and deep-throated shouts. Incessant sharp cracks of small arms fire, the galloping of mounted horses and rumble of cannons that belched bluish puffs of smoke added to the dreadful battle chorus.

As the infantry columns engaged in close range fire, war cries muffled the rattle of snare rolls and shrill of fifes. Through sheets of acrid smoke, the frontal assaults continued until many of the combatants on both sides were fighting at arms length. Amid the deafening volley of rifled-muskets and mortar-fired explosives, field-musicians set down their instruments to become stretcher-bearers. In the sheer chaos, they stepped over the agony of the dying while loading the moaning and twitching wounded into ambulance wagons.

The constant popping of muzzle-loaders began to agitate Golliwog. When her shaggy black cords started to shiver, I whispered into an ear, "It's just Hollywood shit."

Behind the soldiers' encampments surrounding the mock battlefield, authentic replicas of sutler carts and covered supply wagons were parked next to rows of yellow school buses, pickups and gleaming horse trailers. In the bustling activity at the reenactment site, I could see crowded spectator stands, hot dog vendors, carnival rides, living history exhibits such as traveling blacksmith forges, cotton candy booths and military impersonators posing for photos under red tent canopies with Coca-Cola logos. Some of the attendees came in the style of hardcore preservationists while others viewing the historical attractions wore modern civilian attire.

As I continued to watch the bloodless carnage that was described in gory detail by a narrator over loudspeakers in the multi-tiered bleachers, some of the women near me began coughing as wafts of discharged Pyrodex cartridges that smelled like the burning coal of potbelly stoves pervaded the wooded ridge.

"Stick with Olde Eynsford, rebels!" the guy standing next to me yelled while sinking his fork into a wedge of rhubarb pie that crumbled on the painted china plate.

"Never call them rebels, my good sir," rang a voice in the crowd.

With shrill warning barks, the puli lifted a paw as an immense shadow blotted out the captive audience watching the skirmish lines from the sun-dappled mezzanine. The spreading darkness was cast by something that skirted the treetops while floating directly overhead.

As I peered through gaps in the foliage, my first thought was that the ponderous vessel was a blimp like those that appeared at sporting events. However, I quickly realized that its unusual proportions and bristling appendages closer resembled an aluminum-skinned dirigible or one of those fanciful old-fashioned airships that emblazoned the covers of vintage pulp magazines.

When it turned with a graceful curve, I could see lateral structures that projected from its oblong frame. These and an array of mechanized fin-like protrusions were constructed of a flexible metallic material that flapped in tandem in some biomimetic process. Near the aft fishtail rudder was a boiler stokehold for steam-powered blades. As these brass screws rotated beneath the floating hull, a rhythmical hissing sound could be heard over the tumult of the ensuing conflict.

With its expansive ribbed protrusions, globular carriage attached to the main frame by ornamental iron girders and clockwork propelling machinery, I couldn't understand why those gathered at the edge of the clearing didn't appear to be amused by what was obviously an elaborate prank.

"Jee-whillikins! I am deceived by my optics of a queer sight on this valorous morn," uttered the man with the lorgnette. "What kind of aerial maverick wanders over our leisurely outing?"

"What is in these drinkables is a better question?" asked another as he sprayed the lemonade from a frosted tumbler into a patch of violets. "Something stronger than creek water, I surely suspect."

A black girl wearing a gingham skirt and a servant's turban removed a Samsung tablet from her apron and held it up so that the airship was framed on its touchscreen.

"Why are you looking at it through the devil's window, child?" a pretty face with carmine-tinted lips asked.

As the aerial curiosity maneuvered into position, some in the crowd began pointing excitedly to a figure that could be seen pulling levers and peering at gauges in copper fittings while standing behind a nautical steering apparatus in the gondola. Wearing a black bowler and goggles, the pilot was garbed in a leather tailcoat adorned with brassy utilities. Like the retro-futuristic appearance of the various engine controls, the techno peripheries on his gauntlets were analogous to the steampunk twist.

Even odder than the pilot's flying outfit was that I could see details (such as his facial expressions) with startling clarity. It was as if my vision had somehow been greatly enhanced, though I couldn't figure out what might account for this, or why the curious optical effect only pertained to the operator of the hulking airship.

If it wasn't someone's idea of a joke (the peculiar visual boost had caused me to question my initial take), what was the purpose of some marvelous aerial steamer in a scripted Civil War battle portrayal? The jumble of cog wheels and tumbling rods, sprocket teeth and helical gears was more like the creation of an artist sculpting with industrial scraps than a period prototype of some flying contraption built in secrecy by a mechanical genius.

As the airship leveled off before gliding over canvas shelters, on the back of its carriage I could see painted in the decorative typeface of an old circus poster the name:

DR. R. FINLEY HUNT
RICHMOND, VIRGINIA

"Surely, I hope the operator of this cloud-borne perplexity tosses rotten eggs on the Billy Yanks," the man that I encountered on the path said with a twist of tobacco still in his bulging jaw. "Better, yet, the captain lucifers sticks of dynamite with the bang of a hundred sparked Howitzers."

A field artillery crew was the first to become engulfed in shadow. Surprisingly, rather than being stricken with terror by the winged behemoth as it descended, the Union soldiers continued to work in unison with sponge and projectile rammers before a friction primer was inserted into the breech. As a portly Sergeant wearing a soiled kepi was about to pull the lanyard, he 'took a hit' that caused him to lurch backwards and collapse near a two-wheeled limber. Though I'm sure those reenactors who followed the guidebook appreciated his etiquette, I was baffled as to how he could close his eyes and realistically play dead at the very moment the imposing structure sailed overhead.

Making a low-level sweep over the billowing smoke that arose from the mock engagement, the pilot of the airship turned a screw valve that released from the gondola what looked like a primitive torpedo onto the advancing blue forces. There was a blinding flash that caused a mad scramble from some of those around me.

Golliwog snarled at the swishing noise made by cumbersome drapery as women with coiffed bouffants ducked under drooping tree limbs.

While stepping on gilded plates of jelly tarts and cream puffs spread out on a luncheon blanket, a mustached fellow pulled a half-pint bottle of peach schnapps from a pocket of his waistcoat and took a healthy swig. As he did so, a lady wearing a damask bodice looked him squarely in the eye.

"If you must take a drop of the creature," she snapped with a southern twang, "kindly keep it in a proper tin flask. After all, we are supposed to be progressives, are we not... and the same goes for that Hokies tee shirt beneath your muslin. As we learned in training school, neither are reverented. If you do so again, dear, I shall give you a sockdolager like the mysterious conqueror just did to those Federal scallywags."

"The only reason I'm letting you talk to him is because you're still young and I don't want you to make the same mistake and throw your life away like he did," a middle-aged woman said as I followed her into the living room of a single-family home near Spotsylvania's Lake Wilderness area. Wearing denim paperbag shorts and a white V-Neck tank, she led me through a messy kitchen and down a narrow wood-paneled hallway. "But it's nice of you to bring him an iced-tea. I could have made him some Lipton, but he has a thing for theirs."

"Glad to bring it – their tea slaps," I said.

"I hope you don't waste an entire lifetime like Dad did on what is clearly a hoax," she continued. "It sounds trite, but before he became obsessed with finding the treasure, he had a good job and loving wife. They lived in a nice house with a big yard. Now he doesn't have a pot to piss in and has to stay in my converted garage. Spent all that money on a backhoe only to have it blown up by dynamite. Lucky he didn't kill himself – the only time he's had any luck with this, actually. There have been many others that let those damn 23 pages ruin their lives, too. All of them on the same wild goose chase with nothing but dead ends or scraps of rusty pig iron. At least he read some Shakespeare while look-ing for another source document… you know, the key. No, the only vault he'll ever find is his own grave buried six feet deep… just like the hoard is supposed to be."

"Yeah, I've heard all that before – the historical problems, but why would someone go to so much effort for a fake? And why is the government so interested if it's all a hoax? Have you seen all the NSA documents that were released?"

"I'd imagine they're keeping track of people just in case something else is found with all the trespassing. Things like Civil War artifacts dug up on state and federal land. They don't want people to keep what belongs to the government. With what you do, Jack, you know the laws."

Before we entered the garage, she turned to face me.

"These days he just rambles. Nothing he says will make any sense. I doubt he can answer your question."

When we entered the garage, her elderly father was seated in a dingy recliner in front of a card table that was cluttered with maps. Wearing a tan BLUE RIDGE MTNS trucker hat that was too big for his head, he had a scraggly white beard and wraparound sunglasses on a sunburnt face.

"Hello sir," I said while handing him the cup of iced tea that he wanted. "I'm Jack and I'm on the same wild goose chase."

"Did you notice they dropped the apostrophe?" he asked.

"No, I didn't," I replied, confused by the question. "You think that's a possible clue?"

"Bojangles did away with it without saying a word. Wasn't necessary, I guess, but their iced tea is still legendary."

"How are your itchy toes?" his daughter asked.

"That tough actin' Tinactin really works."

"I'm planning on hiring a handyman to put in a window," she said to me. "And maybe lay down some carpet. He has a fold-out cot with a comfy mattress I got on Amazon."

"You're looking for answers," the old man said after taking a gulp from the cup of Bojangles iced tea. "Don't try to fix anything. Everything you need is right there in the papers. Any mistakes were done on purpose."

"Have you searched the Black Horse Gap... searched it thoroughly?" I asked.

"It's not there. The location of the cube is inside a triangular letter. When I get myself a proper boat I'll search this Daleth for what's hidden away. What it contains is not to be believed. Like everyone, you look at numbers to be replaced by letters. But what's not there is just as important. Look for what you don't or can't see on the numeric grid. Yeah, Bojangles got rid of the apostrophe."

"I told you, Jack," his daughter said.

"Well thanks for your time, sir. My dog is in the pickup, so I'll let you get back to it."

A debonair fellow in a town coat helped a woman in a voluminous hoopskirt get out of a stylish Victorian buggy that was parked in front of Sharpshooters Bar & Grille. Although the simulated battle maneuvers had ended, the couple was still acting out their civilian impressions in the rustic setting of one of Spotsylvania's most popular hangouts.

Known for their authentic peanut soup recipe and great selection of beers on tap, I had stopped by the dog-friendly alehouse for a burger and draft Bud, unable as I was to afford any entrée that came with a bowl of consommé beef topped with craft pilsner and goober froth like those with BMWs in their garage could. Not yet, that is, though I was hoping things would soon change.

After having a crochet shawl placed over her shoulders, the prim and proper southern belle nearly dragged the silk taffeta cascade over a fresh pile of horse droppings that were speckled with flies.

"Watch old Nell's road apples, my darling," the man gestured to the moist greenish clumps before she concealed her blush with a decorative hand fan.

Walls in the brick-accented taproom contained dusty Civil War-era artifacts that hung alongside projection screens that were all showing a Nationals baseball game. Passing a couple of ladies in frothy chiffon who were sneaking a Marlboro, I carried Golliwog through the open back doors and set her down in the sunny beer garden that was paved with gravel and shaded by potted trees. The communal benches were filled with participants in the staged battle, so I found a rough-hewn table and sat down on a tree stump stool that was veined with moss.

As a local bluegrass band played patriotic Civil War songs of both sides, I noticed that many of those singing along were what the stitch counter types referred to as "polyester soldiers", meaning, rather than a bedraggled lot with gaunt faces and lice-infested, uncombed hair beneath rumpled forage caps, they were tubby, clean-shaven fellows with Oakley sunglasses and unsullied kepis. Wearing brown tennis shoes and wedding bands, they shared bratwurst platters and drank an assortment of micro-brews. Gathered among these mainstream reenactors were a few progressives in authentic uniforms (right down to period-correct underwear, I would bet), tapping their muddy brogans to the fast tempo of banjo, fiddle and lap steel.

A waitress in a period twill skirt and ruffled blouse arrived at the table and placed a bowl of water on the ground. As she and another female server went on about how cute Golliwog was, petting her dark matted strings with their lacy gloves, I noticed the black guy sitting nearby seemed to be having trouble reaching for his glass of orange juice. While groping for it, he knocked it over; its contents pooling on the paper table mat. Thinking he might be having a seizure, I jumped up and hurried over to see if there was anything I could do.

When I asked if he needed help, there was no response. Unable to speak, his face was contorted in a painful expression as he repeatedly attempted to grasp something in the pocket of his windbreaker. Finally, he managed to pull out one of those wrapped apple pie snacks like you see in convenience stores, but was having difficulty unwrapping it with his stiff fingers.

As the servers looked on with alarmed expressions, I ripped open the waxed green wrapper and eased the thing into his mouth. Slowly, he began to lick the sugary glaze on the crust before swallowing some of the goopy apple filling.

Two soldiers rushed over to help out. Both had stubble on their grimy faces and strong body odor (living history!). One was wearing a dark indigo-blue uniform with tarred white gaiters that crunched the shiny gravel, while the other was dressed in a gray coat with baggy trousers from which a cavalry sword scabbard hung. His officer's slouch hat was folded on the left side at the brim, with a dark grosgrain ribbon on the right. Each of them appeared to be sticklers for detail, with treasured brass insignias that were probably correct for 1864, but not for 1865.

"Reckon his catalepsy's from the honey piss?" the Union soldier with the epaulettes of a major asked the Confederate in a voice that could be heard over the Dixie banjo picking.

"Might be a low blood sugar attack," the cavalry officer agreed while helping me gently push the processed junk further into his gnashing teeth, being careful so that he didn't choke. "The high fructose in this shit is as good as glucose."

When the guy started to come around, I asked him what his name was.

"Pye," he mumbled, still a bit woozy. "Pye."

"You need some more pie?" I asked while glancing up at the waitresses.

"No… no, that's my name," he grimaced. "Jeremy Pye. I've got this condition that sometimes gets me a little muddled because I didn't have anything to eat."

"Are you in need of some vittles?" the Confederate asked, quickly falling back into character. "Their Johnny Reb flank steak isn't half bad."

"Neither is the Yankee Pot Roast," the major from the Northern army was quick to add.

"No… thanks… thanks, but I already ordered a burger," Jeremy said while picking up a napkin to clean his face.

He looked to be in his mid-twenties, was smooth-faced and had short natural hair. There was sadness in his brown eyes, but perhaps they were still glazed over from the hypo attack.

"Your food's coming right out," the waitress said while sopping up the spilled juice.

"For a minute I thought we were going to have to cart you to the field hospital to have a leg sawed off, seeing how your fingers were fumbling to get the remedy," the major chuckled gruffly. "You're still having a better day than I had. Though I managed not to get stung by grapeshot… or these people's hard tack, for that matter, some yellow jackets did me right good through my under drawers."

"And I'm sure that burger beats the stuff in our battalion cook's kettle," the rebel cavalry officer joked.

"Were you able to galvanize, sir, you could have sampled our tasty slumgullion," his counterpart teased. "By the way, is that Hardee of yours Tuscaloosa gray?"

"Richmond," the southerner sneered at the perceived slight.

"Well, you take care, my friend," the Confederate patted Jeremy on the back.

"Who won this time?" Jeremy asked.

"Inconclusive," was the reply in unison.

"Even with that cray airship dropping bombs on the blue guys?" I asked.

"Why there was nothing of the sort," the major said with a puzzled look.

"Are you talking about that damned helicopter that was buzzing about taking photos for the sponsors?" the other asked.

"Neither of you noticed a gianormous airship flying over the battlefield?" I asked with an incredulous expression. "Or trenches lit by the mother of all pyrotechnics?"

"I think he's suggesting one of the ironclads sprouted wings," the major laughed. "Seems as if someone's made too many visits to the hard cider booth," he joked to the Confederate officer as they headed back to their fellow preservationists seated at the communal benches.

"Here, Golliwog," I motioned for the dog to join me at Jeremy's table.

"The dog's name is Golliwog?" Jeremy asked while pointing to his ear as if he wasn't sure that he heard me correctly over the music.

"Yeah, it's my grilf's puli. That's what she named her. Not sure why, though. Maybe after one of those Muppets?"

"So, then you don't know what a golliwog is?"

He typed the name into an early model smartphone in a scuffed cloth case and brought up a gallery of images on Pinterest. The photos showed creepy-looking dolls that had round black fabric faces, big white pop eyes, red clown lips and unruly frizzy black hair. They were dressed in striped minstrel suits with floppy bow ties. Looking at the pinboards of what some labeled as being obvious 'darky' caricatures, my first thought was, 'Did Merrily know about these things?' The similarity of their

18

woolly hair and the dog's black coat made it clear that it wasn't just a fluke. Knowing how touchy people were these days, she could have at least told me in order to avoid any situations like this. I didn't know if this guy was going to get in my face about being a racist or be chill, but guessed he wouldn't get too salty if he believed me when I told him that my bowling alley didn't have white balls and black pins.

"Sorry, dude, we didn't know about these things."

"Don't get shook, man. Why be sorry?" he smiled. "She's more dreads than dog. Your girlfriend snatched it. Better than Woggie."

"Yeah, I guess so," I nodded. "Marley would have been even better."

"So, who just saved my bacon?" he reached out to shake my hand.

"I'm Jack."

"Super ruling, Jack. With the pie."

"What are these fuzzy clowns anyway?" I asked while pointing to the images.

"They were characters in children's Toyland books that became popular dolls in Europe in the late nineteenth century... like Teddy Bears later became here. They used to sell them as antiques online before people began to raise a fuss."

A server arrived with Jeremy's order.

"I'd like to get a burger, too," I said while pointing to the Farb Burger on the menu, "with nothing on it so I can give a piece to the dog –"

"For little Golliwog here," Jeremy's white teeth flashed as he emphasized the name.

"With waffle fries and a Bud instead of all those fruity craft suds," I quickly added.

"And no dessert for me," Jeremy laughed while gesturing to the empty pie wrapper.

"No yummy cannonball?" The waitress gave him a funny frown before pirouetting in her billowy layers.

"I can't believe those guys playing soldier didn't see the airship," I said. "Because of its mammoth size, you couldn't miss it."

"You were serious about seeing that thing? I thought you were talking about one of those dinky yellow balloons that advertise for Ikea."

"No, this was a mechanical throw-back, is the best I can describe it. It didn't make sense... but a bunch of us at the Belvedere Plantation saw it. Flown by a madcap pilot. Hunt, or something was painted on the back... a doctor from Richmond."

"Robert Finley Hunt, the dentist?" Jeremy's eyes widened.

"Yeah, I think that was the name. How'd you know?"

Once again, Jeremy Googled a name.

"I read about this a while back. Someone in a rare bookshop found plans for a steam-driven flying machine dated 1863 stuck inside a book. It was supposed to be used to drop bombs on the Union troops, but the inventor couldn't get any financial backing because of all the design flaws and such. Like it says here, 'so obvious on reflection that no discussion is required.' But that was back in 1863. Could some engineer today use the sketches – they were auctioned off – to get the damn thing off the ground? It would be a costly undertaking for a reenactment stunt, though some of these people spend crazy amounts for realism. Take classes and shit. You don't have any receipts? No one took a photo?"

"These people were playing along with the others. They talked and dressed funny... didn't carry iPhones... and I was too blown away by the whole scene to think about pulling out mine. Just this one guy had a wooden box that might have been a camera, but it probably didn't work."

"If it wasn't a prank, the other explanation would be that you accidently stepped through a portal into another dimension," he said with a straight face, "where the good doctor's airship was developed and used as a wonder weapon against the northerners. This caused a totally different outcome to the war, which means – in that alternate universe – the cuddly blackface playthings are readily available and smiling little Golli is still used as the Robinson's jam mascot."

"Jam mascot? You mean, like strawberry jam?" I asked.

"That and plum. Golly it's good," he said in a silly high-pitched voice. "You didn't happen to get your passport stamped in this analogous world, did you?"

"What are you, Jeremy, some kind of brainiac that knows all about airship oddities, parallel universes and freakin' golliwogs?"

"I don't want to get too dumbed down in this age of Twitter attention spans. Thing is, Jack, I just like learning about stuff like that. Rarities and collector's items. Things of interest, but especially early printed matter, being that I'm a wannabe antiquarian bookseller. Mostly working out of my van... and my aunt's antique shop. I comb through flea markets and local estate sales, looking for anything of value."

"I'm a wannabe treasure hunter, myself, searching for the Beale horde."

"You're a Bealiever, no kidding. I wouldn't have thought. You know, I once found an original fifty-cent pamphlet of the Beale Papers from 1885 at a yard sale in Lynchburg. Researchers have clocked it as being a hoax but I'm sure you've heard all that before. I'm actually going to an estate sale after I finish my lunch. You should check it out, too. They might have something that helps you with your search, because the original owner was also a local treasure hunter."

"Yeah, maybe I will. You're talking about the Sutton estate, right?"

As the bluegrass group got ready to play their last tune, my burger arrived with toppings on the side. For the entire set they had been dueling with themselves by covering songs with Civil War themes that represented both the North and the South, but now they asked all of the reenactors to join in together for their rendition of "Home! Sweet Home!" As musicians playing everything from dulcimer, mandolin and uilleann pipes exchanged improvised solos, the audience in their array of cavalry vests, infantry kepis and shell jackets toasted one another with swinging mugs of beer. In their shared passion for living history, scruffy die-hards embraced whiskerless newbies, whose lack of concern for detail was normally frowned upon. When the song ended, there was no shortage of "hurrahs."

After cheroots were passed around, the soldiers huddled together for a sepia-tone photograph. As they posed, the hostess in a Victorian ensemble helped the waitresses serve the drafthouse's specialty dessert. This was the chocolate cannonball, a rolled, truffle-like confection into which was inserted a smokeless sparkler.

"You know, Jack, that band slaps," Jeremy nodded as I chowed down on my burger.

I followed Jeremy's old cargo van onto the secluded property where the estate sale was. With a dozen or so cars parked along a circular gravel driveway, I squeezed my rumbling black Ford pickup next to a boxwood hedge at the center and climbed out by a rustic wishing well.

After putting a leash on Golliwog, I walked over and gazed down at the gleaming coins in its cloudy water before continuing to where Jeremy was examining one of his bald front tires.

"Got diddlysquat on this one too," he said while running a finger over the badly worn tread.

On the walk over I could smell burning oil.

"Leaky crankshaft, too," I said while tapping my fingers on the blistered silver paint on the Savana's hood. "Shame to stain the gravel," I joked. "Nice place. I hope the high brows don't make a stink about the dog."

"We might find a bargain at this time of day. The dealers always get here early."

The sprawling grounds were well maintained and encompassed by dense, foreboding woods. Rising from the manicured lawn was a rectangular Federal-style farmhouse with side chimneys and attached wings of matching white clapboards that glinted in the late afternoon sun.

Decorative features on the restored facade, such as attic dormers surmounted by a sculpted balustrade at the roofline, made the otherwise chunky box rather impressive. Looking up at the showy pediment above the curved portico, I wondered why I had come. Buying a gift for Merrilly's birthday in these fancy digs would be tough, but maybe I could find out a little about the treasure hunter Jeremy mentioned. By all appearances, he'd found something of value.

As we approached the house, I could see people moving behind the large window on the second floor above the fanlight tracery. The front door was propped open, so after letting Golliwog sniff all of the potted Black-eyed Susans on the porch, we stepped into the entrance hall.

When no one showed up to greet us in the foyer, we proceeded into a sparsely furnished living room. Gilt-framed paintings hung in the complex pastel color scheme, along with an antique mercury mirror on a tiered mantle, whose lacquered corbels contained hand-carved leaves (cabbage, Jeremy called them). Ceramic jardinières with floral motifs in lilac and Dutch pink had been placed together on the parquet floor. Though I didn't see any price stickers on them, large planters like that would look ridiculous among the cheap décor in our '1st of the month' anyway.

As we continued down a wide hallway, Jeremy was trying to find the library, ruling out doors that had signs marked "off-limits." While searching for it, he kept stopping to admire the architectural details and embellished vintage furniture, commenting on things like, "ebonized", "marquetry" and "scagliola." Soon he found what he was looking for – a spacious room with half-filled mahogany bookcases. The chemical degradation of the old tomes seemed to intoxicate him as he inhaled the slightly musty aroma that was mingled with faint traces of vanillin.

As he went straight for the rows of books, I was perplexed by the room's decorative accents. Light green wallpaper contained shimmering vine scrollwork that reached a curious plasterwork frieze under the verdigris crown molding. Jeremy told me that the design resembled ancient Egyptian lotus palmettes, and pointed to a similar anthemion motif that was featured on ornate pilasters that framed the painting of a typical garden scene.

While further examining the carvings of flowering vines twining about the columns, it seemed as if the wild tangle had sprung *into* the canvas and was currently in the process of smothering the splashes of the variegated blooms originally de-picted. Spiraling vines clambering over more desirable plants were also featured on the upholstery of the curvaceous arm-chairs in the room.

Whoever was responsible for the interior details were so fas-cinated with this honeysuckle-like growth, that it was practically invading the library.

"Might be the only wallpaper I've ever seen that needs a weed-warrior," I joked.

The moment Jeremy pulled out one of the books, either a family member or volunteer quietly walked in and sat down at a checkout table. The elderly woman with a lavender pixie eyed my new friend suspiciously through thick glasses as he thumbed through the pages.

"Some of those valuable early works can be quite pricy," she said in a tone that was almost apologetic.

"I'm not sure who your appraiser was," Jeremy said while further examining the book, "but for this 1896 first edition of *Mosby's Rangers*, they're a bit on the low end. It's not terribly scarce, but usually the hinges are starting... but with this one the binding is solid and the gilt vignette title is still robust. With most copies I've handled, the end pages are usually loose or even detached. The boards are a trifle rubbed... and pebbled cloth lightly soiled, but no bubbling. Other than a sticker ghost on the right front flyleaf and minor foxing it's internally good and presents well. Yeah, for real, I'd list it as near fine and price it at four hundred."

When he finished with his appraisal, I was thinking, damn, his tongue is more silver than his van.

"Should you decide not to buy it, I'll mention that to the owner, young man."

"He's the treasure hunter," Jeremy said while handing me the book.

"So you know about the legend of Mosby's buried treasure?" I asked.

"Yeah, the Gray Ghost," he replied. "Mosby's 43rd Virginia cavalry conducted a midnight raid and took gold and jewels and stuff, but had to quickly bury the spoils after learning there were more Union troops nearby. When some of his men were later sent to dig up the valuables, they were captured and hanged. According to Mosby's deathbed confession, the treasure's still out there, buried under a pine tree near Culpeper. There are lots of holes in his story – like why wouldn't he have gone back to get it at some point – a guy known for his daring exploits and guerilla tactics."

"Retweet, there's lots of shit that doesn't make sense," I said. "It's unlikely that the treasure ever existed."

"Unlike *The Beale Papers*," he grinned. "Then again, maybe the guy who built this place found the right pine tree using clues from Mosby's memoir."

"Yeah, really," I laughed while glancing about at the proliferation of climbing, uncoiling vines on the ornamental metallic wallpaper. "Honeysuckle grows wild along Highway 211... everyone knows that."

When I handed the book to Jeremy, he placed it back on the shelf and continued to look for more finds.

Checking out the collection myself, I noticed something of interest. This was a book entitled *The Bartender's Guide*. On its frayed brown cover, stamped in cursive gilt was: "Price $2.50." Being that my current job was a part-time bartender, I opened it and read out loud from the first page: "How to mix drinks... or the bon-vivant's companion, to which is appended a manual for the manufacture of cordials, liquors and fancy syrups."

Lightly penciled in the corner was the price of $3,500.00. This was so unexpected that I had to do a double take.

"Whoa, this one's over three grand! That's absurd... for a book just about how to mix drinks... that I've never heard of... like the Cobbler," I laughed while flipping through the pages.

"It's the first of its kind... highly sought after," Jeremy informed me.

The lady at the table squinted at her flip-phone and stood up. "I'll be right back if you have any questions," she said while hurrying off in a wake of drugstore Shalimar.

"Here's a walk out," Jeremy uttered while carefully removing a volume with tinted red bands on its full calf spine. "Check out what's been tucked into the back of this book," he said while walking over to me. Opening it gently towards the rear, he showed me a browned vellum page with notched edges that read:

NEVV ATLANTIS
A VVORKE VNFINISHED

"How'd you know it would be there?" I asked.

"It's how the book was issued back then."

"This thing looks really old."

"It's the 1639 fifth printing of the first edition of *Sylva Sylvarum*, but the inclusion of *New Atlantis* appended in the back wasn't mentioned at the time. "*New Atlantis*," he read, "A Work Unfinished, Written by the Most Honorable Francis, Lord Verulan, Viscount St. Alban. It's Sir Francis Bacon's incomplete utopian novel. The rest was not perfected, as it says at the end."

"Who was this guy?" I asked.

"Besides being the Lord High Chancellor of England back then, he was a natural philosopher – the prototype of what today would be a scientist. Many historians don't mention it, but, along with his other cryptic doings, Bacon was drawn to magic and the occult and may have been in possession of a type of discovery device."

"What's a discovery device?"

"You know how a ship's compass dial was used to discover new worlds... to sail beyond the current limits. Well, there's an analogue to this with Bacon's occult faculty as being a tool to guide the human mind in its quest for knowledge. Things like those mentioned in this book."

"So, it's about –"

"It's about the Baconian method to advance humanity. Somehow, maybe using his discovery device, he anticipated things that were made centuries later... in modern times. His fictional account gives examples of technologies that were lost... the wisdom known before the Fall, but that can still be recovered. So, it's about what was before and what's yet to come... the Great Instauration, as Bacon called it."

"What's yet to come?"

"Yeah, the new Atlantis. There's this remote island the rest of the nations of Earth don't know about with all kinds of advanced stuff. Bacon's prophetic vision foretells of scientific know-how equal to ours or even surpassing what we have today."

He turned a few pages and read a passage: "We procure means of seeing objects as afar off; as in the heaven and remote places; and represent things near as afar off; and things afar off as near, making feigned distances."

"The first part sounds like a telescope, but what does he mean by things near as afar off?"

"Projections of images, I guess... or, how about quantum

mechanics… like entanglement… spooky paradoxes that boggle modern physicists."

"Yeah, maybe, but projections make more sense."

"We have also houses of deceits of the senses," he continued to read, "where we represent all manner of feats of juggling, false apparitions, impostures and illusions, and their fallacies. False apparitions, Jack… so they can create artificial imagery and fake miracles – things like that phantom airship you saw this morning – the rebel wunderwaffe," he chuckled.

"To quote the author, 'Some books should be tasted, some devoured, but only a few should be chewed and digested thoroughly', kind of like the silverfish have done to this copy over the centuries," he chuckled while showing me the yellowish stains in the brittle tawny paper, "or maybe it suffered the attention of a rodent. No, actually what Bacon was drawing our attention to is that one needs to read between the lines to extract the reality disguised as fiction. He signals to others with his Lanthorn – the name of a Fraternal Order that met in secret to set their ship's prosperous course to the New Atlantis."

"Did they make it?" I asked as a way of humoring him, to which he responded by shrugging his shoulders and stretching his arms with flattened palms as if balancing something.

"How much are they looking to get?"

"Thirteen hundred. It's been repaired, but that doesn't detract much. There's a turn at that."

"Are you going to snag it instead of getting new tires?"

"Wish I could. I guess I need to get a fix from my aunt, Cleo, or else stick to the flea-market scene," he shrugged while putting the book back on the shelf. "Finding raroria in junk bins."

"You're wanting a book about Atlantis," I said, "but when I was little I met this older guy who was looking for the actual place."

"The sunken continent?" Jeremy asked.

"Yeah. There was something wrong with his memory and he had come here to Virginia but wasn't sure why. When I first saw him – I had this job mowing the lawn at the little library in Louisa where my mom worked – he was standing there looking at the brick wall... actually at the mortar that was used because he thought it looked a little different from other brick buildings in the area. This was due, he said, to a mineral oxide that gave it a special reddish tint. He was looking for some alloy that was mined only in Atlantis, and thought the unusual color of mortar that had something mixed into it was some kind of clue."

"Was it different looking – the mortar used for the bricks?"

"Not really. It had a kind of odd reddish glint in the sun... but that's all."

"The metal was called *orichalcum*," Jeremy said. "This guy – was he looney tunes?"

"He was homeless, but a really nice guy that helped my mom with some things in the library. Okay, so this was how I first got into being a TH'er. There was this other man who used to come to the library to do research about the lost treasures in Virginia. He'd actually had some success as a diver looking for shipwrecks. He liked me, I guess, or my mom, and gave me this ancient Greek silver coin that was one of many that he had found in the Aegean Sea. It was a *tetradrachm* with an owl on it, I remember. Anyway, getting back to the homeless guy, whose name was Granger or something like that – he kept talking about wanting to go back to some place in Illinois called Moos something, so I sold the coin and used part of the money to buy him a bus ticket to St. Louis. It might be the only good deed I've done," I laughed. "Before he left, he wrote my home address on this temporary library card my mom gave him and said that if he ever found the location of

Atlantis, he'd let me know. After that, I never heard from him again. Weird story, huh."

"Yeah, especially the part about Moo town."

"I know. Moosville, I think it was."

When Jeremy's phone dinged, he checked the message.

"I've got to head back to Lynchburg. My Aunt Jema needs help with something."

"What – you just got here."

"This is my third estate sale today… without any luck. Tough way to make a nickel, and now Jema needs the van to deliver this harlequin set. Here, I'll text you my number in case you want to hook up some time."

"Okay, but watch your blood sugar levels and get more of those gooey apple fruit pies, Pye."

Before heading towards the door, I heard him mutter something that sounded like:

"But if they didn't find it – I sure as hell will."

When he left, I decided to see what kind of things were for sale on the second story. Nudging the dog up the central staircase, I redirected her at the landing into a hallway whose atrium white walls smelled like a fresh coat of Benjamin Moore. In what was once a bedroom (painted the same color, but with a glossy pearl finish), several people were checking out the assortment of items on folding tables.

The first thing that caught my eye was a framed advertising label for Welcome Nugget Tobacco. Placed on top of this was a silver-plated miniature lighthouse whose beacon functioned as table cigar lighter. While trying to get a better look at the vintage poster, I accidently knocked the thing over. As I quickly set it upright, and put the chased snuffer back in place, I heard a woman's contrived sultry voice.

31

"That's why we can never have nice things, Jack."

Looking up, I saw a girl in her early 20s seated behind a small antique writing desk. With her fingers, she brushed back messy layers of light brown hair, all the while keeping her wide green eyes fixed on me. When I stared back to try to recognize the pretty face, she crushed out a demi-slim cigarette and made a funny expression before sticking a toddler's red lollipop into her mouth.

"How'd you know my name?" I asked while averting my gaze as she adjusted one of the spaghetti straps on her grey camisole.

"Just guessed, though its no guess that's your F-150 down there," she said while turning towards the window. "Want to try and guess mine?" she asked while removing the cherry sucker.

Before I had a chance to respond, an attractive middle-aged woman with a messy bob stuck her head in the door.

"Callie, have you seen the feather duster?"

"Are you talking about the thingy with black plumage?" she said while looking down at Golliwog. "No, but should I see one with humane microfibers, I'll send a text to your Jitterbug."

"Are you smoking again?" the woman wrinkled her nose while marching into the room in a dark green shift dress. Her facial features resembled the girl's and nature had been good to both mother and daughter in other ways, I thought while stealing a glimpse of the lace décolletage.

"I certainly am not," she replied with a wry smile. "Jack here just took a tiny little puff to see if your grandpa's lighthouse worked. And then he coughed. Tell him what you told me, mother, about how there's nothing glamorous with lung carcinoma."

"Callie, I need that duster," she said in an exasperated tone, "and Jack, you should run... run as fast as you can."

When her mother turned and left the room, Callie once again tousled her voluminous hair.

"That bitch will never find it," she muttered to herself in a cartoonish voice while rubbing her palms together as if fiendishly pleased. "Hehehe, laughs the poor ostrich running around without its black jammies."

She then stuck the lollipop back into her mouth while picking up one of the crayons spread out on the crescent-shaped desk's polished veneer.

"What's your woozle's name?" she asked without looking up.

"Can't you guess that, too?" I replied.

She shook her head as her gaze remained focused on the page she was in the process of coloring.

"If you're talking about the dog... it's... her name is Gollydog," I said, hoping she didn't know about those fuzzy bozos Jeremy showed me, nor seeing any reason to bring up Golliwog's rightful owner.

As she leaned forward in the snug top and was about to select another color, one of the crayons fell off the desk and rolled across the floor. When I reached down to pick it up, I saw that its light blue label said:

BONER PILL BLUE

While handing it to her, I realized it was part of a novelty set when I saw the names of some of the other humorously offensive colors, such as "Miscarriage Maroon." Still, I couldn't help but wonder if she had dropped that particular one on purpose.

When I tried to take a peek at what she was coloring, she quickly closed the book and pursed her lips in another goofy expression. Looking at the cover, I saw it was one of those "stress-free" adult coloring books that contained complex designs. A few seconds later, she opened it back to the page whose highly detailed images were almost completely filled in. Using her politically incorrect set of crayons and palette of fine tip markers, the illustration depicting an aquatic paradise had been magically transformed by a delirium of colors. In a vibrant, kaleidoscopic flurry of amphibious life, the predominant creature was some kind of merman, whose face (colored with "Vaping Douche Violet") was enhaloed by a radiant gloriole.

"That thing's weirder than monsters I've caught fishing in the Rappahannock," I joked.

"I don't know what it is, but I heard its call. It sounded like... like... I don't know what," she said in a manner that was no longer playful, as she pointed to the sea-trumpet (conch) the mysterious being was holding while gliding from the distant golden pinnacles of some fabled underwater kingdom (Atlantis had surfaced again!). "And it said something about being in a glass container... to be studied. Yeah, I'm probably a smidge crazy. It runs in the family, Jack."

As I waited for more of her childlike antics, her resolute gaze remained transfixed on the mythical sea-god slipping through a glittering mass of marine life in the limpid depths. The spell was finally broken by the sound of her mother's voice.

"Callie."

Once again her mom entered the room.

"Mother, go buy a fucking Swiffer," her daughter uttered in a voice that startled a few of the people checking out decorative ephemera and tarnished oddments on the tables.

"Always be Lilith, never Eve, like it says on her favorite tee shirt," mom said to the onlookers. "That's my lovely daughter. A bit quirky at times, like when giving her undivided attention to coloring sea fairies in crystal palaces. Darling child," she said with an insincere grin, "could I persuade you to help me with something that doesn't involve feather dusting?"

After untangling strands of her hair, Callie stood up in lace-trimmed jean shorts and flashed a strained smile at those staring at her.

"You're still here," the mother said with waning patience. "With each tick of the clock, it's going to be that much harder to ward her off, Jack."

As dusty beams of sunlight streamed through the Palladian window in the adjoining room, several people were hunched over unlocked display cases filled with Civil War artifacts. Standing behind them, I was pretending to be checking out some rusty medals and worn metal tokens as a militaria expert was helping a potential buyer with one of the brass buttons.

Seeing the array of relics, I figured that's how Callie knew my name. A few years ago, in my late teens, I had been featured in several YouTube clips as an amateur detectorist. Though my permissions finds were usually of no major value – silver Mercury dimes, Rosies and a couple of Barber halves – I once rang up a choice Civil War button that wasn't too toasty, along with some other drops in the same plug. After getting skunked so many times, I got tired of door-knocking on someone's property for basic coin-shooting, and decided to put all my free time into searching for Beale's legendary horde.

"It appears to be dug," the authority said, "but often newer buttons were buried intentionally to give them a patina and make them more valuable. It wears its historic surface well... and the gilt plating here makes a nice exemplar for the serious collector."

"My grandfather would sometimes bury them on the property", Callie's mom explained. "Not post-war buttons stamped from the old dies, but actual relics just to give us kids something to do when we visited. He would draw up little maps with clues and markers to see if we could find them. Those that did could redeem them for a prize."

I've got a prize for you, I said to myself with a wry grin as I pulled from my pocket a metal slug that was trash my detector should have ignored. *Why not,* I thought while slipping it into the jar with a blank expression when nobody was looking. I couldn't remember where I had dug it up, but I kept forgetting to throw the damn thing away because it didn't come out in the wash and rattle around like the rest of my spare change did. Though it wasn't in my nature to play little tricks like that, the thought had suddenly come to me. Out of the blue, as the saying goes. Maybe I was inspired by the prank at the recreation of the Battle of Spotsylvania.

"Where's the funny button?" Callie mumbled to herself.

"I don't know, Callie," her mom replied with an annoyed look. "Check one of those pickling jars."

"As for these tokens," the expert continued, "you've got a variety of patriotic slogans and store cards... like this one for a saloon, but besides those with striking errors, the sutler tokens are the most sought after in the bunch."

"Hey, it *is* here." Callie said with a surprised look on her face. "I found it – it's right here," she repeated, this time with an excited voice while pulling out a metallic disc about the size of a quarter that had been placed in a mason jar along with the more common civil war tokens.

'How funny,' I laughed inside. There was already one like mine in the jar. It was a different color but just as worthless. Someone else must have had the same idea. The world is full of practical jokers.

"I saw that earlier," the specialist said. "It doesn't have any designs and it's lighter than a feather. Maybe it's from a degraded die. Ordinary people made some tokens and there weren't any rules. There were also odd metal compositions. I've seen white metal, copper-nickel and German silver. Tin-plated, zinc-plated and even rubber, believe it or not. But, to be blank on both the obverse and reverse, that doesn't make sense," he said while examining the disc, whose surface emitted subtle fluctuations in a curious luminosity, "unless it's not actually a token, but just some machine punch out. Is this made of plastic?" he scratched his chin, "As far as I can recall, I haven't seen anything like it in a CWTS catalog."

"It's just one of those things people use to cheat Coke machines," her mom said. "Before he was bedridden, my grandfather made a fuss about it just to impress us children. Told us it had supernatural powers. I remember he'd place it on his dresser and have us kneel down as he intoned some mumbo-jumbo along with parlor-game theatrics. Suddenly the object of our wishes appeared in a room that was already hazy from his cigarette smoke. These were usually trifles like taffy suckers that he had bought at Gink's country store and stashed away for just such occasions. He said he found the thing under a hemlock tree after hearing a whippoorwill singing about a treasure that was nearby. Of course, he had to chop the head off a fire-breathing copperhead before he could obtain it. This was just part of his crazed web. Whatever it is, it's not anything we need to hire Pinkerton guards to protect, that's for sure."

"Sounds like your granddaddy was quite a character," the guy said while handing the disc back to Callie.

"Heavens, you have no idea, Mister Pribble "

"It's a treasured family heirloom," Callie informed the stodgy authority.

"Well, if you want it, take it," her mom said while sweeping the bangs from her eyes. "Let it collect dust somewhere else... and you can go back to what you were coloring now."

"Fine," Callie said while slipping the disc into her pocket.

Upon hearing that the grandfather was more of a bullshit artist than an actual treasure hunter, I was about to leave when a muffled voice behind me caught my attention. When I turned to have a look, there was no one there. Realizing the tinny voice was coming from an antique Philco floor model radio that was placed in the corner of the room, I moved closer towards the faint glow of the console's dial lamp. It was hard to believe the damn thing still worked, but when I leaned my ear towards the pops and hiss coming from its tattered grille cloth, I could make out what sounded like an elderly man speaking with a wheezy voice. His conversation seemed oddly casual for a radio program, almost like the show contained unscripted dialogue?

"Della, can you fetch me a glass of water from the kitchen... and remember not to tell grandma about the noisy bubbles the tablet makes while it's busy alkalizing."

"Plop, plop... Fizz, fizz," a child giggled over the static.

"And when I'm feeling better," the man with the nasally voice continued, "I'll ask the magical doojigger to make Grumble's Star show itself tonight."

"And the other things, too, grandpa?" the little girl asked.

"You mean the glowing trails that mark the paths of the grey piggies while zipping through the sky?"

"That's when you put the doojiggy in the same jar with the plops that go fizzy. How come?"

"It likes to hide there, sweetie, and look just like them... until they're gone. That's the game they play."

"Back to the sky go all the grey piggies," the child giggled.

What made these crackling voices even stranger was that in the background I could hear a totally different radio broadcast. The announcer was talking about the horseracing results from a place I'd heard about called Shenandoah Downs near Charles Town. After commenting about the matchups in the stakes, he segued into a nostalgic advertisement for Lucky Strikes cigarettes: "The taste to start with... the taste to stay with…"

As I strained to listen to the drifting voice talking about the thoroughbreds that would be running "tonight" (on a racetrack that was demolished many years ago), the audio signal grew faint with additional background static. Turning one of the knobs to scan stations had no affect, and soon there was no reception, with only the hum of vacuum tubes coming from the scuffed walnut cabinet.

Though it was about time to take Golliwog for a walk, before heading home I stopped back at the estate's library to have another look at the Francis Bacon book that Jeremy showed me.

Opening it towards the back where the author's unfinished shipwreck tale had been appended, I skimmed passages written in old English until I found the section where the technological marvels of the *New Atlantis* were listed:

'We have also sound houses…we make divers tremblings and warblings of sounds, which in their original are entire… We have certain helps which set to the ear do further the hearing greatly… We have also divers strange and artificial echoes, reflecting the voice many times…'

Although there was a slip of paper with the book's current price, I noticed that an earlier price of -65 was penciled at the top of what Jeremy called "the engraved frontis." When Callie walked in and sat down at the checkout table, I wondered if I could finagle buying it at the much lower price. Sticking the piece of paper between the aged vellum pages somewhere near the middle of the book, I walked over and set it down on the table.

"It's marked sixty-five dollars," I said while placing a credit card on top of it. "And it's not even finished."

"That will be six shillings and five pence, or you can pay the wholesale price of salted herring if you'd rather barter for it as they used to do at the tavern on Fleet Street," she said while examining the publisher's imprint at the base of the title page. "With your pardon, sir, no rotten cabbages, though," she added with a bad cockney accent while running the plastic through a mobile card machine.

"The rest was not perfected, it says. What – am I supposed to finish it myself?" I joked.

"Aye, that may be, but 'tis a fair price being paid with this strange fancy ye have."

As the card was being processed, I thought about commenting on her green eyes, but quickly thought better of it.

"For your perusal, I thank thee, sir," she said as she handed me the book.

"So, what's going on with all the rampaging greenery in here?" I asked while gesturing to the repeating pattern of climbing vegetation on the decorative wallpaper and relief carvings of virescent tentacles bordering the ceiling.

"It used to be his favorite," she replied, "the breath of honeysuckle. But before he passed, my great grandfather had recurring dreams of the things. Uncoiling vines spreading over everything. Crowding out other plants and things. His wife, Deliza, wanted him to go to the nervous hospital – what she called psychiatrists back in those days – when he woke up saying the creepers had climbed to such heights that they smothered the light of the sun. These were his nightmares. Always one to paint a negative picture of him, naturally my mother interpreted these bad dreams as his subconscious mind trying to tell him something. The invasive species represented his vices… his smoking, drinking and, worse of all, his gambling problem. Spending his days betting on horses – even if he was winning – affected his relationship with those who cared about him. They were being drowned out just like the honeysuckle was doing to the world in his reoccurring dreams. But I have a different take. Rather than representing bad habits, the dreams were some kind of warning."

"What's your mother's name?"

"Della. Della Sutton."

"Well, it was nice to meet you and your mom and hear about gramp's stories and dreams and things."

As I called to Golliwog and turned to leave, she tapped me on the back.

"Plato died before finishing his Atlantis, too – his warning about how all things end… and not just things in the distant past. Anyway, methinks Neville's *Isle of Pines* might be a better utopia, at least for me," she said with a mischievous twinkle in her green irises. "A place where everyone goes about naked all day with nothing better to do than… well, no spoilers here."

While walking back to my pickup, I started to feel guilty about the deceit involved to obtain the book for a greatly 'discounted' price. The idea had been to sell it to Jeremy for half of the listed amount, or maybe to cash in at some used bookstore (hell, if I even needed money after tonight's dig).

Once I finished reading about the futuristic devices in the *New Atlantis* (Jeremy's mentioning of which had piqued my curiosity), if I returned the volume when the same estate sale continued next weekend, I would score points for my honesty after showing Callie the slip of paper I found stuck between its pages. I wasn't sure about some fatal attraction curse like her mom joked about, but love-charm whammy or not, I definitely wanted to see her again.

Instead of heading directly home, I stopped at the wooded ridge where the civilian reenactors had gathered earlier to watch the mock Battle of Spotsylvania. When I climbed out of the pickup, Golliwog began acting strangely, quivering and refusing to budge from the cab. Thinking she might still be agitated from the morning's events, I left her inside and proceeded towards the sloping trail.

When I entered the opening through the trees, I was surprised to see that the place seemed undisturbed. Glancing casually about the clearing as gleams of sunlight slanted weakly through the foliage, there was no evidence of those that had come to observe the spectacle. No broken pieces of china, cigar stubs, ham bones or even fruit rinds.

Even more puzzling, there was only one set of shoe prints on the still muddy ground and they looked like my Reeboks. Moving to the edge of the ridge that overlooked the park, acrid drifts of Pyrodex still lingered in the waning daylight that was streaked with purple, rose and orange tints. In the distance I could see what remained of the reenactors' village.

Those who weren't quite ready to drive back into the 21st century were listening to a nostalgic string band performing near some canvased wagons. Though some of the Bluebird school buses and pickups pulling aluminum trailers were exiting the grounds, lots of people were still milling about the fair-booths, food kiosks and living history expositions.

Before leaving, I saw a small hole in the ground near a gnarled old oak that lovers had carved a heart with their initials into the bark. From the looks of it, a detectorist without ethics didn't bother to fill in their clean plug. Thinking that I would do it for them, as I glanced about for the small clump of earth, there was none to be seen. That's when I noticed that, unlike the rest of the sodden clearing, both the circular bore and loamy soil along its edge were completely dry.

At the same moment that I noticed this peculiar detail, I had this feeling that I had seen the hole before – even numerous times – though this wasn't possible because I had never been to the place until this morning. Along with the sensation of *déjà vu*, for no apparent reason, I was suddenly overcome with an increasing sense of agitation. While trying to shake this off, the flash of a 'hazy grey blob' appeared in my field of vision, causing me to take a step back from the knotty oak. After rubbing my eyes, I quickly left the clearing.

While driving home, my thoughts drifted to the day's strange series of events. First there was the zany flying machine (actually, the more I thought about it, despite the open pilot house, with its propelling-screws and mechanical oars, the overall design of the thing was more like the imaginings of an early period submarine than an airship, which made the fluid dynamics of its passage through the air even more baffling). Next was the striking illustration of some fish-like creature as part of Callie's coloring therapy.

There were those faint voices from the past on the old radio, with one having the same name as Callie's mom. Not to mention the announcer at a ghost racetrack. How fucking weird was that? Even more bizarre, though, were the grandfather's nightmares of rampant vines taking over the world. And I almost forgot about the shiny whatzit that Callie wanted for whatever reason (maybe just to try and conjure more doctor's lollipops). Yeah, it had been quite a day for sure, but the night might be even more eventful. I began to get excited just thinking about returning to the excavation site near the Appalachian Trail, where my partner and I were hoping to find a buried treasure worth an estimated $65 million.

CHAPTER II
BEALIEVERS

*"Shall I write about things not to be spoken of
and divulge what ought not to be divulged?"*

Julian (362 A.D.)

*"Unlike any other pursuit with practical and natural
results, a charm attended it, independent of the ultimate benefit
he expected; and the possibility of success lent an interest and
excitement to the work not to be resisted."*

"The game is worth the candle."

The Beale Papers (1885)

I thought Blue Willows View Estates was a funny name for a
trailer park until I noticed the even more pretentious Deer Brook
Manor hanging on a sign in front of similar welfare castles a
couple of miles south. At least the place wasn't the Schlitz-guz-
zling mulletopia with Saturday night turkey bowling that I half
expected when I first started going out with Merrily. There were
no rebel flags draped over meth kitchen windows or rusty pickups with translucent red tape covering broken taillights. Neither
was there any pink flamingo lawn statuary on the fresh cut grass
to make fun of, though there were a few traileresque flourishes,
such as the Chrysler hubcap birdbath on a wrought-iron pedestal in front of our doublewide.

When I turned onto the "quiet lane", I could see the coruscating dance of fireflies over a marshy area in the nearby field where the sweep of my headlights was reflected in the eyes of several deer licking a salt block. With the scent of flowering dogwood mingling with the smoke of charred burgers from the nearby Dairy Queen, I parked on the stretch of gravel and grabbed the leather-bound book. Following the excited dog through the opened screen door, I headed down the narrow hall towards the bedroom.

"It's me, Merr, bringing home the Bacon," I announced. "Francis Bacon, that is."

"Golliwoggie!" Merrily uttered in her squeaky 'dog voice' while turning from the vanity where she had been applying lip plumper. As the barking little dynamo tried to jump into her lap, she picked her up and set her down on the barmaid's apron that was already tied around her black work slacks "Did you miss your mommy – yes you did, didn't you. Yes you did. How about a special treat for my woggiedoggy– "

"She just had some tenders from Cracker Barrel," I said.

Pulling one of the strawberry blonde pigtails over her Royalene's THIRST RESPONSE tank top, her arm was a sleeve of tattoos as she began stroking Golliwog's dense woolly coat.

"What's this about bringing home the bacon?" she asked while finally acknowledging my presence.

"It's a book about Francis Bacon. He was an olden guy who was way ahead of his time and also knew about a time long ago that was ahead of our time, so it's pretty cool. And he might have brought a repository of stuff of how he learned this hidden knowledge to Virginia that hasn't been found yet."

"Repository?" Her mocking utterance was followed by a snort of laughter. "Where's my fucking boyfriend, Jack Atkins – the guy who left this morning in his pickup truck? I hope you didn't use my credit card again," she snapped before grabbing the book. "Strike that – it's pretty shabby. You're gonna read this huge thing?"

"Maybe. Just to know what's in store for the planet. Bacon was a man of rare learning."

"He looks like one of the three musketeers," she said after opening it to the portrait of Bacon with his cloak's frilly decorative ruff and stovepipe hat. "Or a creepy leprechaun," she snickered. "Even one of those guys on that cigar box you keep your finds." Rolling her eyes, she tossed the book next to the opened Roma's Pizza box on the messy unmade bed.

"Careful, there's some cracking to the outer joints," I cringed while inviting further teasing.

"The poor thing. Sorry," she smiled blandly. "Oh, you won't believe what the delivery guy told me," she said while squeezing her feet into some pink chucks lying by the chair.

After everything that happened today, I would have believed her if she told me the driver was a piebald kangaroo.

"Yeah, what's that?"

"At one of his stops, instead of seeing a normal ant hill, the ants were making a little pyramid… a tiny little copy of the bigger ones like in Egypt… that's what he said."

"That's cray."

"And then this Cali girl on TroVe –"

"Callie?" I interrupted.

"Yeah, some chick from California was talking about giving birth to this alien thingy. Well, it wasn't alien, but wasn't human either. Anyway, weird shit's gonna start happening, she said during the interview – like what those ants were doing." While looking into the mirror, she contorted her face into silly mask of mock horror while also checking to make sure the tips of her pigtails were even. "Royalene's is gonna be slam-packed tonight and you're taking off to go dirt-fishing in some holler – getting all revved up about finding something all the other nutters can't find. Missing good work tips just to get beeps from pop-tops or whatever it is –"

"You mean canslaw?"

"And that's when you were in your groove, babe. There will only be one other barmaid… Jesse, and with Royalene being away, she'll be doing shots of peach cobbler shine until she's useless, not that she isn't anyway. Bitch has trouble making a damn rum and Coke."

"I know where to get her the bon-vivant's companion if she's got an extra three and a half grand."

This time she pretended as if she didn't hear me.

"Tell her to toe the line," I said.

"Shit, where's my poke? Oh, and how did the Nats do today? Get bigger tips if I know."

"How did you come up with the name, Golliwog?" I asked as she looked for her purse in the cluttered room.

"It was my brother's idea. Why?"

I typed the name into her tablet and pulled up the same images on Pinterest that Jeremy showed me.

"That's why."

"Rag dolls with black locks? How cute. Look, that one's got a straight bob with flipped ends. Golliwog means sweetheart, Raiden said, and everyone knows Golliwog's my bae."

For the past year my treasure-hunting partner Baldwyn and I had been gridding likely sites within a four-mile radius of the chimney remains of Buford's tavern in Montvale, Bedford County. Using historical survey maps and new imagery from Global Earth, we had based our search zone on a series of numbers in *The Beale Papers* that Baldy (as I called the aged fortune seeker) speculated might be surveyors' road bearings and/or latitude and longitude coordinates. Recently, we had narrowed down potential targets situated within an equilateral triangle (formed by an overgrown stagecoach road and old Cherokee trails) near a small caldera in the Goose Creek Valley. However, these ghost outlines visible on satellite maps also proved to be a 'wild goose chase', as did previous purported locations at the foot of the Peaks of Otter in the Blue Ridge Mountains that were plotted by the supposed coordinate-based cipher.

After tirelessly searching for the vault entrance (or a grave-sized plot filled with covered iron pots), we had nothing to show for our efforts except for a 1935 Buffalo. As we choked on dust while crawling in abandoned mineshafts, dug holes around the gaunt ruins of Colonial-era brickwork, and ran our search coils in a graveyard on Federal property, there had been warning shots by landowners, snarls of menacing guard dogs and deer ticks that attached themselves to our skin while plodding through dense forests. Feeling that nothing had been overlooked, Baldy had finally resorted to paying for a séance conducted by a lady psychic in order to find Beale's elusive cache.

Though the medium's services were costly, Baldy convinced me it was an avenue worth pursuing. The woman hadn't asked him any telling questions beforehand as a way of obtaining information, and there had been no gimmicks during the session (that he could detect).

Without any tangible manifestation, the spirit of a "valued friend" of Thomas J. Beale indicated that the prize was buried in iron hearth kettles at a depth of six feet close to where the

Black Horse Tavern once stood. The foundations were near the Appalachian Trail, not far from Black Horse Gap. As for the X marks the spot, this could be located by "Quaker Guns that were employed at times during the unpleasantness." Because the medium said she didn't know what Quaker Guns were, she attempted a pencil rendering of the impressions she received.

The crude drawings looked like short dark poles lying near a mound of earth. Knowing that Quaker Guns were a deceptive tactic used during the Civil War, in which pine logs were painted black to resemble the barrels of cannons, the sketch further convinced Baldy that the channeled communication from an "esteemed associate" or otherwise would be our next target. Especially, he told me, since the Black Horse Gap was in close proximity of the main reference point in the deciphered text.

With these new revelations, we headed back to the narrow roads that twisted through the rolling hills in Bedford wine country. Passing scenic overlooks, lakes and picturesque farmland, we eventually turned onto a gravel stretch that ended at the trailhead to Black Horse Gap.

While hiking under the shady canopy of trees, we veered onto a fire road that was also a popular mountain bike path. After a slight uphill climb, we passed through a fence onto private land. Ignoring the No Trespassing sign nailed to a stately oak, we continued with our exploratory mission.

Not far from the oak, we spotted three short logs that had been stained black and placed near an earthen mound (exactly like the psychic described). With my detector adjusted not to discriminate, a crackling tone indicated there was ferrous metal at a depth of several feet beneath the heaped pile of debris. Along with this choppy audio signal, when I bobbed the search coil over the rounded area, the numerical values kept changing, a telltale big iron response. Thinking we might have found the entrance to Beale's vault, we made plans to return the following night with digging tools.

Fog rolling down from the hillsides was a perfect cover for the dig. With his face glazed by the faint light of a crescent moon, Baldy watched as I took a pickaxe to the mound. Surprisingly, the dirt and rocks that covered it were easily penetrated. As the loose stones and mineral deposits gave way, it wasn't long before we uncovered rusted hinges attached to fragments of rotted wood that we guessed might have been the remains of an old wooden cellar hatch.

Through an opening that was just wide enough to squeeze through, our pivoting flashlights revealed the steps leading down to a narrow vault, whose muddy grey floor was littered with hoops and staves of old oak casks. Perhaps, this was the foundation of a storeroom that was adjacent to, or beneath the old tavern, Baldy suggested with a faint smile. With further sweeps of the light, the sharp beams landed on a dusty iron pot set amidst the debris. Bending our heads, we stepped down into the dank, tapering confines. Unable to control my excitement, I squatted and removed the kettle's cast iron lid. Much to my dismay, it was empty, save for a scrap of brown paper onto which something had been written in old-style cursive:

'Do not store up yourselves treasures on Earth, where moth and rust destroy, and where thieves break in and steal.'

"What's this – a joke tag? What's the fucking deal here, Baldwyn? The ground's been salted."

"Seeing just the one pot in the cellar hole – I didn't think that was a good sign," he nodded while picking up the kettle. Turning it upside down, he shined his flashlight on the bottom, "There's no slash on the casing," he muttered while running a finger over the surface.

"Yeah, so what?"

"Gate marks were phased out when the molding method changed to lip injection. Meaning, this thing isn't that old."

A creaking noise on the steps caused us to turn at the same time someone else's flashlight clicked on. Behind its blinding glare, I could discern a figure hunched in the scant opening. In the wavering glow of our own beams, this appeared to be a black guy wearing a khaki green uniform.

"Y'all want to come out now... and bring that pot," he said. "I know about finder's-keepers, but that don't make no never mind when you is on federal lands."

When we emerged from the cramped space, I saw that there were three of them. All were dressed in uniforms of the U.S. Park Service. Two were black, with the third being a white guy with a lumpy face under his khaki stocking cap. Unlike the suede sneakers the others were wearing, dirty white Nikes protruded from his wrinkled green Dockers.

"Are you volunteers?" Baldy asked after getting a better look at their uniforms. "Can I see a badge?"

"This here's Uncle Sam's badge," one of the black guys said while pointing to a colorful patch on the right sleeve of his field shirt. "You's not first time visitors. We watched you on yesterday, takin' your slow and you better not have snatched the bonanza from the jug," he said while peering into the empty kettle, "where the Good Lord said it would be stashed."

"Gentlemen, digging is not permitted without a permit," came a stern, deep voice, followed by the crunch of footfalls as a forest ranger stepped from behind a tree with military-grade night vision goggles under his flat-bill hat, "nor is impersonating a federal officer, even if your state-issues are Skittles green," he added in a half-teasing tone.

Other Federal law enforcement officers appeared on both sides of him, their drawn weapons visible in the thinning mist.

"Your insignia of office is on the wrong side, dummies," the ranger chuckled while gesturing to the patch on the left arm of his tan button-up. "And what are those other badges supposed to be? It looks like you pinned mini forest rangers certificates to your shirts. Impersonating mini rangers, too… pretty low, fellas. And, try as we might – we sure as hell aren't issued designer sneakers, are we Arne," he joked with one of the rangers pointing a rifle.

"We ain't toting no guns, sir," the nervous fellow said, "and Donnell don't even step on stink bugs. We's not polices. We's from the Baptist Church here, looking for a faith promise to get a new organ. Tambourines ain't gonna drive the devil away. Do you hear me what I say?"

"I know your pastor," the ranger said, "and don't think he'd approve what you're up to. Not with the legal tangles. I don't want to make light of this, but it seems the Lord has been guiding folks like you to sink holes in this area for miles with nothing ever showing up except for a hefty fine to pay."

After aiming a flashlight into the pot, he pulled out the piece of paper and read the message out loud: "Do not store up yourselves treasures on Earth… where thieves break in and steal. This psalm sounds like damn good advice."

"It's not from the sommets. That there's Matthew," one of the Baptists corrected the officer.

"Okay, these boys are from Club Jesus. What's your story?" the ranger asked Baldy.

When he didn't answer, the ranger held up the piece of paper.

"Okay, fine, let me tell you. You've been conned, and this isn't the first time it's happened to a Bealiever. They painted those logs black. I watched them with my cat eyes here, adding a nice touch by brushing 'em in places with that fake mud stuff they sell at the Wal-Mart to people who want to cover their license plates. The so-called psychic you paid – she's going to tell you the treasure was moved elsewhere and charge you even more for another sitting. So, rather than giving you a ticket, or having you pay restitution once it comes to the attention of the federal magistrate in Roanoke, let me give you some additional advice. And, by the way, I no longer need a cheat sheet for this. There is no treasure. Never was. No puzzle to solve. The whole thing was an elaborate hoax to sell newspapers. The *Lynchburg Virginian*, which, at the time, was failing. The story and ciphers were concocted by the paper's new owner, who was also the sole writer and editor. Before purchasing it, he wrote fiction, including dime novels about buried treasure. Ads for *The Beale Papers* – a pamphlet that sold for fifty cents – appeared in the paper hundreds of times. They were placed there by the only person who could afford to do so – the paper's owner. With the amount of treasure involved, he knew people would flex their greed muscles, which they've being doing now for nearly two hundred years... even with all the evidence by scholars and the historical record against the locality cipher being real. To ignore the facts, only brings trouble and heartache and large holes. Now, before these officers escort you back to the loop, is there anything you'd like to say?"

"Yeah," one of the black guys said, "I told Donnell that I saws you in the woods, but he said you's just a deer."

☙

"No difficulty will be had in finding it, my ass," I laughed while glancing over at Baldy. Taking a large gulp of Beale's Golden Lager, I braced for a rut in the dirt and gravel road. "We might as well be looking for doubloons in bird nests or from talking trees. Hell, or some doomsayer's coins buried in fucking Mason jars."

Under a star-filled sky, we were pedaling our bikes on a bumpy trail, heading back to the fire road intersection where I parked my Ford. In the wide baskets that we hoped would be filled with gold were some of our digging tools and a YETI hopper for the beer.

"Right now, I'd settle for the silver dollar that baseball pitcher threw that didn't make it across the river," Baldy joked.

"That or Pepsi cap number 349," I laughed.

Though I tried to make light of this latest setback, I felt bad for the old guy getting scammed by a phony medium. When he was younger, Baldy had been pretty successful searching for the lost treasure of sunken ships off the coasts of Virginia and the Carolinas. He often described his adventures of diving to the seabed of the graveyard of wrecks that included everything from English merchantmen, Dutch schooners, modern luxury yachts to German submarines. As part of privately financed expeditions, finds included gold doubloons, silver bars and cases of Jamaican rum, with his share of the biggest haul being from the hull of a Spanish galleon that was blown off course from the Florida straits by a hurricane. While exploring the Chesapeake capes on his own, he had found spoils on inlets frequented by roving pirates that plundered wealthy colonials and plantation homes.

His favorite prize, though, was a ruby that washed up on a beach on "Wreck Island" after a winter storm.

When I told him about the gonzo airship that I saw, he let me know that he didn't dismiss such oddities as misinterpretations. Something strange had happened to him during a salvage effort further out in the Atlantic that he never spoke of because he didn't think people would believe him. He promised to tell me the whole story someday, which I was keen to hear because whatever it was that happened caused him to quit hunting for sunken treasure – unless, that is, it was buried inland.

"What in the world is that?" Baldy shouted while pointing to a bright white light that seemed to descend from the glittering night and was heading directly towards us at a pretty good speed. Above the prismatic halo of the glare could be seen a cluster of twinkling blue lights. After coasting over a small dip, we squeezed the brakes and pulled over in a forest clearing where several people were seated outside tents pitched by a rain shelter. As the blinking lights drew nearer, we realized it was a cyclist on a mobile coffee kiosk whose decorative canopy was festooned with blue LEDs. Though I'd seen such vending trikes before, it seemed odd for some Trail Angel (if that's who it was) to be on the Black Gap loop.

As a few campers huddled around the humming cart, I pulled another beer from the cooler, taking my time in drinking it to give Baldy a breather.

"Who's ready for some midnight nibbles?" the Trail Angel asked. "A little trail magic from the perk-mobile. Let's see – I've got fresh brewed coffee, flavored nectars and energy boosts, though that might not be such a good idea at this hour... or is it, guys?" he snickered. "There are gluten-free sweet treats that would pair nicely with some pureed cantaloupe juice. And I might have a surprise... so hooray!"

"We be hydrating now," a vaguely familiar voice uttered. Turning around, I saw it was one of the Baptists that just tried to punk us. "Free refreshments just like at church, y'all," he announced to the campers while stepping up to the mobile café with his two friends following close behind. "Last time it was chopped barbecue, greens and hoe cakes, but that was a different rollin' kitchen. I'll be taking some of that grape nectar to… oops… spill my Hennessy in. And one of those big round glazed things."

"Are you guys really even church goers?" I asked with a bemused grin.

"This be one of the pastor's ardent spirits," he smiled while pulling a pint of cognac from his back pocket.

"Y'all gonna play the game to the end?" the one they called Donnell asked Baldy.

"Not without the key," he said. "Maybe we'll go hunting for Mosby's loot, instead… or that farmer's fruit jar fortune in Prince George County or wherever the hell it is under a boulder that's carved with a horseshoe," he bullshitted the kid.

"And I might go detecting along the banks of the James River on some Sunday morning while you dudes are busy smoking blunts," I added.

"Lesson learned about *The Beale Papers*." Baldy raised his thick brows.

"Could be that ranger just don't want us pokin' around," Donnell said, "cuz he be lookin' for the golds in the same place."

"Hey, Buddy, like I told you before, don't give the dog your circus peanuts. They're not good for her," I gently admonished Merrilly's teenage brother after catching him trying to feed Golliwog one of his orange marshmallow candies.

"Circus peanuts are good, Jack," he said with an odd tone. "They're fluffy, like a sponge or a pillow."

Merrilly and I had been together for a little over a year and the entire time I had never seen the kid without a package of the sugary things. It was one of the quirks of his ASD. Raiden had been diagnosed with autism as a child and although he experienced the usual symptoms of the disorder, he seemed to lead a fairly normal life. I don't know if he was a savant, but he was really good with numbers. So much so, that Royalene hired him to do the accounting at her bar.

"Yes, they're good for people, but bad for dogs."

"How come, Jack?"

"I don't know. Maybe it's all the sugar or food coloring, but don't give her any. She's got her bone." I gestured to the rib Golliwog was gnawing on after having waited patiently for us to finish the barbecue plates we ordered for Merrilly's birthday dinner. "Keep them all for yourself."

"Circus peanuts are good," he repeated in the same monotonic voice. "Fluffy, like a sponge or a pillow."

I didn't need anything else to go wrong on her birthday, like Golliwog getting sick from eating sweets. The celebration had gotten off to a bad start during breakfast when Merrilly noticed that one of the petite letters ('l') was missing from the 14-karat gold name necklace that I bought her. She didn't make too much of a fuss when I assured her that the jeweler could fix it, though I'm sure she thought the mistake was my fault.

As I finished the last Beale's Golden Lager out on the small patio, I could hear her and her friend Jesse doing shots in the trailer while adding last minute decorations to the cake. The *cake*! Would she bring up her misspelled name again when I saw it written correctly in gel icing? If not, it would definitely surface again at some point, being that I'm certain she filed it away in her brain for just the right time and place.

Picking up the small net that I fashioned using a badminton racket, Raiden turned his attention to catching more fireflies. He already had what looked to be dozens in the glass jar, which currently outnumbered the flashing display in the backyard.

"You don't have enough of them?" I asked.

"Not yet, Jack."

"There's one with its taillights on right next to you," I shouted as one lit up a few feet away.

After chasing its fiery dance in the warm breeze, he caught it with the net and watched carefully to make sure it got into the jar before screwing the lid back on. (It had taken some doing, but he finally was able to follow my instructions of angling the lid just enough after turning the jar upside down so that those already captured didn't escape while he added a new one.)

When he returned and set the jar down on the table, he picked up a screwdriver and attempted to punch a hole in the lid.

"You don't need to poke air holes," I said. "They can breathe and lightning bugs like humidity. That's why I put the damp paper towel inside. So, Raiden, buddy, you wouldn't happen to be a little red, would you?"

"Tomatoes and fire trucks are red. Fire trucks and tomatoes are red."

"You keep your white sheets on the bed," I joked.

"Yes, the white sheets are on my bed," he said while clearing his throat and flapping a hand. Repetitive habits like this were also traits of his ASD.

"And I know you're afraid of clowns – have a deep-rooted fear of Corky – "

"I don't like clowns named Corky," he shook his head as the hand spasms continued.

"So, how do you know about golliwogs, and why did you tell your sister to name her dog that?"

"She's not named that, Jack, she's named Golliwog. Here, look."

After quickly typing something on my iPhone, he showed me an image of a vintage record album that was entitled *Golliwog*. On the black cover was the face of a pretty blonde woman with a foreign name that I didn't attempt to pronounce.

"Okay, yeah, she's pretty," I said.

"Pretty just like Merrilly. Both are sweethearts."

"She's a singer, I guess… from a while back."

"She's Momma Mia," he replied.

Jesse appeared at the screen door.

"Boys, it's time to sing Happy Birthday and blow out the candles."

The lights had been turned off to enhance the multiple colors blinking inside clear globe balloons that floated above the table with its matching galaxy-themed party tableware. Having gathered around a malted chocolate cake with Robin-egg blue buttercream (I pretended not to notice the missing 'l' from her name), we sang the Happy Birthday song, after which Merrilly made her wish and blew out all 23 candles. Before the smoke cleared, Raiden unscrewed the lid on his jar and released the 23 fireflies he had collected for the occasion. Like shooting stars, they scintillated amid the glowing transparent bubbles with flashing LEDs.

"Look, your candles are flying," he shouted, "Carrying your wish to come true."

"Thanks, Raiden," Merrilly clapped her hands while giving me a look that showed how thrilled she was to have 23 luminous beetles buzzing about in the trailer.

As I cut the cake (starting by sinking the knife into the 'l' in her name) and placed slices on the dessert plates, Jesse spooned Dairy Queen soft serve onto them.

"Do you have room for your dessert from the Grill and Chill, Raiden?" Merrilly asked, "after eating all of those greasy hush-puppies?"

"Yes, room for the chill," he nodded. "Can we watch the ants now?"

"Ants?" Do we have ants, Merr?" I asked as she opened the bottle of "Strawberry Shortcake" wine that I found at one of the stores in Montvale.

"Remember when I told you about the pizza delivery guy telling me that he saw ants making a small pyramid at this job site and you didn't believe it. Well, now, others have seen them too in different places and there are even video clips on TroVe."

Raiden picked up the remote for the flat screen and went to the playlist of a YouTube-like video sharing and social media platform and clicked on a thumbnail with lots of views.

As columns of ants scuttled across a red sandstone surface, the person doing the filming began to speak:

"While hiking in one of Sedona's red rock canyons, a couple came across a rather bizarre sight along the trail. Instead of the usual ant mounds we are all familiar with, for some reason, the colony of ants had done something quite extraordinary with the ground soil from tunneling the nest chamber. They used it to make three pyramids that are apparently a scaled-down perfect match with the famed monuments at the Giza necropolis in Egypt."

The camera then pulled back to reveal three perfectly-shaped pyramids made of reddish sand that were several inches in height. Using a split screen for comparison, the placement of the miniature versions (along with auxiliary structures) on the trail in Sedona matched the layout in photos of the great pyramid complex on the Giza plateau.

As multiple camera angles showed streams of worker ants moving along a 'causeway' that ran between the pyramids and ordinary ant mounds, the narration continued:

"Since their discovery, a local amateur Egyptologist has claimed that the three pyramids and additional edifices had been scaled-down 3,000 times smaller than the real thing, and that the dimensions and proportions matched perfectly with those in Egypt. What is even more amazing the expert said, is that the miniatures are in near-perfect alignment with the cardinal points, off by just a fraction of a degree, thus mimicking the Giza layout. This cannot be a coincidence. If actually erected by ants, this would be more of a mystery than the Giza complex, itself. Skeptics say the structures are obviously man-made, either the work of clever hoaxers or as art installations, suggesting they could easily be made by using existing sand coated with ceramic-infused polymers or other materials, such as clear varnish or even hairspray. Whatever method was used, the mini-pyramids were not constructed and astronomically-oriented by worker ants paid with wheat beer."

Brief comments by other hikers on the trail thought they might have been erected by the members of a pyramidology cult, or as college pranks. "Maybe the ants built them to store grain," one laughed.

"It's just a stupid hoax," I told Merrilly, "made by using sand glued to cardboard cut-outs... smoothed using palette knives like your cake-icing spreader."

As I continued to watch the video, Raiden suddenly began reciting his ABCs while running his finger over the series of numbers in my copy of *The Beale Papers* that was sitting on the coffee table and opened to the first cipher text.

"ABCDEFG," he repeated as he slowly moved his fingers over the strings again,

"HIIJKLMMN –"

"Yes, lots of numbers to play with," I said.

"And some letters and pictures, too, Jack."

"That chick from California said weird things were going to start happening," Merrily said when the video went to a commercial. "Check it out," she said while clicking on another thumbnail in the playlist.

A woman seated in a chair had been backlighted so that her face was in silhouette. In addition, part of her arm was pixelated.

The interviewer was asking about her claim that her memory of certain events as the surrogate mother of what she referred to as a hyper-tellurian being had been intentionally deleted.

"Yes," she replied with her voice also distorted to further protect her identity, "it was tampered with by some memory hack like a forgetting pill. They have their own version of the waters of Lethe in Greek mythology that they either ask you to drink or put into your veins. But my memory was reset by – I'll call him my hero – using a reconsolidation process."

"If it was tampered with as you claim, how do you know you weren't given implanted memories of this event?" the interviewer asked.

"I guess I really can't say for sure, but the neurological process involved was designed for memory retrieval and not confabulation."

"Tell us about this being you gave birth to. How did such a thing come about?"

"A DNA sequence was extracted from an organic substance – "

"Was this DNA preserved in amber like something akin to dino genetics we've all seen in the movies?"

"It wasn't degraded remnants of organic material – not fossilized insects or plant fragments trapped in amber or a fallen meteorite, but the fruit of a celestial plant that was detained on Earth. This bears repeating, a celestial plant detained on Earth," she said while emphasizing the word, "plant."

"Let me take a step back. Genetic material deteriorates fairly quickly, relatively speaking, so unless the conditions are extremely favorable, something this old can't be resurrected by modern science. In this case, the substance was perfectly preserved. There are places on the Earth that were left by these beings that are very hard to detect... that blend in well with ordinary features by pretending to be something else and so far only a few have been found. These shadow structures, with their mimetic mesh, were built with some type of dark energy or matter in place of ordinary construction materials and once served as restricted zones for these beings. Again, they coexist within our conventional reality and, along with their energetic solder, have other novel physical properties that make some invisible to the human eye, as well as unperceivable to modern detection equipment. Anyway, it was inside one of these synthetic dimensions that the specimen of fruit was found – again, perfectly preserved."

"For the epigenetic modification, was a variant of CRISPR used? The protein found in the immune system of bacteria."

"As for the actual genetics involved, all I can say is that a more advanced gene editing system than CRISPR was used. A tool of high specificity so that the targeted change was made without direct contact with the genes. First they were looking for what they called 'The Maker's Mark' in the piece of fruit. Next was to locate the 'god of the gaps.' The extracted DNA sequence was inserted and then they flipped a switch – the kiss that awakens 'Sleeping Beauty.' Bioelectrical signals were involved in the reprograming of the code."

"How did the discovery of this fruit come about?"

"Well, to quote from Psalms: 'The spirit of man is as the lamp of God, where with he searcheth every secret.' I don't know what covert group or secret cabal the geneticists worked for, but I can tell you that I didn't realize the danger… understand the repercussions involved by becoming artificially inseminated and giving birth to this more advanced life-form than we humans."

"As its surrogate mother you have serious regrets?"

"We're not talking about mere biological augmentation to create a transhuman here. These aren't wearables that biohackers want. As I speak, the ultra-terrestrial is still an infant or maybe a child, depending on the rate of growth. As a human child plays with toys, it plays with human minds for its enjoyment. Plays with our neural-circuitry. You won't believe its toys… the things it plays with in certain people's minds. And as to growing pains, look at the fabled childhood of Jesus as chronicled in the *Infancy Gospel of Thomas*. Breathing life into clay birds and stretching a wooden plank to help his father as a way of showing off – that wasn't so bad – same with being a little wisenheimer while quarrelling with his teachers, but what about some of his other doings, the more spiteful, nay, malevolent stuff, like cursing to death the little boy who accidently bumped into him on the street, or causing the hand of the person that broke his water jar to shrivel up, or turning children into pigs and climbing sunbeams while pushing the others kids off them. When their parents complained, they were blinded. Precocious – yeah,

I'd say. Okay, Jesus might have restored them to health, but as far as growing pains go, do you really want to take your chance with provoking the wrath of this hyper-tellurian? I don't expect most people to believe me, but watch the news. Strange things are going to start happening. Really strange things, and as Ultra-1 develops, who knows what it will be capable of and what it will choose to do with its enhanced abilities. I can only hope it will be empathetic to the human condition… to our human limitations, which was the intentional design by our true creators."

"Where did these beings come from?"

"Well, I don't think they're what we call aliens. I believe they're indigenous to the Earth… remote ancestors from a long long time ago."

"What is she on and where can I get some?" Merrilly laughed when the clip went to a cringy advertisement about how our deodorants are killing us.

Raiden grabbed the remote and went to the clickable thumbnails of recommended videos, choosing one that showed swarms of ants at a complex of mini-pyramids and associated structures that were aligned exactly like the scaled-down versions in Arizona. However, unlike the unfinished ones in Sedona, these (found at a picnic area in Memphis, Tennessee) were 'plated' with an outer layer of quartz sand grains that reflected the sunlight.

"More ants!" Raiden uttered. "That person in line at the Grill and Chill said I was one ant short of a picnic, but even with six thousand three hundred and sixty four they're still short. Next time I am at the Grill and Chill I will tell the person in line why they are still short."

"What an asshole," Merrilly said while wrinkling her nose in disgust after hearing about the comment made by someone being disrespectful to her brother at the Dairy Queen. Instead of agreeing (though I also found the remark to be offensive), I had to repress a smile while wondering exactly how many ants were in the camera frame at the time.

Before heading to work a few nights later, I watched a podcast channel that showed an aerial shot of similar pyramids and satellite edifices. A caption read:

CAPTURED BY A DRONE CAMERA IN CAIRO, SOUTHERN ILLINOIS.

This was followed by:

THE REGION IS KNOWN AS 'LITTLE EGYPT'

These scaled-down structures also had a white casing of reflective crystalline silica. Aligned like those on the Giza Plateau in Egypt, the largest pyramid shone the brightest and was topped by a capstone that mimicked polished gold. Besides the gleaming pyramidion, the layout in southern Illinois featured two mini-Sphinxes that were parallel to each other.

The next camera shot showed how the entire complex, along with thousands of worker ants, had been obliterated. All that remained was a jumble of shoeprints in sand that was flecked with grains of quartz and a golden substance that might have been mica or pyrite. Subtitles displayed at the bottom of the screen claimed that the person responsible for stomping on it was a local fundamentalist Christian who believed, "the pyramids had been erected by ants under the directions of wily Satan as part of a scheme of fraud and deceit."

"According to Raiden's figures, the bar is coming up short on Peach Shine and Bold Rock," Royalene told Merrilly and I as she brushed her straggly grey bangs from her granny glasses. "Now, I don't mind the occasional free shot to the more devoted regulars," she said while fiddling with the faux pearls on her eyeglass chain strap, "but let's not overdo it with the Midnight Moon going into hard cider, okay."

As Merrilly walked back to her end of the corrugated metal bar, I could hear her mutter something about "that bitch, Jesse, putting tips in her poke instead of pooling."

Royalene was the elderly owner of a popular neighborhood bar in Louisa. The regulars didn't come in for the dingy brick walls plastered with photos, the country-heavy jukebox or the Sharpie-decorated bathrooms. Their butts sagged on cracking vinyl stools for cheap booze, mostly domestic beer, hard ciders and well drinks. There were very few frozens, except my special "Blue Ridge Sunset" with its splash of flaming peach moonshine. We didn't have free peanuts like most of the other dives, but when Royalene "made groceries", complimentary slices of her made-from-scratch pies were a big hit with the barflies (with my personal favorite being bourbon walnut).

"You want to know what you saw, don't you?" the man seated at the bar asked while stirring his drink with the manicured nail of his index finger. He had ordered some imported rum called "Gosling's Black Seal", calling it "the dew of the still-vex'd

Bermoothes" after getting my attention with a friendly, "Ahoy there… mind if I drop anchor here?" When I told him we didn't have any fancy dew like that – just dark Bacardi, he settled for it without a condescending smile and asked me to mix it with ginger beer and garnish with a wheel of lime, but added that technically it wasn't "a Dark 'n Stormy."

The middle-aged fellow carefully selected a potato chip from the small bag next to the black straw fedora he had removed after walking into the bar wearing a black suit. Oddly enough, the hat like his suit appeared to be perfectly dry even though it had been pouring when he first stepped into the joint. He had a shaven head and no facial hair. In the glare of neon, pale features with pink undertones contrasted with his all black attire. From his manner of dress and neatly-groomed appearance, I immediately pegged him as a D.C. government type, though, even after asking me lots of personal questions, I never asked about his means of employment.

At times it felt like he was trying to determine a medical problem. "Did I have trouble sleeping? Did I have a bipolar disorder, or suffer from occipital seizures, or frequently get migraines? Was I diagnosed with Parkinson's? Did I use recreational drugs?" He asked me this a couple of times when I told him about the exceptional clarity of the airship and its occupant, whose details I could see better than should have been the case from the distance that I had observed it.

"I know what I saw," I replied while grabbing some cans of PBR for a few locals shooting pool.

"Sightings of phantom zeppelins at the end of the nineteenth century were attributed to mass hysteria or practical jokes, with some concocted by newspapers to increase sales. The captions to these wild stories about flying locomotives read 'Take it or leave it – believe it or not.' Unusual aerial phenomena tend to change with the technology of the times... so why would the otherworldly intelligence behind this be playing around in a Civil War reenactment with some ridiculous flying contraption when a sleek antigravitic triangular object would be more in keeping with the pattern of those meddling in human affairs? It doesn't make sense... unless they didn't know it was a reenactment," he chuckled. "In which case, what's the message being sent by choosing sides?"

"If I was tripping, how come I saw the name of the dentist from Richmond whose detailed plans for a steam-powered airship just like the one I saw were recently found? If it were a hallucination, wouldn't that be a hell of a coincidence? And what about the dressed up picnickers that also saw it? Maybe the thing was a hologram, like in the movies."

"You mean like the face of Allah projected onto the battlefield to incite fear into the enemy? Non-lethal weapons? The problem with that is no one doing the fighting saw this convincing deception and, as for the playacting by civilian reenactors enjoying their ham sandwiches while watching the battle, a complex scenario like this hasn't happened before. So who's fighting shadows here?" he mused while cautiously choosing another chip from the bag (which he must have brought in himself, because we didn't sell the Walker's brand of Salt and Vinegar crisps he was eating). "Are the perceptions benign or does the illusion signal ill intentions? But getting back to this thing that doesn't match modern accounts, sometimes we're unaware with what's going on around and inside us. You want to know what you saw, don't you?" he asked while gazing fixedly at me.

"Probably some kind of a large box kite," I nodded while shrugging my shoulders.

"Just one more thing. You say this flying machine was on the side of the rebels. Did you ever wonder why or feel like cheering them on? Playing along with the civilian reenactors picnicking on the hillside?"

"No, I was wearing my Reeboks and had an iPhone. So, no."

"Well, thanks for telling me about this," he said while pulling out some cash to settle his tab and handing me a crisp $20 dollar bill for a tip. "This helps with putting some of the pieces together because phantom zeppelins aren't seen today. Sightings of aerial wonders change with the technology of the time. That makes sense, right?" he repeated for the umpteenth time.

After he put on his fedora and left, I peeked through the window as he got into a shiny black sedan that, unlike the other cars in the parking lot, wasn't beaded with rain. When he pulled away, I kept thinking about why I had subjected myself to his probing questions. I normally didn't get psychological evaluations from strangers drinking at the bar. And then there were the mind games. Even though I was consciously aware there was something unusual about the way he spoke – using verbal skills that were more effective than a super salesman – I willingly played along with the covert technique. It was like he was secretly hypnotizing me to make me change my story (I had written about the mysterious vessel on my old Facebook page about metal detecting), or to encode some kind of message. Or both. Or maybe he was just an oddball that amused me with a conversational style that was so different from the slurred jabbering of grizzled alkies that I answered his harmless questions about a crazy sighting that I no longer cared much about. I wasn't sure what was going on with the guy, as I tried to recall some of his quirks, such as the strange manner that he chomped on snack chips, until a clap of thunder broke my thoughts.

71

"What the fuck is this doing in the tip cup?" Merrilly shouted over the doleful old-time country song playing on the jukebox.

From the solo cup of tips that got dumped every two hours, she pulled out a pale green $20.00 bill of Monopoly money and held it up for me to see.

"Did some fuck give you Monopoly money for a tip and you didn't even notice?"

When I arrived at the Sutton home for round two of their estate sale, I saw that Jeremy had also made the drive. Walking past his cargo van, I noticed four new tires, along with a magnetic sign advertising his aunt's antique business that was placed over sections of corroded silver paint. JEMA'S ATTIC, it was called. The acrid smell of burning engine oil lingered in the warm gust of freshly baled hay coming from nearby fields. Hopefully, fixing the leak was next on the list, before the shame train went up in flames.

On the way to the propped open front door, I saw a black Ford sedan parked along the circular drive that was similar to the car the stranger at the bar drove. I couldn't remember if it also had a special license plate, but both vehicles had darkly tinted windows.

The first person I saw inside was Callie's mother, Della. As she brushed back her messy bob, frazzled from having to handle all the particulars of the sale, I handed her the Francis Bacon book, explaining that I had bought it for considerably less than the asking price due to that number having been penciled on a slip of paper that was stuck between the pages. After thanking me for my honesty, she said that if it didn't sell by the end of the day, I could keep it.

That way, I'd have another excuse to see her daughter, she added with a telling wink (which, of course, I pretended not to get).

When I walked into the library with its detailed ornamentation of unbridled honeysuckle, Jeremy was checking out one of the remaining tomes on the shelves.

"New treads on the Savana, I see."

Startled, he closed the book and turned around, seemingly not recognizing me at first, or, perhaps, his attention was still absorbed by what he had been reading.

"And good sugar levels, I hope."

"Shit, Jack's back," he said as a smile spread across his face. "Where's the little gyal? Yeah, I guess my aunt didn't want me to have a blowout on those turnpike slicks while hauling a high-dollar armoire and cheval mirror with lots of cabbage."

"Hey, if you changed your mind about the *New Atlantis*, miss Sutton should be placing it back on the shelf soon."

"I'm more jazzed about this George Wither book."

Opening that which he had been so engrossed in, the brittle, tawny pages bound within olive crushed morocco with gilt fillets to the board edges smelled as old as the Francis Bacon book.

"Wither was one of the "Good Pens" that Francis Bacon was the secret leader of. It's a 1635 first edition, and, amazingly, it's got the original two volvelles bound into the back," he said while showing me a couple of woodcut spinners attached to a radial dial in the book's appendix.

"What are those used for?" I asked while bending to get a better look at the square frames that were equipped with crude mechanisms similar to a modern wheel of fortune.

"The wheels are used to play a game," he explained while turning one of the pointers with his long brown finger. "The book is laid out in the form of a lottery – an honest and pleasant recreation, as the author states so not to be accused of any wrongdoing by the nobility. This was an interactive experience back in the day of Tewkesbury mustard."

From the corner of my eye I saw Callie walking by, peeking into the library while sucking on one of her cherry 'doctor's pops'.

"I'm gonna check out some Civil War stuff upstairs," I told Jeremy, "but don't leave without saying goodbye."

"The daughter's no fustilugs," he winked.

Upstairs, dozens of people were looking for valuable items in plastic bins. I didn't see Callie watching the thrill of the hunt for jadeite salt and pepper shakers, so I went into the room where the Civil War artifacts were kept. Of the half dozen people gathered around open display cases, a hansome elderly fellow wearing Cartier sunglasses stood out. Lantern-jawed with neatly trimmed silver hair, I assumed he was the one driving the black sedan. He looked like a government type, or ex-black something or other. His dark dress shirt was still crisp in the humidity and had a curious, though pleasant, aseptic fragrance. As the sun beamed through the Palladian window the hand-painted camo pattern on his oxblood-stained leather boots was spotless.

The appraiser was showing him the circular depression marks on a brass military button.

"Notice the depression channel on this one. The back mark lettering indicates the manufacturer as Scovill from Waterbury. With its untouched patina, and, yet, prominent device, it's a splendid example of a dug button."

"Others were found in a trunk," Della said, "filled with letters from prisoners. Along with them was an old brown coat that had several dozen Union buttons sewn onto it."

"Here's a strange question for you, Mister Pribble," the man with the gold-tinted aviators asked with a gravelly voice. "Have you ever seen a button without shanks or a sutler token lacking any surface markings? Just a flat disc with the face and back not brazed."

"I don't know why that would be," the authority replied with his monotonous tone, "being that the point of the store cards was to advertise an arcade or grocer. It would have to be from a badly degraded die, but I haven't any like that in the CWTS catalog. What you're describing sounds like a metal punch-out to trick parking meters... like the young lady here has," he gestured to Callie as she walked into the room in a sexy grey lounge romper.

"If you're talking about the lucky doojigger, I don't know what happened to it. I put it in the pocket of my shorts, but later, it wasn't there. Maybe it will come home like a lost puppy."

"I'm sure it will, Callie," her mother nodded, "Roll right up and lay down by your bare feet."

"Don't be acerbic, mother."

"It's nothing of any value," Della said to the man with the Cartier shades, "unless you don't have enough change to buy a cold drink from a vending machine."

While listening to this, I turned the knobs on the antique Philco radio, trying to get an audio signal, though when I placed my ear against the worn grille cloth, there wasn't even the slightest static.

"That radio doesn't work, Jack," Della said while noticing me playing with the knobs.

"It got reception the last time," I replied. "Some guy talking about a race at Shenandoah Downs."

"Shenny?" Della's eyes widened. "That track was torn down many years ago. And, sorry to say, the old Philco is just as dead. It's funny, though, because Grumble did listen to night racing from Shenny on it back in the day... that and Charles Town. He made lots of money wagering. Said he had a secret for his luck. This wasn't the usual L-shaped fishbone, buckeye nut or Appalachian charm to grow sweet melons. Grandmother said it was gambling prayers, not common ones, that he recited during favorable appearances of a star, which I think they both mistook for something else."

"Sounds like gramps was into voodoo," I joked, noticing that the government-type appeared to be keenly interested in what she had just said.

"Growing up, I never saw any frog heads or crow brains if that's what you mean. Whatever his trick for picking winning horses was though, it sure seemed to work."

"Well, that's certainly refreshing, " the man said while directing his gaze at Callie as she adjusted the revealing button up V-neck outfit before sitting down at a small desk.

"What, a grown woman with crayons and a coloring book," Della smirked.

"You don't see too many young misses these days whose bodies aren't covered with tattoos. Maybe this boomer's out of touch, but it all seems a bit much, and have you seen the latest light-emitting tattoos that glow a greenish color like a horny firefly? I guess they use some kind of OLED display that flexes with the person's skin."

"They're called bio-hacks," Callie said while selecting a crayon, "and soon they'll be used to monitor a person's health."

"Probably have other applications we can't imagine," the man nodded in agreement.

"My daughter prefers her lovely colors in books instead of on her body."

"Maybe it just can't be seen," Callie said with her widening eyes focused on the book. "It's undetectable to most… in a particular spot… like behind the ear or under my foot… or somewhere even less conspicuous, wink, wink."

"Well, something that discreet beats flashy or trashy… being painted from head to toe. Just a tiny rose, butterfly or symbol like the All-Seeing Eye of the ancient Egyptians in a special place."

"I'm not telling, so don't ask."

Maybe my imagination was getting the best of me after what happened at Royalene's the other night, but it seemed like this guy was also probing for information in a way that Callie didn't notice. By mentioning his dislike of flashy body tags, it even occurred to me that he might be referring to Merrilly. Was he making a veiled threat? How could he even have known that I'd show up? I quickly dismissed the idea as my mind playing tricks. Trash patches on women were commonplace, a dime a dozen, especially at our hick Hilton. Most likely, he was just an old letch that had a problem with the new generation of tatted up girls.

When he glanced down to see what Callie was working on, for a second he appeared to be shocked. Then he silently nodded his approval, like one trained not to let their facial expression give anything away. However, judging by his initial reaction, something had made quite an impression. So much so, that I wondered if it was same mind-blowing colors that I had seen, along with added details to the illustration (when I last saw it, she had started to draw fantastic sea flora and marine creatures *outside the lines*).

"I see you used the rather offensive gray-colored one with this," he said after removing his gold mirror shades and pointing to one of the novelty crayons spread out on the small antique desk.

"Oh, heavens, Callie, that's disgusting," Della said while shaking her head, "Worse than the others."

"It came with the set, so –"

"Sorry, Mister Pribble." The mother raised her hands as if to surrender.

"This ranks as one of the strangest conversations I've ever had at an estate sale," the authority said, "and, believe me, I've heard some doozies, but no need to apologize. I'm anxious to hear what comes next."

"Have any of you ever seen one of those Civil War brass acorns that maybe spies used?" I asked.

"You're talking about the so-called rectal acorn, like the one in the museum whose purpose is still unknown," the man said while pushing the Cartier pilots back over his nose.

"I'm glad you didn't start with speaking of which," Callie said after pulling the cherry sucker from her mouth by its safety cord loop, "because that's not the special place. And, it's not a vadge badge either."

"Callie!" Della shook her head again while staring down at the floor.

"No, really," I said, "I once found one something like that while detectoring. The thing was crusty, but made of brass and looked like an acorn."

"Is that what you do, young fellow?" Mister Pribble asked. "Search the ground for buried caches?"

"I used to hunt permissions before I became one of the Bealievers and chased after that hoard. But, I'm done obsessing over that after realizing it's just a scam."

"Have you ever heard of the Gillogly Strings?" the man with the scratchy voice asked.

"Nope."

"Gillogly found something highly unlikely in the middle of Beale Cipher One. The letters of the alphabet from A to Z damn near in the correct sequence. The chances of this being random are practically zero. Either the codemaker got lazy as some think or there's something there that continues to elude both cryptographers and supercomputers, like a sub-cipher embedded in the surface cipher."

"Why don't you go digging for the gold?" I asked. "Get your fingers dirty in some cellar hole."

"It's not what's buried in the ground like the stuff you find with your search coil. It's what's buried in the field of numbers… a second or maybe even third layer of encryption that requires a multi-step process to uncover. In your spare time, you might want to give the matter some more attention. Do it at your leisure," he emphasized, "don't obsess, and you might be rewarded for your efforts."

"Jack, I've an idea," Della said. "We're having a final get together before the property goes up for sale. There will be some kids, so would you bring your metal detector? Come early and we can plant prizes for them to find. A treasure hunt party kind of like what Grumble did for us before he started having problems."

"I've a couple of Garrets I can bring. We can seed the grounds with fake pirate booty. Maybe even find a few real drops… pocket spill and such, or Civil War artifacts if the place hasn't been hunted out. Do you know if there's an old trash pit?"

At that moment, Jeremy entered the room carrying the book with the gilt arabesques on its crushed olive morocco cover.

"Excuse me, is the price on this firm? I'm interested in purchasing it."

"Is that the book with the paper wheels? I used to play with those as a kid."

"Yeah, the emblems and illustrations are disposed into lotteries – both moral and divine," Jeremy read from one of the pages.

"How about a thousand even," Della said, "and I won't ask to give it one last spin."

∾

While driving home after work at the bar, I made the mistake of asking Merrilly if she really needed another tattoo after she told me that she was planning to have a sit down with her artist.

"Seeing how I'm paying for it with my own tips," she said, "which I make more than you because of my tits, tats and stats about the Nats, you don't need to worry about whether I get a new one or not, or where it will go, which will probably be a place you don't seem that interested to look at any more. I don't get salty with you for buying a book you can't read or for going to a dayger next week to sweep for kiddy prizes."

"I told you there also might be some real drops there."

"Yeah, rusty bottle caps."

"I've seen the property and I'll bet it's not as stingy as you think. And I'm just worried about you getting another infection, Merr, that's all – "

"Okay, now what's that?" she said while pointing to something hanging in the night sky as we approached the Dairy Queen that was closed at this late hour.

"Jack, do you see that – near the Grill and Chill?"

"Yeah, what's going on with that?"

Whatever the object was, it remained stationary at treetop level. With minimum streetlights (and little moon) on the "quiet lane" that led to our trailer court, it was hard to make out details. When we got a bit closer, at first I thought it might be a drone with multiple rotor pylons, like one of the larger octocopters you see on Amazon, but quickly ruled this out because of its size. From my angle of view, its visible profile resembled a Black Hawk helicopter with a reshaped surface.

As it continued to hover without making a sound, the most unusual feature was its circular tail section. After a long whip antenna retracted back into the belly's enigmatic dark finish, the rotorcraft lifted higher and started heading right towards us.

"Why's it coming this way?" Merrily uttered with a trace of alarm in her voice.

Getting a better look at the thing as it barely cleared a power line, the unique front cowling had a sleek, truncated triangular design, whose graphite panels matched the fuselage's armor plating and infrared-reducing fairing. There were no identifiable markings or blinking navigation lights. As its skids passed directly over the pickup, I couldn't hear anything except for a soft swishing sound.

"Idiot's flying at an unsafe altitude," I said. "Probably coming from Fort Eustis."

"Shit, Jack, they're watching you because of that stupid thing you said you saw."

We continued to watch it as it skimmed a grassy field before disappearing over a forested area.

When we walked into the trailer with our nerves still a bit rattled after being buzzed by the stealthy helicopter, Raiden was sitting on the couch watching a new TroVe clip of another ant colony building a mini-pyramid complex aligned like those on the Giza Plateau.

"Where's Charlotte?" Merrily asked. "Walking Golliwog?"

"She went home after the Amazon delivery man came."

"What are you talking about? So, then, where's Golliwog?"

Normally the dog would come running when Merrily walked in, but for some reason she was sleeping soundly on the kitchen floor.

"She's sleepy, huh, Merr," Raiden said.

After Merrily roused her, she scooted across the floor, slipping a couple of times.

"What did this delivery man look like?" I asked, "Was he wearing a blue polo shirt with the Amazon logo? Not the cardboard Hitler mustache one."

"The cardboard Hitler mustache was a logo, but it's gone now, Jack. It was the arrow pointing from A to Z. He also wore army boots... and gave me a purple cow."

"What's that?" I asked.

"It's a purple milkshake. Not as good as Grill and Chill, but still good. He gave Charlotte one, too, but she didn't remember liking it. It's a purple milkshake."

"That's cray, Raiden," I said. "Retweet – what does that mean?"

"It had grape juice in it with vanilla ice cream instead of strawberry, which isn't purple," he said with his compromised speech.

"Raiden, c'mon, buddy."

"He doesn't make up things," Merrily said with a twinge of anger.

Sitting on the coffee table was my copy of *The Beale Papers*. In the middle of a cipher field of numbers on one of the pages someone had drawn with a pencil several lines that intersected to form a crude depiction of the most identifiable symbol of Freemasonry. There were also some numbers written at two points on the emblem that could have been map coordinates.

"Did you write in this?" I asked Raiden.

"Yes, Jack. I hope it's okay," he said after clearing his throat and flapping his hand. "The Amazon driver with the blue polo shirt and logo of the arrow pointing from A to Z must have liked it because he took pictures of it. He also wore army boots, Jack."

"Oh my God, it was one of them," Merrilly said while picking up Golliwog, who was still a bit wobbly. "Like the guy at the bar asking you all those questions. He was in my trailer with my brother and my dog. He drugged Golliwog. Came in the helicopter, didn't he? That military black thing we just saw!"

"I don't know about that," I said, trying to calm her down.

"Oh, you don't know – that's so fucking typical, Jack. It was either one of them or a burglar. Shit, I better check my jewelry," she said while rushing into the bedroom.

"Where's the package this Amazon driver, brought," I asked Raiden.

"He left it outside where it would be safe."

Moments later Merrily returned with her face buried in her hands.

"My stuff's all here," she said weakly, "but it looks like someone went through your cigar box. Doesn't look like they took anything, though. The silver Morgan's still here so I don't know what they were looking for," she said as tears trickled down onto the smattering of freckles on her cheeks.

After Merrilly settled down and Raiden fell asleep on the couch, I went outside to have a look inside the portable Weber grill on the patio. Lifting the cover, I saw a small package from

Amazon, whose shipping address said: YUMYUM FACTORY. Setting it back on the grill, I quietly closed the lid until I could sneak it inside.

CHAPTER III
PROSPERI-TEA

"For books are not absolutely dead things,
but do contain a potency of life in them
to be as active as that soul whose progeny
they are; nay, they do preserve in a vial
the purest efficacy and extraction of the
living intellect that bred them."

John Milton

"You have often
B*egun to tell me what I am, but stopped*
And left me to a bootless inquisition,
Con*cluding, 'Stay, Not yet.' "*

Shakespeare's *The Tempest*

"Sherman: It's a man wearing a disguise!
Mr. Peabody: Francis Bacon, if I'm not mistaken.
And I never am.
Shakespeare: Bacon! You'll fry for this!"

Mr. Peabody and the Wayback Machine
Animation series episode from 1961

The Sutton family gathering was in full swing in the spacious backyard of Della's large house. Friends and relatives were seated at dappled picnic tables under a large weeping willow tree, where they gossiped and talked politics over the sugar-high screams of children running around a rusted old swing set on the freshly mowed lawn.

"That's a screamer," I told the small boy when the metal detector emitted a high pitch beep. Though he was barely able to handle the lightweight 'Junior' model that I used when I first got into the hobby, the alert repeated as I helped him swing the search coil over the patch of grass that I had earlier liberally salted for the treasure hunt party.

"You've rung up something good, even with these ultra-violet killers messing with the thing. Let's hope it's a valuable coinball. Okay, use the pointer when I start digging."

Using a serrated spade to remove the already loose plug of earth, I quickly pulled out one of the replica 'silver Spanish doubloons' that I had planted earlier. After brushing off the dirt, I handed it to the kid with the delighted smile.

"Wow, nice find, mister happy face. Look at that antique silver finish. Blackbeard probably dropped this hundreds of years ago after sailing his flagship up the North Anna River. First, we replace the clump of dirt because we're responsible hunters, then we flag and bag. Since stores these days don't take pirate booty, take it to Ms. Sutton over there and she'll give you a crisp five-dollar bill. This place is turning out to be a honey hole," I winked at several adults who had gathered around to watch the kids unearth their prizes.

"Someone ring the dinner bell," a potbellied fellow in camouflage fatigues (including a chef's camo toque that he must have purchased from a Bass Pro Shop catalogue) shouted while grilling meat on a brick smoker. "Though the smoke is the only thing keeping the horseflies from eating me. Those zappers ain't doing their job, Della," he said while rubbing his puffy, stubby cheeks, "and it appears this summer God's super-sized the pesky fuckers."

"There are children present, Lewis," Della reminded him while walking up in a floral chiffon cardigan with a lowcut white tank beneath. Her messy bob was cut shorter and now had lilac streaks.

"And I've got fancy hotdogs for the small fries, if they don't like my venison steaks," Lewis said while shooing away the noisy fly that kept buzzing around him.

"I hope to see my meat in your mouth, Della," he winked after taking a gulp of beer.

"How many times have I heard that," Della cringed while playfully kicking him in the shin.

"And lemon clouds for dessert," she smiled at a little girl adjusting her floppy straw sun hat.

"I hope there's also some blackberry cobbler to go with those heaping white mounds of —"

"That would be Chantilly cream, Lewis."

"Not that I'm giving away secrets, but, along with my other spices, a pinch or two of hickory-smoked salt does wonders for grilled deer hearts," he said to no one in particular. "These I've seasoned here aren't tartare, but have just a little tooth. Put 'em on a mini potato roll with some coleslaw, and you're in business... if you've already got a jar of bourbon and ice, that is."

"Kids, come get some Firecracker Franks," Della shouted while the robust flies attempted to alight on a tray of hotdogs on skewers that were wrapped in breadstick dough topped by half-melted Colby cheese stars.

"Martha Stewart to the rescue," I teased her while picking up one of the charred things.

"Then have one of Lewis's deer heart sliders, Jack."

"They're a little rare for me — almost still beating."

"Why don't you take your wiener and go find Callie."

After grabbing a couple of iced hard seltzers from the aluminum tub, I headed towards the forest at the edge of the lawn. Just past some horseshoe pits, a path wound through the woods that had been cleared of much growth. Following this for a minute, I found Callie sitting on a bench in a clearing that was shaded by the droopy branches of a hemlock tree. Wearing a pink tee shirt that said 'APPROACH WITH CAUTION', she was smoking one of her demi-slims. As I walked up, offering her a can of Bold Rock, she tugged at the distressed Levi shorts that barely covered her tanned thighs. Though she was barefoot, a pair of wedge sandals lay under the bench where she wiggled her painted toes in the dirt.

"Watch out for the poison ivy," she said while untangling a strand of hair, "and that hornets nest. I warned them about the repellent lamps so they might be a little perturbed."

"Want something cold?" I asked while handing her the hard seltzer. "I also brought you a gift," I said while pulling out a small box from my pocket that I had wrapped with festive paper left over from Merrilly's birthday. "It's been in my detecting apron for a while so I hope it's okay."

After carefully unwrapping the paper, she removed from the box three fancy pink lollipops that had crushed rose pedals inside.

"Flowers and candy... or flowers in candy," she said tonelessly. "Why bring them for me?"

"Oh, I was just feeling kind of bad for any kiddies out there at the doctor's office being deprived of a cherry lollipop because you've conjured the motherlode with that whatzit of yours."

"Yeah, they just flicker into being... Presto!" she made a motion with the cigarette like that of a stage magician tapping his wand. "Strange thing is, I haven't seen Grumble's funny button for a while. But, I know I didn't just lose it. So, how are the kiddies doing with your detectors?"

"The newbies are finding lots of pirate drops."

"That hunter with the army chef's hat – Lewis – he's a friend of my uncle. He's gross. Bombards my mother with plebeian sexual innuendos like knowing a nice rack when he sees one. Yeah, as if a man with hair on his tongue could have her as his grill. He thinks he's so swol, but he's just a blobby Elmer. Shoots poor innocent deer and then cuts their hearts out. Stashes the meat in his freezer until we have a gathering. They'll get even with their stalker someday – the deer will – probably plotting their revenge as we speak. I heard he even once shot his neighbor's dog when he couldn't find a harmless deer."

"The gadflies sure like him. I'm glad I didn't bring Golliwog."

"I thought your woozle's name was Gollidog?"

"Sometimes," I laughed.

"Those glizzys aren't killed humanely either," she said while wriggling her nose with a disgusted look. "I told her to serve grilled beets, but instead she called mister smoky bones. Or asparagus and shiitakes… and Lentil burgers for the kids."

"Yeah, you might be able to convince them it's a burger and they're not being punished for something."

"What about stuffed tomatoes – they're festive."

"They sound exciting. Vogue Perle Menthe," I tried to pronounce the name on the box of her demi-slims. "Sounds yummy, but those are worse for you than the burnt glizzys."

"Ever heard a tobacco plant scream, Jack?"

Turning to avoid the stream of mentholated smoke she exhaled towards my face, I noticed several holes in the ground that had a white residue around their edges. Bending down to take a closer look at their smooth edges and uniform shape, the shallow depressions resembled dirt plugs that weren't replaced or cutouts made by a core sample drill.

"Did someone else get permissions to detect here?

"They've been here for ever. Since the 1960s, I've heard. They were made by the astrodilla."

"What?"

"The stories I heard were that Grumble saw a lightball darting about here that was brighter than those flashlights Amazon sells. It bounced up, down and sideways. When he came to check it out, the intense sparkle was gone but he saw this rolling greyish shape that caused his vision to blur. His skin was prickling, but he still chased after it. Once it stopped rolling, it suddenly changed shape, becoming this silverish creature that was covered with scales so that it looked like what he called an armored pig. That's what he called armadillos that he'd seen in photos. He said it hopped kind of funny, almost gliding as it circled around his feet before it slowly lifted up and changed shape again before it floated through the trees. After the lightball was gone and his eyesight returned to normal, he found these glowing rings on the ground. When he touched one, his fingers became numb. Later, samples were taken of the circles that you can still see. The white crust here had weird properties. They were more acidic than normal and also had high levels of calcium, even though no cows browsed here. They still don't absorb water. Not even a drop. Here, watch this."

As she poured some of the Bold Rock into one of the depressions, the bubbly liquid instantly congealed into a globule and spurted out like a frog jumping from a lily pad.

"That's cray," I said while examining the glob of seltzer lying next to the hole.

Before I poured some of my own seltzer into another hole to see if it, too, would fling the stuff out, I heard what sounded like a woman singing while approaching from the twisting path. When Callie recognized the voice to be her mother's, she quickly dropped the cigarette and covered it with one of her espadrilles.

"Callie's sad, and I'm glad and I know what to please her," the words to a child's ditty went. "A bottle of wine to make her shine and a pretty little boy to squeeze her."

"Mother, please stop. We're not churning butter or whatever you did when singing that idiotic song."

"Daughter, why do I constantly smell cigarette smoke when in your presence?"

"That's the stench of cooked deer permeating your clothes, along with the nasty marinade whipped up by the butcher of Massaponax Creek."

"Why don't you come have some green bean and wild rice salad that Darla made especially for you?"

"I was planning to do just that as soon as we're done."

"What are you doing besides sneaking a smoke?"

"I don't know about Callie, but I'm trying to figure out why this hole won't swallow boozy seltzer," I laughed. "It just spat a mouthful of Passion Fruit back at us."

"Oh, brother, not the astrodillo thing again. The rings are caused by some kind of fungus, probably from the conifers or freak lightning strikes – ball lightning, it's called."

"Why do you always have to be so glib when you talk about what happened here?" Callie bristled.

"Because I have a hard time believing in nature spirits or space animals or whatever you think it was. Grumble saw lots of things that weren't really there. Even prize walks by black slaves with ragged garments in a nearby field – this in the 1960s, mind you. The same field where he said a rebel soldier found that button or token that's really just a common vending machine tricker. These things happened after he fell into a dark hole in his own mind, but that's a family matter."

⁓

While most were having dessert, the seeded hunt was about to come to an end. During the last girl's turn, at the spot where I buried a Mercury dime, the tone indicated a non-ferrous target.

"You've rung up something good, sweetie. Sounds like silver to these trained ears...maybe even Lady Liberty, herself. Do you know what that is? It's an old Mercury dime worth a lot more than ten cents," I said while digging up the plug of earth. While scrapping away more dirt, instead of finding the expected Merc, there was an acorn-shaped object whose brass surface had a greenish patina. Its slightly corroded side looked familiar, being almost identical in appearance to the piece I had found several years ago that was now back in my top dresser drawer at the trailer. From what I had been told, it was most likely a Civil War hat badge, but possibly a device used by spies to smuggle secret messages in their rectum. When the pointer buzzed again after another sweep, I quickly found and removed the 1945 Mercury dime that I had planted, giving it to the girl with an excited look on her face.

"Here you go – a genuine Merc," I said while pocketing the crusty brass object. "Now, go have another lemon cloud."

As she scampered off with her prize, the little boy that found the first pirate coin walked up.

"Sir, when I checked on the web, it said I ought to get more than five dollars for one of Blackbeard's coins... like a lot more, sir, because it's a pirate's and pirates get more for theirs, so maybe I can get it back –"

"That's for the really shiny gold ones like Ray found," I explained, "And I just learned yours is made of zinc, so five bucks was a good deal. Someone messed with the settings. It's an entry-level detector, but it's not a toy."

When he walked away with a confused look on his face, I approached Della, who was fending off more advances from Louis.

"Are you keeping the fakes after paying the tikes?"

"I thought I was supposed to – in exchange for the cash."

"Yeah, but if the little shits are going to Google everything, you're gonna need to make a larger withdrawal from your bank."

"I'll bet that's how little Ray knew the *Queen Ann's Revenge* never set anchor in the North Anna River. Next, they'll be consulting with Darla's decorated squid over there."

After most of those who had children had packed up and left, a handful of us were seated under the sprawling canopy of the willow as the sun started to dip below the horizon. Peeking through its long, delicate branches to make sure her mom wasn't around, Callie lit one of her demi-slims.

"Don't let your mom or aunt see you with that," the husband of Della's older sister, Darla, said over the clanging of horseshoes tossed by a couple of teens. "Last time I told her the smell was from fufu juice rubbed on my kisser, but she wasn't buying that. I sent her on a fool's errand, but she catches on quick, so after another drag or two I'd ditch the thing."

The clean-shaven guy with ruddy cheeks was wearing a dark blue nylon jacket that contained colorful patches honoring his service in Vietnam. Wondering if his Navy pride extended to placing military challenge coins in the slots of his Penny loafers, I glanced down as they tapped the ground to the rhythm of croaking frogs. Both were devoid of patriotic tokens.

"There were chemical irregularities found in the insoluble rings, and they still retain these unusual properties, like repelling water – as you saw – but the story gets even weirder," he told me while using his emblazoned Navy cap to scratch wisps of snow-white hair. "Grumble said he was going to shoot the varmint if it returned – this armadillo or whatever it was."

"Tell him about what else he saw – on the ground," Callie said, "that you guys never talk about."

"You mean the purple lines? Oh, we never believed that," her uncle said while making a dismissive hand gesture. "Its puzzling characteristics – the playful behavior of the energetic light – he said it made a crackling noise like crushed glass. This sounds to me like ball lightning. It's a rare phenomenon. Not much was known about it back then, or even today. Even though he swore its movements weren't haphazard – that it was looking for something – maybe his lucky button because this happened during the time that it went missing, even though he was careful not to lose it and kept it in a safe place. The reason being that it was his good luck charm and responsible for his winning streak at the track. But, scuttlebutt had it that this was just an excuse – the cover story for the kitchen magic he was doing... the dark fixins. I later found out that Darla and Della had taken the thing from his hiding place and were playing hide-and-seek with it down there in the trees where the light was later seen bouncing around."

After taking a sip of iced sweet tea, he continued: "Grumble had a brother named Grayson who was the total opposite of him. He didn't smoke, drink or gamble. He attended church regularly. He wasn't one of those hippie-like Jesus people in the

'60s that strummed guitars and sang about Jesus being the good drug. If he gave away free donuts, it was as a missionary in places like Haiti. He wasn't what we called in the Navy a pollywog, meaning he went to foreign places... Do you hear that whippoorwill?" He paused. "Or is it a mockingbird that's mimicking a whippoorwill?"

"Maybe it's even messin' with the frogs – it's a little early for their croaks," I said.

"Yeah, could be. Have to be doing a lot of them, though," he joked. "Heck, I've even heard 'em sound like car alarms. Damn thing will be going all night. Anyway, where was I? Oh, yeah, when Grumble told his brother about his run-in with the critter doing all the digging, Grayson assumed he was just seeing things because of his serious alcohol problem. But, even so, it inspired him to write a children's book with funny armadillo characters.

This was one of those 'it's okay if you don't fit in' kind of books and how to react when hurtful things are said or when you get clobbered by the neighborhood bully just because you're different from the other kids. Okay, so when Grayson tried to get his brother to walk the straight and narrow – to find Jesus and what not, Grumble flatly rejected him, and said he had something to show him that would destroy his own faith. He also said that his way of praying was far more effective and that with his method those in charge hear one's voice more clearly. Along with this, he rambled on about strange places he said he saw through tiny windows – things no one could have imagined. This was probably just another one of his cockamamie schemes, though some of the things he talked about were pretty heavy stuff for someone with his limited education. And as for things in the night sky – before all this started, he had never imagined anything further away than Neptune," he laughed. "Whatever it was that he showed him... well, shortly after, Grayson dropped out of sight. Broke off all communication. And not long after this, the characters featured in his popular book began to appear in those doper funnies that were peddled to long-haired types. Only now, they weren't straight-laced avengers of the neighborhood toughs. They were counter-culture freaks that smoked grass all day and used offensive language. I've heard that some think that there's something more going on with their crazy antics than just to make dopers giggle, but what that could be I don't know. Though the comic strips were written anonymously, same as his book, one of the armadillos was named Darla, so we all figured it had to be Grayson's doing, but as to why the 180 from decent picture books to radical hippie garbage – what caused such a drastic change in his personality is anyone's guess."

"What do you think gramps showed him?" I asked.

"I wouldn't hazard a guess, Jack, but Grumble used to tell people around here that he had his own star that at times ap-peared only over his property. If he could somehow pull off a trick like that – that might cause someone to rethink things."

Just then, the mockingbird started up again with its long series of phrases. Only, this time, instead of imitating the sound of other birds (or croaks of frogs), it mimicked something that sounded like the mechanical drone of a helicopter with dampened rotor blades. Making the mimicry even stranger, the steady *thwop-thwop* was accompanied by a repeating series of complex machine-like tones.

"Listen to that silly thing," Callie's uncle said while getting up from the picnic table and pulling back a handful of thin branches to gaze at the dark outlines of hemlock trees. "Now, it sounds like some kind of machine. Almost like a chopper with its *whup-whup* pared down. And do you hear that weird beeping noise it's making? How goofy is that."

"That's funny, I actually saw a helicopter that kind of sounded like that last week," I said.

As the songbird continued to replicate the repeated cycle of machine-like tones, Callie seemed to be growing uneasy. She jabbed the cigarette against the bench and flicked it away. As orange sparks scattered across the lawn, she waved away the smoke and nervously squeezed my hand.

"Did it look like some derivative of a Black Hawk MH-60?" the Navy vet asked.

"Yeah, I figured it was from Fort Eustis."

"Yep, probably something stealthy. Reduced blade-vortex interaction, the whisper mode's called, and those mockingbirds are doing a pretty good impression."

Without saying a word, Callie got up and made a beeline towards the house.

"She's not turning in this early, is she?" her uncle asked. "Without saying any goodbyes."

"Nature call would be my guess," I said.

"Right, the head."

When she didn't return after a half an hour, I gathered up my metal detectors and headed to my pickup. When I opened the door, I smelled cigarette smoke and saw Callie curled up like a ball in the front seat.

"That's a strange place to be doing yoga," I joked.

"Can you drop me off at a friend's house?" she asked after pulling a child's red lollipop from her mouth. "I don't want to listen to that thing for another night."

"You mean the bird? It's just doing its thing. Copying other stuff."

"I know what it's imitating, because it landed here a few nights ago. Only, it wasn't your regular whirlybird, and not always colored black. It had this coating that looked like our drive-way seen in a large mirror – some pearlescent coating that even reflected the fireflies around the wishing well here. That guy you saw at the sale who was asking me if I had any tattoos – he was with the doctors, or whatever they were. When he mentioned something about the crayon – the offensive gray one – I thought he was going to push me inside a hot oven."

"What are you talking about, Callie?"

"It wasn't an oven, but the tube was dark inside and glowed orangish like an oven. It was one of those machines used for medical imaging."

"MRI? You were given an MRI scan?"

"Without a fucking call button. They were looking for a tattoo on my private parts... even on the insides – after first checking the palms of my hands and forehead... not just the skin, but under the skin, Jack. Maybe they thought I had some kind of wearable stuck on me with electric paint like those smart tattoos used for track-ing, or to monitor medical problems like fitness bands do but I told them I didn't have diabetes or high glucose levels."

"This sounds like a dream, Callie. Sounds like a really strange dream?"

"That's what I was thinking at first – it seemed like a dream, but I picked up some white pebbles from the driveway, here and left a trail back to my bedroom like Hansel and Gretel did with breadcrumbs in the forest... so I would remember what hap-pened, and in the morning they were still there – the pebbles were. When they were done, they wanted me to drink a Dixie Cup of purple stuff, but when they weren't looking I spat the stuff on the floor."

While returning from the Food Lion, Merrilly lifted the back of her Royalene's tank to show me the new tattoo on the small of her back. When she had told me that she was going to get a "strippers barcode", I assumed she was referring to one of those common 'tramp stamps' that women get just above their ass. However, as it turned out, she meant it literally. The tattoo was a QR code for a crypto currency account that she had set up in order to earn extra money doing some pole dancing at a nearby strip joint that accepted Bitcoin tips from customers. Before I had a chance to react, she pulled out a box of Vogue Perle Menthe demi-slims from her purse.

"I found these on the seat this morning when I borrowed the truck to get some Grey Goose and moisturizer. What were they doing in the cab?"

"I don't know, Merr... Oh, I know... Yeah, they must have been left there by one of the Sutton family members that I gave a ride to after the gathering."

"Is she pretty?"

"Why are you throwing away candy?" Raiden asked as I tossed the remaining rose petal lollipops that I had tucked inside a pair of gloves in my dresser drawer into a plastic grocery bag.

"Because they're dirty, buddy – have pieces of leaves and floor sweepings inside them. I was going to give them to Merrilly, but now I'll have to get something else. Don't tell her, though, and ruin the surprise."

"The ants would lick them, Jack, but then they'd be set on fire by the red dragon. Circus peanuts are good, they're fluffy like a sponge or pillow," he said after clearing his throat and flapping his hand.

I wasn't sure what he meant about ants being "set on fire by the red dragon" until he clicked on a recently uploaded video on TroVe that showed columns of ants bustling around a newly discovered mini-complex of pyramids in a picnic area. Evidently, with new sightings now occurring across the country, people were taking sides, with some destroying the scale-model monuments (along with the nearby ant mounds) while others formed circles around the layout to protect them from being stomped on.

The drone shot of the pyramids cut to a man spraying poison on ant mounds near his backyard pergola.

"Here in Arizona, we don't want our Pharaoh ants building these damn things in our pantries, so we spray their hills with industrial strength pesticide. We're also commencing to start ant-killing parties at potential sites just so they don't get any ideas. We'll be setting up bait stations with the likes of honey syrup, melted *raspados* and my daughters' favorite cereal, Sugar Smacks, basically, anything sweet from Bashas to attract them before we wallop 'em or the monsoon washes 'em away. We'll put down advanced granular poison for the workers to feed the queen. Sorry, your Highness, but no omelets today. Yep, we're gonna eradicate all the colonies and a gazillion eggs with them."

The next shot showed a man wearing a battered cowboy hat proudly displaying the propane weed torch (Red Dragon brand) that he held with a pair of large oven mitts.

"We'll take the devils out with flame weeders like this baby. Totally vaporize the things. No more A-rab funny business here in Apache Junction, folks."

With another cut, a woman in a tie-dyed tee standing with a circle of protesters around some ant mounds in Sedona stated their position:

"If they're all not hoaxes – which I don't think they are – then we need to study the high-degree of precision of these little wonders... the near-perfect accuracy of the alignments with the Autumnal Equinox that was constructed without blueprints or even a basic gnomon."

"Is this a joke gone viral?" I asked Raiden. "C'mon, get real, people."

"The birds should put the people asleep so the red dragon can't set ants on fire," Raiden said.

Before I could ask what he meant by this, he grabbed the remote and clicked on a thumbnail from the playlist. Birds were singing, but their songs didn't sound right.

"Birds are learning a new trick it seems," said the narrator with a British accent. "What you're listening to isn't common chirping – not a lullaby for sleeping babies in the nest. When using the BirdGenie app, the audio spectrograms don't recognize these avian voices with their multi-element phrases, slurred pitch contours and lack of dissonant intervals. Here, we have cardinals, finch, grosbeaks, sparrow and thrusts, but take a look at what the circular structure of their repetitive melodies have on any stalking felines."

The camera angles widened from the various singing birds to show common house cats falling asleep on the ground.

"Tabbies, Calicos or exotics – the affect of the cradle song puts their prey soundly asleep, thus allowing the birds free rein on any nearby tasty insects."

"What's this twit talking about?" I asked Raiden. "That shit's got to be fake, too."

❧

Wearing a new pair of embroidered skinny jeans, Merrilly kicked off her baby pink glitter high heels and plopped down on the sofa where I was watching people in several states battle over the ant pyramids. She had just returned from her pole-dancing job and once again couldn't wait to check her cryptocurrency account.

"I'm liking this low-key currency thing, and so do our customers. Not only do they get a discount, there's no digital trail for their nosey wives to see. Sorry, peach – it's encrypted."

"People are coming to blows over these hoaxes," I shook my head. "Injuries are being reported – some serious with people having to go to the hospital."

On the flat screen, a dude with a droopy mustache was crushing a bag of snack food by doing an improvised dance with his snakeskin boots.

"Here's a little mashing dance I come up with for bags of chips from the 7-Lebanon. Making ant feed from Bugles for the rest of the nest, and then we'll see just how smart they are."

"Even ants won't touch that salty crud," I mumbled.

"Speaking of no cash," Merrilly said while popping open a beer, "let me know when you have the other half of the rent. So… did you find anything of value in those peoples' backyard?"

"Just another one of those brass acorn things, but it's just as roached as the first one."

"Finders keepers," she joked. "Well, that's better than a hunk of pig iron… I guess. Another wasted dayger. If you had done your shift, you'd have the money to pay your bae or whatever it is I am. Someone tipped me a twenty for the best carousel slide to the knees he'd ever seen," she said while running her fingers over the floral applique on the new blue denim.

"And he's probably still enjoying it while sitting on a dirty toilet," I said.

"Uh-oh, friction." Merrilly shot me a sidelong glance. "Hello, AdBlock!" she shouted when the video went to a commercial about stomach noises.

"How about Cali?"

"Callie?"

"That chick who says she gave birth to whatever it is. We watched part of it – it's supposed to be like an alien."

"You said she was a nutter."

"She is a nutter, but I like the way she talks."

Using the remote, she fast-forwarded the video of the interview with the woman who was disguised to protect her identity (including a patch of blurred colored squares on her arm). As she spoke with a filtered voice, a quote on the screen read:

Strange things are going to start happening.
- Siriana

"What, if any details can you tell us about the artificial insemination of this ultra-terrestrial being?" the interviewer asked.

"The procedure took place at the same lab in the Bay Area in a secure area known as the Stork's Nest. This was a dual-use facility with the front being synthetic biology for designer children. Some truly brilliant geneticists worked there, although how many times in the past have gifted minds engaged in monstrous enterprises. One interesting thing is that some of the top scientists had a glass eye that I came to realize was used as a biometric feature to grant access to the strictly off-limits Stork's

Nest. Again, this was where the team conducted experiments with electrical signals on things like Picasso frogs while attempting to rewrite their code."

"I'm trying to imagine what this more advanced life-form's physical features looked like?" the interviewer said.

"Either I wasn't shown the baby or that part of my memory is still blacked out – wasn't restored. But I do recall seeing ultrasounds that made me think àbout what it says in the Bible about the gods creating humans in their image... after their likeness. I also don't know what sex it is. It might be able to reproduce asexually – where a male and female union isn't necessary – like Komodo Dragons do. There was also talk about this jellyfish – I forget the species – that has relative immortality. If physically compromised, it has the ability to transform itself back into a polyp and start all over again."

"Earlier you mentioned the favorable conditions that preserved their DNA. Is there anything more you can tell us about this?"

"They referred to these pockets of synthetic dimensions as shadow architecture. Again, they're built with some kind of energy instead of steel, wood or bricks. Some have a mimetic mesh integrated into them as a type of optical camouflage, but it also does more than just mirror the surroundings. It must have seemed like... well, do you know the tale from the *Arabian Nights* about the fairy, Paribandi? How the sultan asked the jinn to deliver to him a magic tent... or pavilion... even though he considered such a thing to be an impossible feat, even for a fairy. But to his amazement, Paribandi presented him with a tent that met his requirements... Fold it, and it seemed like a toy that could be held in the palm of a child's hand. Spread it, and the armies of the sultan might repose in its shade. Such are the mind-boggling properties of this shelter, and it's in a similar safe haven... one of these structures that Ultra-1 is currently being kept."

"Why keep this a secret?"

"That would depend on who's in charge of the program. If it were the military they would be interested in any technological advancement issued from its unfiltered neurological wiring. They might even use it as bait – to lure others like it back to the planet for a reunion with our glorious creators. From subtle impressions I received while carrying it, I sense that – even in the womb – it's aware of such duplicity. If it's some esoteric syndicate that's actually pulling the strings, they would have their own agenda, perhaps hoping it would be the vanguard that ushers in a new golden age. Again, as its surrogate mother, I can only hope certain challenges Ultra-1 presents to humans aren't insuperable, though I do have my doubts."

"Were you given the chance, what would you have named the baby?"

"Asphodel. The flower with beautiful blossoms that's often chosen for funerals."

As the video was about to end, I received a text from Jeremy letting me know that he had a potential buyer for my Francis Bacon book. If I was still interested in selling it, I should let him know so we could set up a time for me to bring it by his aunt's shop. I quickly replied that I wanted to sell it and would bring it to the address he provided on Sunday afternoon. Good timing, I thought. If the deal went through, I could get Merrily off my back and catch up on some bills that were past due.

Nestled along a scenic old route in Lynchburg, just past a roadside produce stand, I found Jeremy's aunts' shops without too much trouble. Pulling into the shady gravel drive, I parked under some flowering dogwood trees by his faded silver van. There were no other cars in the lot, so I figured the antique business wasn't open on Sundays. Taking the last gulp from a cup of Bojangles lemonade, I gazed at the cluster of old grey wooden structures with tin ceilings that might have once been large storage sheds for a farm.

The colorful sign on the one to my left read: CLEO'S FIX-INS, with the one to the right being JEMA'S ATTIC. Between them was a rustic cottage with a sagging porch. When I climbed out of the pickup, a scruffy gray tomcat darted from the weed-choked shell of a vintage gas pump in front of the main group of washed out buildings.

As I started towards the antique store, I heard Jeremy call me from the entrance to the other shop.

"Jack, I'm over here."

When I walked up to the door with the book, I handed him a wrapped sweet potato pie that I got at Bojangles.

"Some crisis pie for Pye. Its got a sugar spread."

The smell in here is just witch wash. Cologne... like Florida Water to remove any negativity," he said as I entered what looked like a dimly lit old-fashioned apothecary with a creaking wood floor and exposed ceiling beams.

"So, I just finished loading a green candle with a petition to get the highest price for your book, and I'm about to inscribe it with a spiral of success sigils using a coffin nail that was recently replenished by a spirit in a graveyard at Heritage's Baptist Church. Then we'll dress it with money-drawing oil and check the smoke patterns to determine the efficacy of the spell. Some Lucky Hoodoo for you, Jack."

"Fuck are you talking about, dude?"

"I'm just messing with you. You should see your face. You look so shook. I was just helping myself to one of my aunt's maple donuts. You want one?"

"I just had my own one of their desserts. This place isn't creepy," I laughed while pointing to dolls cobbled together from scraps of fabric and clutching fistfuls of decorative joss paper money.

"My aunt Cleo is a well-known conjure doctor. She specializes in rootwork and cleansing with down-home methods. There's a nursery out back. She also sells assorted spiritual needs here, and in mail-order catalogues, though I'm trying to convince her to get an online store."

Walking down a cluttered aisle, we passed shelves containing dried roots, potions, candles, incense and other curiosities that were kept in a pink washtub.

"Sachet powders, body butters and black cat perfume," Jeremy began naming the various items used for spell-craft. "Bible ashes, caterpillar heads, salamander eyes, chamber lye – I think that's Cleo's piss – Chinese hell money, aerial spray potions, bergamot floor scrub, cherry root, dying breath, mad water, steel dust, egg mucus, puppy drum, black-eyed peas, prosperi-tea, raccoon penis bones, seeds for the sweetest melons and silver dollars painted with menstrual blood. Just the staples like blessed candles, though not human tallow, and lots of dressed bundles. Mojo amulets for just about any need you can imagine. Maybe I can interest you in a gold-plated Pro-Tecto Bible like many soldiers in WWII carried?"

"Does any of this shit actually work, or do people just believe it does?"

I heard the Pro-Tecto Bible stopped a few bullets. Think about it, Jack – what is money based on? What gives it any value? Nothing tangible. Money is based on belief – a collective belief. Belief is energy, and energy can be manipulated."

"I wonder if the Sutton's gramps, Grumble, used any of this stuff to bet on the ponies?"

"Money-drawing tricks? Shit, who knows, he might have used gamblers' hand wash or consulted some enchiridion to catch lucky numbers like the *Petit Albert* to seek the favorable dispositions of the stars. Perhaps he dabbled in scriptural sorcery. Used the lawd's hoodoo like this spell from Job to beat a slot machine... He hath swallowed down riches and he shall vomit them up again. God shall cast them out of his belly. Cleo once told me about this reverend that boiled a bible to extract its power into a liquid that he used for a floor wash."

On a counter containing decorative colored bottles and calabashes filled with shiny trinkets, he thumbed through a Rolodex whose smudged index cards contained recipes for mysterious hoodoo tinctures along with the corresponding petitions written in old-fashioned cursive lettering.

"Is there anything in there to make a girl want you?" I asked, even though I had no intention of engaging in such superstitious nonsense.

"Talking a love-charm ... an attraction spell for mutuals? Yeah, but you're going to need a dressed pink candle and one of those shriveled raccoon dicks," he laughed.

After jotting down a "sweet jar spell" from the Rolodex, he walked down a cluttered aisle to get something. When he returned, he carefully rolled a pink candle and the piece of paper that contained the petition for attraction in some tissue wrap and handed it to me.

"Seriously?" I grinned. "A Whammy?"

"The important thing is to maintain focus... not to let your concentration be distracted by the wandering nature of the mind... not even for an instant. Also, don't be vague... You need to be specific with your desire. Cleo has told me about clients casting money spells without naming an exact amount only to find a lousy penny on the ground. Another thing... once started, there can be no self-doubt."

He selected a stem from a bin that was labeled "Iris Virginica" and placed it inside an ornate brass cash register.

"Blue Flag root for the till to keep the money coming, though I'm not going to charge you for the candle for attraction. You'll have to find your own pink ink," he said while closing the antique cash box, "and any personal concerns. Come, check out Jema's Attic before we go to my cabin."

When we stepped inside the antique shop, I could smell the musty, attic-y odor of old shellac along with a resinous scent like amber mixed with a trace of lead from paint, locks and hasps.

"The smell's a little funky – like an attic, but I like the chemical bouquet of things old," Jeremy said. "Though sometimes I need a little Murphy's or apple cider vinegar. Jema doesn't use Cleo's cleansings here, so that the residue of the former owners remains."

When he turned on the lights, I saw that the place was brimming with period furniture, hand-forged ironworks and vintage housewares. Display cases contained an assortment of tabletop curios, including opalescent glassware, wooden toys and utilitarian folk-art.

"That's my favorite," Jeremy smiled while pointing to an empty old bottle with a porcelain lid whose product was labeled: PEADEN LEMONADE. "Yeah, I'd be yeeting that."

Behind the cases were several dusty upright pianos along with a cable coin-operated ragtime nickelodeon player piano whose rosewood cabinet was colorfully embellished. The sheet music placed on it was entitled *Ebony Echoes*.

Near some homespun quilts, I was surprised to see a round-faced male black doll dressed in striped purple corduroy overalls and a mauve bow sitting in a rocking chair. With its untamed, frizzy hair, buffoonish red lips and big white-rimmed eyes, I recognized it to be a golliwog.

"Hey, your aunt has one of those dolls for sale."

"I don't think it's for sale. Jema loves that damn fuzz ball."

Even more surprising than finding the golliwog doll were several concrete statues of dwarf-like lawn jockeys holding lanterns. All had glossy black faces with exaggerated features and wore buffoonish gaudy colored clothes.

"Your aunt sells these?"

"They're still popular, though now days many of their faces have been repainted nearly-white with blue eyes. Either that or they're afflicted with the skin disorder called vitiligo. But even with the scrubbing from history folks can't do much about the flat noses and big red lips. Unless the jockos get the same treatments as Wacko Jacko did."

As I started to laugh, I was startled when the ragtime player piano suddenly cranked up on its own accord and began playing the syncopated rhythm of an old-fashioned cakewalk.

"You might think it would be the other way around," Jeremy said with a mock expression of fear on his face, "but the haunted shit happens here and not at Cleo's."

A short distance behind his aunts' shops, we walked on a sandy path through some scraggly trees, one of which had a tire swing attached to a limb. Blue mud wasps darted about, causing me to swat at them and make sure none got inside the plastic grocery bag that contained my valuable book. Seconds later, I could make out the shady raised porch of Jeremy's log cabin.

Sitting beside a burbling creek, wild tangles of climbing honeysuckle covered sections of the wooden façade where humming bees went about their business. Having trudged up to the porch on some warped planks half hidden by ragged patches of black-eyed Susans, a couple of painted Adirondack chairs placed behind a stained plywood table with cinder block legs looked inviting.

"Welcome to my creek-side chalet," Jeremy joked while holding the torn screen door open. "Back yard's mostly a cat-tail marsh."

The rustic cabin's interior was modestly furnished with second-hand items, but not the restored antiques that I had imagined would be the case. There was ample makeshift shelving for the antiquarian books that he sold, along with some flea market bric-a-brac on display. The desk on which his computer sat was a repurposed library card storage chest. Hanging above it was an enlarged old photograph of a short thin black man who had his teeth filed to sharp points. Naked from the waist up, the smiling figure with short nappy hair was holding what looked like a spear.

"Who's this?" I asked.

"It's a family portrait," Jeremy flashed a toothy smile. "Actually, Ota Benga was a Congo pygmy who was sold in the early nineteen hundreds and put on display as a savage cannibal at the St. Louis World Fair. Later he was caged in the Monkey House as an exhibit for the Bronx Zoo… though at times he was able to roam the grounds. After complaints by the black clergy, he was allowed to leave his orangutan friends. His teeth were capped and he was given a cotton suit and a bit of an education right here in Lynchburg. Being depressed – go figure – he committed suicide in 1916. With a borrowed pistol, he shot himself square in the heart."

"Jeez," I shook my head. "That's cray."

Beneath the black-and-white photo the following was written in type:

"The Darwinian theory is absolutely opposed to Christianity, and a public demonstration in its favor should not be permitted."

James H. Gordon
Clergyman

"You want some lemonade... that's not Peaden?" he joked.

"No, I'm good."

After turning on a swamp cooler, we got down to business.

"The buyer's willing to pay fifteen hundred. Like I said, minor worming in the margins, spotting and shit like damp staining don't detract much. You might be able to get more, but that could take some time for me to find another buyer. What's the death? My cut would be twenty percent."

"That amount sounds good. Tell your buyer we've got a deal. So, Jeremy, tell me again why you don't want it?"

"I have a facsimile that I bought for less than ten bucks. This gives me all the information I need."

"Need? For what?"

"*New Atlantis* is a work unfinished, but many Baconian scholars think he completed it and the manuscript was brought to America shortly after his death. Maybe even carried by Bacon, himself, if he didn't die on Easter Sunday from a common cold after stuffing a chicken with snow. By the way, there is no record of his funeral. The full-length version was preserved by a mercury bath – all the pages being treated with mercuric chloride as a biocide and the bound silvered leaves secured in copper cylinders in a brick vault beneath the cemetery of Bruton Parish in Williamsburg. Besides this copy, with its master plans, are other valuables, such as the original copies of Shakespeare's works and proof that Bacon was the illegitimate son of England's Queen Elizabeth I. Did you know that Virginia was named after her?"

"We learned that in the 5th grade. So, what's the deal with the Shakespeare stuff? I guess his old shit is worth a lot – "

"Shakespeare was a hired mask. All his writings should instead be attributed to Bacon and his secret collaborators – like-minded thinkers who called themselves the Good Pens."

"You're saying Shakespeare didn't exist?"

"Willy Shagspur existed, but he was illiterate. Couldn't even write his name without someone guiding the quill. As one member of the Good Pens said about Shagspur, the most learned of works could not have been written by the least of learned men. But the Bacon Group paid him handsomely to be the face for their Invisible College. The ruse worked and few people knew about the encoded passages in the famous plays. Under the guise of fictional characters, truth was enveloped by obscurity, thus it shined in the shadows… in a veiled manner. Bacon's occult fraternity was known as the Lanthorn. They secretly conceived and set in motion a great plan that was to come about at a future time. As Bacon wrote in *New Atlantis*, 'the end of our foundation is the knowledge of causes, and secret motions of things; and the enlarging of the bounds of human empire, to the effecting of all things possible.' Did you get that, Jack? Knowledge of all things. That was his vision for humanity – to master all aspects of science. Many find this perverse, like it's some kind of blueprint for the Illuminati and alien lizards that will bring about the apocalypse. To them, the intent of Bacon's glorification of technology – even the ethical progress of science – was to subvert and eventually displace religion. But to me it's about reshaping things... enlightenment and prosperity... mastery of our own destiny."

"Unlike the current generation of Twitter dummies," I joked, recalling his past concerns. "Okay, so how does one go about finding this vault full of goodies?"

"By deciphering what's written on certain headstones at the church in colonial Williamsburg. Anagrams are called to the reader's attention by the key-words, 'Dear Reader' that are more prominently chiseled in the stone than the other grave inscriptions and which give directions to the treasure's whereabouts. It's already been discovered that one of the anagrams says, 'Dear Reader, learn from this tomb the exact location of old Bruton's foundations.' Besides these coded instructions, we've my secret weapon here."

He picked up his worn copy of the George Wither *Collection of Emblems* book that he bought at the Sutton's estate sale.

"Like I already told you, this edition still has functioning lottery spinners that facsimiles usually don't have. The author was part of Bacon's Shakespeare Circle. Poetic riddles in the book are said to foretell future events. There are even illustrations of towns before they existed... streets, taverns and other buildings, including the old Bruton church."

"Okay, I'm confused. Before it was built? C'mon, how's that possible?"

"They were pre-conceived at an earlier time, with the design to be constructed later. It's not prophetic – it was deliberately planned. To quote Wither: 'And aftertimes, though me this age despise, will think these pages had been prophecies.'"

"It's still a little foggy to me."

"There's an even better allusion," Jeremy said while opening the book with the gilded flourishes on its paneled crushed olive morocco cover.

"By, sometimes, looking backward, we behold those things, which have been done in times of old; by looking wisely forward, we foresee such matters, as in future-times will be... Other clues are given in the lottery verses – in the form of advice given in one's fortune."

"Easy as pie, huh, Pye?"

"Want to give it a try?"

"Sure, I'll play the game, but first can you crank up that swamp cooler. Don't you think it's kind of hot in here?"

"The unit is topped out," he said with a sympathetic shrug before flipping the heavy pages to the lottery dials with attached woodcut spinners appended at the back. "Super ruling, Jack... Now, close your eyes like it says to do so in the instructions."

When I shut my eyes tightly, he told me what to do next.

"Now, use your index finger to turn the paper spinner... Be careful, the thing is really old, Jack... and stop when you want... when it feels right."

After rotating the wheel for a few seconds, I stopped with my finger still pressed against it.

"Okay, so your lot is number four. Now move to the bottom one and do the same thing."

Though I felt kind of stupid, I followed his instructions.

"The book is divided into four sections and you landed on three."

He turned to the page indicated and began reading:

'By this thy lot, we may misdoubt,
Though lookest not warily about;
But hudlest onward, without heed,
What went before,
Or may succeed;

Procuring loss, or discontent,
Which, circumspection, might prevent.
Therefore, with gratefulness, receive,
Those counsels, which our morals give.'

"It says to go to emblem four... and here's the key-phrase:"

'He, that concealed things will find, must look before him
and behind.'

"Fuck does that mean?" I asked.
   "Whatever you're doing... proceed with caution."
   "That's cray."
   "That's Bibliomancy."

Later that night when Merrilly was at work, I unwrapped the
pink candle from Cleo's and read what was written on the piece
of paper. After lighting it, I was supposed to write my first name
and her last name without lifting the pen from the white paper.
Next, I was instructed to draw a circle around both names.
While focusing on my desire, I was to recite the words: "This
simple spell will put the seed of attraction in (someone's) heart
and get them to notice me." After fifteen minutes, I was to extin-
guish the flame with a snuffer instead of blowing it out so as not
to break the spell.

A couple of days later I received a text from Jeremy telling me that he had my money. He wanted to know if we could meet at Sharpshooters so he could pay me and buy me a Farb Burger. He also said that something very bizarre happened to him the day before, but that he would tell me about this when we met in person.

Having seated ourselves in the beer garden at Sharpshooters Bar & Grill, after handing me an envelope that contained the money, we both ordered Farb Burgers, with Jeremy asking for a glass of orange juice (telling the confused waitress that he promised not to spill it) and me getting a draft Bud.

"So, get this," Jeremy said with his voice lowered. "After dealing with some Amish guy trying to sell me some sewing notions at my aunt's shop, as I watched him leave with his horse and buggy, a second later this other guy comes in. Ahoy there, he says. I didn't hear his car pull up and there were none but my van in the parking area. He wants to know if we have any Civil War tokens, in particular one that was blank on both sides, which is a weird thing to want. I mean, c'mon, a sutler token with no ads. When I said that we didn't have any, he shows me this little square black box that he said he was going to put the token in. The thing looked like one solid piece – like it didn't have a top or any way to open it, but it was so damn shiny of a black color that I could see the reflection of his fingers on it."

"What did he look like?" I asked.

"Pretty basic for the most part. Bald headed and clean-shaven with pale skin that was almost a waxy pink. He had a kind of official look like he was with the government or something. Wore a black jacket, but he didn't sweat even though Jema's evaporative cooler was also on the fritz.

Anyway, after I told him again that we didn't have any tokens, he said that if I did, or knew of any other meddlers that did, that it would be our patriotic duty to let him have it so that he could put it inside the cube – that was the word he used – like it was some kind of special container. He also repeated a couple of times that the room smelled like a hospital, which I thought was odd. It was like he was talking to me twice or speaking on two different levels. Before telling me "we cannot give a name" – even though I never asked for one – he showed me a photo of some dude wearing a hunting outfit and asked if I had ever seen him before. When I said no, he said, just as you do not have a token, so he no longer has a heart. Then he left. So, I'm thinking that he was just some crank but when I looked through the window – and here's the really weird part – I see this old black truck pull out of the lot. I mean, really old – from the 1930s. It looked identical to this vintage metal truck that Jema had in the shop – a die-cast toy that we sell as a box plant holder – a farmhouse decoration, which I had dusted earlier that day.

When I went to check it out again, just to see how close it looked to the real one I just saw, it was missing... fucking gone. No cap, Jack."

On the way back home, I kept thinking about how the description of the guy at Jema's was so similar to the stranger at Royalene's that grilled me with questions about my airship sighting.

Although Jeremy's 'darksider' seemed more intimidating – more like a bully – his method of "talking twice" (to use Jeremy's words) was the same way he had probed my head.

When I walked into the trailer, Raiden was watching some TroVe clips on the flat screen. Setting some of my metal detecting accessories down (which I had finally removed from the pickup), I was surprised to see an item that I recognized from the Sutton's estate sale placed on the table. It was the silver-plated miniature lighthouse, whose beacon served as a table cigar lighter.

"I found this at the doorstep when I got home," Merrilly said while doing a shot of Grey Goose, "along with a note to you from Callie."

"What?" I feigned surprise, "the girl from the video?"

"Noooo," she said while softly adding vowels in a nuanced manner to let me know that I wasn't fooling her. "Callie, who I'll bet smokes menthol demi-slims. It needs some polishing, but could be worth a grand. I did some checking online. Lucky for you… and for me, because after you sell it you can pay me what you owe."

Confused by why she left the thing at my trailer, I read the note that was written *with pink ink*:

Jack, here's what you were so attracted to. It's modeled after PHAROS in Alexandria. I here they're going to rebuild it. Needed to leave mother and home. That mockingbird was driving me crazy. – Callie Sutton

"Not much of a speller," I heard Merrilly say while pouring another shot. "Then again, neither are you."

Ignoring this, I was about to take my canvas apron into the bedroom when Raiden suddenly became agitated by something he was watching.

"Those deer want to burn us! Mer, Jack, the same deer are in the field outside, so we can't leave the trailer or they'll cook us, too."

"What's he talking about?" I asked Merrilly.

"Raiden, calm down. Why are you so upset at the deer?" she asked.

"The same deer that burned the man are in the field."

When I turned to have a look at what was on the screen, I saw a female news reporter interviewing a man wearing a hunting outfit as they stood at the edge of some woods. The caption read:

UNEXPLAINED DEATH IN MINERAL VIRGINIA

"The first thing I noticed was a strange smell in the air – it was sweet and musky, and I know this sounds weird, but it was almost like a marinade with liquid-smoke and other spices... garlic, maple syrup, cumin... even a trace of copped rosemary, which is what I use. It's terrible to say, but it actually smelled pretty dang good. The man wasn't moving, but that's not unusual. Maybe he was glassing, I thought... but that smell. Then I saw that he was holding a rifle – not binoculars – while still standing upright, even though, of course, it's not deer-hunting season. When I saw his face – that's when I knew he had been zapped by something. Bingo-bango, he got blown, but not by any prize trophy buck. It had to have been by some pulse beam weapon being tested. His face was red as barn paint and swollen with globby blisters. I heard there were third-degree burns on one hundred percent of his body and that his innards were cooked in their own juices. Cooked from the inside out like a microwave oven does. Pieces of his super-heated flesh were stuck to his Bass Pro Shop hat."

This was followed by a quick shot of the close up of a black mesh cap (onto which a buck with large antlers had been embroidered in white thread) with what appeared to be clumps of flesh fused to the cloth.

The next shot was of a different man being interviewed in his home by the same reporter.

"Lewis might have just been in the woods laying down dope. Spreading deer attractant hoping to fatten up a dandy with nutrients because a bag of 'Black Magic Deer Co-Cain' was found nearby his body."

"Raiden, buddy, this isn't real news. It's just some scary show, so let's watch something else," I said as he began throwing his circus peanuts at the images of deer moving serenely about in a field on the screen. As he got more upset, Golliwog started to growl, nipping at table legs as her corded black coat ran around in circles.

"Golliwog, chill, mon," I shouted. "Wah Gwaan."

"That's a local news station," Merrily said. "This happened just a few miles away."

"Merr, c'mon. That ain't it. Here, buddy, watch the birds make the cats go to sleep," I said while clicking on a different thumbnail from the TroVe homepage menu.

When Raiden calmed down a bit, I took my metal detecting stuff into the bedroom. Reaching into one of the pouches, I pulled out the brass acorn-shaped object that I had dug up on the Sutton's property. As I was about to put it in the drawer where I kept the other one, I noticed something through a small gap in the corroded metal. Upon closer inspection, it appeared to be a fragment of paper. When I managed to pull it out, I saw that numbers and letters had been written on it.

25° N 71° W

I wondered if the ordered pairs were part of some secret message smuggled in the butt-hole of a spy or scout for either the North or South. Planning to Google them later, when I placed the object into the drawer, there was no sign of the other one. Then I remembered the night when we saw the stealthy helicopter and Merrilly thought that someone had been in the trailer. Did this person take the thing?

Then a second thought occurred to me. Since the two brass acorns looked similar, could the one that I unearthed from the lawn (that I had seeded with the fake pirate coins for the party) be the same one that was taken from the drawer, with the scrap of paper containing the map coordinates placed inside for me to find?

When I checked online, the coordinates were for the Bermuda Triangle (also called the Devil's Triangle), a region in the Atlantic Ocean famously known for the strange disappearances of ships, planes and their crews that has been the subject of numerous conspiracy theories. When I saw this, I thought that the message was someone's idea of a joke. Either that or they wanted to make me look foolish for claiming to have seen the zany airship, thus validating my suspicions that the brass object had indeed been stolen, only to be replanted where someone knew I would find it. Like the stranger that appeared at Royalene's, this person was hell-bent on destroying my credibility, probably hoping that I would go public with something that was as equally far-fetched as my last claim (a message that I had received inside a rectal acorn, no less, with the insinuation being that, like the sighting of Dr. Finley's flying machine, I had also pulled this out of my ass).

Though I was sure someone was messing with me, things became a little more confusing when I recalled that Raiden had written some numbers into my copy of *The Beale Papers*. He also said that the intruder had taken a photo of them. If the sequence of numbers next to the points on the Freemasonic emblem were also latitude and longitude coordinates, I needed to find out what position they marked.

In checking online, they indicated a location in the Atlantic Ocean just east of Bermuda, perhaps one of the adjacent areas in the notorious triangle. The close proximity was intriguing enough to do another Google search, this time to see if I could pinpoint a particular disappearance. The only thing I could find was a sea wreck that occurred in 1609 of a vessel called *Sea Venture*. It was on its way to re-supplying the colony of Jamestown in Virginia when damage from a violent storm caused the captain to ground the vessel on a nearby island. The ship's crew and passengers were stranded there for a year, until repairs were made that enabled them to continue on to Virginia. Before they arrived, accounts of the island's abundant natural resources reached England, and led to the colonization of Bermuda. Though an interesting bit of history, I couldn't find anything to connect the beaching of the *Sea Venture* to Beale's treasure, or, for that matter, the reason for someone's apparent interest with the markings. Because of this connection, I planned to ask Raiden how he came up with the numbers the next time he visited. Currently, he was avoiding the trailer because of his fear of the deer that browsed a nearby field where local residents let them feed.

Before putting my computer to sleep, I did a bit of searching for the Shakespeare controversy that Jeremy mentioned. To my surprise, there were hundreds of articles whose authors sought to unmask the Stratford pretender. Among the reasons for their doubts was the lack of documentation, with many claiming that there was virtually no evidence to support the traditional view. How could it be that nothing survived but a few shaky signatures on legal papers? They also wondered how a man with no formal education could achieve such a literary output?

Hundreds of questions remained unanswered, too many for someone regarded as the greatest writer in English language. Mark Twain went so far to say that during his lifetime, the Bard of Avon (Shakespeare) was never regarded as a person of consequence, and that he was all but forgotten "before he was fairly cold in the grave."

On the contrary, Francis Bacon's towering greatness was much celebrated during his lifetime, as were the achievements of the other illustrious figures of the 17th century that were candidates for the true authors of the poet and playwright (the concealed "Good Pens").

Anagrammatic codes discovered within the plays by Shakespearian detectives and amateur cryptographers were presented as circumstantial evidence to support their claims, along with discoveries of various anomalies in Latin inscriptions on monuments that supposedly contained steganographic ciphers.

As the online debate raged on, I found something that possibly linked Raiden's map coordinates with one of Shakespeare's works (or whoever the true author was). His last play, *The Tempest*, was inspired by the ferocious gale that grounded the *Sea Venture* and left its crew and passengers trapped in paradise. The enchanted island on which the play takes place was ruled by a powerful figure named Prospero, who, as he engaged with supernatural forces, claimed that the influence of an "auspicious star" was responsible for his fortunes.

When I grew tired of the Shakespeare argument, I turned on the flat screen and clicked through some thumbnails on the homepage of TroVe until I found a new video that contained an update on the story of the hunter that had been cooked alive by something in the woods.

In the video, a UFO researcher suggested that what the hunter assumed to be a deer was actually an alien robotic probe with an organic outer shell that mimicked the features of a whitetail deer. Trail cameras that showed bucks with abnormal antlers, strange eyes and discolored hides had captured some of these clever deceptions elsewhere. There was also video footage in which actual deer in the presence of the alien look-alikes are seen "raising all kinds of devil", such as bellowing and stomping their hooves while circling around the imposter.

"Similarly, many of the cattle mutilations that have long baffled ranchers were the result of covert military actions, whose teams were tasked with carefully extracting the technology concealed in synthetic innards of the imposter that had infiltrated the herd. This is why there is never a drop of blood found at the grisly scenes. In order to conceal this mimicking by self-replicating androids, the phantom surgeons are also involved in the ghostly butchering of actual animals, which explains those de-fleshed carcasses found in pastures with their eyes punched out, reproductive organs excised with surgical precision and other parts cored away with bloodless cuts."

"You have got to be freakin' kidding me," I said while walking over to the kitchen window. As I peered out at the field, in the gathering dusk I could make out several deer slowly coming out of the oak-hickory forest. Skittishly, a buck approached some "Chuck-A-Nut" (what a neighbor once told me he used as feed) that had been scattered next to the salt block. After looking around some more, it began to eat while the others patiently waited their turn.

While working the night shift at Royalene's the following night, a couple of regulars seated at the bar were giving me a hard time about Merrilly's pole dancing.

"I need to get me some of that butt-coin for the merry-go-round," a guy named Delmer joked.

"Yeah, at first I was a doubter, but now I'm a bitiever," the other laughed. "It's mooning alright, and I want to be the one experiencing the spike."

"Pump and dump," Delmer laughed. "Don't worry, I won't let her catch me crypto-jacking. So, Jack, have you tried scanning that tat, or does she accept other payments from you?"

"It's called bio-telemetry, Delmer," I said.

"No, Jack's a non-coiner... just an ex-shitcoin detector," his friend replied.

"I guess I'm not smart enough to stare down into a hole while doing road work," I said with a straight face while loading some dirty glasses into the under-counter washer.

"You don't need to be as long as the merry-go-round has chalk dust," Delmer said after downing his draft Pabst.

"Instead of pernicious rage, I shall ignore your foul bombard," I quoted some brassy Shakespeare that I read on the Internet.

"What's that supposed to mean?" Delmer said with a stupid look on his face. "Well, get us another round and I'll see to it that you get a big tip. I think I might have me another twenty in Monopoly money in my wallet," he elbowed his friend in the side as both cracked up.

At that moment, Raiden walked out of the small office where he had been doing some accounting.

Before pouring the flat Pabst, I went over to ask him something.

"Hey, buddy, do you remember that night when the Amazon driver came?"

"Yes."

"Why did you write those numbers and draw those lines in my book?"

"There are lots of numbers and letters and funny pictures, too... some are scary, Jack. But, I didn't draw the shape. The man with the army boots in the blue polo shirt with the logo of the arrow pointing from A to Z did that."

Before climbing out of the pickup when I got home, I scanned the nearby field through a pair of binoculars to see if there were any deer feeding. Though I didn't see the glint of eyes from my headlights when I turned the corner, I was also curious to know if any might be standing just inside the tree line. With none in sight, I got out and headed to the front door. On the way I noticed that all the lights inside the trailer were turned off. Merrily should have been home from her other job by now, so I wondered where she was. When I walked inside and flipped on the light, I was surprised to see her sitting on the couch next to the dog.

"What's going on?" I asked. "Why are you sitting in the dark? Did something happen at work?"

"Yes, something did," she said with a shaky voice.

"Did some drunk get out of control? Try to touch you? You've got those bouncers."

"That man who came to Royalene's that night. He was there. Only, this time he was sunburned, his face as red as a lobster like he just got back from vacation in the tropics. I don't know why I let him... why I talked to him, but for some reason I did."

"Was he asking you stuff about me?"

"Um, no. He was asking about my tats, actually."

"Okay, something weird is going on. What's with this sudden fascination with tattoos and Civil War tokens? The guy is cray, Merr."

"Yeah, well, I think he might be something different than crazy. Listen to this," she said before turning on a recording she made with her smartphone.

"I came to this place full of motorcycle people," a man's voice stated over a Nicki Minaj song, "with their poisons and confusers to see if you could pass the test –"

"I perform my routine on the pole but don't do anything else," Merrilly told him.

"I wouldn't travel all the way to Africa just to steal a banana from a monkey," the guy said. "This is a screwy business and others in the bushes with their heads covered by green yarn will be watching you."

She then turned off the voice memo.

"Heads covered by green yarn?" she shook her head. "After he told me this, I half expected him to pull out one of those flash guns like in the movies, but instead he just said that he couldn't tell me his name… or the color of his shoelaces. When I looked down at his feet, he was wearing Bermuda sandals."

"Did you see what he was driving? Was it an old black truck? Like a really old black truck?"

"One of the door guys said it was a regular car. It was black, though. A black Buick or something like that. I don't know, but I know he came because of that thing you said you saw."

"I wish I had taken a photo," I said, "but if I did, I'll bet someone would find a model or drone of a gonzo airship in my closet. What I saw was unfakable. I keep wondering why those reenactors didn't say anything. There's nothing online or anywhere. Well, as long as the guy isn't carrying a sickle, I'm not going to worry. That's probably the last you'll ever see of him."

"Yeah, sure, Jack, he won't be back," she said with more than a trace of sarcasm.

CHAPTER IV
ANNAGRAHAM

"We form an association of brothers in all points of the globe...
yet there is one unseen that can hardly be felt, yet it weighs on us.
Whence comes it? Where is it? No one knows...
or at least no one tells. This association is secret even to us,
the veterans of secret societies."

Giuseppe Mazzini

"... For the residues of these archaic temples
of Atlantean magick were still broadcasting."

Michael Bertiaux

While pouring a shot of Grey Goose, Merrilly informed me that she was going to stay with her mother for a while. The snooping around by shadowy government types after my sighting of "whatever it was that I *thought* I saw" had been a cause for concern for a while, but the stranger coming to The Platinum Club was the final straw. The man had so rattled her nerves that she needed to get away from me. Her other reason for leaving was that Raiden refused to visit because of his fear that the deer in the nearby field might use "beamed energy" to cook us alive. She hoped this crazy notion would soon pass. Although her mind was made up, she assured me that this decision was only temporary, and that she would be back when things returned to normal. In the meantime, she said I could stay at the trailer as long as I paid my half of the rent.

When she asked what my plans were, I told her that I was going to keep bartending part time at Royalene's, but that I was also considering joining a friend on a new treasure hunt that involved Francis Bacon's hidden vault under a church in colonial Williamsburg. Though she didn't seem interested in hearing the details of this latest venture, she did ask me what the treasure was supposed to be. When I told her that the vault was believed to contain a complete copy of Bacon's *New Atlantis*, along with the original manuscripts of Shakespeare's works, she gave me one of her 'are you serious?' looks and muttered something about "trading gold for beans." She then headed to the bedroom to start packing.

A couple of days after she left, I was searching the TroVe homepage when I came across another mini doco about the deerstalker's strange death. Rumors had it that similar incidents had occurred in Culpeper (where Merrilly's mom and Raiden lived) and Tuckahoe. At first I thought the video was meant to be funny by taking an absurd story reported on the Internet and making it even more preposterous. But the more I watched, the more I realized that the person making it (an ex-postal worker) was serious about seeking justice for the victims.

Unlike the UFO investigator that suggested the hunter had been irradiated by a particle beam weapon projected by an alien robot disguised as a deer, this new guy thought that a biological construct was responsible, in particular a sub-species of hominid that lumbered about in the dense woodlands (although he didn't explain how this sasquatch managed to brown the hunter like a Christmas turkey). In his opinion, military Special Forces should hunt down the creature. Once captured, it should be put on trial in a court of law using the same legal system that humans are afforded.

To bolster his position, he informed his viewers that for over 500 years and up until recently modern times, animals, including cows, pigs, donkeys, dogs and even vermin and insects (locusts and weevils) were tried by jury for their offenses. Some of the accused animals were acquitted, while those found guilty were either exiled or hung depending on the severity of the crime.

When the video ended and the creator gave the usual spiel about getting subscribers, I felt that my initial thought was correct. Only, its farcical nature wasn't meant to be a comedy *per se*. Rather, it was a tried and true tactic to stymie further investigations into the matter by making what was surely a laughable situation even more laughable. But why go to the trouble to discredit something unless it actually happened?

Over the next two days I watched a few other videos that featured little known oddities. One of them was about cans of Pork & Beans. Without any announcement by the parent companies, major brand names of canned Pork & Beans changed their labels to Beans & Pork. "It's almost as if the change happened overnight," one TroVer commented while his camera panned rows of household brands with the new label that had been stocked on the shelves of the various retail giants. One of the comments read: "Why'd this change for honesty's sake take so long? When hillbilly contactee Buck Nelson told reporters about his joyride inside a flying saucer in the early 1950s, he said that one of the major concerns that the space folk have with Earthlings is our deceptive food can labels, such as Pork N Beans when the contents are 90 percent beans and 10 percent pork. BTW, the MIB that later showed up on Buck's doorstep in the Missouri boonies said it was okay for him to tell his story so long that he NEVER TRIED TO PROVE IT. Maybe we're finally in the aliens' good graces."

Even weirder than that story were reports coming in from all over the globe that people had been receiving postcards from deceased family members that were mailed from heaven. As the creator of the podcast explained, "The cards don't have a return address or postmark, but all contain the same symbol, which some have identified as the signature of an angel. The particular watcher-angel is named Ramiel, the angel of visions and hope. There are also no descriptions of heaven written on the postcards – not even the mundane green hills and flower-strewn fields that one often hears about. Maybe heaven isn't all that it's cracked up to be, what with its tacky sparkling grounds filled with hierarchies of ruling class angels and zombie-servants that are branded like cows. Even were I a true believer, I will probably be a leftover. The reason why? As you can see for yourself, I have a rather flat nose and according to *Leviticus* those with blemishes, including flat noses can never come close to God. People with scabs aren't accepted either, which as you can also see, I have one from a nasty tumble on my skateboard. For those who think this is just a hoax, consider this: the signatures of the dearly departed on the cards all match with examples from the same individuals when they were still alive."

Pausing the video, I peeked through the blinds to see if there were any deer in the field. Being that it was the early evening, not surprisingly, a few had gathered to feed near the salt lick. I was thinking about taking the Meepo to the D.Q. for a burger, but decided instead to make a peanut butter sandwich and wash it down with a tangerine La Croix. Sitting down on the couch with my dinner, I resumed the podcast.

"Now, this would be a nice story if it weren't for one little thing. According to the Bible, no one is in heaven... except for

Christ. What, you say? That's right; at no point does it say in the Gospels that anyone has gone to heaven. The spirits of the dead are in limbo, either still in the grave or in an intermediate state... yep, like a waiting room, with or without soft clouds. These aren't Bible bloopers, and I'm not cherry-picking scriptures from the *King James Version*. You see, blind fools, to borrow one of Jesus's insults in Matthew, there's this thing called Judgment Day, and when it happens, Christ will be returning to Earth for a new act of creation. That's right, he's heading this way... instead of the other way around, and I read about this from a Bishop with a cope and mitre, no less. So, if heaven's not open for business, why do so many people think their loved ones are looking down? We can chalk this up to Luke 23. When Jesus says to the good thief on the cross next to him, 'Today you will be with me in paradise.' But, depending on where the comma is placed, if Christ won't be resurrected for another three days... paradise must be *something else*. So, who's sending these postcards from the afterlife? Snickering Satan? Dyslexic angles? Beats the hell out of me, but keeping checking back as I search for answers."

The video ended with the following quote:

"No one has gone up into heaven but there is One who came down from heaven, the Son of Man (himself — whose home is in heaven)."
- JOHN 3:13

One of the comments said that there were other shenanigans in the Authorized Version. In Psalm 46, the word SHAKE is 46 words from the beginning, and SPEARE is 46 words from the end. Shakespeare was 46 years old when the King James Bible was translated. Either this cryptogram was the work of Francis

Bacon, or it's someone's heads up that we're just the cascading green code of someone's simulated reality.

After the usual notification spiel, instead of flipping on the Nats game, I clicked a thumbnail whose caption read:

MIRACLE AT THE MOTORWAY

The video began with a fellow with saggy jowls and dark facial stubble sitting in his wood-paneled den. After bending to spit some Redmen snuff into a dirty glass, he looked straight at the camera and went on a tirade about a Nascar race he had attended:

> "I don't care what the television replays show – you can examine the edited videotape all you want, but I'm here to tell you that the race was stolen. Devin got royally screwed. Hundreds of us in the stands on that Saturday saw exactly what happened, and despite what the godless media and those with their lattes in the skybox that are part of the fix say, there's no doubt whatsoever that the green Impala driven by Devin Gasil for Christ won the race, and he did so by driving in reverse gear. Come August, hundreds, maybe thousands of us will be protesting the decision and they'll be more than a shower of beer cans on the track, I'll promise you that. What we were witness to was nothing else than a miracle at the motorway."

The video turned out to be about a controversial Nascar race in which, despite plenty of footage to the contrary, hundreds of spectators claimed that during a wreck-filled photo finish (without a caution flag), the "JESUS JERKY" car finished first. The so-called miracle was that the driver had completed the final lap driving in reverse and managed to negotiate the pile up and cross the finish line without so much as a scratch on his car. However, tape from the original broadcast, news race coverage (from all but a few stations) and camera footage submitted by fans at the speedway told a different story. Even so, hundreds steadfastly insisted that the miracle occurred, going so far to suggest that what really happened could only be seen by the eyes of the true believers of Jesus Christ.

Before continuing, the video went to a skippable ad. As a large stone rolled away from a cave entrance, two shiny figures helped the resurrected Jesus walk from the sepulcher. A tall wooden cross that was also walking followed the three men. From the sky a deep voice rang out:

"You have preached to those who are sleeping?"
"Yes," the cross replied.

(Gospel of Peter 9:35 – 10:42)

A caption appeared that read:

JESUS JERKY
(No artificial preservatives)

Beneath this was written:

"You must eat my flesh."

A lanky figure with an unlit cigarette stuck between his teeth was reclined in his suburban man-cave. As he was being interviewed, the word 'NASCAR' on his light-up baseball cap was blinking.

"Gordo was probably crapping the diapers under his fire-suit when he saw Devin coming at him backwards. And there was no yellow. Yet, he still took a victory lap. The sham outcome is not only bad for the circuit, but an affront to the almighty. The next time I see someone with a Gordo bumper sticker," he smiled bitterly, "this Bubba just might let them hear my chrome horn."

Having enough of this lunacy pretending to be news, before shutting the Samsung down, I clicked on the podcast of "Siri-ana" (the girl from California that claimed to have given birth to an ultra-terrestrial being) to hear once again what she had to say about "strange things are going to start happening." When I got to that part of the interview, I heard her say something that I missed the first time. She said that while pregnant with this new life form, one of the impressions she received from it was that "it lived in visions."

Lived in visions? What did that mean? Was that what this was all about? Were the strange things being reported visions generated by this thing's mind? (I thought about the tricked up airship that I had seen.) To believe this, you'd have to accept that Siriana was telling the truth. That she had been artificially inseminated with non-human DNA extracted from a piece of fruit and had given birth to this creature in a secret government lab – an idea that was even crazier than ants building miniature pyramids and postcards being mailed from heaven.

If the TroVe videos weren't elaborate hoaxes by their creators and social media influencers to try and out do one another to get subscribers, then maybe they were made as a test for psychological warfare conducted by the government on an unsuspecting populace. And the same shadowy group involved was using the power of suggestion in public places to fool people – like this guinea pig – with similar experiments, even though they later tried to convince them that what they had seen wasn't real. Though a more plausible explanation, this, too, seemed like a bit of a stretch I thought while taking a quick look through the blinds to see if the deer had gone back into the woods. It appeared as if they did, for I saw no eyes aglow under the full moon.

During our first meeting to discuss the details of Bacon's hidden vault, I mentioned the weird 'coincidence' of Shakespeare's name being in the Bible. Jeremy, who already knew about this, said that Bacon had edited the official version. Anagrams, substitution codes and acrostics were a passion of his and part of his genius. They were embodied in his various works to convey information that it wouldn't have been prudent to lay bare. The puzzles were not devised as games, he reiterated, but out of necessity for later generations to unlock. In the time of the ancient Greeks, secret communiqués were tattooed on the shaved heads of couriers who were dispatched as soon as their hair grew back. In Bacon's day, bilateral ciphers were employed. Ever since the first concealed messages were discovered, the anti-Stratfordians have had a field day finding others in the folios and quartos. Again, Shakespeare was just one of Bacon's various masks, and steganography one of his tools.

But getting back to the vault under the Bruton Parish church, I told Jeremy about my doubts of finding anything under Anna Graham's tomb because somebody had already beat him to it (back in the 1930s) with nothing to show but part of the brick foundation of an earlier structure.

More recently, some New Age types had also tried to excavate in the churchyard without permission, which reminded me to let him know that I didn't want anything to do with illegal midnight digging, especially in a place that was designated as a national historical landmark.

While doing some research online, the evidence seemed pretty thin, I added.

After voicing my concerns, Jeremy said he was well aware of the story involving the discovery the original church's foundations. Though the lady responsible claimed to be clairvoyant, she had actually determined the whereabouts of the vault by deciphering cryptic messages on the grave markers that had been strategically placed in the churchyard (along with clues contained in other old documents). Needless to say, both the vestry and city officials were dubious of both methods of detection, believing the woman was prone to flights of fancy. Yet, there could be no denying even from her most ardent detractors that she had managed to unearth something precisely where she said the vault was located.

"It was the Rockefeller Restoration Project that tried to stop her quest to find Bacon's treasure vault," Jeremy said. "The foundation acquired most of the properties – damn near bought all of Williamsburg supposedly to restore it to its colonial past and become a major tourist attraction."

Once again we had met in the beer garden at Sharpshooters. Instead of ordering the same old Farb Burger, Jeremy was going to try the wild game pie.

"I'll let you try it," he said.

"You think there's venison in it?"

"Yeah, it says braised venison, mushrooms and redcurrant jelly. Might even be some hare or partridge in the filling to make it really wild."

"No, that's okay. I'm probably going to get a sammie. Chicken salad panini without the slices of granny smith apples. Don't want to see apples in my beer either."

"Shit, you're gonna get the Farb Burger, aren't you," he grinned.

"Yep," I replied while quickly closing the menu. "And a bottle of Bud."

"Anyway," he continued, "the restoration officials allowed her to dig beneath the tower floor where they knew nothing would be found – and even she knew this because it wasn't the original structure, with the newer church having been erected in 1715. When she pointed this out, they denied an earlier brick church existed. They also claimed that all records before the present church were missing. The question is: was this to protect the priceless collection, or did someone deliberately destroy them so that they'd never see the light of day? To ensure that secret vault would remain written out of history."

"Okay, that's the thing that gets me. Why?"

"Because the powers that be didn't want anyone to know how big a part Bacon's secret society played in the founding of America. That they were the guiding spirits. They wanted to sweep this under the rug, but that's where Wither's book of emblems comes in. One of the emblems shows a combination of both churches in the middle of a cluster of buildings, narrow streets and alleys that's a dead ringer for colonial Duke of Gloucester Street – now the main drag in Williamsburg. Remember, this illustration was published long before any of these structures were built. Some of the officials were blown away at certain details in the picture. Like you, they couldn't conceive how such a thing was possible. Others said the features in the town square shown in the emblem filled in the blanks of certain discrepancies that had long puzzled the restorers. Still, the church elders insisted on more concrete proof than her metaphysical ramblings before they'd give their consent to allow more excavating. Fortunately for her, she discovered at William and Mary College a drawing made by a visitor from Germany in 1699 that featured the original brick church. Listening to the ghostly whispers from the headstones, she studied the rubbings of the encoded memorials and followed the trail of clues – "

"The other guiding spirits," I joked. "The inner Masonic group or was it Bacon's Wild Goose Club?" I asked as my way of letting him know that I was still somewhat skeptical and didn't wish to take part in the proverbial chase.

"You're still on the fence. Yeah, I get it, Jack."

"Honestly, I am, but what you've said is still better than the news I see about butterflies without colors and modern highways that abruptly end in wheat fields. But, go on – I'm listening."

"As she took measurements and made calculations, others shadowed her every move, sneaking around corners and popping up from behind mulberry trees and shit. While some encouraged her strange methods to see where it might lead them, most wanted her to go back to where she came from… California. To satisfy the rigid conditions of the officials, she enlisted the aid of an engineer to conduct a surface test – what was called an equipotential survey."

"What was that?"

"An instrument that used an alternating current to detect anomalies in what should be undisturbed soil –"

"Sure, sound waves that bounce back. An early version of ground penetrating radar."

"That's right, mister metal detector. The results indicated a foreign body at a certain depth – possibly the fabled vault beneath the Anna Graham tomb, which is just west of the current church, and that's how she found the glazed brick foundations of the previous church.

So, they rounded up some diggers and went to work until one of the shovels hit the brass fixtures of a casket. When this happened, the officials called it quits. Like I said on the phone, they abruptly halted any further excavating under the pretense that they couldn't allow any graves to be disturbed."

"So, what makes you think the vault hasn't been emptied? That these people with the Rockefeller group didn't go back and raid it once they knew the location?"

"Yeah, maybe leaving behind only a single brass brick to mark it, like the one under the steeple entrance. Philanthropic project, my ass. No, something tells me they'd rather keep it hidden, but that's what I want to find out."

"Even if it's still there... which I kinda doubt... no one will give us permissions. I can hardly detect for lousy coins anymore in public places."

"Nobody said anything about digging in the churchyard. That section's not even open to the public these days."

"How do we gain access then?"

"Underground passageway."

"An access tunnel? From where?"

"According to two sisters that once lived in one of the restored colonial houses right across the street from the entrance to the Bruton churchyard – lot 355 to be precise, a stone's throw away – as children they used to play hide-and-seek in a tunnel they found in the cellar. Only, the thing is, no one else could find it. Not even the entrance to a drain system, which was pretty common – arched drain tunnels in basements. So, I did me some thinking."

"Yeah." I gave him a knowing look. "What did the spinner land on? The dial mechanism in that book."

"Bibliomancy? No, I use that sparingly. But there was this: Even from the tomb the voice of Nature crieth," he recited the words, "even in our ashes live their wonted fires. That's not from Wither's book – it's from the Elegy written in a country church-yard. There's a connection. So, I'm thinking the entrance is an ash catcher in the center of the fireplace. A cast iron trap door that's big enough for a person to squeeze through. If not a dump door, maybe a sliding wall of bricks that swivels inside the fire-place to reveal a passage."

"How do we get inside the house? Take a guided tour and slip away?"

"I have a friend that's a security guard there."

"Did you tell him about your ash trap idea?"

"Hell no, I've more brains in my elbow. But, he'll help us. First, we need to do an exploratory mission. I'm thinking during the Fourth of July celebration. You got something better to do that night?"

"Yeah, make good tips at work. I've been perfecting this pa-triotic cocktail. Red, white and booze. It's a variation of the fire-work Blue Blazer in that Bon-Vivant's Guide."

"You don't want to learn how to make fudge the old-fash-ioned way?"

On a quiet residential street, Jeremy stopped his van alongside a marked patrol cruiser.

Climbing out of the driver's seat, he quickly slid open the squeaky cargo door and pulled out something that was wrapped tightly in a patterned quilt. When the passenger door of the Williamsburg security vehicle opened, he placed the object inside and gave a thumbs up to his friend before he sped away.

I was told that the old Amish quilt was rolled around one of the concrete lawn jockey statues from his aunt's antique shop. When the time came, this was going to be used to give us the all-clear signal. If we saw a green ribbon attached to 'Jocko's' hand, it was safe to enter the unlocked house. If the ribbon were red, we'd have to wait because it meant that night security teams on foot or riding mountain bikes were nearby while conducting their routine patrols of the colonial buildings and houses in the Living History Museum.

"Some historians claim they were used as beacons for fugitive slaves seeking refuge in safe-houses," Jeremy said as we took a shuttle to Duke of Gloucester Street for the faux-colonial experience. "If old Jocko was holding a green ribbon, it was safe to enter and hide or move through the secret network. It's a good story, but to keep in 100, it's probably not true. Just another myth. Likewise with Freedom Quilts used as signals to runways. At least these things weren't commonplace."

"I wondered where you got the idea," I said.

"Lots of people think the so-called Underground Railroad was some kind of Grand Central Station with conductors, stations and stuff, but it hardly existed at all below the Mason-Dixon Line. All the action was up north, and the conductors were mainly free blacks. Sure, white activists helped out – mostly Quakers, so it was an interracial coalition, but the real beacon for an escaping slave in the south was the handle of the Big Dipper, which pointed north."

The ambiance was pretty much what I expected, not as tacky as some tourists traps that I had found myself in, though the amount of merchandizing was more relentless. Being that it was the Fourth of July, the place was packed. Visitors that didn't take the tour in horse-drawn carriages strolled along the recently paved pedestrian-only lane. Shaded by red and white oaks, they paused to watch the presentations by costumed tradespeople in front of replica shopfronts and historic alehouses draped in the king's colors. Ruffled bonnets and tri-cornered hats were everywhere, as were police cars and security patrols.

Over the din of street performers and clopping of horse hoofs pulling gilded carriages, whose wooden wheels rimmed with iron rolled over the dusty asphalt (no cobblestones on "DOG Street"), Jeremy told me that he was going to get something from the replica visitor's center.

"I'm going to grab some lemonade," I said, "so long as it's not Peaden."

As I walked through the noisy bustle towards an old-fashioned lemonade stand, a square-set British soldier with a ruddy complexion grabbed the shoulder of a young boy with tawny hair who wore a glazed wool jacket over his linen shirt despite the sultry weather. As the redcoat tightened his venous grip, a gaunt figure wearing a green broadcloth coat retreated behind a group of tradesmen wearing brown wigs beneath their tricornes. It was this bewigged man that had discreetly pointed to the boy who, at the time, was leisurely spinning a whirligig on a string.

Though I knew reenactors performed as part of the immersive experience, the surroundings suddenly took on the same dream-like quality as the hazy forest clearing filled with Civil

War buffs watching the mock battle of Spotsylvania. Not only was the peculiar vividity somewhat unsettling, the facial features of the soldier play-acting closely resembled the man that I had first encountered while chasing after Golliwog, with a noticeable difference being that he was clean-shaven and didn't have a bulging wad of chew in his powdered cheek. I also noticed that he had a pennant of a golden trowel affixed to his gabardine waistcoat.

"In the name of good King George, might I enquire of your business with this peddler?" he asked the boy's mother, whose pretty face was partly obscured by a wide-pleated cap.

"I am known as Lydia, sir – my husband is a cooper and I have business with this man," she replied while gesturing to an itinerant peddler astride a fully stocked wagon.

"A charming name for such an artful-devious wench. I ask again, m'dear," he said with waning patience, "what business durst thou have with this Yankee scoundrel? Thou hesitates – speak on before mine suspicion grows."

"Very well, if it pleases you – to purchase essential wares –"

"More buttons from a mercer, perhaps," he grinned while rubbing the gilt brass buttons on his bright red coat, "stamped buttons to be enswathed with decorative fabric."

"No sir."

"There be chatter from Loyalists of silver balls… hollowed out silver balls filled with slivers of parchment that contain a hidden message… strategic plans of a special committee. If this be swallowed like a crystalized treat just now – apricot or marzipan – I shall cut it from the lad's stomach, or seek among his spilled guts from the buck and ball of ole Brown Bess here," he bellowed while running his fingers along the walnut stock of his flintlock musket.

"'Tis not his business, sir, not the business of a tender soul —"

"Enough, woman!" he barked with surging contempt. Watch thine tongue," he stomped his black gaiters, sending up puffs of dust. "Enshrouded brass buttons. Just what treachery might be smuggled inside?"

"Prithee, sir, the boy knows not. Of that I am most certain."

Taking out a pocketknife, the redcoat snipped off one of the buttons and crudely tore apart the fabric to reveal tiny slips of inked paper.

"Well, well. What spycraft 'tis this, I ask," he said with triumph glinting in his eyes. "Spycraft of no triviality from the Sons of Liberty."

When he saw me give the boy a thumbs up, the soldier straightened his cocked black hat and fixed upon me a malevolent gaze.

"Pardon my trespassing upon such matters, but might thou also be one of these conniving Whigs, or perhaps, with thine raiment, just a recreant coxcomb thou are? Thou could at least put on knit stockings and buckles on the latchets to maintain the illusion. If fortune wishes it, us trust, thou shall be witness to further such betrayal as the sleight used by the crafty wench here with the lad's buttons."

Confused by his bringing me in to the performance, I watched as the woman took the boy's hand and attempted to escape into the ring of spectators. As her wide hoop dress rustled softly on the paving, the murmurs of the onlookers went completely silent. When I turned back to the British soldier, he was nowhere to be seen. Instead, where he had been standing, a guest speaker smoking a long, curing pipe was giving a lecture about George Washington's Culper spy network.

"Besides invisible ink, mask letters and hollowed out quills and those silver balls, a patriotic woman hung a black petticoat and handkerchiefs on her clothesline as a signal of troop movements and such for the Continental Army. The Culper spy ring code for this woman was 355... 355, that's what rhe number decrypted to."

The sounds of patriotic festivities could be heard amid the throngs of tourists as I met up with Jeremy in the Merchant Square. Passing those shaded by colorful umbrellas on the brick patios of quaint eateries, we continued into the historic district until reaching the manicured grounds of the Bruton Parish Church.

"Like I mentioned before, the older headstones with the anagrammatic cues are chained off from public view," Jeremy said, "but my app says Washington will be at the candlelight recital later if there's anything you desire to ask him."

"Maybe what tourist taphouse doesn't only serve applejack-maple pints," I joked.

A short distance past some colonial houses, whose gabled roofs and dormer windows reflected the evening sun, Jeremy stopped in front of one that seemed a bit larger than the others. Behind its white picket fence, brick pathways divided trimmed hedges and a boxwood garden. Strains of a harpsichord could be heard coming from the sitting room.

"This is it," he said almost in a whisper. "Shall we go for baroque without tramping on the parterre?" he asked with a posh British accent. "Enjoy the expression of that harpsichord... take in the repertoire... the musical ornament known as trills."

"I don't know who has the worst British accent – you or Callie," I said.

"Who's Callie?"

"Callie Sutton."

"The girl with the crayons? Is she the reason you asked about an attraction spell?"

"Yeah, it worked great," I said with obvious sarcasm. "Guess I should have bought one of those raccoon dicks. I did get a parting gift, though."

Producing two tickets that he purchased at the Visitor's Center, he opened the gate where a Union Flag waved in the gentle breeze. Moments later we were inside, being led into the sitting room by an elderly black house servant in well-tailored livery. In the sitting room, scented bayberry candles illuminated the polished antique furnishings.

A costumed interpreter wearing an elaborate rococo gown greeted us as a black female servant offered us our choice of gingerbread or brandysnaps from a pewter tray. As she bent down in her calico uniform, I noticed that she wore a silver collar.

As other tourists milled about the room, Jeremy looked for security cameras and stole glances at the fireplace, in which unlit pine torches were wedged in the hearthstone.

We didn't stay long.

Once outside, Jeremy paused under a mulberry tree and scanned the yard.

"That silver necklace looked pretty expensive for a servant," I sneered.

"You think they bought the maid a Tiffany choker?" Jeremy smiled. "The collar was engraved with her master's name and address," he said pointedly.

"So, what are you thinking?"

"I'm thinking that a welcoming lawn jockey wouldn't be terribly out of place here. Now, how about some wenching, or maybe we find a chophouse with good mutton pie or ale potted beef before the fireworks start."

"Super ruling, Jeremy."

We decided to eat at one of the pubs that advertised an authentic atmosphere. I ordered a salet, beef trencher, pickled root cellar veggies and Bud in a salted mug, while Jeremy opted for Pottage Pye (one the Founding Fathers' favorites, the jovial waitress in her period costume informed him). "Just like the homemade potato chips and Diet Pepsi," I joked, growing tired of the historical tidbits in this pricey time capsule.

"So, listen to this," I said over the fiddler in the corner, "when you were at the Visitor's Center, I found out that the number 355 was the codename for a woman in Washington's spy ring. That's the same number of the house with the access point to the tunnel —"

"One of the access points," he reminded me.

"Right, but could the tunnel the little girls played hide-and-seek in have once been used by spies?"

"And I thought I was getting carried away with codes. Sure, it could have, and the Rockefellers might have been aware of this... and a century later it was used again by escaping slaves. And during prohibition it was probably used by bootleggers, but that doesn't mean that it wasn't originally made for Bacon's vault."

"Yeah, but with so much traffic, who's to say anything is still there. Slaves probably didn't give a rat's ass about the Shakespeare plays, but any royal trinkets were surely pocketed."

"I hear you," he said after taking a sip from his rum-infused 'Witches Revenge', "but I didn't say the tunnel still led directly to the vault. It was probably sealed up long ago. Once in the tunnel, that's what we're going to find out. With our measurements and shit, we should be able to determine when we're directly under the Anna Graham tomb. If walled up, we figure out how to break in. What concerns me the most is a verse from Shakespeare's *The Tempest*: 'Deeper than did ever plummet sound, I'll drown my book.' Just how deep is the vault?"

Just then, a bearded figure in a parti-colored doublet approached our booth. He was holding a portable brass planetarium that worked via a clock mechanism.

"Gents, might I interest you in the motions of the planets or news concerning recent celestial events? As you can see, I hold in my hands a portable orrery."

"Not to be chuffy, but not now," Jeremy said. "That retro orrery slaps, though."

"Perhaps then a nightly diversion that consists of harmless debauchery? A little game of dice." The interpreter winked before moving to another booth with his mechanical device.

"I've studied the reports," Jeremy continued after being interrupted. "The historic building survey. Everything from drainage basins in the foundations of outbuildings to the bonding used in the fireplace's bricks. Oyster shell mortar joints – shit like that, Jack. And there's a bit of mystery about the size of the bricks used in one of the fireplaces. The important thing is that the house has been restored... altered, but not completely rebuilt like most of the others. But, even if it had been, wouldn't the fireplace's original ash trap still be utilized?"

When the waitress arrived with our "salets", we could hear the first whistling and bangs of fireworks over the Market Square of Palace Green.

Dressed as security guards on late night foot patrol (with the patches sewn on the correct sleeves), when we reached the house we saw that the lawn jockey had a green ribbon tied to its free hand. By placing Jocko there, so far, Jeremy's friend had come through with his part in the caper. Having arrived a bit later than originally planned, we could only hope the all-clear signal was still in effect. (If we got caught, the story was that we were Instabloggers doing some urban exploring.)

When we opened the unlocked back door without hearing any alarms go off, we entered the house and proceeded directly to the fireplace in the sitting room. After removing the pine torches from the hearth and sweeping away a thick layer of ash, we lifted the dump cover by its cast iron handles and shined a flashlight into the dark opening. As Jeremy thought would be the case, through a flurry of dust, we could see a couple of iron handgrips that had been bolted onto the brick surface. Able to discern the ground below, we dropped our backpacks and listened for the thuds that told us we wouldn't be descending into centuries of dumped ash. Confident that the ash catcher was for the most part a 'trick', we squeezed through the scant opening. After securing our footing on a wooden ladder, we climbed down into the dank gloom of a narrow tunnel that was arched with timber supports.

Though the passage extended to both our left and right, we headed in the direction of the churchyard. From our starting point, Jeremy switched on a walking pedometer, hoping he'd be able to pinpoint the location of the Anna Graham tomb in the cemetery above us by using the device along with the calculations on his notepad.

As we proceeded, the gravel-strewn floor was muddy in spots with shallow puddles in others. There was no graffiti on the rotted beams, and little signs of past activity, though at one point we could make out the remaining square patterns of a child's hopscotch grid. For the hell of it, I picked up a stone and tossed it into one of the partly visible squares. With the bobbing of my flashlight, I jumped onto the next one with one foot without hitting a line.

As Jeremy continued to check his measurements, it wasn't long before we reached a collapsed section of the tunnel that was further blocked with stacks of unused reinforcement beams.

Hammering away at the rubble between the wooden posts with a pick was of little use, as was using the tool to scoop out the tightly packed clay. Obviously, someone wanted to prevent others from continuing. With disappointment etched on his face, my friend eventually accepted that we had no choice but to turn back.

When we reached the starting point, we decided to see where the opposite direction would lead us. Unlike the straight shot we had just explored, the tunnel going the other way suddenly began to twist. The ceiling was also lower, causing us to bend our heads as it snaked beneath the colonial street.

As our eyes strayed about in the wavering glare of our flashlights, we noticed the corroded webbing that covered an inclined shaft that might have been an air vent. After another ten minutes or so advancing in the damp confines, once again the passage came to an abrupt end. However, instead of terminating with packed earth and wooden props, there was a wall of mortared stone. Though there was no discernible crack, when Jeremy pressed his hand against the rough surface, to our surprise, it moved slightly with a rusty hinge sound. When we gave it a stronger push, the false-wall swung open on its creaking socket. After exchanging nervous glances, we wedged our bodies through the opening and ventured hesitantly into what appeared to be either a wine storage area or basement root cellar.

The musty smell of old fabric mingled with the cloying of dried flowers as we made our way into the shadowy clutter. Behind wooden casks and crates, a large partition blocked our view from the other side. However, as we inched forward it became apparent that we had entered an artificial grotto of ingenious devising. The flickering glow of electric torches set in rocky alcoves glanced off hanging stalactite incrustations and mineral crystallizations in the encircling rockwork, with the imitation craggy surface further enhanced by prismatic moisture stains and patches of velvety mosses.

When we rounded the corner of the tall curtain, we found ourselves standing before a curious assemblage. Some of the figures were seated on couches draped with green damask while others in seventeen-century dress stood on the pebble-encrusted floor. With their lifelike features and authentic costumes, for a second I thought the waxen figures were living, breathing creatures. Facing a backdrop that depicted scenes of bacchanalian revelry and pagan pageantry that nearly reached the sparkle of mica on the ceiling (representing the star-filled sky?), peculiarities in the chamber's imaginative design – enchanted frescos and macabre curiosities – made me wonder if the colorful tableau might be props for a ghost tour or an escape room game?

"It's Bacon's Invisibles," Jeremy whispered while pointing to one of the wax sculptures dressed in a dark purple cloak embroidered with geometric lace. Bound by a decorative collar ruff, the curly-haired figure's bearded countenance was fixed in an inscrutable expression. As he moved close enough to touch the flesh-toned acrylics, rheumy brown eyes peered from under a tilted black high hat.

"Is that your man, Bacon?" I asked while training my flashlight on his pursed lips.

"Besides Lord Bacon and his brother Anthony, we have Ben Jonson, John Lyly, George Wither and maybe that's Henry Neville," he said while pivoting his dusty beam to some of the other figures dressed in their period finery. One was wearing a plumed flat hat set at a jaunty angle. With a ruddy complexion and thin ginger mustache, he sneered in jest at what he was observing.

"This could be Edward DeVere, the 17th Earl of Oxford… another courtier and member of Bacon's secret writing guild, the Shakespeare Circle I keep telling you about. I'm not sure about this one," he said while gesturing to a man with a pointed beard wearing a Tudor flat cap, "Sir Thomas North, maybe? Another one of the Good Pens. Only one member is missing – John Dee, but he was into other types of spirits."

"But, what's all this supposed to be?" I asked after shining my light at what they were witness to.

In front of a carved oak lectern, a plaster baboon wearing gaily decorated clothes and a motley fools-cap with a wide brim shaped like a figure eight was raised on stilts while in the process over overturning a silver chalice filled with a crimson libation. Beneath its sub-human appendages was the detached hand of a skeleton. Engaged in some grisly gambling game, the bony, slender fingers were fitted with jeweled rings while scattering wooden dice, whose faces had landed under blood-red tapers.

"I'm guessing it's somebody's re-creation of the subterranean tavern of the Wild Goose Club," Jeremy shrugged. "Window dressing – a façade for the Lanthorn, Bacon's occult Lodge."

As I examined the morbid trappings and curious burlesque, the dimly glowing eyes of owls perched in niches seemed to be watching us from odd corners. All the while, candle-blackened plaster castings of satyrs and fauns wreathed with plastic vines looked on with impish grins.

Above the garish display at the podium, ivy-entwined Corinthian columns framed a pedestaled marble statue of a goddess draped in cascading white folds having an iridescent sheen.

On her head was a gilded helmet and coiled by her right foot was a serpent. The spear that she held was positioned in such a way that light danced upon the steel, giving the illusion that it was vibrating.

"It's Pallas Athena with her helmet of invisibility," Jeremy said, "the spear-shaker... Goddess of wisdom."

"I still think it might be part of a ghost tour," I said.

"Though he endeavor all he can, an ape will never be a man," Jeremy quoted a passage he'd read that accorded to the image of the audacious baboon. "The fantastic monkey is from one of the emblems in the book. It's the Stratford imposter, Willy... a vain shadow... the motley clown standing on stilts. We're inside a magic puzzle box, Jack," he muttered while raising his gaze to the triglyph frieze on the projecting roof of the Doric façade. Incised beneath the depictions of honeysuckle vines on the horizontal beam was the Latin word: NOVATUS

As Jeremy wrote this on his notepad, there was the creaking sound of someone opening a door behind us. Hearing someone stomping down the short flight of steps, we quickly ducked behind the plaster columns before crawling under the backdrop. While lying there, I lifted the heavy fabric just high enough to get a look at the person. Though it was hard to make out features, I recognized the Cartier shades with the gold mirror lenses. I could also see the camo pattern on his boots' oxblood-stained leather – the same pair worn by the lantern-jawed spook that was asking Callie questions about tattoos at the estate sale.

When he opened a hidden panel in the lectern, I saw the glowing digital display of a high-tech radio transmitter/receiver.

"If thou beest Stephano, touch me and speak to me, for I am Trinculo – be not afeared – thy good friend, Trinculo."

Though the florid old English sounded funny with the man's scratchy larynx, his hoarse 'delivery' was anything but humorous.

"If thou beest Trinculo, come forth," said the static-free voice on the other end.

"Be advised – the strange fish is out of water," the man said into the mic. "Taken for test drive of the Trouble Bubble at the Little Egypt site."

Probably thinking this was a coded message, I saw Jeremy hit the button on his phone's recorder.

"Copy," came the reply. "Let's hope it has its learner's permit. Any news on the eye that sees beyond the horizon of time?"

"Negative."

"The ship will be drawn to Prospero on the island of illusion in the sea of troubles through his high charms. Dost thou like the plot, Trinculo?"

"Excellent."

With this said, the man closed the secret compartment in the podium and headed for the stairs.

I felt bad for Jeremy on the way home. He was hoping to find treasures sealed in copper cylinders and to breathe 17th-century oxygen, but, instead, he got the sickly scent of plastic foliage and painted beeswax lips that uttered not a sibilant whisper. There were only more questions. More codes to unravel, if that's what the man in Cartier sunglasses' references to a Shakespeare play were intended to be. Either way, the wordplay was as puzzling to Jeremy as the cryptic imagery in the artificial grotto was to me. The one thing that we did determine, after counting our steps in the historic district once we returned to the colonial house, was that the cavernous recess had been constructed in the cellar of a nearby alehouse called The Tempest Bar.

The following night I watched a documentary about Bacon's *New Atlantis* (and, no, I didn't smash the notification bell even though I was told that by doing so I would have good luck for seven years). In the discussion, those who were critical of the author's imaginings of a utopia pointed out some of the work's dark undertones, suggesting that the ideal civilization of Bensalem (the name of the uncharted island) wasn't all that it seemed. The inhabitants were, in essence, contented sheep giving their unquestioning allegiance to a controlling government in exchange for the comforts of technological achievements. Dystopian elements included a structured hierarchy, political authority (using deception and subversive tactics by rarely seen leaders), exclusion zones, restricted travel, surveillance and censorship, not to mention the strange laws and customs of the population.

As I listened to those address the problems with the island's scientific advancements (albeit in an oblique manner), I wondered if Jeremy was aware of such connotations, or if he conveniently overlooked them in his conviction that Bensalem was the blueprint for an idyllic society?

Although the guest speakers had varying opinions of the metaphorical nature or underlying meaning of the work (admitting that it was up to individual interpretation), all agreed that there was something fishy going on behind the scenes.

Throughout the narrative, whenever something juicy was about to be revealed to the crewmembers, the governor of the Bensalemites was either interrupted or called away on other business by a mysterious messenger. While this could be taken as evidence of censorship by the powers that be, it could also serve as a literary device by the author asking his readers to also think about that which is *not* mentioned. Indeed, the story's lack of information was both confusing and intriguing. Some believed the more ambiguous aspects of the text – information that wasn't revealed due to the constant pauses (conversations that are never resumed) – symbolized the inner workings of a secret society, whether Freemasons, Rosicrucians, or the enigmatic Lanthorn group that Bacon was believed to have founded.

To go along with this line of thinking, the inhabitants of the *New Atlantis* were said to be full of piety and have ideal qualities. Such merits were used to justify the rare admission of strangers. At first the crew was denied access, and only after proving themselves worthy and taking an oath were they granted a license to come on land. As the official explained, it had been a long time since others stepped onto their happy island. Towards the end of the story, one of the crew was given permission (even encouraged) by an official to reveal all that he had seen (or, rather, been *told*) about the island to the rest of the world upon his return. However, earlier it was emphasized to him that the reports of outsiders before him weren't believed (that they were "taken for a dream"). Therefore, as one of the contributors asked, why should he (or we) think things would be any different this time around? Thus another discrepancy that was certainly intentional.

A couple of days later I invited Jeremy to the trailer for some grilled burgers and beers. I wanted to know where things stood with our search for the hidden vault after coming up empty on our first attempt. I was also keen to hear his take on the negative aspects of the *New Atlantis* that were mentioned in the doco. If Bacon's intellectual movement had anything to do with some New World Order scenario, I didn't want to have anything to do with it, especially after all the shit that had recently happened to me and some of those around me.

I had already told him that I was almost certain that the man using Willy-speak in the grotto was the same guy that asked lots of questions at the Sutton house – looney stuff about Civil War tokens without markings and tattoos of ancient mystical designs.

What I hadn't told him was his cluing me in about the Gillogly sub-cipher embedded in the Beale encryption, and the numbers written on a scrap of paper stuffed inside a brass acorn thing that was taken from my cigar box of dug up coins, only to turn up later where I was expected to find it. (Numbers that represented latitude and longitude coordinates in a stretch of the Atlantic that encompassed the points-of-reference scribbled into my copy of *The Beale Papers* by my girlfriend's autistic brother). I could understand Raiden sharing them with me, but not the government type.) That's what I needed to figure out. How did that lottery key-phrase in Jeremy's book go again: 'He that concealed things will find must look before him and behind.' After seeing (and hearing) the hijinks in the basement of the alehouse, I was becoming more convinced that there was a connection between the coordinates of the beaching of the storm-tossed *Sea Venture* near Bermuda in 1609 with Bacon's mysterious Bensalem, and the bard's swan song of Prospero's enchanted island (one other than merely serving as inspiration for whom ever the playwright might be). In all likelihood, the set of numbers contained the key (more so than the anagrammatic inscriptions on the grave markers in the Bruton churchyard).

"You're late, fucker," I smiled at Jeremy as he parked next to my pickup. "I thought you might have taken one of those new freeways that end in the middle of an alfalfa field."

"Naw, I stopped to pick up a can of beans and pork," he joked back.

"That will go good with my Holy Cow burgers on purple buns. You weren't tailed by any old black clunkers hauling a giant flowerpot, were you?"

"No, but with all those owls watching us, they know who we are. Might as well have posted the entire caper as an Insta-feed."

"They probably had us chipped with RFID tags before we filled up. You still don't think the timing of aviator glasses speaking in Willy code was a coincidence, do you?"

"I never condemned it as being improbable. Here, put this in your fridge," he said while handing me an 8-pack of Beale's Gold Lager.

"Bacon's agenda wasn't the nefarious stuff some of his detractors claim," Jeremy said while building his burger at my kitchen table. "He might have had his fingers in a lot of pies, but the new tool he left behind wasn't about a surveillance state or that totalitarian shit you hear about in paranoid rants. World banker reptiles, the floating eye on the dollar bill and milk carton kids... though that's fizzled. It wasn't some grand scheme having to do with the Rothchilds and Bilderbergers... by the way, this burger slaps, Jack," he said after taking a bite. "And you slayed those tators, too. Bacon's thesis was about the Great Instauration... restoring or renewing things like that written in the grotto: NOVATUS. He was the herald of a new golden age that he saw coming... and it didn't include satanic rituals involving any damn onion pizzas."

"Just the Wild Goose Club," I said while scooping more of my sliced potato mélange onto his paper plate.

"As with any convivial society, yeah, sure, there might have been some drinkin' bouts. A few hearty pints of ale to release steam from their intellectual pursuits. But compared to those that imitated the Wild Goose... or is it geese?... their nocturnal revelry was nothing like Sir Francis Dashwood and his Med-menham Monks, with their Hell Fire Punch, naughty ditties, wenching and religious burlesque. Their proud monkey mascot wore a black chasuble and bishop's funky biretta. How's that for gross perversion of a Catholic function? Unlike Bacon's cir-cle, they were a gaggle of rakes. It was all about indulgence and deviation, though they weren't even true revolutionaries. They were just a bunch of dabblers and dilettantes. Wealthy drunken pranksters that dressed whores as nuns and pigged out at ban-quets that included Holy Pyes.... and if I still have room, what's for dessert?"

"Want to know what I think?" I asked Jeremy after taking a gulp of beer.

"Yeah, sorry bruh. You were going to lay out something for me besides this tasty grub."

After showing Jeremy the slip of parchment with the map coordinates (25N, 71W) and the numbers and crude depiction of the Freemasonic square and set of compasses joined that Raiden had marked inside the cipher field in my copy of *The Beale Papers*, I opened my tablet and showed him that the first set of coor-dinates was for the Bermuda Triangle, with Raiden's sequence placed at a position on the masonic device that represented a somewhat more specific area near Bermuda. I then told him that it was the spot where the *Sea Venture* was grounded on its way to Virginia after taking on water during a storm. The reason for the coarse change to a northerly direction, I explained, was be-cause of the Spanish threat in the West Indies. After reminding him that the man speaking on the radio in the artificial cave had mentioned "Sit the dial to NBW", I also told him about the plight of the ship's passengers while stranded on the island being the inspiration for Shakespeare's play, *The Tempest*. When I was done, I could see the wheels turning in Jeremy's head. "The only problem," I said, "is that the center of the square and compass is still just a stretch of open sea in the Atlantic."

"Deeper than did ever plummet sound, I'll drown my book," Jeremy recited a line from the play. "You're thinking the vault might be buried under water? You trying to make a Bealiever out of me, Jack? Wait a minute…"

He turned on his phone and scrolled through some recent photos until he found one that showed the cluster of dice that had been tossed by the skeletal hand in the lurid display in the grotto. There were 5 positions altogether, and after enlarging the image we could discern their individual faces. The first one was a 2, with the second one being a 5. The two that were touching each other were a 6 and a 1, with the final throw also being a 1.

"Twenty five and seventy one," he mumbled.

He then turned on the phone's voice recorder to play back part of what the voice on the other end of the shortwave radio had said during the seemingly coded messages:

"The ship will be drawn to Prospero on the island of illusion in the sea of troubles through his high charms. Dost thou like the plot, Trinculo? Sea of troubles," Jeremy uttered with excitement in his voice. "The Bermuda Triangle. What could be more tempestuous?"

Just then there was a brief tapping on the door, followed by someone turning the knob, which caused me to rise from the table.

"Hmm, something smells yummy," Merrilly said with a big smile. "Did you save some for me?"

"Hey, it's Merr," I said while sitting back down. "A nice surprise. The coals are still going if you want me to throw a burger on?"

"No, I already ate... drat, missed the hobo potatoes again. No, I just dropped by to pick up something."

"This is my partner in crime," I said. "Name is Jeremy Pye."

"Hi, Jeremy, I'm Merrilly, as in life is but a dream, but with two l's, even though Jack here always forgets that."

"Nice to finally meet you," Jeremy smiled. "I thought Jack was just making up shit about having himself a bae."

"When he makes things up, its something more unbelievable than having a girlfriend, which explains why we had men with their heads covered by green yarn hiding in the bushes. Jack, can I have a word with you... alone."

After telling me that she didn't think we should be a couple anymore, and that her mom was selling the trailer to move to North Carolina, and that Royalene wasn't too thrilled with me for missing shifts during my daygers, and that I still owed her money from a credit card (but that I could pay her back after I found the book "in the secret cave" – with the extra time given being her version of finesse for breaking up, so I gathered), she mentioned that she was pretty sure that she had seen my friend Jeremy at the Platinum Club (where she pole danced), snaking lap dances when not gawking at the afternoon McDances.

While the idea of my friend hanging around at a strip club was surprising, it wasn't as much of a shock as the news that I only had two weeks to find a new place to live.

After Merrilly hurried out the door without saying goodbye (and without taking anything), I sat back down at the table and gave Jeremy a "what the fuck just happened?" look.

"So, I've got this antique table cigar lighter," I said. "You think your aunt might want to buy it?"

When I showed him the thing, after fiddling with its chased snuffer, he also took a look at the note that Callie had left with it.

"I might have secret messages on the brain these days, but this could be one meant for you. Did you notice how she spelled hear?"

"What do you mean?"

"Have you heard about the Pharos Lighthouse in Alexandria?"

"The Cleopatra thing in Egypt? That's where it was, right?"

"Yeah, there was one in Egypt – it was one of the Seven Wonders of the World – but now there's one in Alexandria, VA, like she says. It's a nightclub… Hey, did you know that Cleopatra lived closer in time to the first Pizza Hut than to the building of the great pyramids?"

"Really? I should use that in a bet at Royalene's. I could use the money. That Comfort Inn in Williamsburg set me back. Cleopatra lived closer to the first Pizza Hut than to the pyramids –"

"Closer in time," Jeremy emphasized.

"I know. I know. A nightclub? Really? Is it a peeler club?"

CHAPTER V
OXYRHYNCHUS

"I believe a change has gotta come
Get ready for the new things…
I believe a change is gotta come
They'll be fascinating things"

Gary Wright

Just to see if Jeremy was right about the note from Callie containing a hidden message, the following night I made the two hour drive to Alexandria. Parking near the waterfront of the Potomac, I walked to the trendy nightclub whose three tapering tiers of light brown stone were designed to resemble the scaled-downed edifice of the Pharos Lighthouse of ancient Egypt. In the gathering dusk, the rotating orange beacon at the apex shone with a fiery intensity above the brick facades of the Old Town boutiques, restaurants and other bustling entertainment venues.

Standing motionless in front of the entrance were two black doorkeepers (bouncers?) who looked to be identical twins. Both had statuesque physiques that were accentuated by short linen kilts wrapped around their waists and gold bands entwined like snakes against muscular biceps that glistened like polished ebony. Their feet were shod in leather sandals and each had their arms akimbo as if mimicking the royal guards of a Pharaoh.

As I approached, they simultaneously opened large wide doors that were painted with an earthy brown glaze. Their synchronous motions (and silence) were a bit unnerving, as were the bronze visages of cobras that served as decorative handles.

Once inside, I walked across the glazed mosaic tiles of a hypostyle hall, whose pillars resembled traditional buff-colored papyrus-reed stalks with floral-bud capitals. In niches along the faux-limestone texture of the wall cladding, electric torches on each side cast shadowy patterns on variegated frescoes that depicted scenes of daily life in ancient Egypt. Attached to the wall paintings at regular intervals were plaster scorpions coated with metallic gilding. These desert scourges protruded from the flat surface with their barbed tails bent menacingly forward.

"What took you so long, Jack?" a calm female voice asked.

Startled, I quickly turned in the direction of the voice. It took a second to register what I was seeing against the painted vignettes. Through a tangled mass of light brown hair, Callie's green eyes were staring at me, though I couldn't understand why her bare feet were dangling directly above her head. Finally, I realized she was locked in a yoga position that required doing a perfectly balanced handstand with her spine arched back in such a contorted manner so that her lower body was curved like one of the disproportionate scorpions' tails. It seemed impossible that a human could hold such a pose. That and the shiny chestnut-colored jumpsuit that fit tightly against her sculpted body made her appear like she was just another one of the frescoes' slithering creatures.

"You've haven't been doing that the whole time, have you?" I joked.

"Only for a minute, actually," she replied while spitting out the strands of hair in her mouth.

A second later she fell out of the pose by adjusting her spine and lowering one leg at a time. Standing face to face with me, she fluffed her messy hair. While doing so, an extended exhale through her mouth smelled faintly of her menthol demi-slims. When I took a step back, almost bumping into one of the ornate columns, she gave me a quizzical smile, perhaps not realizing the reason for my sudden unease was her radiant presence.

"It's an advanced inversion known as a Handstand Scorpion," she said matter-of-factly.

"I would say impressive, but a better word might be impossible. Are you okay? What do you do here, besides pretending to be a scorpion?"

"A little bit of everything, but mostly a lot of nothing."

"Sounds pretty cush," I smiled.

"My mother knows the owner, and he offered me a job as his personal assistant. I helped with some of the designs and teach him about the socials... the newest platforms and checkboxes for exposure. Not just re-heated stuff like most clubs use to promote their brand... because this isn't your average club. I added koshari to the menu and a sesame paste appetizer that's healthy."

"I like the guards you have at the doors."

"Unlike the doorkeepers painted on actual temple walls and tomb scenes. It doesn't make sense, but would you believe they're usually shown as being asleep on the job or even blind. No lazy sloths here at Pharos, besides me, of course."

"That doesn't make sense for a guard, especially if they're blind."

"Listen, I've got beer in my office. Let's go there before the maquillage parade starts. Pretty soon there'll be droves of wannabe Cleopatras in here."

"Yeah, let's get away from that," I deadpanned. "So... your note with the lighter. Why be so cryptic?"

"I didn't want your partner to get shook."

"You mean ex-partner," I informed her.

"Hopefully not because of my lighthouse?"

"No, because of me," I replied.

Displayed prominently above the heavily curtained entrance into the upscale club was a large painted *wedjat* eye (Eye of Horus) with its distinctive markings.

"I feel like I'm being watched," I said. "Why are people so fascinated by this mystical eye? Always using the design for their tattoos."

"It's called the *wedjat* – the all-seeing eye of the ancient Egyptians. I recently learned it's about numbers, with painted strokes that subdivide it into arithmetic fractions... but a part is missing... a fraction that equates with the pupil, so the vision that is All-Seeing must be of something else. Something magical, I was told, like a window to the beyond where the gods dwelt. Maybe an old scrap of papyrus has the answer? There's a landfill in Egypt that has lots of well-preserved stuff that was lost at the original Alexandria. That's where we got some of the stuff that we used as decorations for the club."

"I see," I chuckled.

"The *wedjat's* portions were probably used to tally grain for beer, but I also heard it's a symbol for a secret area of the brain, and the image of the painted eye shows this very spot."

On the way to Callie's office I got a quick glimpse of the interior's Egyptian-themed design. Besides numerous hanging video screens, the most attention-grabbing feature was a floating barge dance floor behind a palm-fringed strip of sand that sloped downward from the main bar. Instead of the DJ playing remixes, a belly dancer with exotic features was performing under colored lights. Through the circle of onlookers, I could make out the gleam of torques and hear the jingle of the coin sash as her toned muscles undulated to the accompaniment of a strident reed-flute. Wearing diaphanous harem pants and a sequined crochet bra, she waved a long chiffon scarf, drawing applause from those admiring the serpentine articulations of her bronzed torso.

When we got to Callie's small office, she opened a mini-fridge.

"I've got cans of Sakara Gold and bottles of Stella. Both imported from Egypt. The Sakara is rather pale... if you prefer blondes, and the Stella is the Egyptian's answer to Budweiser."

"Really? Then, I'll try the Stella."

After handing the bottle to me, she picked a small tomato from a clump of dozens that were bunched together on short vines that she held like a bouquet of flowers.

"Want a tomata," she asked after popping one into her mouth. "It's CRISPR-edited."

"What's so different about it?"

"Just how compact they are – but not how squishy."

"No, I'm good with these suds. You should keep the lighthouse lighter for your desk. It fits perfectly with the theme. Use it when you sneak a smoke. So, what's extra here? People suck down boozy seltzers, eat your veggies – no glizzys, I take it – and dance under lasers?"

Bending over behind her desk, she quickly removed the figure-skimming jumpsuit and put on a pair of lace-trimmed jean shorts. After zipping up the pants, she pulled down a slinky black tank from her messy hair and smoothed it around the contours of her breasts. While doing so, I got a whiff of body lotion that smelled delicious. When she stood up, I smiled at what was written on the shirt:

MY (red heart logo) BELONGS TO AN EMBALMER

"The club goers here like our pomegranate beers, but they get really turnt seeing themselves and their friends placed in the time of the real Pharos Lighthouse. They like seeing themselves doing things from that period. They might be a peasant or a pharaoh and all the effects are dynamic."

"How's this switcheroo done?"

"We've got cameras placed all about the club, and their captures – the raw images of our customers – are altered by a computer graphics program that projects them back onto the screens... but now with a different look. The compiling happens in real-time... well almost... though it's really quick... without markers... well, kind of, but not like those used for most CGI tricks –"

"You're losing me, Callie, you mean like deepfake shit?"

"It's easier if I just show you, but once they have the motion captures, rather than animating a digital character – an actor in a film, say – detailed overlays are added to a person hanging out in the club by fractal algorithms... and then the person is placed in a different setting, with a backdrop created by terrain generators... taken from render-farms or high-res stock imagery. The finished simulation – when all the elements are fleshed out and blended together – is super-realistic. A company called ULTRAFX designed the compositing techniques, which actually consists of just one imaging artist and his assistant. I don't know how the process works, but the guys talk about things like polygonal meshes, cartesian coordinates and surface topologies. And they make sandstorms in our cocktail blenders."

"So, this isn't crayons and coloring book stuff."

"Well, that's another thing," she mumbled almost inaudibly, "that I can't help."

When we walked back into the club, it was filled with people. Callie wasn't kidding about the wannabe Cleopatras. I must have counted five of them seated at the bar alone. With their sheer skirts, richly costumed breasts and striking features, I could see why the place was so popular. There was also no shortage of mystic eye tats like the stylized Egyptian design above the entrance.

After exchanging a few pleasantries with the bartender, Callie ordered me another Egyptian Budweiser (no, I didn't want to try the date wine) and a glass of iced hibiscus tea for herself.

While waiting for the drinks to arrive, she drew my attention to the imagery on one of the large overhanging screens. What I saw looked like a scene from a movie. A canopied pleasure barge was silhouetted against the lavender twilight as it skimmed across the milky-green waters of the Nile.

An ancient Egyptian queen on board the oared reed boat was reclined on a settee covered with zebra pelts. As she nibbled on honey-cakes and figs, kilted fan-bearers (who resembled the club's black doormen) cooled her shapely-bronzed curves with purple heron feathers.

Callie told me to look closely at the queen's facial features. In studying them, I could see that her cheeks were rouged with henna and her eyes were heavily painted (with stibium, kohl and malachite). Upon her gold-tipped plaits was a fillet that sparkled with the fire-delighted jewels encircling a protruding *uraeus* (upright asp). Along with the bright luster of dripping ear pendants was an elaborate gold collar necklace with blue faience beads.

After getting an eyeful, Callie pointed to a girl who was also seated at the bar. Though she wore sparing makeup and was dressed in a beige shirt and blue jeans, I could tell that it was the same person that was on the screen. The blending of the real and imaginary was seamless.

"That's cray," I said. "She's the queen of the Nile. I see what you were saying about what they can do with their effects toolkit. And she's not even looking at the screen… probably doesn't know she's been… changed."

"She's more interested with that cherry tequila, but wait until she gets a look at herself with the digital makeover. Then again, she might find queenie here's facial paints to be hideous. Plain Jane's not even wearing lip gloss, and there are plenty of Walgreens in this Alexandria. The owner, Mister Zuffante, is using this place as a test. A trial run to work the bugs out for a bigger club he plans on opening on a private island in the Atlantic. Somewhere near Bermuda. And he wants me to go there with him… as his PA… but I'm not sure if I want to. It could be a good opportunity, I suppose," she said with her gaze now fixed on a bronzed sculpture beneath the bottles of liquor and a stemware rack that appeared to be some odd species of fish with a downturned snout that had, for whatever reason, an erect human penis in its mouth.

"Might be," I shrugged.

"It's the Oxyrhynchus fishy," she smiled after noticing my confused look, "that swallowed one of the gods' glizzies after his brother murdered him and sliced it off and tossed it into the Nile. But his wife used magic spells to make a new glizzy – yeah, hopefully an upgraded one, right! – that she attached to her dead husband and used it to impregnate her self with their child… the little miracle… but don't worry, I won't be trying that at home… Hey, who's that I see?" she clapped while pointing up at one of the large screens.

Against a backdrop of moonlit sand dunes, Callie and I had been processed with the advanced renders. On the screen, she was wearing a sheath dress and had a cone-like object on the top of her vivid black hair. Between her breasts was a filigreed necklace with an emerald green scarab amulet. I was dressed in a short tunic and my head had been shaved. Instead of the can of Sakara Gold that I was drinking at the bar, in the virtual world, I lifted a clay vessel. We were playing some kind of board game that involved tossing black and white sticks (instead of dice) and moving pieces along the grid of squares.

"What are we playing?" I asked as she moved one of her pawns with fingers whose long nails had been lacquered with henna. In a nice touch by the graphic designers, ribbons of flame were reflected on the wooden game board from lighted wicks floating in saucers of oil.

"It's called *Senet*," she replied, "and I'm winning."

"That's because you know the owner. Hey, did you know that the ancient Egyptians had a similar version of this layering thing? Only, it was a little cruder... more static. Just look at the decorations in the club. In the tomb paintings, people have heads like animals."

"Ha ha ha," she half-smiled.

"Okay, did you know that Cleopatra lived closer in time to the first moon landing than she did to the building of the great pyramids?"

Suddenly, Callie grabbed my arm while gesturing up at the screen.

"The fucker's back."

"Who?"

Instead of seeing myself moving pieces on the board, someone else in the club was now playing against Callie. Only this time, the game wasn't *Senet*. In place of the board was a brass tray filled with sand. In the middle, two scorpions were engaged in a deadly contest as Callie's character and a man dressed in a black leather tunic prodded them with painted sticks.

"It's one of the men from the helicopter. I also saw him here a few days ago."

Looking closely at the man's features, I recognized him as the government-type that had asked me lots of strange questions at Royalene's.

"Where is he?" I asked while glancing about the club.

"There he is," Callie said while pointing at the barge. "Wearing the funny hat…by the dancer."

Watching the shimmying hips of the gauze-winged belly dancer was a man in a dark suit and black bucket hat. Instead of having pale skin like he did that night when he probed my mind, as Merrilly had said, he had a deep tan like he just returned from the tropics. While bathed in colored lights, his sinister veneer made him stand out from those around him.

As her eyes remained fixed on him, Callie got up from the barstool.

"Let's go back to my office."

While smoking one of her demi-slims, she paced about with a frightened look in her eyes.

"What's he doing here?" I asked.

"I know what he wants, but I don't have it. And if I told you, you'd just laugh."

"Is he looking for one of those eye tattoos? One like most of the women here have," I asked with a calm voice. "Or one of those Civil War tokens without any markings."

"It's not a tattoo, so I don't get that part… and it's not really a token… or a button… but I thought it would be safe there. I got the idea of hiding it there from the stories about the ancient garbage jump at Oxyrhynchus in Egypt that I told you about, but it needs me to move it to someplace else. You'll laugh – I know you will. Can you drive me somewhere in the morning?

I'll get you a room here using the company card and meet you there in the morning. Just don't ask where we're going until I tell you. Okay? I'll explain later."

CHAPTER VI
WHIPPOORWILL

*"Twilight whippoorwill... whistle on
sweet deepener of dark loneliness"*

Matsou Basho

I still had no idea why Callie wanted me to stop at the gutted ruins of some old country store on a deserted stretch of road not far from her family's estate. The place was probably the hub of rural life back in the day, but now the two-storied, white-washed structure was barely standing.

Parking next to the rusted shells of a couple of old gas pumps, I turned towards what remained of a full width front porch that was shaded by a corroded metal roof.

"If you're looking for a snack, I doubt they'll have too good a selection," I joked.

"This used to be Gink's general store. My mother hung out here when she was little. They bought popsicles and cokes and stuff for nickels. There might not be too many choices, but the parking lot – it's a good place to hide a certain something, don't you think?"

Spreading out from the decaying facade in all directions, layer upon layer of old bottle caps covered the once gravel drive. While the faded logos of some of the more recent ones glinted in the sun, the flattened crowns of those embedded for nearly a century were encrusted with a dull reddish–brown patina.

"It's a good place to hide a bottle cap," I replied.

"You're right about that," Callie said as she climbed out of the pickup. As she made a beeline towards the side of the building, I got out and followed her. Bending over an area of mostly older caps, she appeared to be searching for something.

"It's not here any more," she said with a confused look. "I know I put it under one called Pick-Upper which was next to this one here with a little birdie called Chirp that says it was bottled in Alexandria...that's touching this Wise-Up, a Hoot of a Cola one, but now it's gone and there's this stupid Sprite one where Pick-Upper it should be. It wanted to be here to hide, instead of being at Pharos," she said while turning over several indistinct caps, "but now it wants to be moved again."

As I looked down at the assortment of caps on the ground, once again I wondered if Callie had mental issues of some kind. Either that or an arrested development condition that would account for her childlike behavior at times. Her coloring with crayons and doctor's office lollipops were no different than teens that still needed a comfort blanket or sucked their thumb.

As she continued to look for something, I reached down and flipped over a few caps: Nesbitts Orange, Sundrop Cola, Flip and NuGrape Soda.

"This place is a detectorist's hell," I said. "So, what are we looking for?"

"Pick-Upper. Oh, here you are. I found it, Jack. Pick-Upper must have been picked up."

She showed me a blank reddish-copper disc about the same size as one of the bottle caps. It looked like the thing she'd found in a mason jar full of common sutler tokens at the estate sale.

"So, then where's Sprite? I don't see it anymore."

"Who cares?"

After sitting for a spell on the creaking planks of what remained of the store's back porch, Callie spread out my fingers
and placed her great grandfather's treasured doojigger into the
palm of my hand, letting me know by means of her solemn expression that I should feel privileged to hold it. Whatever the
thing was, it was extremely light, especially for a metallic alloy
(?). When I closed my fist, I could barely feel it. It was as if I were
holding a wisp of frozen smoke.

"After Grumble died, it went into hibernation for a long time
– pretending for a while to be one of the shiny buttons in a sewing
box. This was once some angel's halo, I'll bet you didn't know."

When I looked at the thing more closely, I realized that
its blank surface was coated with a glaze of sorts, whose faint
effulgence changed according to the angle of view. The reac-
tive effect was strangely compelling; somewhat like the shifting
colors of dichroic glass I'd seen in pieces of modern jewelry. As
I continued to peer into the puzzling sheen, I noticed an image
developing within the depths of the micro-layers that quickly re-
solved into what looked like a speckled human iris. Even without
a pupil, the quivering golden membrane appeared to be strangely alive. If this was some kind of optical trick, it was quite clever,
especially when the glinting eye blinked before engaging with
my captive gaze. As I tried to resist the magnetic intensity of its
luminous fixation, a series of smaller diameter spheres appeared
on the disc, orbiting along the edge of its lustrous surface with
a curious fluidity. Though I couldn't make out what was being
shown within these tiny, brilliant displays, I found myself squinting at the specks of movement in one of the 'windows' in particular when I was startled by the sound of a beeping horn.

Looking up, I saw a boxy old powder blue Plymouth with
chromed accents and white-wall tires screech to a stop on the

bottle cap-paved drive near the store's back entrance. The strange thing was that my first glimpse of the vehicle was of its passenger side, when it should have been the driver's side from where I was sitting. Though this bizarre optical anomaly only lasted for an instant, I was at a complete loss as to why the car initially appeared that way from my vantage point.

I could hear classical music playing on the tinny radio when an elderly guy in a crisp white suit and straw fedora climbed out. The man quickly rounded the hood of the car while pointing his finger at something in the forest on the opposite side of a narrow dirt track. When I tried to see what this was, I noticed that the trees seemed flat and lifeless. There was also something about the dappled effect from the light and shade that didn't seem quite right.

"Whippoorwill, come out of there with that trunk," the man shouted with a nasally, high-pitched voice. After lighting a cigarette, he called out again. "I know you're in there, Will, you little tree-peeper. Come on out, and let's take a gander of what's inside that chest you found."

When I looked to my left, instead of seeing Callie sitting next to me, two old-timers with grimy, pudgy faces were slouched in aluminum chairs on the flyblown porch. Both were wearing soiled, baggy grey work clothes and tractor caps whose creased bills were smudged with oil stains. One had his grubby fingers wrapped around a bottle of beer while the other scooped potted meat onto a cracker. Both seemed to be unaware of my presence as I sat there frozen in disbelief.

When I jumped up and glanced about, everything around me appeared slightly warped. I also realized that the surroundings had changed to some extent. I shut my eyes tightly for a second, hoping that when I opened them things would return back to normal.

"Grumble's got a keen eye," the hick with the gelatinous spread croaked. "I didn't even see that colored boy."

I tried to get my bearings, but nothing made sense. When I nodded as a way of saying hello to one of rustic types sitting on the porch, there was no response. I could hear the ringing of a cash resister inside the store and see flashes of movement through its screen door. *How could it now be open?* The only thing that I could think of was that the computer graphic whizzes from Pharos were messing with me with their optical shit, and that Callie was in on the joke. If so, the simulation was mind-boggling. Far stranger than my sighting of the crazy airship and the 'time-shift' incident with the British soldier in the Merchant's Square. But how could their artificial imagery be inside my head? I could hear the birds chirping on the power lines and smell the strong body odor from the local yokels lazing on the porch. As my anxiety began to escalate, I swallowed hard, fighting to stay calm.

When I swayed dizzily towards the door to look for Callie, the surroundings tilted and my legs went rubbery. I could hear the blood pounding in my ears and felt so light-headed that I thought I might pass out at any second.

After regaining my equilibrium, I opened the squeaky door, catching a glimpse of a faded sign hanging above it that boldly stated: POLITICIANS NOT PERMITTED ON PREMISES. Once inside, an elderly clerk standing behind an old cash register was staring suspiciously over the rim of glasses resting on the tip of his nose at a couple of small boys holding wrapped Fudgesicles.

"Wind, water and words are free," the man repeated a couple of times with an auctioneer's staccato voice while leaning over boxes of pine tar soap and bins of penny candy, "but everything else costs money. Part with your shiniest nickel, sonny, and you can peel back that frosty jacket."

As he spoke, my eyes were fixated on the smoke that curled from the Fudgesicle's paper wrapper. Seeing the vapor streaming from ice crystals, whatever was happening inside the store was incredibly realistic.

After touching a ribbon studded with dead flies that hung from an exposed beam right above a tray of smelly egg slices and piles of smushed bologna sandwiches, the kid pulled a nickel from his pocket and set it on the cluttered counter.

The storekeeper's empurpled lips contorted with humorous contempt.

"Be sure to count your change," he said in a jeering matter while placing his index finger on an empty spot. When the next boy stepped up, he repeated the same lines that he'd probably used a thousand times.

Before continuing across the dingy linoleum floor, I caught sight of a spotless Nolde's Bread calendar hanging above the Coca-Cola ice chest. Seeing that its date was June 1967, I did a double take. Instead of trying to find Callie among the aisles of dusty canned goods, I hastened back outside, where the two backwoods folk still didn't seem to notice me.

Trying to maintain my composure, I watched as one of the kids with the Fudgesicles kneeled behind the rear bumper of the Plymouth. Making sure that no one was watching, he pulled something out of his back pocket. As he did so, he kept an eye on the man in the snazzy white suit (Grumble?) that was standing by the tree line next to a bare-chested young black kid wearing tattered pants. Both were examining a long-tailed brown coat that was almost completely covered with shiny brass buttons. Evidently they had removed the garment from the mottled old footlocker opened at their feet. Whatever it was that the boy behind the car held, he quickly began attaching it to the chrome tailgate.

Curious to see what kind of mischief the kid was up to, I walked over to have a look. When I got there, he was pressing down on the edges of a sticker from a die-cut trading card set that featured cartoonish parodies of popular consumer products. This one depicted a green sprout-figure stomping on a bunch of equally cartoony peas with terrified faces.

"What's going on here?" I asked, hoping for any explanation that might explain the absurdity of the situation.

"It's a Wacky Packy of the Jolly Mean Giant," the kid said with his squeaky larynx. "I'm a friend of the Suttons visiting here from my home in Mfkzt." (Pronounced "Moof-kooz-tee"). "That's in Southern Illinois. The S is silent. My name is Addison Albright, and I have a friend named Kelby Timmons who's really smart."

He stood up straight and licked the melting Fudgesicle, using the back of his hand to wipe away the streak of chocolate on his cheek.

"So... I'm here now at Gink's store, but at the same time I'm also speaking to you when I'm older," he said with his adolescent voice cracking. "A lot older, actually. It's how the *Anunna* device you have works – these home movies – I know because I also have one, and it's not a piece of inanimate earth. It's actually a divine possession, but it's my best friend, Kelby, who's gonna tell you something about the strange fish."

Seeing the man in the white suit and the black kid walking towards the car while carrying the trunk by its leather handles, the boy hurried off to join his little friend at the side of the building.

"What's he gonna tell me?" I shouted. "Hey! Hey, what is it?"

"I already told you, Jack," came the soft reply from Callie. I flinched at the subdued tone, dazed for a moment to find her sitting next to me. Speechless, I breathed in the faint lavender aroma of her "everywhere" body lotion as it mingled with the rotting planks. Standing up and glancing about, I saw that the surroundings were as they'd been before. How much time had elapsed, I wondered? "You just don't believe me," she said while lighting a demi-slim and exhaling a mentholated stream. "Like I said, it used to be some angel's halo...but not the harp playing ones."

"You weren't there... with me," I said after getting over the initial shock of whatever had caused the radical changes that I had somehow experienced. "Didn't see any of it – how incredibly clear it was."

"The thing in the sky?" she asked.

When I glanced down at the disc, the revolving dots with their hyper spectrum of colors were gone. So were any subtle fluctuations or shimmering quality on its blank surface. It looked as unimpressive as it did the first time I saw the damn thing. Just a metal slug used to fool vending machines.

"Okay, okay, I believe you," I said to Callie while driving to her family's estate, "if you say the Pharos geeks had nothing to do with it, fine, but if it isn't some hypnosis gizmo, we need to tell someone about it because it's cray – the things the little fucker can do. Those guys at the club would shit their pants if they saw what I did... like the mist coming from the Fudgescicle, and what about the smelly pits of those pumpkin head hayseeds. Now, *I* need one of those doctor's cherry lollipops of yours because I'm starting to think there might be a real problem with my head –"

"Tell who, Jack? The helicopter guys?" she said while rolling her eyes.

"I don't know," I said while raising both hands in exaspera-
tion. "It must have come from somewhere off Earth. Maybe one
of those crashed spacecraft like you hear about with the weird
metal. Someone kept a piece and I'll bet the military is still busy
looking for it. That would explain a lot of the shit that's been
happening lately, wouldn't it, like the helicopter guys. Wait a
minute, your mom's sister's husband – I forget his name – the
guy who was in the Navy in Vietnam – "

"Uncle Harland – "

"Can you call him and say I want to ask him a question?"

"I'll call him right now if you want."

She rang his number and switched on the speakerphone. He
answered after the first ring.

"Hello, sweetie."

"Hiya there, skipper. Hey, my friend Jack who you met at the
family gathering – he wants to ask you something… It has to do
with Grumble, I think."

"Sure, okay."

"Hello, sir, do you know how he got his good luck charm?"

"It was some black kid whose family lived in a shack back in
the woods. His name was Will, but everyone at Ginks – that was
the name of the general store – called him Whippoorwill because he was always watching us from the trees and we couldn't
see him until he popped out. You know how the brown mottling
of whippoorwills blends in perfectly with tree bark. The little
kids thought he was some kind of boogeyman, but he was just as
frightened of outsiders, I guess. Anyway, he found an old chest
from Civil War times that contained letters from Confederate
prisoners and a brown jacket that was almost completely covered
with Union buttons. Grumble bought the trunk and its contents
for twenty-five dollars and a dozen or so cans of potted meat and

sardines. Will loved those Vienna sausages… and a jug of apple cider, I think."

"Okay, thanks," I said. "I was just curious."

"Bye, Uncle Harland. Kisses to Darla."

"Well, shit, the kid from Southern Illinois that I told you about — he said we were in someone's home movie. Maybe the device captured the entire sequence of being sold to Grumble, and even things that happened inside the store. It's a wild idea, but we're flying a helicopter on Mars, so I guess it's not really that wild."

For some reason I tried to remember the name of the town in Illinois that the kid at Gink's store said he was from. Moof something or other, which reminded me of a similar sounding place that the stranger I met at the library where my mom worked when I was younger wanted to go. Was it Moosville, or Moof something? Anyway, it was probably just a coincidence.

Though the Sutton estate was in the process of being sold, some of the furnishings were still in place, including a couch that Callie said I could sleep on. All that remained of Grumble's once impressive library was his mahogany desk. From one of the drawers Callie pulled out a letter that was stuffed inside a manila folder.

"I found this among Grumble's stuff here. I think it was written during the period he was having all those bad dreams about climbing plants."

"Oh, yeah, the honeysuckle that was smothering him," I said.

"He talks about men from the government visiting the house and asking questions about if he had recently seen anything out of the ordinary. It also says they wanted to know about any tattoos he had, though they didn't seem interested in the nautical star he got on his arm during his time with the Merchant Marine. The one that was shaded like a compass rose. He says they kept checking the palms of his hand, which he thought was odd, but, as he says here," she read from the letter, "they weren't chuckling... and later the one named Bevin from King Neptune's Court couldn't be warded off with the fairy tears of Chief Powhatan."

"The tattoo, again," I mumbled.

"I know, and the guy in the helicopter, or whatever it was, he checked my palms, too."

"Yeah, I remember you telling me that. They were looking for tattoos in all kinds of places."

"All kinds," she emphasized. "The rest of the letter is pretty weird as well... like this part where he mentions the space animals. Here, you can read it for yourself."

"Civil war rages on this rebel soil. It's my belief that the stalkers are looking for the keepsake sewn on the Confederate prisoner's jacket placed in a camp chest. Their dazzling astrodillas zigzag over the property, which they mark with purple checkerboards – the bedeviled critters. You'd think the toads wore diamonds here. It's not for a gambler's lucky charm or the recipe for Deliza's spiced peaches that they have come. The doojigger holds the secret of the true nautical star. An angel protects this learning. I have seen its glorious halo. The object changes location or goes unnoticed. Hides from the swooping panzershwein combing the rebel soil with their pigheaded ganders..."

"What does he mean by civil war?" I asked. "Not *the* Civil War, I hope... I mean, he sounds schizoid, but with what that thing does, I get it... and what's with this nautical star?"

"Let's go look for it," Callie's eyes widened as she placed the letter back in the folder.

"Look for what?"

"Grumble's star."

On the way to an open field on the property that Callie chose to experiment with Grumble's doojigger, we stopped at a ramshackle barn to look for a favorite bicycle from her childhood.

Being that it was getting dark, I clicked on my flashlight while entering its cluttered interior. As the faint beam illuminated hooks and racks that were festooned with cobwebs, I was amazed to see the dusty frame of the same old Plymouth that pulled into Gink's store. As it sagged on flat white walls, I trained the light on its chrome bumper, equally amazed to see that the "Jolly Mean Giant" sticker was still firmly attached. Once again, my mind reeled. Here was tangible evidence that what I had witnessed was something akin to a home movie – one that I didn't just view, but experienced as if I was actually present when it was being recorded. I didn't know how else to explain it – the sensation of being there in the footage.

"Can you believe it – it's the sticker I watched that kid put on," I said while staring in astonishment. "There it is – it really did happen."

"I forgot about the powder-blue whale," Callie said. "Do you think the sticker was someone's way of making fun of his scary dreams? The rampaging vines?"

"Who, the little kid I saw – or older guy I heard?"

"There's my Sweet Thunder," she said when she caught sight of her bike leaning against the dirty webs on one of the walls. "Just be glad it wasn't up in the hay loft."

After moving some badminton equipment, a wheelbarrow and hand crank ice-cream maker, I rolled a little girl's pink bicycle out of the barn and gently placed it in the bed of my pickup.

Having been parked in a recently mowed field for a couple of hours, we tried to activate the doojigger but were unable to get a response from anything we did.

The gradient effect of the various layers that had thrilled my eyes earlier could not be seen in the faint moonlight and there was no sign of the revolving displays with flecks of activity that had somehow placed me as an unperceived spectator in someone's three-dimensional home movie.

Fiddling with it while sitting on the tailgate, I felt like a caveman that had been handed a smartphone, although owing to other, more perplexing, features that the doojigger exhibited, that tired analogy wasn't really fitting. iPhones have passcodes to enable (and prevent) access, but the operating system of the thing that the kid called an *Anunna* device seemed far more flexible, causing me to wonder if it represented a sentient machine. Although I didn't tell this to Callie, the impression I received earlier in the day was that some mysterious connection had been established between its internal functioning and myself. At the same time, I also sensed that it had absorbed every aspect of my mind, and that my unfiltered thoughts determined its actions.

However, due to its current lack of response, I was getting tired of fooling with the thing as Callie pedaled her little bike around the F-150 with great agility, looking silly on the child's "bread loaf" seat while ringing the bell with a lit cigarette stuck in her mouth.

"There's another one!" she shouted while pointing to where she had just seen a shooting star.

"That makes seven for you already," I said while popping open a can of Bold Rock seltzer that I found in the Sutton's fridge.

While wiping away some of the spray from the surface of the disc, its composite layers flared with a chromatic mosaic that quickly dissolved before reappearing as a boundless expanse of stars surrounding a moon that was in a different phase than the crescent presently hanging over the field. Amidst this impressive celestial display, a dark oval shape suddenly appeared. As the aperture widened, something that resembled a glowing orb swiftly emerged. Though my eyesight was enhanced by some unknown means (once again), the magnification wasn't sufficient enough for me determine what this shiny object was as it rapidly descended from the increasing expanse of darkness.

"Callie, come here… quick… it's doing something. There's like a tear in the sky… an opening, and things are pouring out."

As Callie hurried over, dozens of pulsating dots began to glide out of the ominous portal. When she reached for the doojigger, it quickly went blank, as if both of us touching it at the same time had short-circuited the device.

"What'd we do to make it go away?" she asked while shaking the disc in her palm.

When I looked up at her disappointed face, I was stunned by what was transpiring a short distance away.

"What the fuck."

In the middle of what should have been an empty field, a large plantation house stood on sprawling grounds. Bathed in moonlight, the imposing facade and complex of outbuildings could be seen through a grand entrance flanked by boxwood hedges.

In front of the stately columns of its expansive porch, dozens of indistinct figures (a mixture of blacks and whites) were illuminated by the pale glow of oil lanterns as they gathered on the spacious lawn. As I watched, the blacks assembled in a square formation as the whites seated themselves at a large table.

I could feel a surge of adrenaline as I glanced about at the vague outlines of crude cabins, kennels and a tobacco barn. Having just experienced the activity at the country store, I figured the antebellum mansion was another projection that had unfolded in a spectacularly realistic manner from the device Callie was holding. I could hear the insect shrill, though the persistent rhythmic patterns were strangely out of sync. I could also smell the sweet scent of uncured tobacco that permeated the landscaped grounds.

"What's that smell?" Callie asked.

"You smell the crop, but can you see what I see?" I asked while clasping her shoulders and turning her around.

For a moment she stood there frozen.

"Where did that come from – maybe the guys at Pharos?" she tried to rationalize.

Seeing my truck glinting in the more familiar surroundings behind us, I realized we were coexisting in two distinct settings. One didn't look more real than the other, though the boundaries were distinct enough to recognize in places that hadn't melded together perfectly. Looking up, I saw that there were two 'different' moons, each shining in its half of separate starry skies.

"All this is your thing's doing," I said, "and its tricks are getting weirder."

As I pivoted my body, the shifting perception of the two actualities became disorienting.

"Two moons makes me dizzy," Callie mumbled as she slumped to the ground, " I don't think I like two moons."

As I watched the navigation lights of a high-flying commercial plane move across the sky, the second it entered the 'other' sky, both the red and green beacons, along with the strobing on the wingtips winked out.

"Do you see those people over there?" Callie asked, still visibly agitated. "What are they doing just standing like that in the yard dressed funny? Do you know what they're doing, Jack?"

"It's just some kind of reenactment, or practice of a reenactment... maybe – "

"Maybe?"

"I told you about the calendar and everything at the store. This doojigger stuff might be from the past, too."

"Can't we just drive away? I don't want to get trapped here."

"If you want to, but don't you want to check it out?" I said while reaching for her hands to pull her up. "It was your idea to come here –"

"I just wanted to see what Grumble's star was about. Not to see these creepy people. Why do you want to check it out?"

"To see what his star is all about, too," I said, hoping the casual bravado might hide my own anxiety. "Or what the deal is with tattoos of mystic eyes, or even the airship... something, at least. The thing seems receptive to our thoughts. Callie, you can do it," I nodded, trying to ease her concerns. "Let's try it for a minute to see what happens... It might be dope, and if the struggle is real, and you want to come back to my truck, we will. Come right back here, I promise."

Squeezing the disc in the palm of her hand, she reluctantly nodded her willingness to go along with whatever I had in mind.

As we headed towards the plantation, she nervously attempted to light one of her demi-slims.

"I'll bet there's lots of your Vogue Perle Menthe in that tobacco shed" I joked.

"I need to quit," she said tensely.

Besides the sweet cloying smell of the tobacco crop, the fragrance of evening primrose mingled with odious whiffs from the hencoops. I don't know if they sensed our approach, but several dogs began barking. Before reaching the dirt track that was bounded by boxwood hedges, we both paused and took a deep breath.

"Here goes," I said. "You ready?"

"Just as long as I can still see the truck when I look back."

Giving Callie a look of reassurance, we proceeded cautiously, hesitating for a second at the abrupt change in the terrain. While stepping onto the wide swath of shadowy grass, I noticed that the temperature was warmer and the air was considerably more humid. Continuing to the colorful gathering, we paused in front of a bald-headed black fellow in a harlequin checkered frockcoat sitting on a bench at a fancy upright piano.

"Don't worry," I said, "he can't see you... well, unless our shapes are like ghosts."

"He sure smells like I can see him and when did you become such an expert on whatever this is?"

"This afternoon," I shrugged.

"Okay, I believe you – they don't know we're here," she said with a giddy conviction, "but I know your F-150 is right over there because I can see it."

"Be careful not to bump into anyone – who knows what might happen."

Glancing about at the surroundings, we both realized that everything was way too authentic to be a reenactment. We had walked into a moment in the past that was captured by Callie's little device. The question was: was this event just a random occurrence in its memory, or did it have any relevance to our interest in Grumble's star?

As a flurry of moths wheeled in the faint cast of a tin candle lantern, dark, bony fingers struck a diminished chord with dramatic flare. This was followed by the motley pianist's left hand playing a bouncing two-step rhythm, while his right hand improvised with complex ragtime syncopation.

The traditional cakewalk contest began at a languid pace. Each of the fourteen black couples tilted their heads back while talking a few steps forward, moving solemnly in a tight formation with proud demeanors. All were dressed in handed-down Victorian finery. The men wore long, spit-tailed coats, chaplain black trousers and silk top hats, while their female partners were lavishly bedecked in ruffled belle gowns and feathered velvet bowlers. The men held walking sticks and the women spun lace parasols.

As the slow procession paraded across the lawn, the contestants picked up their pace like the spoke wheels of an old train gaining steam. Their poised movements also became more pronounced. Instead of soldierly precision with dignified expressions, the couples began strutting and prancing about in an exaggerated parody of the restrictive, rigid formality of high-society ballroom promenades. Effortlessly, they danced with challenging moves to the improvised piano staccato, all the while continuing to caricaturize the attitudes of their white oppressors.

Moths batted softly against the lantern's glass panes as dark fingers continued to hammer the keys in a frenzied waltz. To this wild rhythm, the prize-walkers became even more animated, the men waving their canes and doffing their hats with over-accentuated bows. As they high-stepped in comical fashion down the aisle of lined up couples, members of the plantation owner's family seated at a table clapped and whistled when some performed acrobatic somersaults.

On the table an elaborate cake was set on a silver pedestal-footed stand. Arranged on its jam frosting were halved wild plums and a few shiny baubles, including one that looked exactly like the doojigger.

"What if we took it?" Callie asked, raising her voice to be heard over the raucous tack piano.

"I don't know –"

"You should have tried to buy or take something from Ginks to see if you could bring it back."

"Yeah, I know, a receipt, but at the time – I didn't know if I was coming back."

"Don't say that… you're freakin' me out, Jack."

Unlike those whites that were enjoying the performance, one seemed to view the derisive antics of the dancers with amused contempt as he gulped something in a brown stoneware jug. The bitter disposition etched on his visage was so unsettling that we walked over to the mansion's wraparound veranda. There, a young, pretty Caucasian woman in a flounced dress was sipping lemonade while speaking with a southern accent in hushed tones to an elderly black servant. As he listened to her, the man scratched his grizzled stubble.

"Luella shall tally the votes and announce Silas and Clora as the winners. That little gimcrack the Quakers found along with the dialogues of the celebrated playwright at the tracks under the Duke of Gloucester Street serves well to mark the location of the real prize of this walk-around, indicating precisely where one is to sink one's fork in the event that any company desires a slice of Patsy's dessert course."

"If they have already been told about which side of the tree moss blankets," the black fellow said while rubbing the vertical furrows on his forehead, "and to pay heed to which direction the handle of the gourd that sparkles points to, why, Miss Sadie, was there any need for a map to be squirreled away among them baked raisins, apricots and cherries?"

"Truly, coded spirituals help, Hubert, but we've an obligation to our cargo to provide other articles – further assistance for the journey far away from this gaunt picture."

"Happy world it may be, Miss Sadie, but the overseer can coax things if them catchers –"

"I am as acutely aware of the flogging post as I am of the cruel wrongs endured by others."

"Let's just hope he doesn't get a taste for plum cake, and pray the star of freedom doesn't fall out of the sky like those stars are doing over yonder."

When the music stopped, the couples quickly returned to their original square formation. At the same time, the pulsing chirps of crickets went silent, only to be replaced a complex machine-like sound that caused some at the gathering to cover their ears. Though I couldn't tell where this artificial chittering emanated from, the strange tones seemed to be mimicking the nocturnal swarms in the same exaggerated manner as the prize-walkers mocked their keepers.

"Will you look at that, Miss Sadie," the old man pointed excitedly to the lawn, "What devilry straight from Bensalem lands on the greensward with crisscrosses like Patsy's waffle iron?"

Looking down, I noticed that an intricate mosaic had been projected onto the grass – the expansive pattern being clearly defined by luminous purplish lines.

Hearing the startled gasps from the assemblage, in my peripheral vision I caught sight of an array of glowing objects floating above the adjacent woods.

As Callie and I watched their graceful coordinated movements in awe, I recalled the moonlit silhouettes of the spawn that swooped down from the black void on the surface of the doojigger. When one of the gleaming spheres drew closer, she tugged my hand. As it hovered over a grassy slope with a sibilant vibratory rhythm, I could see biomorphic appendages protruding from its shimmery carapace. Its throbbing, living radiance was palpable, bringing to mind one of Grumble's space animals. As it pounced, I found myself standing next to Callie at the back of my pickup. The plantation was gone and there was no visible life anywhere. The only sound came from a light breeze that rustled the nearby treetops.

Hardly a word passed between our lips on the way back to the house. We were both trying to absorb the strange experience we shared. Callie's main concern after seeing the swarm of glowing 'creatures' and the grid laid out on the lawn was that a methodical search for the doojigger had been conducted. According to her, the device had done everything in its power to avoid being detected. When I once again brought up the idea of contacting someone about its advanced capabilities, she emphatically shook her head to the contrary.

So resounding was her negative response – almost bordering on hostility – I was made to promise not to tell anyone about what she asserted was our secret… and ours alone.

Moments after we arrived at the house, she went straight up to her old bedroom, claiming that the bizarre episode had left

her utterly exhausted. Though I was craving something salty –
like Bojangles' seasoned fries, or something sweet like Trader
Joe's Macarons, I was also feeling sleepy. Without taking off my
clothes, I laid down on a couch among stacked Bekins boxes in
the living room.

I wasn't sure how long I was out before being jarred awake
by the sound of the front door closing. Bolting from the couch I
rushed towards the closest window. Peering into the darkness, I
saw Callie getting into the passenger side of a black sedan. With
its tinted windows, I couldn't make out the driver, but the car
resembled the one that I saw at the second estate sale.

Though my legs were weak from adrenal fatigue, as it pulled
away, I hurried outside and jumped into my pickup. Intending
to follow the car, when I turned the key, there was no response.
Same thing after several more tries. The battery was dead. As I
watched the sedan's taillights fade in the distance, I called Callie's cell. When she didn't pick up, I slumped back in the seat.
Trying to figure out what to do, I noticed that she had left one of
her coloring books on the center console.

While flipping through the pages of underwater kingdom
drawings that had been colored in with considerable skill, I noticed that, yet again, she had added highly detailed elements
in the blank spaces outside the lines. Although the sea-fantasy
themes were similar, one of the completed illustrations was par-
ticularly baffling. After staring at it for several minutes (and at
different angles), I still couldn't figure out what it was supposed to
portray. It appeared to be a collage of sorts, surely of an aquatic
setting, but unlike the other frozen kaleidoscopes, the mishmash
of shapes and colors were of such an abstract nature that they
made no sense whatsoever. And though there was no clearly defined image that I could readily discern, there was something

about the overall composition that made me think it had been done that way for a particular reason. But, what the hell was it? Even the words, 'Blue Cocoon' scrawled at the bottom didn't help matters.

CHAPTER VII
VUDUVERSES

"In opposition to all humanistic culture,
we are lured ever to the brink of chaos.
We want to go where we are forbidden.
We want to know what has been denied to us.
We seek, in a word, the more."

"Beings said to be speaking from remote areas of space
are really speaking from remote areas of our minds…
this wonderfully one mind, fills all space and exists at all times."

Michael Bertiaux

"What Artist now dares boast that he can bring
Heaven hither or constellate any thing,
So as the influence of those starres may bee
Imprison'd in an Hearbe, or Charme, or Tree,
And doe by touch, all which those stars could do?
The art is lost and correspondence too."

John Donne (1611)

Five days had passed and I still hadn't heard from Callie. Her cell went straight to voicemail and I didn't have her mother in my contacts (did she have my number?). Thinking she might have inadvertently left her phone at the house when she left in such a hurry, I went back the next day, only to find no one home and all of the doors locked. I also went to the Pharos Club twice, but none of her co-workers knew where she was. One thought she might be on vacation, but couldn't provide further details.

All kinds of scenarios ran through my mind, including the possibility that government agents had taken her because of the *Anunna* device (who probably chipped her while she was being examined). Conversely, instead of CIA goons snatching her away, maybe she had arranged to be picked up by a friend (whose black sedan just happened to have darkly tinted windows) and was avoiding me because she thought that I was going to contact someone with authority and spill the beans about Grumble's doojigger. This might explain why she didn't appear to have been forced into the car, but, instead, seemed to leave of her own free will.

Until I heard from her, all I could do was to keep calling and check back at the club. I thought about calling the police to report a missing person, but decided against it because of Callie's quirky, impulsive nature. I also didn't want to answer questions about the events that led up to her disappearance. If I told them the truth, they'd probably have me carted away to some rubber room (same if I had contacted the military – only to have the damn thing play possum and look like a vending machine slug or flattened soft drink crown). Still, the thought of her being held by shadowy officials had me growing increasingly concerned. With her previous vanishing act, she'd left me a clue. This time all I had was a coloring book with a puzzling design that probably had nothing to do with her going missing.

While packing up my belongings, I caught part of a new video on TroVe about how the city of Bethlehem in Pennsylvania had built a nice house for Jesus to live in for as long as he wanted when he returned to Earth. A spokesperson said this was to make up for the shameful actions of the biblical Bethlehem, where Joseph and Mary were denied guest lodging after their relatives learned about her unusual pregnancy (evidently, the residents of the American Bethlehem had no qualms with Jesus' latest unwedded mother). Though, admittedly, the house was no "celestial mansion", it was said to be quite comfortable. In addition, Fig Newtons were being handed out to the entire population of Bethlehem to feed the Savior should he come a door knocking. After the news of the free snacks was made public, a group of vegans began protesting the handouts because the Newtons crunchy filling was said to be full of dead wasps.

When I started the video from the beginning, the host explained how many residents in Bethlehem believed that the prophesized Second Coming had been jump-started by geneticists using a process involving somatic cell nuclear transfer (and caffeine!) at a clandestine military lab.

Jesus' DNA wasn't extracted from the Turin Shroud or from some relative's chalk-box ossuary, they claimed, but from a type of fruit that the whistle-blower 'Siriana' spoke of in the viral report about her being the surrogate (virgin) mother to an advanced life form. Their evidence of what essentially amounted to cloning the Savior came from biblical references about "the True Vine" and "Fruit that is Ripe." The host concluded the video by joking that he prayed this new improved Jesus wouldn't throw any toddlers' tantrums like those described in the Infancy Gospels (which were also mentioned by Siriana in the doco). He also informed his viewers that modern figs were commercially grown without any insects being involved in the process.

The next podcast I watched was also a response to the 'Siriana' piece, and how she was believed to be responsible for a new religious movement. The Enochites, as they called themselves, were increasing in numbers and spreading the word of a biblical patriarch's ambiguous visions by speaking in a strange ancient language. In the podcast, the host said he was "flabbergasted" that the so-called Enochian language – which many members believed to be the Earth's primordial tongue, while others took it even a step further by claiming it to be the celestial speech of angels – was currently the number one selling foreign language learning program. That meant it was more popular than Spanish, French and German, even though most linguists argued that it wasn't even a true natural language.

Before commenting on the linguistic criteria, his scholarly-looking guest, a self-proclaimed expert on the subject, said that they needed to first "back way the fuck up." He then proceeded to give a crash course on the history of the Enochia:

"Enoch was the great grandfather of Noah who walked with God and spoke with angels. While still alive, he was elevated to heaven and given a tour. What he saw terrified him, and before swiftly exiting the biblical stage, he left dire warnings for mankind.

Flash forward to 16th-century England and a man named John Dee. Dee had a brilliant mind and was a contemporary of Sir Francis Bacon in Elizabethan court circles. In fact, he was the Queen's spymaster, given the personal codename 007. He was fascinated by ciphers, and rapt in secret studies. Owing to his reputation as a magus, he was the inspiration for Shakespeare's fictional wizard, Prospero, in *The Tempest*. In fact, enticingly concealed in the play are theatrical parables making it an esoteric manifesto concerning new worlds. As a side note, in the biliteral cipher that many scholars believe that Bacon embedded in the epitaph of Shakespeare's gravestone, the scarcely pronounceable names of some of the Enochian angels appear.

Along with his various scientific pursuits, Dee sought to communicate with spirits and discover their knowledge. His diligence finally paid off when he received a vision of the mighty angel

Uriel after enflaming himself in prayer. Uriel revealed the method to establish contact with the divine messengers and instructed him about the specific occult equipment that was required. Along with temple furnishings that included a scrying table and optical devices, Dee would also need an assistant to serve as the medium. Enter one Edward Kelley. As Kelley peered into the depths of a convex crystal, various angels would appear on the surface and point to letters that were arranged in grids, often in reverse order. Before fading away, the celestial script appeared in a glowing brassy yellow color that Kelley traced. At other times the message was dictated backwards as a safety precaution, for the angels warned that the efficacy of the Words of Power were too dangerous to be pronounced directly.

Generating the Enochian Calls from the scrying sessions was a daunting task and lengthy process when factoring in all the safeguards. Being potent prayers, the Calls energized portals from which the peculiar forms provided answers to Dee's questions. Well, to some of the questions, at least. How do we know this? Dee kept meticulous records of the experiments. Filled his spiritual diaries with copious notes of the rigorous procedures.

His lexicology included phonetic features for the English translation of what he thought was the pre-deluge language spoken in Atlantis. And just as the spiritual beings took great measures to avert problems, seasoned occultists in modern times also warn that the Enochia is not to be trifled with. Dabblers that are normally protected by their own ineptitude might trigger unwanted forces while singing in the angelic tongue. Besides bringing chaos into their lives, having the celestial hierarchy within tangible grasp can have even more devastating consequences if the magical system is misused."

"Okay," the host interrupted him. "I was going to ask you what might happen if the wrong shitheads started gazing into the Devil's looking-glass or spewing out occult gobbledygook they memorized from the Enochian language tools? I assume all the words and names are in these new Rosetta and Babbel–type apps."

"The language tools and online translators, like the Enochian dictionaries themselves, are limited to the conversations from Dee's diary entries. We see no prior existence of the Enochia before Dee began conducting his experiments."

"Okay, so these angels granted visions… revealed things and gave us a bizarre lingo," the host said in a casual tone that reflected his skeptical attitude. "What I really want to know is where are they when not called upon? What are they doing? Just hanging out? Watering the lawn? Do they have an independent existence outside the human mind? And if so, suppose two or more people dial up the same angel at the same time. What's the spirit-etiquette in that case?"

"To answer your question, though not as glibly, we should keep in mind that previously unknown life forms such as microscopic organisms were first discovered around the same time that Dee was conversing with the Enochian angels. Until we had the technological means to detect microbes, no one imagined such things, even though they existed right under our nose. Bacteria… Protists… today, scientists estimate we've only discovered one per cent of the various species of fungi. Besides astrobiology and a cosmic menagerie, it's possible other forms of life exist somewhere on the Earth… behind the scenery, so to speak… that are perhaps more intelligent than humans… beings higher up on the food chain that we might want to prepare for."

"That's a scary thought," the host interjected, "and wouldn't it be funny, or ironic, that there might be those inhabiting these other realms who think that some of their fellow entities are crazy for believing in the existence of humans."

"It's quite possible. At times I've wondered if Enochian is the language of our genetic code, and if so, Dee's angelic constructs might have been pointing to junk or dormant DNA sequences that play a part in the evolutionary process... causing a mutation leap. Could awakening our darker DNA from its slumber have been one of the scientific equations behind the drama that unfolded within the depths of the scrying zone?"

"What kind of things would Dee and his side-kick ask these angels? Don't tell me – let me guess – they wanted to know where treasure was buried."

"As you would get tired of listening to the squeaks of a mouse, the angels were annoyed by such requests, considering baser gold to be mere trifles that they swept out their doors. Even so, for a while they told the two what they wanted to hear... stringing them along like master manipulators to secure their cooperation for reasons that weren't apparent. For their agenda, whatever that was."

"Making empty promises... So they're deceivers."

"The angels are tricky fuckers. They were, however, quite interested in Dee's dream that he shared with the greatest minds of the period. They wanted to know all the details from whoever was steering the ship... pun intended...in their grand design for the colonization of the New World... North America, which they referred to as the New Atlantis."

Before I got to hear the rest of his response, there was a brief knock on the door, followed by Merrilly entering along with Raiden and Golliwog.

"Hey, it's Merr and the whole gang," I said.

"My catered spread for tomorrow's showing," she said while

setting some bags of groceries on the kitchen counter. "Tea sandwiches… ham with Dijon mustard, brie and slices of green apples. And a fruit charcuterie board from Wegmans."

"Tea sandwiches for a trailer open house? You should have just got some of those cocktail wieners for people to dip into a bag of cheese sauce. That or spread some Miracle Whip on white bread," I laughed.

"Eww, I have a creep that tries to flick that stuff on me while I'm performing. No shit. He brings in a squeeze bottle. I'd have him tossed on his ear if he didn't also flick crumpled Jacksons. This is at the Dancing Bear – not at Club Platinum."

"I want to see the dancing bear," Raiden said after clearing his throat and flapping a hand, "but Merrily won't take me there."

Merrily and I couldn't suppress a smile at his naivety.

"I've also got honey-drop lemonade and Royalene's truffle brownies – "

"Jeez, gourmet lemonade, too. These people wouldn't know the difference if it was Peaden."

"What?"

"Circus peanuts are good, Jack," Raiden said in his usual monotone while offering me a piece of his orange marshmallow candies. "They're fluffy like a sponge or pillow."

"Grill and Chill is good, too," Merrily said while pulling out a hamburger from a Dairy Queen sack. "Sorry, I should have called to see if you were hungry… since you can't eat my spread."

She giggled after realizing the sexual connotation of what she just said.

"That's okay, I was just getting ready to order a pizza from Roma's."

"How do you get *ready* to order a pizza?" she shook her head while knitting her brows with an annoyed look.

Walking over to the table, she noticed Callie's coloring book, which was opened to the vibrant illustration of the underwater scene teeming with varicolored fish. From her confused expression, it was evident that she was also having trouble making sense of the brilliantly hued schools that were jumbled together in a conceptual enigma.

"Looks like you've got something to keep you busy while you're not working. Interesting," she said as her eyes narrowed as part of a forced smile. "Maybe you should frame it, only don't hang it in the trailer."

"You know it's not mine," I snapped.

"Is it the girl's with the fancy cigs? Blue Cocoon – wow, I wish I could afford that," she said while pointing to what was scrawled at the bottom of the page.

"So, you know what a blue cocoon is?" I asked.

"The facial moisturizer? Stuff's really expensive."

"Look at that funny person," Raiden said while running a finger over the riotous colors.

"You see a person?" I asked. "Where is it, buddy?"

"It is looking at all the fishes... with the others... from the window in its room."

After looking at the confused mixture of marine life on the seabed (again, from different angles), I still couldn't see these people that he was talking about.

"Merr, do you see a person in all this?"

"No, but looking at it, it's making me dizzy," she replied after squinting at the puzzling aquascape, "What ocean was she in... or what was she on in the ocean? But if Raiden says someone's there, I believe him. Hey, that reminds me, mom's treating some of the family to a vacation rental on the outer banks. A cute beach cottage called Sea Venture at Nag's Head."

"Sea Venture? You're kidding… really? That's cray. That's the name of the old ship that was beached from a storm off Bermuda. One of the Jamestown supply missions – it wrecked in the same spot on the map that Raiden here marked with numbers in my copy of *The Beale Papers*. You know, the book about the buried treasure."

"This *is* those numbers, Jack," Raiden said while tapping the page in the coloring book.

"Callie's drawing is the numbers?" I smiled, thinking he must be confused.

"So, what are your plans?" Merrilly asked.

"I don't know. I'm hoping to get a job at this new club in Alexandria. Instead of draft Pabst, the regs drink pomegranate beer punch. And I might stay with Jeremy for a while."

"Oh, that reminds me. Your friend Jeremy was at the Platinum Club the other day. He seemed awfully interested in Desire… the Asian girl. He told her that he was looking for a girl that was a water sign."

"A water sign?"

"Yeah, Desire is a Pisces, the sign of the Fish in the zodiac. From what she told me, he's into some pretty kinky stuff… for a bookworm," she said while taking some of Raiden's French fries.

"You better hurry up and finish that Grill and Chill before you know what comes out to feed."

"I don't like deer, Jack, and I don't think deer like us."

Though I was tired from packing, before going to bed I clicked on TroVe. The mentioning of "Mfkzt" at the start of the video caught my attention. Being a small town in southern Illinois, its name sounded similar to Moosville, the place I thought the homeless guy with the memory issue that I befriended as a boy wanted to go back to. Though I never heard from him after buying him a Greyhound ticket, the pronunciation of "Moof-kooz-tee" rang a bell. It sounded more like the actual name of the place where the guy was looking for fabled Atlantis than Moosville.

According to the filmmaker, high strangeness was occurring in boonies of Mfkzt that was right up there with the supernatural happenings of Utah's infamous Skinwalker Ranch (I'd seen several recent docos about it as a paranormal hotspot). For instance, the rural town of less than 5,000 people had become a United States Space Force location, with a complex of high security buildings and a secret runway that only appeared at certain times in the middle of a soybean field. Besides fenced off cargo terminals, there was a large hangar for advanced military craft. However, rumors circulated around town that the facility was part of a space archaeology division within the USSF whose task it was to preserve artificial orbital debris in a kind of galactic museum. But others believed this was just a cover for its real mission – to search for alien techno-signatures.

Adding to the mystery was what a maintenance worker claimed to have seen inside the hangar. Instead of glimpsing robotic space planes or other exotic aeroforms, much to his astonishment, he saw a ramshackle Victorian house complete with its adjacent garage that was situated on a well-tended yard along with a couple of sycamore trees. As smoke from a brick chimney drifted across its steeply pitched roof, diffused sunlight (filtered through narrow panels in the hangar) was dimly reflected on protruding oriel windows that had a fanciful gingerbread trim.

While trying to make sense of what he was seeing, he noticed lots of repetition in details, as if certain features of the yard – such as trees and bushes – were mirror images. After watching birds flitting from branches in oddly repeated loops, he ventured tentatively onto the creaking planks of the wraparound porch, whose white columns with ornate spindles appeared to be freshly painted. When he peered into one of the windows, he could make out drab furnishings and mildewed wallpaper. Chunks of plaster that had fallen from a ceiling swathed with dirty cobwebs littered the stained wooded floor. Among the neglect, a mahogany television console with a 1960s rabbit ear antenna flickered in front of a shabby chartreuse recliner. On the screen were grainy scenes of "an old movie that seemed to have sunken treasure theme." No one was watching this, and the house's only resident seemed to be a Siamese cat that popped up on a windowsill, scaring the "bejesus" out of him.

As strange as it was to see a decrepit large house and its freshly mowed lawn as a protected asset inside a hardened military shelter, what happened when he backed away from the sagging veranda was even odder. Looking down, he noticed that his soiled uniform and muddy work boots were now immaculate, as if they had somehow been laundered spotless. How this was possible, he hadn't a clue, but he sealed both the clothes and boots in plastic bags when he went into hiding after going public with what he observed.

After sharing the ex-maintenance worker's remarkable tale, the video's narrator spoke about other bizarre incidents told by the townsfolk that might offer a possible explanation as to why a secure aviation hangar had been constructed over a forbidding old house.

Located on a semi-rural road called "ShadowCrest", for years the Victorian was known to locals as the "Loony Tunes House" due to a series of strange occurrences associated with it.

Many claimed to have witnessed anomalous phenomena in the front yard – in particular what they described as an eternal-looping generator effect, in which birds (usually cardinals and blue jays) seemed to have identical (not just similar) flight pattern contours. This has been compared to the cost-cutting measures used in old cartoons, where the exact background scenery is repeated.

Others spoke about one of the past owners – a gaunt oddity named Maxx Schaufler, who was the town's undertaker and had been given the nickname, "Molewhisker" for the unsightly protrusion that grew from an ordinary mole on his chin. Though he had become reclusive in his later years, in the 1950s he was the leader of a notorious Hot Rod Club called WILL O' THE WISP that raised hell on the back roads. The local paper even did a story on him and his old funeral coach that had been converted into a chrome-festooned street machine, but the article was slanted with humor as a way of poking fun at gullible readers. Nefarious activity attributed to the "grim-beeper" was compared with tales about Abraham Lincoln's ghost visiting family dinners when chicken fricassee, biscuits and apple pie for dessert were served.

But not everyone was laughing. Many Christian residents believed that Schaufler's Victorian was originally built over the pit where the Biblical Fallen Angels were imprisoned for their past transgressions. Making their case for the preternatural nature of the house, they cited that several attempts made to burn the place down had all failed. It seemed that the gasoline-drenched wooden structure couldn't catch fire. They also thought that the rumors about the undertaker being a body snatcher were true, even accusing him of chopping up and consuming human corpses with bowls of Dinty Moore stew.

For this reason, every time "Unholy Moley" cruised through a local hot dog and root beer joint in his spectral hearse, the name on the blinking neon sign inexplicably changed from "King Coney" to "Corpse King." Someone even had old Polaroids that showed the less-appetizing brand.

Tales of Schaufler's flashy hot rod resurfaced when a farmer reported a bizarre incident that occurred at his property on the outskirts of town. In the recent account, the man had been scouting deer at night while positioned inside a ground blind that blended perfectly with the wooded area. Through one of the see-thru panels, he observed an object floating over the field that he said was hard to describe. It resembled a metallic soap bubble that was "bigger than a 1000 gallon propane tank." Sections of it were softly illuminated, including biomorphic appendages that fluttered in a graceful manner as if mimicking a bird's wings. Though confusing to behold, the craft seemed to be under intelligent control. His impression was that it was some kind of "living machine."

After watching it float silently from his panoramic view, its movements suddenly became erratic. There was a blinding flash that was followed by a whirling vortex of brilliant silvery filaments as the thing quickly began to reassemble itself. At the same time, suspended in mid-air above the scattered debris were minuscule symbols that repeatedly changed shape. According to the witness, the tiny unintelligible figures were like a graphic representation of something seen on computer screens, "only there weren't no screens – they just dangled there still-like in the wind while switching through all kinds of colors." When he left the hunting blind to check out the wreckage, instead of finding what he assumed to be a high-tech shuttle craft or secret military drone, he was shocked to find an old style hearse (in perfect condition) that he later identified as a 1951 Packard Henney. The car was funny looking – tricked out like a 50s greaser's street rod. Its matte black frame had been lowered, and the side service door contained spectral green lettering that read:

WILL O' THE WISP

On either side of its metalwork grille, antique black lanterns that functioned as headlights were unusually bright, casting intense bluish beams into the woods.

When he leaned towards the open window to see the dash panel, he "nearly crapped his pants" as a guttural shriek came from the exaggerated grimace of a furry green creature that suddenly popped up from the driver's seat. He described the thing as being a life-sized puppet that had an oversized head and comically grotesque face with bulging bloodshot eyes. With a croaky voice it uttered what sounded like a "German word" that was followed by fits of malicious laughter.

Seeing the headlights of approaching military vehicles, the man hurried back to the camouflaged structure, where he observed the goings-on in the field. Through night-vision glasses he watched dozens of security personnel wearing uniforms with a unique color scheme focusing their attention on something inside the old car. There was also some kind of robotic figure that seemed to be erasing those peculiar symbols that were still levitating above the ground.

One of the guards got so close to the ground blind that he could hear a transmission over the static on his hand-held field radio. When a recording of what he heard was later played back on the farmer's phone's voice memo app, it sounded to him like a coded message:

"What have we here? A man or a fish? Dead or alive?"

The initial reply from the military figure on the ground was garbled.

"A fish, he smells like a fish, a very ancient and fish-like smell," was the reply. A fender bender to the Trouble Bubble. Not what I would have expected from humanity-plus."

"Dost thou like the plot, Trinculo?" the guard asked.

"Excellent."

Some of these words I had heard before. The guy speaking funny lingo in the grotto under The Tempest Bar in colonial Williamsburg called himself Trinculo, which I later found out was a character in Shakespeare's (or Francis Bacon's?) play about an enchanted island. He also mentioned something about a "strange fish", just like the kid at the country store did when passing along a message to me during my experience with what he referred to as the *Anunna* device. I'm sure Jeremy would want to know about these new developments — the mentioning again of Trinculo and the strange fish — though I still wasn't ready to tell him about the recording of the boy at Gink's because of my promise to Callie not to talk to anyone about Grumble's doojigger. For the time being, this was still our secret.

As I continued to watch the video, the farmer said that a body was removed from the hot rod. Though he couldn't make out details, whatever it was had been carried away on a stretcher and placed inside a military Humvee-type ambulance. Next, a tarp was placed over the car — blue-hot headlights and all — before it was hauled away on a flatbed trailer.

The last segment of the video delved into yet another mystery having to do with the small town. This concerned a rural cemetery with unkempt grounds that was surrounded by corn-fields. Among its weathered headstones, one stood out. Evidently, its marble surface hadn't aged a bit in 50 years. Though none of the townspeople knew who was buried there, its flawless inscription read:

YWLLWY * ELXXLE

Even more puzzling was that when anyone attempted to get close to the grave marker, they suddenly felt a deep sense of dread that, in essence, paralyzed them, so that, try as they might, they were unable to get within several feet of it. Explanations for this included an infrasound frequency in the area whose intensity caused extreme anxiety and this restricted any further movement towards it.

Not long ago, a local entrepreneur offered a challenge to those who were curious, or felt they could penetrate the containment field and touch the grave. He charged them each five dollars and said he would pay five hundred dollars to anyone that could lay their hands on the marble. To date, no one has collected the money and the young businessman recently purchased a brand new BMW.

This mystery was on a par with the "Loony Tunes House" that was being concealed in a military installation and the "grim-beeper's" morphing hot rod hearse. The podcast channel that aired it normally didn't cater to conspiracy theories or fringe discourse, so I didn't know what to think.

One of the responses from a subscriber was: "So, does this mean that orbital patrols by our space fleet are pretending to be Rat Finks in old jalopies?" Another comment mentioned that Mfkzt was located in that part of southern Illinois known as "Little Egypt."

Being the same town that my childhood friend was planning to look for the remnants of sunken Atlantis, I couldn't help but wonder if all the paranormal activity was somehow related?

"You got something in there that works better than a raccoon's dick?" I asked Jeremy's Aunt Cleo as she searched through an assortment of Lucky Hoodoo items that were stuffed inside an upturned black top hat with orange flame piping. Along with colorful witch bottles containing botanical infusions and occult distillates, also arranged on the cluttered counter where an antique brass cash register gleamed were money-drawing oils, tonics and assorted rootwork potions.

"Jack here wants to be deeply loved," Cleo's sister Jema cooed while adjusting bead-framed glasses that matched the vibrant design on her flip-flops, "without buying no heart-shaped box."

Wearing a tangerine-colored Dashiki caftan tunic with an eye-catching West African artwork print, Cleo pulled from the silk topper a hard brown root that was shaped like a man's testicle.

"Those roots look like my balls," Jeremy laughed.

"Well, it is a man's thing, honey," Cleo cackled. "If he wants me to put a root on her, I'd advise High John the Conqueroo. If it helped him win the heart of the Devil's daughter, Big Johnny ought to work wonders with this Callie gal. I'll mix it with other fixins in a charm bundle, which reminds me, Jema, I'm gonna need more flannel. And I'll do up a love attraction spell on petition paper, but if you want it to rhyme it'll cost more," she joked while spinning a Rolodex filled with smudged index cards containing various hoodoo recipes.

"I don't see Jack toting a bouquet sachet," Jeremy said. "Maybe instead of throwing roots, how about reaching into the toolbox for something more potent."

"Your nephew wants me to draw her name on a Friday with the feather of a hoopoe stained with its heart's blood on freshly prepared parchment," Cleo muttered while looking her sister straight in the eye. "Now, you tell me," she said, raising her voice, "where I'm supposed to get hoopoe blood? There aint been no hoopoe spotted in America since... never. I aint dumb to the fact, and there aint no blood of the diddy-wah-diddy things on that Internet, neither. Lately, Jeremy's more preoccupied with hoopoes than with hoodoo, reading about the dirty birdy in that reefer comic book his eyes have been glued to." She eyed him disapprovingly. "Asking me about setting lights and squiggly lines... recipes and mischief from those handbooks that aren't the *Petit Albert*. I told him he better make safety checks cuz I don't want to have to wear haint blue all day or put up no bottle tree out back next to that peristyle he's a-making. He don't know what he's foolin' with," she uttered while once again staring Jema in the eye.

"There's nothing wrong with consulting Solomonic-style magical papyri, Aunt Cleo," Jeremy said.

"Um hum, if fitly spoken," Cleo replied. "But I've seen your fancy sketches, and it looks more like appealing to the vodou spirits than to Solomon's helpers. Besides, I aint got enough cormeal to build no ship for Damballa."

"You better take precautions like she advised," the more softly spoken aunt said. "These spirits expect things for their service and are vindictive when offended."

"Now, back to Jack and his gal," Cleo said while impatiently tapping her antelope-leather heeled sandals against the creaky floorboard. "If we ain't layin' tricks, does he have any personal concerns, like a strand of hair found in that Ford pickup? But you best make certain it is her hair so we don't have no crossed conditions to deal with. What about any foot-track dirt, or if Jema's got an old Barbie in the shop we could make a doll-baby as a stand-in – "

"A poppet!" Jeremy uttered.

"What's that?" I asked.

"A vodou doll. She's just messing with you, right, Cleo?"

"A voodoo doll with a toddler's cherry lollipop in its mouth," I laughed.

"And holding a crayon," Jeremy added with a toothy smile.

"For now, let's just stick with the roots, or maybe I'll get her a heart-shaped box... if I ever see her again," I shrugged.

"Cleo, when you go out to your conjure garden, can you pick something for my greens three?" Jema asked. "Just the right touch to take some of the bitter out for Jack here."

"You cooking your leafy treasure, Jema?" Jeremy asked. "Jack, you'll like her dandelion leaf after eating that greasy Bojangles for the last few days."

"I just like their iced-tea," I said.

"That aint no Prosperi-tea," Cleo mumbled, "I'll tell you that much. Yeah, he'll be gobbling them greens... gobbling 'em down."

"Greens three with a hundred on the plate and some of my soppin' cassava biscuits," Jema nodded proudly.

"That's beans and pork," Jeremy said after seeing my confused look.

"White cassoulet beans," Jema added with a sassy, all-knowing wink.

While staying for a while at Jeremy's cabin, when I wasn't looking for a bartending gig, I helped his aunts with various odd
jobs. With Jema this involved refurbishing antiques and making
deliveries while for Cleo I assisted in any way that I could with
her preparing spagyric extracts, herbal tinctures and sweeten-
ers, as well as combining the ingredients used for dressings, dust-
ings and rootwork colognes. I also helped Jeremy construct a
screened in gazebo behind the cabin, including adding a corrugated metal roof and verd antique marble pedestal at the center
of the structure. For whatever reason the frame was painted
bright red (The color of "hexerei barn paint used by pow wow
doctors," Cleo said).

Though he never told me what he was planning to use the
gazebo for, I assumed it would be his private space for medita-
tion. But, if it was to be a spiritual retreat, I couldn't figure out
why Cleo would sometimes watch us from behind the Carolina
Silverbell trees with a disapproving frown, as if there was something unsavory about her nephew's latest undertaking.

When Jeremy wasn't working on this, he spent most of his
free time reading the same old comix book over and over (the
last letter being distinguished for X-rated, I learned online).
Though he was careful to never leave this lying around, judging
by glimpses I got of the psychedelic artwork on the cover, it was
one of those flimsy old doper 'zines from the 1960s like others I'd
seen for sale at Jema's Attic (hence Cleo's bitter expression every
time she saw him absorbed with the thing). The simple concerns
of a rogues' gallery of cartoon characters engaged in mayhem
made his obsession with the drug-inspired slapstick all the more

puzzling. When I flat out asked him what the story was about, his only reply was that "It wasn't what it appeared to be."

While I was staying there I figured we'd be planning our next move in the search for Bacon's hoard. However, for some reason he no longer seemed excited (or even interested) in continuing the treasure hunt. Something had gotten into him, and I couldn't help but wonder if he had been warned or threatened by someone not to pursue the matter any further?

After I told him about the recent video I'd seen with a witness that recorded a military person making a reference to a "strange fish" while using other words spoken in Shakespeare's play, *The Tempest* (or, rather, Bacon's work) and that these were the same bits of dialogue that the shadowy figure in the grotto under The Tempest Bar used, he said that he was done chasing after quasi-anagrams and acrostics that others teased out of the plays. When I reminded him about the set of numbers that Raiden had jotted down in my copy of *The Beale Papers* next to a crude drawing of the Freemasonic emblem – ordered pairs that seemed to be longitude and latitude coordinates marking a location just off the coast of Bermuda – and its possible connection with the line of dialogue from *The Tempest*, indicating that Bacon had hidden his treasure deeper into the ocean than any anchor ever sank ("and deeper than did ever plummet sound I'll drown my book"), he shrugged it off as still being too vague.

Ditto with the numbers pointing to the Devil's Triangle that someone had written on a scrap of paper I found stuffed inside the Civil War-era brass 'acorn.' His only comment was to ask if I had ever considered the vast amount of ocean within the Triangle's boundaries? Even the Gillogy sub-cipher that was submerged in the Beale encryption (that Raiden might have found) no longer seemed to be of any promise to my friend.

As for Bacon's cache of manuscripts having been ingeniously concealed in a vault, he hinted that with a certain type of vault, immersion of parchment in a mercury bath might not be necessary for preservation. Though he wouldn't elaborate on this cryptic statement, I took it as a sign that perhaps he wasn't totally distracted from the original objective by the silly antics in the "literature of hippiedom" as Jema called the freak comix her nephew was preoccupied with.

On those few nights that he slipped away from the cabin alone, I wondered if he might be following up on leads by himself. More likely, though, he was going to strip clubs. When Merrily had called to invite me to spend a day at her family's beach rental on Nag's Head, after accepting, I asked if she had seen Jeremy hanging out with any peelers. As it turned out, he had recently been at The Platinum Club talking again to the dancer who called herself Desire.

As I waited for him to share any new findings, I came up with the idea of inventing a special cocktail that I could take samples of to the upscale clubs that I planned to submit my resume to (this, instead of carrying a lucky bean in my pocket or being anointed with Cleo's 'steady work oil'). One of these bars was the Pharos Lighthouse (where I could also check to see if there was any news about Callie).

The various elixirs, tonics and love philters concocted for Cleo's hoodoo spell kits had been my inspiration. If I could apply the same sorcery to my drink, I might be able to make a name for myself as a mixologist. What I needed was a more modern version of one of those blends in the Bon Vivant's Companion. An infusion from a plant or mineral extract that gave the cocktail a certain zing... a happy hour mojo, or, even better, a spark that had an uplifting affect on one's being unlike any other (legal) alcohol mash-up. With Cleo's experience of the beneficial properties of roots and herbs, perhaps she would help me craft it, or at least allow me to experiment from the catalogue of botanical curiosities in her backwoods apothecary.

While experimenting with some of Cleo's botanical tinctures for a rum drink in Jeremy's kitchen late at night, I heard strange sounds coming from out back. Over the insect shrill, the faint strains of a woman singing in some foreign language were discernable along with the squawks of seagulls and words intoned with a tedious monotone. When this continued, I went outside to investigate. Walking around the colorful vegetation in Cleo's pollinator bed, drifts of pungent incense mingled with the cloying of moonlit blooms.

The incongruous mélange coming from a marshy area grew louder as I followed the winding path through a stretch of woods that led to Jeremy's freshly painted gazebo. When I reached the clearing, seeing that the small structure was aglow, I ducked behind one of the silverbell trees.

Through the fine mesh screen I could see Jeremy and an unclothed woman engaged in what appeared to be some sexual activity. With her sharp facial features, almond eyes and silky black hair, I figured the female was the Asian dancer that Merrilly had told me about. As her lithe body leaned against the central post, bluish flame shadows from a circle of jellied alcohol canisters danced on her glistening nakedness. Her tongue wagged obscenely as Jeremy moved the palm of his hand over the shapely contours of a honey-skinned form that was partly adorned with scarlet-colored serpents. Though he never actually touched her lewd undulations, a series of peculiar hand gestures caused a noticeable change in her breathing pattern. So bizarre was this unusual foreplay (or perverted madness?), I couldn't stop watching.

As if performing a lurid ballet, long dark fingers glided fluid-
ly over the green beryl pendant that glinted between her jutting
breasts. When he positioned these manual gestures in specific
ways, she reacted with spasms of pleasure. With each convul-
sion, the serpentine markings became animated, writhing on
her shapely physique like some flickering magic lamp projection.
As Jeremy continued with the disturbing (air) massage, strange
utterances issued from her mouth. The torrent of unintelligible
words had a droning quality that was followed by hissing noises as her tongue flicked grotesquely. The eerie sibilance started
to freak me out, as did the illusion of the painted snakes that
uncoiled and slithered on her rippling flesh from hovering fingers contorted into impossibly complex postures. Before l backed
away, the speech of her trance-like state became more robotic. With a distorted, metallic sound, I thought I heard her say,
"We're sorry. Your call cannot be completed from a payphone at
this time." This was followed by a loud *ker-chunk*, after which she
chuckled delightedly.

The next morning while Jeremy was still asleep, I went out
to his gazebo to have a better look at the unusual furnishings
I'd glimpsed at night. The first thing I noticed was that the plywood floor had been painted half white and half black. Placed
at the four cardinal points were vibrant occult diagrams formed
by a colored chalk. One of them was a doodle of a large sailboat
outlined in an indigo hue whose X-shaped anchor was visible
beneath wavy lines. Encircling these geometrical motifs were
cans of Sterno, whose bluish tongues of flaming ethanol had long
been snuffed out. Though disturbed in places, I stepped around
the chalked traceries to check out the junk shop altar.

Placed next to crab shell lamps was a goblet of Florida water
in which floated a miniature bright plastic steamboat. Sea-green

plates containing sugary offerings that included banana chips, rice pudding and gold-foiled chocolate coins were bespeckled with crawling flies. Next to a slice of white cake was a bottle of naval rum and opened can of Diet Coke.

In the sunlight that filtered through the silverbell leaves, I watched as a large fly moved across the iridescent sheen of a small metallic fish that was affixed to the breccia marble pedestal. Along with this were other ornaments having a marine theme, including pink cowrie shells, nautical medals, glasswork dolphins and brightly painted little mermaid figures. What the hell kind of game was my friend playing, I wondered? Hearing Jema calling my name, I headed back to the shop to make a delivery.

When I heard the crooning of seagulls and drum-like sounds coming from the gazebo a couple of nights later, I knew that Jeremy was back at it. As before, a woman with a deep glottal voice was speaking in tongues like some 'charismatic' church members have been known to do. Either that, or what I heard being spoken was magical gibberish by means of those Enochian language apps that were being talked about on TroVe. Besides these monotonous utterances, there were other puzzling noises that didn't sound organic in nature. Whatever they were, this time I didn't go anywhere near the creepy shit.

Because of these on-going sexual frolics, but mainly due to the ineffectiveness of the cabin's swamp cooler in the sweltering heat of the Dog Days of summer, I began sleeping on an old couch in the antique shop. Having fallen right to sleep after a long day of delivering furniture, I was awakened by what I first thought to be the squealing belt of yet another faulty cooling unit. However, I quickly realized the roll mechanism of one of the player pianos must have cranked up on its own accord due to some glitch. Or maybe the pianola keys were being rippled by the invisible fingers of a ghost, I half-joked to myself. Jeremy had once told be that Jema's Attic was haunted, and accordingly, rather than the expected detuned cacophony of some traditional rag, the fast flourishes sounded fiendishly complicated, so much so, in fact, that it seemed as if multiple pianists were simultaneously responsible for striking the notes of some devilish shuffle. Could the peculiar juxtaposing of chords and edgy contrapuntal melodies emanating from a corner of the room be the work of a trio of disembodied specters?

As the frenzied jazz runs continued, I got up to go turn the damn thing off. Stumbling in the dark through the clutter of antiques, I was startled for a second by the sight of the fuzzy golliwog doll swaying back and forth in a rocking chair. Though I couldn't make out the exaggerated ruby lips on its round black face, comically large eyes formed by chalk white circles seemed to be staring back at me. Having stepped around the freakish doll, I was surprised to see Jeremy seated behind one the player pianos. When I rounded the upright's dusty walnut frame, I was even more surprised to see that it was he who was playing it.

With a vacant expression on his face, his left hand climbed with hectic bass lines in broken time while the right hand improvised at an equally fevered pace. I didn't know that he played, let alone how accomplished he was. Though the riffs of his dueling hands were often at variance, the fingering was flawless, especially when considering how hard he was stabbing at the chipped keys. As I kept checking to make sure he wasn't playing along with the pneumatic motor, he stopped in the middle of dissonant arpeggios. When I checked his eyes, I could see that they were glazed over, leading me to believe he was having another low blood sugar attack.

"You okay?" I asked. "There's left over okra stew in the fridge, or should I get one of Cleo's maple donuts?"

"No, I'm fine, Jack," he said while staring down at the yellowed keys.

Still thinking he was coming out of a hypoglycemic episode, I leaned over to inspect his rheumy brown eyes.

"I didn't know you could play," I said.

"Yeah, neither did I," he replied. "The piano wasn't on auto pilot?"

"No, it was all you."

With all the carrying-on at night from Jeremy, it was a relief to get away for a couple of days. While hanging with Merrilly's family at the beach cottage on North Carolina's Outer Banks, on the first day we knocked out the usual tourist stuff, such as watching for dolphins, hiking on a trail through the salt marsh and flying kites from the sandy dunes.

While her mom prepared homemade crab cakes for dinner – a welcome improvement from the childhood version of serving canned salmon cakes with Miracle Whip spread on hamburger buns that Merrilly taunted – I made my new rum cocktail as a change from their spiked seltzers and as way of testing the special syrup that I added to the mix of citrus juices.

While drinking them (without much comment), when I described the features of Jeremy's exotic lady friend, Merrilly confirmed that it was Desire. She also said that she had told her how Jeremy was "gifted in finding her hot points", adding with a derisive smile "maybe my new friend really could help me find buried treasure."

After the sun went down, there was a thunderstorm warning for the Nags Head area. With gusty winds rattling the windows, a few of us went down to watch the spray of crashing waves. Despite having had one too many of my rum drinks, we had enough sense not to risk any rip currents while going for a night swim, and were content to let the foamy breakers rush around our knees. Though the sustained winds never reached storm force, the waves were high enough that early the next morning Merrilly and I took Raiden to look for beached sand dollars.

As the sea foam lapped gently at his feet, he gathered as many of the flattened sea-urchin skeletons that he could carry without them crumbling in his hand, believing his older sister when she told him that the intact, round shells were coins that spilled out of a mermaid's poke during the night's rough seas.

Seeing Raiden's stash, a beachcomber with a handlebar moustache, who happened to be a marine biologist on vacation, informed him that his sand dollars were members of the *Clypeasteroida* order, and that newly-hatched larvae were able to clone themselves if threatened by predators by separating into two smaller versions, thus reducing the chance of both of them being eaten.

When Raiden responded by asking, in all seriousness, if each would be worth fifty cents, the scientist laughed as if this was the best joke he'd heard in a while. Raiden, for his part, appeared to be confused.

When Merrilly and her mom went shopping and to have their nails done, I drove to the Pirate's Cove Marina in nearby Manteo. I wanted to sample one of the specialty Navy Grogs at a popular tiki bar on the waterfront deck overlooking the Roanoke Sound.

Sipping the drink while watching some of the returning fishing charters, I saw a man on the dock that looked a lot like my old friend Baldwyn. When the fellow walked into the patio, I realized that it was Baldy.

"Hey, Baldy," I called while waving him over to my thatch-umbrellaed table.

Rubbing his chin stubble while looking at faces in the open-air seating, once he saw me, he headed my way with a surprised look on his ruddy complexion.

"Since when did you become an angler?" I joked.

"Hey there, Jack! I was thinking, who else calls me Baldy? Spirits up... at noon, I see," he laughed while reaching out to shake my hand. "No Beale's Golden in these parts, huh buddy," he smiled while pointing to my heavily garnished cocktail.

"Sit down and let me buy you a sandy bottom."

"I was just gonna grab some lunch."

"A gulper, then – with lunch. So, what are you doing here?"

"Well, I just had a meeting on a boat with a movie producer – no fooling – and his pretty young assistant about a job as a technical advisor for a film that's in pre-production as they say."

"Is this movie about a treasure hunt?"

"Yeah, how'd you know?"

"Not the Beale treasure?"

"No, it's about something that happened in the past."

From the look on his face, I could tell that he was debating in his mind if he should continue.

"Remember when I told you about something I'd seen during a salvage operation off of Bermuda in the 1960s? The Levant ship wreck with the silver pieces like the drachma I showed you."

"You said there was a bluish glow to the waves at night... that it was really an intense blue, but that's all."

"That's right, and this fluorescence wasn't from plankton, I can tell you that. While underwater during the next day," he continued after a short pause, "me and the other diver noticed something that struck us both as being really odd. It was a large school of reef fish of mixed species...how they were moving with such precise rhythm... their foraging behavior was too coordinated... too damned synchronized to be natural... like a looping sequence —"

"I've heard something like this, only it was with birds."

"If that wasn't weird enough, all at once they just froze in place... went completely motionless... not even quivering but just hanging there fixed in place. Then they started up again, only to freeze seconds later. This happened repeatedly. It was the darndest thing I've ever seen. Well, until... they vanished in the blink of an eye... the entire aggregation with their colorful markings just blinked out. What caused this I haven't the faintest, but it might have been some trick of sorts... a cloak... camouflage, because in their place there was an imposing shimmery structure... translucent, like it was constructed with walls of stilled water. I don't know how else to explain this thing. There was nothing about it that looked right. We only glimpsed it for a short time before — you guessed it — it became obscured by the school of fish. But, before that, we saw figures... some in uniforms that were pointing at us through even clearer viewing ports, and there was laboratory equipment in the weird blue lighting... machines that I didn't recognize. Talk about your sailors' yarns."

When the waiter came by, after Baldy ordered a chowder and Michelob, I asked if there was demerara syrup in my Navy Grog, to which he said he'd check with the bartender.

"That's what the movie is about?" I asked.

"I'm not supposed to say anything, but my scuba diving partner at the time, who's now deceased, filmed this thing with what we called his ocean-eye 16, a 16 millimeter Arriflex, and I got a couple of stills with my Nikonos. The footage was later confiscated by the military, who claimed that what we saw was a secret underwater research facility complete with aquanauts and supplies delivered by trained dolphins kind of bullshit. But it also housed Navy personnel as a listening post used to track Soviet subs. The ektachrome film he used caused the weird bluish tones, they said... even though we knew it was color corrected. Anyway, that was the reason for the military brass classifying the stuff he shot. Part of the footage that he managed to keep a duplicate of was later inserted into a sunken treasure film made in the 60s. It was called *The Curse of Ba'al,* because during the recovery of shekels scattered on the ocean floor – or whatever they called the riches – they disturbed this barnacled statuette of some Phoenician storm god. I was told that the film was terrible even by B-movie standards, with cheesy dialogue and bad accents. There was lots of stock footage that didn't match, and a Captain Nemo rip-off hero. It wasn't released and most Hollywood types and film historians doubt it ever existed. It wasn't in theaters because it was a total piece of crap, though – but because of the reel of film containing the secret sea lab that was spliced into it. In the movie, the lifted footage was supposed to be Nemo's underwater lair where the Nautilus was docked. It was set in the East Aegean Sea, but actually filmed off the Florida Keys. Now this producer I met with wants to do a remake."

"If it sucked back then, why are they remaking it?"

"After a lot of detective work, they found a film reel on an antique projector locked in a safe. It had the title on the leader. Thinking it might be the only surviving print, they had it digitally transferred. Then they cooked up this idea to use the basic premise with the brazen idol nonsense and hype the classified footage, claiming it's not of some 1960s sea lab, but an alien structure that was discovered back then and still used today as a secret military base."

On the way back to the beach rental, I saw a local playhouse whose marquee advertised the performance of Shakespeare's *The Tempest*. When I asked Merrilly if she and Raiden would like to see it, I was surprised when she agreed that it would make for a nice afternoon (albeit after sweetening the deal by offering to take them to a trendy seafood restaurant and carnival afterwards).

After taking our seats with the hundred plus in the audience, I was worried that Merrilly and Raiden (myself as well) would be bored if unable to follow the complex narrative delivered by a Shakespeare troupe using outdated Elizabethan-era wording. However, with the opening scene's way of presenting the first of many supernatural events that figured prominently in the plot, I began to think it might not be so bad after all.

In the darkened theater, a spotlight focused on a beautiful young woman whose face had an enchanting glimmer. Dressed in sparkling tights, she was portraying Ariel, one of many fantastical characters that appear in the play.

While holding a toy wooden ship in her hand, she suddenly began rocking it back and forth with a series of violent movements against a swathe of indigo fabric that was also shaken wildly by a couple of stagehands in black bodysuits as a theatrical signal for the raging waves the "ayrie spirit" was conjuring up. With flashing strobe lights simulating lightning strikes and thunderclaps booming over the venue's sound system, as the lissome figure continued to manipulate the prop ship, she sprouted gossamer wings before moving with a balletic fluidity to the side of the unlit stage.

When the colorful stage lights came on, the 'Boatswain' was holding a wooden helm beneath a flapping tattered sail that was lowered. As he and the ship's master shouted to one another over the shrieking wind, their bodies wobbled to further indicate the storm-tossed vessel.

During this dramatic opening scene of Ariel's magic feat (having "flam'd amazement aboard the ship"), blue-costumed children playing sea-nymphs with coronets of cockleshells squirted the distressed mariners with toy water guns until the plastic tanks strapped to their backs were empty. Providing a bit more comedic relief, a couple of them tossed scaly fish at the sailors.

After a set change in which minimal scenic pieces were used to depict another part of the exotic locale of the exiled ruler, came the act that I had been anticipating.

From doing a Google search, I knew that it was the dialogue in the subplot involving the shipwrecked king's drunken butler and court jester that was being used as coded references to something by both the military personnel in the southern Illinois video and the government type with the fancy oxblood leather boots in the artificial grotto. This humorous exchange occurred when the bumbling jester, Trinculo, first encountered the 'primitive' native of the island.

The misshapen figure named Caliban was freckled with large brown spots and had prosthetic horns jutting from matted strings of hair. To further stress his feral nature, he was dressed in a baggy gabardine cloak onto which the costume designers had glued shells, thorns, toads and beetles. As a final touch, he wore a cardboard crown at a jaunty angle.

When the buffoonish Trinculo entered the stage in his motley attire, he was holding a bottle of "Kill Devil" rum. Though this anachronistic touch drew some laughs from the audience, I thought it was odd that no one seemed to have noticed his modern-day translation of the original wording:

"What do we have here, a man or a fish? Whew, he stinks like a fish – an old salted fish – not a fresh caught one. A strange fish. If I were in England now, as I once was, and I had even a painted picture of this fish, every fool there would pay me to look at it. In England, this strange monster could pass as just another man. Any strange beast there can be considered a man. The people there won't give a penny to a lame beggar, but they'll throw down their Barclay's bank credit card to gawk at a freak show exhibit."

The code words taken from this might have been chosen randomly, but given all the tie-ins involving mysterious islands that were similar to the setting for the play, I didn't think so. Either way, after watching and listening carefully to the scene – looking for some hidden message – nothing jumped out at me. Maybe my mind was playing tricks on me like those that haunted the castaways, brought about by a spirit that served the magician Prospero. However, just when I thought I might be reading too much into certain things, I was confronted by yet another 'coincidence.'

This came about during another paranormal event staged by Ariel, when the tricky spirit impersonated a mythological Harpy. While strapped in a harness and lowered over a banquet table, before a sweep of its glittering wings caused the platters of food to disappear, I noticed that the victuals consisted of bacon-wrapped sushi, jars labeled "bacon jam" and even what appeared to be bacon candy. Even if this was an inside joke by the director, I doubted such blatant heresy happened often.

After the play ended, we decided to get a cold drink in the lobby as our dinner reservation was still hours away. When Merrily said that she felt sorry for the "wild man" of the island, even though he plotted to kill his captor, which, she added, he had every right to do because his land was taken from him and he was forced to be a slave, an elderly woman wearing a WHAT'S PAST IS PROLOGUE tee told her that such issues were what the drama was really all about.

A warning about colonialism... indigenous people suffering from oppression after New World voyages... even exhibited as deformed savages to civilized Europeans... like animals in a zoo.

"That's why at times the rebellious Caliban speaks in verse as eloquent as the other *dramatis personae*," she said, "to show that he isn't less than human."

When Merrilly wasn't sipping her lemon vodka spritzer or picking at the garlicky shrimp, she cast nervous glances at the dozen or so aged Green Berets wearing camo fatigues with woodland patterns that were carrying on at a large table next to us.

"What's the matter?" I asked.

"I was just thinking about what that creepazoid said about men in the trees with their heads covered by green yarn that would be watching me. Green yarn, Jack, like their hats. They're watching you and me... and Raiden –"

"That's cray, Merr. They're having a reunion... talking about the Robin Sage exercise when they were candidates at Fort Bragg. Free Pineland. You know, the fictitious country here. They probably have left over dons to pay the bill."

"Well, I've had enough fictional places for one day... and oregano butter," she said with a familiar sneer. "They look kind of sus to me. Let's get the hell out of here. The food at the carnival will be better than this shit."

With double shots of Grey Goose in her cocktails, I knew there was no point trying to further rationalize the presence of the ex-soldiers.

After paying the bill at the cash register, when I went back to the table to leave a tip, I was freaked out to see what looked like Callie's doojigger placed on a mat.

When I picked up the lustrous thing, it felt light to the touch, but had a course texture where the *Anunna* device felt like frozen smoke. Looking closer at its metallic sheen, I realized it was one of Raiden's sand dollars that he had painted with multiple layers of glossy acrylics and left as a tip for the waitress.

Ever since we left the play, Raiden had been repeating parts of the dialogue that he had memorized line by line. Besides his amazing recall, he had an uncanny ability to match the accents of the various actors. Although Merrily had at first applauded his impression of the island's "wizard dictator" and other characters, she had since grown annoyed and was staring blankly out the passenger side window.

"Great, Jack, now I'll be hearing him repeat that old talk for months. And all for some overcooked shrimp. Well, you tried at least… and I liked those twinkle leotards that feisty pixie had on."

When I didn't respond, Raiden started up again.

When I returned to Jeremy's cabin, one of the first things I did was to open Callie's coloring book to the ambiguous illustration of the sea fantasy. Bearing in mind what Baldy had told me about how schooling fish might have been some holographic display to cloak a mysterious structure, I examined it from a different perspective. Instead of concentrating on the multicolored flurries, I shifted my focus to the gaps *between* them, as well as to the paler shades that extended onto parts of the iridescent scales of certain fish and distorted their shapes. When these 'insignificant blanks' were viewed as a connected whole, something popped. A separate image appeared. It was like one of those optical illusion brainteasers. I could discern the faint outlines of a rippled glassy structure with what appeared to be silvery figures engaged in various activities within.

Once the hidden image was revealed, being that the aquascape was strikingly similar to what Baldy had described, several things raced through my mind. Was the ingenious design a conscious effort on Callie's part, and, if so, how did she know about the structure? Did she see it in a vision, or had someone told her about it? Her uncle was in the Navy and might have been involved with the project or handled sensitive material at some point. I even entertained the idea that she saw it in the *Anunna* device. Maybe there was a connection between the two oddities.

The more I thought about it, the more I realized that whatever was going on involved members of her family. Hadn't her mom tried to warn me about something, telling me that I should run to getaway from Callie as fast as I could? Jeremy probably knew something about the family's secret as well, which is why he went to the estate sale to search for clues in their bizarre library.

Then I remembered the old book he bought that had drawings of places long before they were built. Like tossing dice, he used the lottery spinner at the back to seek guidance. Bibliomancy he called it. Hoping to find some answers, myself, when Jeremy was out somewhere, I went over to the area where his antiquarian books were shelved. Finding the olive green leather one with the gilt designs, I opened it to the appendix where the crude woodcut wheels for the lottery were placed. For the hell of it, I shut my eyes and rotated the top one for a few seconds.

When I stopped, I saw that the number was 55. I closed my eyes again and proceeded to do the same for the lower dial. When it 'felt right', I saw that the indicator pointed to the fourth lottery. When I turned to the page, I was surprised to see that there was no emblem for my number. In reading the directions again, it said that anything over 50 was a "Blancke Chance" and that I was to look no further.

While putting the book back, I glanced up at the old photograph hanging on the wall of the Congo Pygmy who was once displayed as a fairground exhibit and even caged in the Monkey House at the Bronx Zoo. With my eyes fixed on how his front teeth had been filed to sharp points, the fragile volume tumbled to the floor and landed with its opened pages facing downward. When I picked it up, before I had a chance to make sure the fragile rotary constructs didn't get damaged, I noticed that my finger, as if mimicking one of the spinners, was pointing right at verse 55 in the fourth lottery. Even though there was no emblem associated with it, I read the passage:

It seems, Dame Fortune doth not know,
What Lot, on thee, she should bestow:
Nor, canst thou tell, (if thou mightiest have
The choice) what Fortune, thou shouldst crave.
For, one thing, Now, thy mind requires;
Anon, another it desires.
When Resolution thou hast got,
Then, come again, and draw thy Lot

Though I didn't follow the correct procedure, now it was telling me to look further. Instead of taking another turn right then and there, I thought it would be best to wait for another time.

As I grabbed my keys to go to a nearby taphouse for a couple of beers, I caught sight of Jeremy's hippie comix on the kitchen table. This was the first time I'd seen it without being in his reach. Curious as to what the thing was about, I opened it. When I saw the faces of a couple of outlandish armadillos named Darby and Darlina on the inside cover, it took a moment, but then I remembered where I'd heard about these guys. Callie's uncle mentioned how Grumble's disturbed brother swerved from writing mainstream children's books to using the same popular characters in a series of underground 'zines titled *JEET*. If I needed any more evidence that Jeremy suspected the Suttons of being in possession of something of great value, this was it. But was he also aware of the *Anunna* device?

In turning the pages, picture after picture showed the armadillos' zany adventures with speech bubbles containing their salty language. This might have had shock value when the comix were first issued, but in today's world it wouldn't raise a brow.

In the first few panels the couple were seen trying to hitchhike through the Louisiana bayous.

Comical sequences showed that they were having trouble getting picked up because instead of sticking out thumbs all they could do was make weird gestures with their clawed forepaws. As redneck drivers honked and shouted for the hippie freaks to get the hell out of the road, they were called things like "Texas speed bumps", "crunchy bunnies" and "glorified roly-polies."

When they finally caught a ride, the driver turned out to be a smelly bird with a jumbo Afro dyed in a rainbow of colors. Because the armadillos kept pinching one another's snouts, the bird got the hint and stopped to take a dust bath. While doing so, it caught a worm that it later tried to trade for a kilo of cannabis. Later strips had the two shacked up in the hollowed log of a cottonmouth they met while smoking grass and foraging for munchies. In the next frame their crash pad was shown going up in flames because earlier the snake kept catching itself on fire after trying to light joints that were twisted like pretzels.

The comix ended after the couple joined a commune of leapers (not lepers, a speech balloon emphasized, because armadillos spread that disease) that was portrayed as a marshy stretch whose collective was made up of Cajun jumping frogs and silver carp wearing tie-dyed tees and retro headbands. The leapers boasted they could out jump the two armadillos, claiming they sometimes leaped from daylight into the nighttime and landed on a righteous star where a big party was always happening.

When a light in the room caught the page that showed the overly large 'party star' in a certain way, I could make out hidden letters amid its multicolored sparkles while being viewed by one of the armadillos through a telescope. 'Here we go again,' I thought to myself. However, rather than being another clever puzzle to solve, the word revealed in the magnified circle was nothing more than the comix's title (JEET) formed from entoptic dots of similar color.

When I finished skimming through the thing, it was hard to imagine why Jeremy had spent so much time and energy on it. He obviously wasn't amused by the characters' foolish behavior because he had read it time and again without so much as a chuckle. His expression was pensive, as Jema called it when poking fun at her nephew's latest obsession. As for Callie's uncle's 180, maybe his mind had been opened after dropping acid. The comic strips were kind of trippy, but didn't seem to contain anything of a cryptic nature. It was just a bunch of flat-topped Delmers on the bayou harassing stoners. There was the mentioning of a star that members of a commune had wild parties on, but it would be a far reach (pun intended) to draw a parallel of such a whimsical notion to any celestial peculiarity that Grumble might have shared with his brother. Perhaps there was no link with the freak comix to the Sutton's other activities as I had first thought. They were a dead end, even though Jeremy was still intent on finding a clue because of the tie-in with the family's name (if, as I suspected, he was aware of this connection).

Just when I thought Jeremy might have been using the gazebo to actually meditate, I started hearing sounds coming from out back. Only, this wasn't the usual squawking of gulls, mechanical beeps and strangely husky utterances. They were the muffled screams of a woman. There was also the shuffling of footsteps just outside the cabin. When I opened the ripped screen door, I saw Cleo hurrying in the direction of shrieks. Concerned as to what Jeremy might be doing besides being engaged in erotic games, I followed the vibrant prints on her Dashiki tunic towards the pollinator garden.

"That's enough damn dialing of toll-free numbers on that poor lady payphone," Cleo muttered with her head bobbing like an angry hen. "The educated fool's done taken a shotgun to a roach… instead of casting bones… if she's a horse ridden at that pretend quincunx."

As the piercing hysterics grew louder, I quickened my pace on the path that twisted through the trees. While swatting at a large spider web that was visible in the moonlight through gaps in the coppery green foliage, I saw a naked woman stumbling towards me.

As I stuck out my hands to stop her, there was a stunned look on her face. With dark almond eyes darting ceaselessly about, I recognized her as the same girl I'd seen in the gazebo a week ago. Perfumed oils rubbed onto her trembling form mingled with the odious night blooms in the conjure garden.

"What happened?" I asked while averting my gaze from her springy breasts. "I'm Merrilly's friend, Jack."

After staring wildly at me for a few seconds, instead of the harsh vocal burst I expected, a cunning smile appeared on her pretty face.

She lowered her eyelids and pursed her lips.

"Babay, Dezi, Babay," she mouthed with a deep voice that sounded infinitely remote.

While trying to decide if I should offer her my shirt, I heard the swishing of Cleo's sneakers approaching from behind me.

"Is she okay, Jack?" she asked while brushing away spider webbing from her braided headwrap. "Let me get you a robe, honey... and some cool apple cider... and a moist sponge," she said before hurrying back towards the cabin.

"The fish moved," the girl whimpered in a normal voice, though she was still slightly dazed. "It swam back and forth over parts of my body."

"Fish?" I asked.

"My fish tattoo. It moved from behind my ear," she said while pointing a lacquered teal fingernail at her ear, "and started swimming all over me until it jumped into Jeremy's hand. How could it do that... a tat... and I watched it flipping and flopping in his palm. Its eye looked kind of scary."

When I pulled back some of her glossy black hair, on a shaved area behind her left ear I could see a simple tattoo of a small purple fish.

"It's still there," I said.

Remembering how the markings of scarlet snakes were seemingly animated on her undulating flesh the last time I saw her, at first I thought this must have been the same illusion aided by the shadow play of bluish forks of fire. However, the discreet location of the minimal tattoo ruled out this possibility. From what she described, obviously she was hallucinating. But, was this the result of being put in some kind of hypnotic trance that allowed disembodied spirits to use her as a mouthpiece, or was it caused by something else? Something he learned from the freak comix?

Jeremy emerged from the trees wearing a belted yellow bathrobe. To spare further embarrassment he was holding an identical one that he offered to Desire.

"Sorry about that, Jeremy," she said with a shaky voice, still visibly disturbed while putting on the robe. "You saw how my fishy went crazy. I think I need to take a break."

As his gaze strayed past her and became fixed on me, he bent down and hugged her.

"Just tangential stuff," he said while trying to catch his breath. "Yes, unwind for a while. We finally got through," he nodded before resting his head on her shoulder, not merely winded, but totally spent.

"They're not just doper funnies, Jack," Jeremy said while flipping through the pages of the freak comix on the kitchen table. "And, for real, I didn't know the Suttons were involved. I've been dissecting this thing for years – the secondary meaning of armadillos' clowning, like here," he said while pointing to the tiers where the cartoon critters were trying to hitch a ride. "The gestures they're making are called *mudras*, and they can activate specific zones mapped out on our subtle anatomy that project occult energy."

"Zones?"

"The *points-chauds*, meaning hot points, that are connected to us but also extend beyond the visible borders of the human body...like chakra frequencies do. It's all about vudutronic engineering and the parallels with quantum physics. We're esoteric machines, bruh... have magical circuits. Vodou contains remnants of an Afro-Atlantean system that haven't been watered down by Catholicism. There's a lot more to unravel here, like the commune of leapers at the end of the comix. They're not acid-tripping space cadets. They are the *voltigeurs* that can jump into different dimensions of reality through a form of astral projection."

"You got all that from this?" I asked with a skeptical glare.

"This," he said while tapping the opened page, "is an initiation document pretending to be a stoner's 'zine. Yeah, for real, it's all here in the hippie lingo... the punning word play. Go with the flow... power to the people... outta sight... and can you dig it. That's where I looked for signals."

"But why armadillos of all things?"

"Because they're diggers, Jack. The uggo-shovels as they're called by the local yokels. Francis Bacon's treasure was said to be hidden in a very ingeniously concealed vault, right?"

"That's what you said."

"It's locked away in the brain with other dormant potentials that can be tapped. That's what this is all about. Bacon had a discovery device that he used as a navigation tool for his inner voyages – remember, he used nautical terms as a metaphor for his explorations beyond ordinary consciousness – into deeper levels – deeper than any anchor has sounded."

"What about the bird with the rainbow 'fro that picks up the dillos? Does that mean anything?" I asked.

"The smelly bird contains the most secret instructions of all. Yeah, when it takes a dust bath, it's indicating the hoopoe bird that possesses a special worm. Do you know what that is?"

"Well, I have... no idea at all."

"Fasten your seatbelt. The worm is the legendary *Shamir* of King Solomon, a miraculous device said to be able to disintegrate stone with its penetrating glare that was left on the Earth by the Angel of the Sea. But, it's not a species of sea worm that bores through limestone like some think, nor is it some laser-like alpha radiation beam as others claim. The *Shamir* opens a micro-wormhole in the brain. Its tunnels are neural pathways and what it's able to penetrate is the nightside wall, allowing us to establish contact with otherness. We're talking arcane cartography, here, and I've got receipts."

His evidence turned out to be recordings on his smartphone. The whisper-like voices that were discernible over the woods sounds were what came out of the seeress' mouth while in her "oracular sleep." Much of it was glossolalia, he said, that he likened to static, but there were also utterances spoken in Haitian Creole, which indicated to him that Desire might have crisscrossed lines with others on the same psychic bandwidth.

Using an online translator, some of the barely audible words he teased out of the recordings were "star", "party" and "paradise" (*zetwal, pati, paradi*). He explained that in the comix, the leapers wanted to jump onto a star that was a blissful place full of grass they could use to roll big fat joints. Only those with "good vibes" could reach this stoner's paradise, which he concluded also had a double meaning that he hadn't yet unraveled.

If I found all this hard to swallow, I was even more skeptical when he tried to make the case that those government types we heard speaking Willy code on military radio channels were also in the medium's loop. One of them was supposed to have said (in a voice that had a warbling metallic quality), "Canst thou bring me to the party," while another says, "They say there's five upon the isle. We are three of them." After this, according to Jeremy's translator, someone speaking in Haitian Creole said, "Make contact with the returners" (*Fe kontak... ak retoueon*). This was followed by, "monster fish" (*Pwason mons*) and "beautiful fish" (*Bel pwason*).

Several times in the recording, Desire claimed to be dizzy, which Jeremy said occurred when she later claimed to be pulled by some unknown attractor through the dark byways during her magnetic sleep. "She said it felt like she was being sucked into whirling vortices or sensory maelstroms that were like a – "

"Like a tempest," I said with a wry smile.

"These first attempts were exploratory," he shrugged. "A little voyage of discovery. I need to make some calibrations... Tweak the components, but the results are still interesting."

"Just for shits and giggles," I said. "What's the Haitian Creole word for armadillo?"

Using the language translator, he quickly had the answer: "*Tutau.*"

The experiment was interesting. But were they actual utterances from people on the same "brainphone" as Jeremy believed, or was it simply a case of his "seeress" repeating things that she'd heard him say (ideas that bubbled up from his mind)? If not that, could his reading into what might have been random noise have been merely wishful thinking on his part, things he wanted to believe so badly that he convinced himself they were true?

Although he may have laid all his cards on the table, I was still holding back a couple of mine because of the promise I made to Callie. These included her curious illustration, but especially the mind-bending wonders of the doojigger. If Desire wasn't a genuine mediumistic conduit, then what about Callie? Didn't she once tell me she heard a mysterious call – like a conch trumpet – and afterwards she had a creative urge? If this was a trigger mechanism, like Jeremy's vectors of force – the *points-chauds* – and the drawing was inspired by an outside source, than whose fingers were holding the crayons?

Later that night while experimenting with yet another infusion from Cleo's cornucopia of ingredients, I watched a recently downloaded podcast that featured Siriana – the woman who claimed to have given birth to an ultraterrestrial being in a secret government lab. Seated behind a chunky desk, her features were once again disguised. In this latest clip she said that the hyper-tellurian was born knowing exactly what it is. This self-knowledge was intrinsic to its superconscious mind, although she wasn't sure if memories of a prior existence were also indelibly ingrained as under normal circumstances the being would have been self-generated.

When questioned about its non-human abilities, she replied that she was only aware of a fraction of them, but one was that it was able to possess people in the same manner in which some religious people believe demonic spirits are capable of doing for malevolent purposes. Although, in this case, those who are temporarily taken control of don't need to call the local exorcist. Instead, they are the recipients of special gifts they might not at first be able to fathom.

When the subject turned to its possible future, she said there was much debate concerning this. She had heard discussions about attempts to contact the being through the amplification of human mind-energy, including esoterically engineered prayers. These, she added, should not be confused with those petitions to the gods that humans routinely engage in with simplistic gestures and utterances. Such common prayers are merely a corruption of the divine technology – being an inefficacious, crude imitation of the lost angelic science of trans-mundane communication – similar to those natives of Melanesia after World War Two who spoke into coconut shell radios in hope of receiving planeloads of cargo like they once saw landing on the islands. As to how to facilitate a catalytic interface with its brain, she had glimpsed a blackboard that was filled with cascades of abstract biophysics equations. When it came to attempts to eavesdrop on its thoughts, the one thing all had agreed on (even those with conflicting interests) was that it wasn't as much of installing something in a human brain as it was about disabling the shackles of certain neural filters already in place.

"Let me clarify something," Siriana emphasized. "They're not attempting to use these methods to simply chit-chat with the new kid on the block. They want to covertly get into Ultra-1's mind to see what intentions it might have with regards to us humans. What its terrestrial policy is."

The final question from the host was: "If this being represents a trans-human existence, than what do people most need to prepare for?"

After a short pause, she responded:

"The shock of beauty."

According to the narrator, shortly after the interview Siriana disappeared under mysterious circumstances. This after a luminous LED tattoo that had been implanted under the skin on her arm was de-pixelated, and someone recognized the unique geometric symbol as being Enochian in nature. "What is known is that her real name is Zyla Cantrell from Sunnyvale, California. She recently had a boyfriend whose mother was a prominent geneticist at a Bay Area lab called 'Cellectech', before she, too, vanished without a trace. The company's glossy brochures advertised super-babies."

The following night I watched the same video to see if I might have missed anything when Siriana talked about people being possessed by the hyper-tellurian. As I waited for that part of the interview, Jeremy pushed the screen door open while holding a bowl of popcorn in one hand and a couple of Diet Cokes in the other.

"Jema made us some of her cheeseburger popcorn," he said while setting the bowl on the table, "and my aquatic spirit left a couple of Cokes. Agwe has a discerning palate and might be pissed off that I didn't fill a glass with real seawater."

"No nocturnal escapades tonight?" I joked.

"My pythoness is still tuckered from her mediumistic wrestling."

Seeing what I was watching, he plopped down on the couch.

"Maybe it's not sci-fi baloney after all," he said.

"Why do you say that?"

"I've never taken a piano lesson. What she's talking about – it's like the magic vodou drum that some can hear from far away while others who are close by don't hear it at all. Can you hear its call... hear something calling you, Jack?"

"No, but I know someone who might – not a drum – but the call of something else."

"You ever hear back from her?"

"No... I thought we were vibing, but... No."

"Well, at least you got to see it playing with one of its toys."

"You're talking about the airship?"

"We're still missing something, Jack. That's what we've got to figure out."

"So, are you giving up on those comix holding all the answers?"

"It seems like they should continue, but there were only seven issues. As the leapers are getting ready to party on that star, the two armadillos exchange furtive glances... and then it just ends."

"I still think the answer lies in cracking the Beale cipher."

"I get what you're saying. Everything points to Bermuda. As it says in the play, 'It's in a deep nook in the much vexed Bermoothes there she's hid'... meaning, of course, the stormy Bermuda Triangle. But, we still need to pinpoint the specific location. Prospero owes everything to the influence of a most auspicious star... the star that led him to the island. Okay, listen to this. In Bacon's *New Atlantis* there's this strange spectacle seen by people on the island... a dazzling pillar of light rising from the sea at night. Thinking this is a heavenly sign some get into boats and sail towards it. But they only get so far before they find themselves unable to move further. Soon, the powerful beam breaks up... and turns into a group of stars. But, the new constellation, too, quickly disappears. This is another puzzle. Remember, their advanced technology – the perspective house for lights and radiations that can represent things near as being far? Feigned distances, Jack. False appearances. So, was this a natural phenomenon of some kind, or one of their imposters... a staged illusion? Whatever this was inspired me to think about a star map that can be overlaid on the ground to mark a certain location... like maybe the constellation of a ship that's lost at sea and finds the new Atlantis. But how could a star that helps to connect the dots to form this celestial ship regularly disappear, only to reappear again at times?"

"You're saying that when this one star can't be seen... the ship can't be seen either... because it changes the appearance of the alignment of stars... and during that time... when its not there...the ship is seemingly lost... maybe sunk or beached on an island – "

"Yeah, but short of an eclipsing binary or this star sinking below the horizon, how could something like that occur in the night sky without being noticed? Especially to a most auspicious star like Prospero's?"

"Let me stop you here. In *The Beale Papers* it's called the 'locality' of the vault – so there isn't any exact location. But, what if your star map pointer isn't in the sky, but hidden in the numeric cipher?"

Yeah, it could be, but getting back to what I was saying, once these stars were gone, they saw a cedar chest floating in the water that one of the wise men of the society," he emphasized, "was able to retrieve. It contained a parchment written by Saint Bartholomew concerning revelations given by an angel that appeared to him in a vision. You following me?"

"I think so."

"So, who was Bartholomew? The apostle was associated with miracles having to do with the weight of objects, like a heavy silver statue of him that was going to be melted down for money to help fund some war until it was weighed and, inexplicably, was only a few grams. Shit, like that."

When he said this, I wondered (again) if he knew anything about the *Anunna* device and Grumble's Star? I thought about asking a few questions as a way of testing him, but quickly decided to let him continue with his latest speculation.

"As a punishment for spreading Christianity, he was flayed. In Bacon's time, grisly imagery of Bartholomew showed a skeletal form holding his own skin. But could it have been that there was something revealing on his skin like a tattoo of an abstruse symbol... maybe like that Egyptian eye that sees beyond the horizon of time – "

"Or a little fish that swam all over his body," I smiled.

"Desire was just seeing things from all the mental excitement involved."

"Good, because I don't want to waste my time looking for tattoos."

"Yeah, like the guy that spoke in Willy-code... with the camo boots does," he said pointedly. "You said that he asked lots of questions about unusual tattoos – "

"That's what Callie said."

"No, I'm not saying it has anything to do with tats. The flaying represents manuscripts or a book. Manuscripts were literally made from the skin of animals, right? I think Bacon was hinting that, in their quest for truth, the Lanthorn came into possession of lost secrets concerning the mysteries of heaven. Things that were hidden from others. A revelation transmitted in the original gift of tongues. That's why he gave Saint Bartholomew such a prominent role in his book. Anyway, those are my thoughts. You know, grasping at straws again. Hey, you know what it might be time for, Jack?"

"Some of that Navy rum your spirit didn't drink?"

"Bibliomancy."

"Right. Back to rational thinking," I deadpanned, "instead of grasping at straws."

After removing the 'Emblems' book from the shelf, Jeremy once again followed the author's instructions for playing the game. The spinner landed on number 31 of the first lottery:

'You seek a lot, which, proving bad,
Would, peradventure, make you sad;

But, this may please: for, you are taught
To mend a Fortune, that is naught;
And, armed, with such Council, here,
That, you, no *destiny*, need fear.
Now, if you come to harm, or shame,
Upon the stars, lay not the blame.'

He was told to consult emblem number XXXI:

'Hee, over *all* the Starres doth raigne,
That *unto* Wisdome can attaine.'

Though I thought Jeremy's latest premise was quite a stretch, it was good to see his brain working overtime again on the treasure hunt.

The next morning I received a text from a manager at the Pharos Club asking if I could come in for an interview for a bartending job. Though I wasn't keen on a three hour plus commute each way (until I could rent an apartment closer by), I decided to go just to see if there was any news of Callie's whereabouts.

When I arrived in the pouring rain there were no buffed black doorkeepers in linen kilts standing under the awning with their arms akimbo, as was normally the case. Wondering if the club was now closed during the day, when I pulled on one of the heavy doors, it opened. With no one in sight, I headed down the pillared hallway, passing walls that were vividly ornamented with ancient Egyptian motifs and large gilded plaster scorpions. When I walked through the curtain beneath the mystical eye design, to my great surprise, I didn't recognize the place. Gone were the floating barge, palm trees and ever-present Cleopatras. Instead, I found myself standing in what appeared to be a hazy dockside sailors' bar, whose wood-paneled walls were cluttered with nautical artifacts.

Several old salts were seated around a bar drinking mugs of flat beer while some younger patrons that were casually dressed in polo shirts sipped a cloudy dark liquid. Ringed by colorful pennants was a sign that read: FAIR WINDS TAVERN. Through large circular windows that were regularly spaced, I could see various boats docked in the blue mirror of a busy marina on a bright sunny day. The harbor view as seen through 'portholes' from inside the tavern, I quickly realized, was a film set backdrop using rear motion projection on screens behind the glass.

With no manager (or employees) to be seen, I took a stool at the bar. Glancing up, I noticed a movie was playing on the hanging video screens (the only things left from the Pharos club).

As I watched, a couple of scuba divers were floating next to the stumps of mastheads of an encrusted wreck on the murky seabed. The rotting hulk looked to be an ancient Phoenician galley that still had part of a painted eye on its barnacled prow. Suddenly, a gigantic fish that came into frame dwarfed both the sunken ship and divers. Only when the camera angle widened did I realize that the bireme oared-ship was merely a resin decoration inside a bubbling aquarium. The divers were also accessories that swayed as an ordinary-sized Golden 'Mini' Grouper did loops around them.

"Did you think it was real?" a voice rang out. "The shipwreck and divers?"

When I turned, I saw a man with a goatee and black-circle glasses standing there.

He was wearing a Tricot-style Italian sweater and beige chinos. Standing behind him was an attractive strawberry blonde woman holding a clipboard and bottle of Pellegrino water.

"Yeah, it looked pretty real," I replied. "I'm here about a bartending job."

"We already have our bartender," he said matter of factually. "But it didn't look too real, did it? We'll add a pulse-stirring rhythm before the fish appears. Oh, do you mean a real bartending job?" he asked after seeing my confused look. "Natch, I assumed you were atmosphere. Well, someone should be along soon, but in the meantime, for the rehearsal, you can be another customer."

"Good, I've got all hands on deck," he addressed those seated around the bar. "The Phantom Hazer's not bothering anyone, I trust… and I see the sherry pepper sauce arrived… but still no raisin bread for the fish-cake sandwiches. Some of you have the Black and Coke you ordered, though personally I'd rather be sipping a good Chianti than that molasses stuff."

When he turned to confer with his production assistant, I went over and stood by one of the wide porthole windows that 'looked out' at the marina.

As a pleasure yacht passed by vigilant gulls on the dock, I saw a girl sunbathing on the lower deck that looked a lot like Callie. Light brown hair glinted richly from a white captain's hat. When she stuck a cherry sucker in her mouth, I knew for sure that it was Callie. As the boat continued outward bound, I hurried to the next window (another translucent projection screen), and was able to catch its name before it passed from site.

AZURIA
ISLE OF ZIRN
BERMY

"Wopnin, Jack," a female voice uttered. Startled, I turned to see Callie standing there, wearing the same captain's hat at a jaunty angle. Deeply tanned, she was dressed in a fuschia halter and khaki shorts. Brushing back her messy hair, green eyes sparkled with enthusiasm. "You've got the job."

"It's a really long way from where I live now," I said, suddenly feeling hurt by her not returning all my calls.

"The job's not here. This place is closed. It's on a private island in Bermuda. It's a hidden paradise with crystal clear water and pink sand beaches. You'll be working for Mister Zuffante and getting big tips from wealthy jet-setters."

"I don't like yacht-rock or noisy birds... Actually, I like noisy birds more than yacht-rock. Why would I want to go to Bermuda?"

"Because your ace-girl will be there."

CHAPTER VIII
ADONIRAMITE

"On the whole, the extinction of the Adonhiramite Rite can scarcely be considered as a loss to Freemasonry."

Encyclopedia of Freemasonry
(And its kindred sciences)

*"Beware of wavering. Blot out suspicion of us for we are Gods Creatures, that have reigned, do reign & shall reign forever.
All our mysteries shall be known to you."*

De Heptarchia Mystica,
Sloane manuscript 3191

"A spreading Tree Full Fraught with Various Fruits most fresh and fair To make succeeding Times most rich and rare."

George Willingham

"Admittedly, I have acquired a taste for the edible landscaping on this islet – ornamental, yet bitter, like the Surinam cherries in this sorbet," the elderly gentleman seated at the polished teakwood bar said. "So, with that in mind, I have no qualms as to your preference to that spicy chutney over our very own onion marmalade, even if it gets its tang from minced red ants."

"Who told you that?" I asked while pouring him a cup of expensive Sri Lankan tea from a silver gilt pot.

257

"The lady owner of Punyaaloka, who is also a notable geneticist in California, or so I'm told," he said while eyeing my pouring etiquette. "But don't fret, lad, we'll figure out something to do with the excess of onions here," he smiled.

"It just goes better with the papadum than that onion dip," I said.

"Isn't it nice to know there are options," he said after trying a spoonful of the sorbet and dabbing his reddened lips with a starched napkin. "Even when it comes to biscuits," he winked while gesturing to the plate of lentil wafers I was munching on for lunch.

Mogwan was the only other person in the bar at noon. When I first met him a few days ago he told me that he used to be Mister Zuffante's majordomo, meaning his head servant, but that he was now retired from that position, and currently helped make business decisions for the billionaire owner of the private island resort. Clean-shaven and bald, his complexion was pale (oddly enough for spending so much time in the semi-tropical clime), with blue eyes that nearly matched his linen blazer. The suit, like the rest of his attire, was immaculate, having on the lapel a pendant of a golden trowel that, rather than a mason's tool, was of the gardening variety, like those I used when detectoring. Having dealt with the crowd at Royalene's, I found his sense of decorum to be refreshing. Though he'd put away the white gloves, he still retained much of his butler protocol, like when I mispronounced the word "scone" during his previous afternoon tea, he corrected me by saying that the alternative would be "walnut bread when the scones were gone."

While setting the teapot on a warmer, I noticed a lizard scurry across the hand-knotted teal rug before stopping under a stylish coffee table whose green quartz base mimicked a 'seabed' on which a pair of bronze dolphins swam. With the beak of one of them protruding from the clear resin top as if emerging from water, this, like the rest of the posh furniture in "Felicity" (the name of the resort), was over-the-top luxury. The only decorations that might not have cost a small fortune were Callie's coloring book illustrations of vibrant marine life that were hanging in showy gilt frames on the muted siesta and coral pink walls along with some pastel fine art abstractions.

I thought about going over to shoo the skink out onto the side patio, which, like the rest of the grounds, was awash with greenery and filled with the dulcet chorus of birds, until I saw it disappear behind one of the velvet rolled arm sofas.

"I thought I saw a cat out there while you were steeping the Golden Tips," Mogwan said, "if my eyes weren't playing tricks on me. Were you to try to catch that creature all you'd wind up with is a rather striking blue tail... the lizard, not the cat, that is."

As he slurped the tea (which he assured me was the proper way to savor the infusion), a man and a woman walked in. Both were casually dressed, though not wearing the traditional Bermuda rigs I was getting accustomed to seeing. As the woman headed to the patio, the man froze in his tracks at the sight of an umbrella station by the sliding glass door. With his gaze riveted on the black handle that was hooked on the container, he regained his composure after seemingly being paralyzed with fear for a few seconds and stepped up to the bar to order some drinks.

"Four rum Swizzles with top shelf stuff," he said with what sounded like an American mid-west accent. "And give yourself a hundred dollar tip."

Reaching into his pocket, he pulled out a hand-painted sand dollar and placed it on the lustrous grain. The intricate artwork featured a seabird (called a petrel) and the pink blooms of oleanders.

"Do you have a bungalow number?" I asked.

"The thing has a QR flowcode. Just as good as Bermy dollars," the guy said while casting nervous glances at the sole black umbrella in the stand. As he gestured to the Bitcoin terminal, I noticed that the sweat trickling down his somewhat bloated face had a bluish tinge. Since his hair wasn't dyed, I wondered if this was some weird medical condition.

"The lad's a new castaway here," Mogwan said after seeing my puzzled look. "Hasn't sunk his toes in the sand yet. They work here like cryptocurrency, Jack. Some more goodies from the Hoodoo Sea for Mister Zuffante, I gather," he said to the man without showing any concern to the ink-like runnels on his badly perspiring forehead.

"Yes, something very special. Been in the fridge for millennia. Not exactly a wahoo salad, and we'll leave it at that."

After I scanned the matrix within the watercolors on the sand dollar and handed it back to the man, he tentatively stepped towards the sunny patio before continuing with his eyes fixed on the umbrella stand the entire time.

"What's that all about?" I asked Mogwan as I began making the drinks.

"Seems Mister Zuffante's coveting of certain possessions are becoming an unfettered enterprise at Felicity. He's an avid collector of antiquities…. extreme antiquities. The ancient Greeks called such avarice, *pleonexia*, the definition of which is an insatiable desire for things that rightly belong to others. The old boy also has a thing for exotic locales. Untraveled, unpeopled places are becoming harder to find these days and what Mister Zuffante covets the most… well, finding it might be easier than building a really tall tower as those legends in the Bible speak of."

"I was talking about his blue sweat."

"Sweating buckets comes with the territory, I'd rather imagine."

"Bermuda?"

Before he had a chance to answer, a member of the staff approached and told him he was late for an appointment.

"Be sure to churn those drinks well," he said before getting up to leave.

While heading back from a thicket of seaside plants at the secluded cove, I stopped to watch Callie staring intently at her left hand while leaning forward in a folding lounge chair. From what I could see, she was examining a tattoo of one of those mystical eyes on one of her palms that for some reason I hadn't noticed during our picnic. As I continued across the warm sand, I soon realized why. She was holding a butterfly that blended perfectly with her skin, and what I took to be a tattoo was actually one of several eyespots on its delicate wingspan. With my approaching soft footsteps, it lifted from her hand and joined others fluttering among patches of milkweed.

"I hope I didn't scare away your new friend," I said over the chattering of birds while setting down a large zip lock bag full of fruit that resembled clusters of grapes.

"Buckeye says bye-bye, Callie," she said with a silky little girl's voice.

Wearing an aquamarine beach sarong over her swimsuit, she eased her supple, bronzed frame back in the Chaise Lounge.

"The restaurant has their signature cocktail," I said, "but soon so will I. And it won't need a gimmick like ice cubes containing borage flowers."

"You're talking about Punyaaloka's Starflower drink?"

"Yeah, if this Bay Grape makes good jam, let's see what kind of syrup I can come up with."

"They taste kind of yucky," she said while contorting her lips before trying to light one of her demi-slims in the warm breeze. "Hey, here comes Zuzu," she uttered excitedly while pointing to a Siamese cat that emerged from a tangle of large leathery green leaves.

"Zuzu?"

"The tag on its collar says Zuzulia, but I call her Zuzu."

"Is it Zuffante's cat?"

"No, he doesn't have the foggiest idea who it belongs to. It's the island's stray, and it's a sneaky little Miss. It stalks rock lizards and bats at butterflies, but once caught, it won't eat them. Not just jungle dragons – it won't eat anything. I've tried to feed it shark fritters and red snapper, but it just turns away. She looks healthy though, huh. She likes to play hide and seek. Here one minute, gone the next."

"All cats do that."

"Not like this one."

"So, you know that Jeremy is playing again tonight. It should be turnt. Aren't you glad we came as a package deal?"

"I'll be there to listen for a while, but we've all got early diving lessons."

"Hey, where'd the cat go?" I asked. "It was just under your chair."

"I told you! She's got escape hatches all over the island. So, Jack, why don't you like Mister Zuffante? It's not because he wears shorts and silly knee socks with his suits, or has strange ideas about digital wallets is it?"

"I've never met him... but I don't trust him. He wants something of yours. That's what all this is about."

"He wants to protect it. That's why all this."

"Don't be so sure about that. I'll bet you a hog penny."

"I'll bet you a hog penny that you don't have a hog penny," she said after finally managing to light the cigarette.

"Well, if I had a hog penny, I'd bet you one," I laughed. "Are there anymore of those watermelon biscuits left?" I asked while lying down on my blanket. "One without those big-headed ants crawling on them."

"You didn't like my sweet potato pudding, but I'll bet you like my picnic spot. Aesthetic, isn't it," she said while pivoting her neck to take in the secluded stretch of pink-flecked sand, glittering turquoise water and towering palms whose fronds swayed against a lush hillside.

"It's blessed, even though it's not the Isle of Pines where everyone goes about naked and there's nothing to do but... well, I'm still trying to figure out what that might be since you never told me," I said while glancing up at her with a sly grin.

"It starts with a F," she teased.

"How could I not have guessed that? Of course... they frolic."

"Let me give you a hint," she said while getting up from the chair. I could smell the citrusy sunscreen on her glistening flesh as she climbed on top of me and gave me a quick kiss on the mouth.

Jeremy's freestyle jazz was even less structured than his previous romps. As an "outsider artist", the people in the bar were witness to something truly unique, with playing that featured the juxtaposing of chord structures (in different keys) and complex polyrhythms meant to elicit in its listeners what the pianist in the rainbow-hued lighting referred to as an "imminent perichoresis." I wasn't sure how others assimilated the sonic odyssey, but, to my ears, at times, the harmonic congruence evoked a sense of aural euphoria, while the atonal dissonance set me adrift in imaginary realms of terrifying strangeness. Untrained as he was, considering the technical proficiency displayed, I could only wonder what mysterious source my friend had tapped into.

As he continued to improvise (if that's the right word), I was busy prepping for more Rum Swizzles and Dark 'n' Stormys. Though I recognized many of the patrons ordering these cocktails, there were a couple of ladies seated at a table that I hadn't seen before. I was told by Mogwan that the striking older woman draped in the golden sari was the owner of the Indian restaurant that was attached to the bar, but as to the younger girl with the short platinum bob, he said that he didn't know who she was, but added that she must have been someone of importance.

Despite her showy hairstyle, the girl watched the outré performance in a demure manner, clapping her hands softly as others shouted and whistled to show their appreciation. At times when I happened to glance her way, she seemed to be beaming with pride, as if the fevered playing that captivated (or confused) the small audience was the achievement of her own son. I also noticed that the men seated on either side of her constantly glanced about the room like guards maintaining a keen vigilance. As they continued to monitor whatever it was that was of concern, the Bengali woman also appeared to be nervous, though unlike the roving eyes of the men, her apprehensive gazes were mostly at the girl.

During a slow passage when Jeremy repeatedly struck a high key that resembled a submarine's sonar ping, the girl stood up from her chair and began speaking gibberish in a deep-throated monotone. Unlike the speaking in tongues one might hear at a Holly Roller's assemblage, whatever was being said, the words were separated into distinct syllables that were slowly glided so that they flowed together. As the two men tried to silence her, the utterances became recognizable, though vocalized with a prolonged delivery that had a certain poetic quality:

"What water recreateth more, or cooleth ignorance deeper than the knowledge of our celestial speech?"

As both of the men and the Bengali woman tried to forcefully remove the girl from the tension charged room, I noticed that she had a luminous tattoo of a magical symbol on her arm.

Backlit with dark blue LEDs, the tat had been implanted in her skin in the same location as the pixelated spot on the girl from the TroVe videos that called herself Siriana. *Was it her?*

Jeremy quit playing and stood up at the Steinway.

"Is Sir Francis Bacon delivering this message from the angels, or is this some other member of the Lanthorn?" he asked.

As the Bengali woman used her hand to cover the girl's mouth, one of the men started moving his lips:

"With my seal I seal her and she is perfect. I prevail in metals: In the knowledge of them… New worlds shall spring of these… The true light, and thorny path, openly seen."

Before dragging the girl into the hallway, I heard him say to the other man:

"I didn't say anything. It's this crazy bitch."

Until the girl threw her voice, I thought she might have had one of those artificial language apps and was playing a prank. Either that or Jeremy had found himself a new mouthpiece to be sidetracked by mischievous spirits. Whatever caused the man to become a ventriloquist's dummy, even Mogwan wouldn't hazard a guess. One thing was for sure though – Callie picked the wrong night to flake.

Later that night after the bar had closed, while I was taking inventory in the cramped liquor storage room beneath where I usually stood behind the bar (accessible by a trapdoor and small ladder), I heard footsteps and a muffled voice coming from above. When I climbed back up and stuck my head out of the hatch, I realized a man in the darkened barroom was talking to someone on a two-way radio.

"We've got crumbs on the floor over here."

"Roger that. How many?" a staticky voice replied.

"Several, I'm told. Spilled from an action salad removed from the belly of the whale. Taken by a blue dripper, would be my guess. We've got a modified portable surgical suction device to hopefully gather up the little varmints. The real headache is they've got mini gardens in glass terrariums as part of the décor, over."

When I couldn't hear the voices anymore, I climbed out of the storage area and left the bar to see what was happening at Punyaaloka.

As I quietly stepped into the restaurant (which was also closed at this late hour), what I saw was so shockingly improbable that it didn't register at first. In the dim glimmer of wall sconces at the far end of the room, the backs of several disembodied human heads appeared to be suspended in mid-air. As several shades of close-cropped hair floated about, beneath them, wavering like a colorful mirage, aspects of the restaurant's themed décor moved in unison with the heads. I'd heard about the military testing active camouflage, but to see the effects first hand was truly mind-boggling. In addition to the bobbing heads standing out from the mirroring of the ornate furnishings, I could see a pair of hands operating a high-tech machine that was being rolled across the floor's patterned veneer on caster wheels. The device had a colorful display and hand-held narrow cylindrical tube with a powerful illuminator at its tip. As other pairs of hands moved the cushioned Mughal chairs, the vacuum cleaner-like wand was pushed under a dining table.

"Looks like our blue dipper also removed an eating utensil," a voice said over the Motorola.

"That figures," one of roaming heads replied. "You can't hunt angel-eats without the blades."

At that moment, I caught sight of a flash of movement. Having emerged lightning-fast from under a serving trolley next to a gilded rosewood cabinet, at first I thought it was some kind of weird insect that I'd never seen before. As it scurried across the mosaic wood flooring, I got a better glimpse of it before it disappeared behind a decorative jardinière. It looked like a minute viridescent organism with an anatomical structure that was about a half of an inch tall. I had no idea what the thing was, but, again, all I could think of was that it had to be a bug whose shape appeared distorted against the marquetry inlay.

Seconds later I saw something else that looked rather odd. Lying on a clean white tablecloth was a metallic object about the size of a dinner fork. Strange gleams radiated from its sleek, tapered handle, at the end of which, instead of tines, was a complex array of tiny rotary blades.

"What are you doing here?" a voice rang out over the screech of chairs being moved.

After switching off the active camouflage, the man was dressed in a dark uniform with insignias that I didn't recognize. Judging by the unique fabric (used as a cryptic screen?), my guess was that he was part of some elite military unit, perhaps a member of the "Silent Service" that Mogwan had once mentioned.

"Do you work here?" he asked with an even tone.

"Yes, I work at the bar."

"Well, go back to what you were doing at your classy bar. Better yet, go home and try to forget about this sci-fi channel shit. There's nothing to see here that's worth that kind of trouble, buddy," he said while reaching down and softly tapping a part of the handle on the futuristic-looking implement. Doing so caused its hyper-alloys to fold (morph?) in an uncanny manner, after which it was considerably smaller than the object's original size had been. This he attached to his uniform, onto which the thing stuck like a magnet.

"That flexible bugger is canceled, too," the guy said with a threatening glare.

"Could Zuffante be involved in the black market trade?" I asked Callie over the loud whistling of tree frogs as we drank hard seltzers under the blanket of stars at the cove. As gentle breezes carried the redolence of dewy ferns and flowering plants, silvery facets of moonlight reflected on the water seemed fitting for their prolonged serenade. "Maybe metals with unusual properties kind of things. The reason I ask is because I might have seen something out of the ordinary last night."

"Mogwan talks too much," she said while wiggling her toes in the rosy sand. "Rex collects all kinds of stuff. His favorites are what he calls out of place artifacts… things like –"

"Like what you have," I said a bit forcefully, to reiterate an earlier point. "Okay, besides that, what I'm talking about are other objects that are beyond anything we're supposed to have. Maybe he makes deals with people that come here to do business. A private island would be a great place for that kind of thing. I saw this doco a while back about the military's interest in exotic materials of unknown origin. We're talking off-world things, here. They're called meta-materials and are supposedly secretly stored in the labs of aerospace companies whose engineers are trying to figure out how to replicate the stuff.

One of those involved claimed that some of the debris found was deliberately seeded by the military to private industries to see what they might develop. Because of the technological jump these things represent, trafficking in them is hugely profitable."

"But that's not what this is," she said while opening her palm to show me that she was holding the *Anunna* device. It had been a while since I'd last seen it and I could tell by the look on her face that showing it to me was her way of letting me know that no one had taken it.

"Yeah, I know, it fell out of an angel's pocket. Unless it's just a curious gizmo that hypnotized us into thinking we were somewhere else."

"So, that's why certain people want it so badly?" she said with a sarcastic tone. "And not just people, but those other things. No, Jack, I don't think so."

I knew she was right, even though I had tried to convince myself otherwise ever since its activated displays had transported me elsewhere. Seeing that faded "Jolly Mean Giant" sticker on the old car in the barn ruled out any possibility that what I experienced was just some kind of trick.

"Don't you think we should tell Jeremy? It might have been brought to Virginia as part of an ancient treasure that was discovered… One of the 'we haves' in the catalogue of Francis Bacon's *New Atlantis*."

"What if he already knows that and has known all along? You think Mister Zuffante is scheming to pry it from my hands, but what if it's someone else… like your friend, Jeremy? Besides, it hasn't decided yet about him, so promise again you won't say anything in case he doesn't know."

"What are you thinking you're going to use it for? I mean… does it do anything else?"

"Wouldn't you like to see Grumble's Star?" she asked while staring down at the disc's blank surface.

"I'm not sure I want to fool with it. But I would like to see if this star of his adds anything or changes anything to a group of stars that are already – hey, what's going on out there," I shouted while pointing to the greenish-blue flickers that appeared on the water just beyond the shore. "Do you see that?"

When I got up to have a better look, I could see the sinuous luminosity of something moving in tight circles beneath the surface. While observing this, suddenly hundreds of brilliant streaks began darting from the depths like shooting stars.

"I thought it would be alright to bring it here," Callie whispered with a confused look on her face while watching the frenetic spectacle of fluorescent gyrations bursting like fireworks in the shallow water of the cove.

"It seemed okay about it. But, they're back. C'mon, let's get out of here."

"Jack, could I trouble you to replenish this," Mogwan asked while having tea at the bar as he habitually did before noon. "Would it be fair to say these glowing pulsations occurred a few nights after the full moon?"

"It was last night, so, yeah, I guess so."

"Well, dear boy, you've witnessed the same dazzling flames in the inky waters that the explorer Zarco, better known as Colon, recorded in his log, though, he, too, didn't know about the bioluminescent slime emitted during the mating ritual of our famous Bermuda fireworms. So, you can check that box. Wait until you're lucky enough to see a glowing megamouth shark."

"I told her it wasn't an aquadilla," I muttered while turning to get the teapot.

"You'll see lots of odd things on the Isle of Zirn."

"Things like bucket hats and rugby shirts?" I joked.

"You'll see what I mean."

While making a couple of shandys in Callie's treehouse cabin, I could hear laughter over the steady amphibious shrill as family members were enjoying themselves down on the beach. "Drinks are served," I called while carrying them out onto a wooden platform. As she joined me, there was a pungent smell of nail polish that mingled with the renewing serum that was part of her summer scent.

"Nothing like a petal bath to unwind," she moaned.

"Is that Blue Cocoon that I detect?" I asked while handing her a glass.

"What's that?"

"The expensive face moisturizer."

She made a face like she didn't know what I was talking about.

"Blue Cocoon?" She furrowed her brows. "Is that what Merrily used? I think you're smelling the Arabian Jasmine."

From our perch nestled among the subtropical coastal flora, we could see Jeremy playing catch with a silver glitter beach ball that belonged to couple of college girls. Orange sparks skittered over the gleaming tide as their tanned bodies moved energetically in the flickering glow of a crackling bonfire.

"I see your friend is hitting it off with Mister Zuffante's new guests," Callie said with a thin smile while leaning forward in one of the rattan peacock chairs that she thought gave the deck "a bohemian touch."

"Yeah, they're frolicking alright. Just like on the Isle of Pines."

"Sorry about flipping out over the glowworm orgy."

"Just keep it in mind should we encounter any *noctiluca* jellyfish during a wreck dive. Mauve Stingers, Callie... not a Bermy lovefest."

"World's foremost expert on jellyfish also adds just the right amount of Victorian lemonade soda to make a decent Pilsner shandy," she said with a bad British accent while raising her glass.

After taking a drink, she glanced about the surroundings with a sense of uneasiness.

"The other night you asked me about you know what ... what else it does. Remember when I told you about the *wedjat* eye symbol? The missing part that's needed... the missing fraction?"

"Right, it doesn't show a pupil."

"What I have sees and records everything of where it's been like a super camera. Has been doing so for a really long time. Besides getting stuff for the club's décor, Mister Zuffante bought something else. A scrap of papyrus that scholars would love to see. It talks about the final gateway that can only be opened and passed through when a certain eye socket," she emphasized, "becomes filled with divine light. He thinks that's why the doorkeepers painted on temple walls are shown as being lazy or even blind. They weren't needed because only this special eye allowed the person – the mariners of RA, they were called – to enter."

"Sounds sort of like what today's biometric systems do… Retinal scans and such to identify a person before they're allowed access."

"What I have needs to be turned into a living eye."

Later that night, while seated on the edge of Callie's canopy bed, between long kisses, we watched a movie that was being shown on a large outdoor screen that was visible through a picture window. As she was about to go have a smoke, we were startled by a thud that vibrated the bed. Turning, I saw the Siamese cat trying to free one of its hooked paws that had gotten snagged in the lilac mesh while jumping through the lace netting.

"Kitty!" Callie uttered while reaching back to try and help it. Once untangled, Zuzulia crawled onto her lap and began flicking its tail.

"I didn't see it come in, did you?" I asked, though I was more confused (or bemused) by the starry sky that filled the movie screen while at the same time being framed against an even greater number of stars twinkling on the clear summer night.

"She was probably hiding under the bed, weren't you you little sneak," she said while stroking the cat's fur, causing it to start purring with a deep, throaty rumble.

"I hope she helps me do combat with those gargantuan roaches because I was about to call in for reinforcements."

"That's weird," Callie said with her eyes fixed on the window.

When I glanced back at the screen, a luminous orb suspended in mid-air blotted out most of the star field. At first I thought it was a scene in the film, but quickly realized that what I was looking at was a three-dimensional object with a faint bio-florescent glow that was hanging silently in front of the screen. Jumping from the bed, I hurried towards the window as a pair of wing-like protrusions unfolded from its metallic skin with a balletic fluidity. As they fluttered, their compact span was suffused with a soft radiance that seamlessly matched the rest of the dully-lucent silver molding. As it slowly rose above the movie projection, the organic nature (or lack of mechanical rigidity) of these delicately kinetic appendages was unsettling. The entire craft seemed more like an animated phantasm than an actual machined object.

"It looks like a flying Twizy," Callie said with a hushed tone as the puzzling aeroform floated with startling maneuverability over a nearby rock formation, "but I don't think it's a baddie." Unlike her unwavering gaze, before it disappeared from sight, I had noticed that one of the characters *in the film* pointed towards the sky with an expression of stunned disbelief. Surely this wasn't a coincidence, I thought while recalling earlier suspicions that I had about the technoids at the Pharos Club.

For nearly a half an hour we hiked in the direction where the glowing sphere had disappeared over a volcanic outcrop. We clambered up a woodland trail that wound between dense stands of juniper and skirted the soggy mud of an inland salt marsh before reaching a moonlit field of coarse grass where we could make out in the darkness a cluster of prefab structures.

Near some Quonset huts, sheds and a large water tank, flashing aviation-green beacons encircled a concrete helipad. As we got closer we were surprised to see in the beams of our flashlights an old car parked in the middle of the landing zone. As we approached the funny-looking vehicle, someone emerged from behind a refueling container.

"You saw that thing, too."

I recognized the voice to be Jeremy's.

"Hell of a beach ball, huh bruh," I said.

"Talk about a fiery chariot, that shit was cray and I've got receipts, but look at what landed."

The car was an old funeral coach that had been converted into a hot rod. The chopped matte black frame was pinstriped in spectral green and on the side service door flamboyant cursive-letters read:

WILL O' THE WISP

Near its chrome grille a couple of decorative black lanterns served as exterior lights, and its wheels were fitted with cloisonné hubcap medallions. Taut strands of rusty barbed wire engirded the roof and a wooden coffin could be seen through a narrow window.

"A speedy meat wagon," Jeremy said while gesturing to the chrome-festooned engine. "That hardcore customizing slaps. Thing's from the fifties or earlier without a trace of rust."

"I guess Rex bought this," Callie said.

"I saw a video about a car just like this," I said. "Not sure about the rust department, but what's really weird is that it appeared right after this farmer had a sighting of a glowing orb like what we just saw. Probably a really convincing hologram with its soap bubble-like tints."

"Shit, is that your more relaxing answer," Jeremy asked with an incredulous smile as if unconvinced that I believed what I just said. "You can kick the tires on this hologram and it leaks tranny fluid –"

"It's just a funny-looking car," Callie interrupted him.

"Wonder who's in the coffin?" I joked.

"Someone dying for a ride," Jeremy said with a toothy smile.

"Maybe you should add comedy to your piano routine," I chided him. "What is this place – some kind of research facility?"

"Zirn is a shore station for something," Callie said.

"Probably for the Silent Service as Mogwan calls those damn chameleons crawling about the island."

"Don't, Jack," Callie uttered as I opened the front door and stuck my head inside to examine the car's showy interior. While checking out the details of the dashboard's gauge bezels, I rubbed my eyes as the instrument panel blurred and began to transition into hyper color displays that I didn't understand. When I glanced up at the windshield, I was surprised to see that the outside surroundings were as visible as if it was noon on a clear sunny day (even brighter and sharper). Oddly enough, the light didn't have any effect on the darkened cabin.

A split-second later, the outline of a dark amber triangle appeared on the driver's side glass and quickly expanded so that it was larger than my head. Within the glowing frame, I was shocked to see a man peering at me through a military grade night vision scope while standing in front of the pastel walls of a small house. In the clear daylight (again, as I perceived the environs), it looked as if he was standing only a few feet in front of the car. I could see moths flitting around a porch light and even hear the pulse of nighttime insects. When I shifted my gaze outside of the triangle's lines there was no one there, but I could make out the house well off in the distance. When I looked back into the triangle, once again the man appeared to be standing right in front of the hot rod's chrome grille. As he lowered the high-powered scope, I recognized him to be the elderly fellow with the prominent chin who was wearing the gold-tinted Cartier sunglasses at the Sutton's estate sale. The same government type that told me about the cipher in *The Beale Papers* and who I later saw wearing his fancy camo-patterned boots in the artificial grotto under the Tempest Bar. Now he was here in Bermy, watching us checking out some futuristic vehicle masquerading as a 1950s street machine. What the fuck!

"Jack, a guard's coming," I heard Callie whisper. "Driving a Twizy."

Looking to the right of the magnifying triangle, I saw a black Renault micro car with its headlights on approaching us from one of the smaller outbuildings.

Jeremy finally had become a Bealiever. The island that we had been 'brought to' was the real-life setting for Bacon's *New Atlantis*, as well as Prospero's enchanted shores. As to Bacon's work, he drew parallels to how everything from a piece of fruit to the color of fabrics one-upped similar items in the travelers' native land ("it's like yours, only better.")

If the ancient treasure had been deposited underwater somewhere nearby, it might have been in the hull of a ship that had been intentionally sunk for that purpose (if it didn't meet with the same fate as numerous other vessels in the Devil's Triangle), or in a specially designed container that was buried "deeper than did ever plummet sound..."

The island contained a military outpost, he further speculated, where the riches of Bacon's utopian 'fiction' were first taken and sorted out. He even thought he had figured out some of the Willy-speak coded messages we had heard. "Strange fish" were the divers that recovered the material and the "monster" mentioned referred to the government scientists that examined the various riddles before the exotic cache was passed on to defense contractors and subsequently integrated into private industry. *Zirn*, as in the "Isle of Zirn", was an Enochian word whose English translation was 'wonders.' "And strange shall be the wonders that are creeping into the new world," he quoted from one of the messages delivered by the angels. "New worlds shall spring from these, New manners: Strange men: The old ways cease, the new begin."

Rounding up the usual suspects from the Elizabethan period, he reminded me that John Dee, who famously had conversations with angels, was one of the leading figures of the secret society and probably responsible for the discoveries of the puzzling artifacts whose original hidden location was revealed during the scrying sessions. Along with the other members of the Lanthorn, Dee had an intense interest in the forbidden knowledge imparted by the rebel Watchers of the biblical Apocrypha, and especially the unimaginable things the pre-deluge figure Enoch witnessed when he walked in the heavens.

The question Jeremy still had was – did the divers find it all, and why had *we* been 'brought' to the Isle of Zirn?

"Violet fingers, black sponges and Chinese hats. What wasn't on that reef?" I laughed over the whipping sails of a passing catamaran while removing my diving fins in the briny silver spray.

"I didn't see a Slippery Dick," Callie replied after taking off her sherbet pink scuba mask. "It's a hermaphrodite," she said while putting on her cute bucket hat. "Born a male, it becomes a female and has to change swimsuits." She looked at me and raised her brows while sticking one of her security blanket cherry suckers into the crooked smile on her pretty face.

"There's been a lot of unexplained things in the Hoodoo Triangle," Jeremy said while stowing way the floating ventilator of his tankless diving system, "but a fish that switches from pink speedos into a skimpy bikini, that's quite a tall tale even for these parts."

The three of us had just finished another diving lesson in the ocean (the third one after our first courses took place in Felicity's infinity pool) and were seated in our dripping neoprene wetsuits on the instructor's glass-bottom boat. The hatch had been opened, giving us an ample view of the colorful marine life in the crystal clear water, which we were told to think of as "a high-def telly on the aquatic channel."

"Your battery-operated buddy system isn't bad for beginners," the dive master said, "but your Bermuda Triangle fish tales need some beefing up if you're planning on telling them around a bonfire with some good ales and zebra mussel pie."

"Something even more scary than a clownfish?" Jeremy asked with exaggerated mock shudders.

"How about Fire Sponges ejecting hot needles into peoples' feet?" Callie chimed in as a couple of shrieking longtails flew over the anchored boat.

"They have the entire ocean but the bastards have to crap on my Bimini top," the instructor said with a disgusted smile while looking up at a couple of sea birds silhouetted against the crimson ball of a sinking sun. "Then they twist the knife by letting you know."

"What about blood red anemones that for some reason quickly evolved," I said while playing the game. "They've developed sharp jagged teeth and first attack a snorkeling charter full of babes in microskins before walking on land and stalking their human prey by moonlight."

"But the remains of feral chickens are found first," Jeremy added. "What was that freaky scraping sound I kept hearing?" he asked the instructor.

"The fish song? That's the sound of herds of parrotfish mobbing the corals and grazing on algae."

"Seriously, though, have you seen some shit down there," I asked him, "like shoals of fish that didn't look right?"

"Not with shoaling, Jack" he replied while staring down at tropical fish darting over delicate branching corals and velvety brownish sponges embedded in the reef on the sea floor, "but with schools of fish. One time, for a few seconds, their glinting shapes suddenly turned an electric emerald-blue or blue-emerald color that pulsed off and on. I don't know what caused this, mate, but I swam away from the flashes lickety-split. And then one time I entered a tunnel – "

"In the ocean?" I asked.

"A tunnel of firmed water."

That night Mogwan and the guy who was among those searching for something of interest at the Indian restaurant last week were the only two seated at the bar. Instead of a dark uniform, the man was casually dressed in a rugby shirt. As I made a couple of shandys for a couple out on the patio, over the strident ethnic instrumentals piped in from Punyaaloka, I could hear everything they were saying:

"We've turned a blind eye in the past as part of the deal that was struck, but this time what's gone missing aren't just baubles for the R&D toy box," the man said while stirring a straight bourbon with his index finger. "One of the blue drippers, we believe, with a special access clearance, removed a paradiser from one of the tanks where those with certain addictions are kept."

"One of the betweeners is missing?" Mogwan asked after sipping his glass of ginger beer.

"An Elxxle-type female."

"How'd someone manage a trick like that?"

"We don't know. In the surveillance footage everything looks honky-dory. All personnel are accounted for. Everyone's doing just what they are supposed to be doing, even the guy that's always picking his nose. Ornamental interfaces, they're easy pickings, so why take an entire body? Accessories, yeah, that I understand."

"Yes, why?"

"She's not exactly dead – not by our standards at least. Even though she's pickled, she smells magnificent. So, she could have been delivered to someone curious about her more desirable attributes – "

"Now see here," Mogwan said while spreading his fingers flat on the polished wood, "what you're implying I find repugnant as well as being a personal affront to Mister Zuffante, so while you have the good fortune to be a guest on these shores, I'll kindly ask you to keep your mind out of the gutter."

"A guest – is that what I am? Perhaps I should take a dip in the pool with a swizzle and charge it on my fancy sand dollar.

God knows, I'd rather be doing that than vacuuming up prey fleeing from bygone salads or keeping track of sensorized earrings plucked from the real housewives of Atlantis while they're vacationing off-world in their own minds. I didn't want to go there. Admittedly, I don't get the concept of *melum* as much as some claim to, but what she exudes – we'll call it glamor – well, something like that might be hard to resist. We think she was smuggled out in one of the delivery vehicles loitering near the beyonder. What SOCOM calls a Black Marlin, but her ass might have been rowed away in a fucking dinghy for all we know. If she was transported wet... hell, either way, like fabled Aphrodite, hopefully she's still in her shell. We've got eyes on the ferry dock. If you should hear or see anything, you know what to do."

"Should anything turn up I'll bloody hell be sure to report it to one of your hyper-enabled goons."

As I walked along the sandy path that twisted to our favorite area at the cove, carrying with me a cooler of beers as Callie requested, she appeared from behind a tree and held a finger to her lips.

"Come look at this," she whispered. "It's right over here. Follow me."

When we reached a certain spot, we ducked behind some foliage that offered an unobstructed view to what she wanted to show me. A short distance away, several uniformed figures were standing near the edge of the sparkling turquoise water, huddled around what looked to be a dead body encased inside a see-through exosuit (personal diving system, although I didn't see a propulsion thruster) that had been placed on the rosy sand. Above this high-tech transparent shell was a column of minute characters like you'd see on a computer screen, though the shifting hyper-colors of the readouts were suspended in mid-air (without a discernible output device).

As I tried to figure out how this effect was achieved, a sandpiper alighted from a confusing pile of rocks and flew right through the visual display. The clear sheathing of the pod also had a few small panels that flickered with peculiar cobalt-blue graphics, and there was what might have been a storage compartment at the bottom of the unit.

I recognized one of the men as the guy I'd seen a couple of times at the bar. As he spoke into a hand-held radio I cocked my head so that I could hear some of what was being said.

"Be advised we've found the missing paradiser and her chart looks good. There are currently no large watercraft in the vicinity so send what's available to the following coordinates before sleeping beauty here wakes up and asks for suntan lotion, over."

"As long as I'm the one doing the rubbing," another guy joked.

On the beach a short distance away were a couple of capsules or 'submarine cars' with twin bubble domes on sleek though oddly shaped frames of a glossy metallic dark emerald color. I hadn't seen any compact (two-person) submersibles like these before, but figured the futuristic-looking things were how the uniformed types transported themselves to the island.

When one of the figures stepped aside, I could make out some of the features of the body within the clear frame. It was a female wearing some kind of shimmery olivine-colored 'skinsuit.' Her complexion was so pale that she looked like an albino, and lengthy snow-white braids were a further indicator of that disorder. The expression on her exquisitely beautiful face as seen through a tear-shaped view-port was one of serene contentment. There was something unusual about her eyes besides their golden-hazel color. They might have been slightly larger than most people's or maybe I got that impression from how strikingly vivid they were.

"Should we start believing in mermaids," Callie asked – maybe a little too loud.

When the men turned in our direction, we quickly slipped away and headed back to her tree house.

"They use the island to test next-generation tech," I told Callie. "Game changing shit. Your mermaid is probably a dummy being used in a prototype for a new landing method for Navy Seals. I've already seen insect-sized drones, changing skins and advanced image intensifiers. It's like the Pineland in North Carolina, and believe me that's not your Isle of Pines. That's what's going on here – it's not what Jeremy thinks."

"What I have has been around a long time."

"That's something else. I don't know if it's an off-world thing, but, if it is, it's used to monitor human activity. In a way – it *is* a living eye. And you can bet the higher-ups would want that if Zuffante opened his mouth."

The moon appeared to be gliding across the mottled sky as I walked out onto the deck of Callie's tree house to check the bottle of shark oil hanging by a nail.

Though the clear golden liquid that was taken from the liver of a puppy shark hadn't turned cloudy – nor was it swirling as an indication of a coming storm – the wind had picked up and was rustling the branches of the aged cedar and surrounding tropical foliage. Hearing another clap of thunder over the incessant whistling of tree frogs, I went back inside.

"So much for Bermudian science. The shark oil is clear even though it looks like we're in for a storm," I said to Callie as she stood in the doorway of the bathroom. "What's wrong?" I asked, seeing the frightened look on her face. "Is that smashed cockroach still running amok?"

She shook her head as a man stepped behind her and put his hand on her shoulder while at the same time letting me see that he was holding the titanium diving knife that she had recently bought. I recognized him as the guy at the bar who paid for his drinks with a QR code on a painted sand dollar. As then, the perspiration that was beaded on his forehead and rolled down his face was tinged blue.

"I don't want to hurt her, but she has something I need," he said with a low and even voice. "The remote for the boat. Not the *Azuria* – for the Iguana."

"That's a push button start, too," I said. "It's on its tracks and ready to go."

"The remote for the ladder and keys to the cabin. Please, don't make me hurt anyone," he repeated, this time almost pleadingly. "Desperate men do desperate things, isn't that right? They set me up with a paradiser I smuggled out of the belly of the whale. They gave me a charge account for Felicity and now they're hunting me," he said while tightening his grip on Callie's shoulder.

"Okay, we want to help you." Instead of trying to make sense out of his rambling, I sought the right words to keep him from getting further agitated. "We're on your side, okay?"

"You don't know what it's like to be inside," he muttered pitifully as the hand brandishing the knife trembled. "But I'll trade you this for the keys – give you the shirt right off my back," he laughed, though it was the tense laughter of someone that had been backed into a corner.

When he stepped slightly to the side of Callie, I saw that he was wearing a silky black short sleeve shirt. There was a picture of a greenish stem of some kind of plant on the front and the fabric looked strange, as if it was suffused with actual moonlight.

"Watch nature's show begin," he said with a proud look. "Those people were some technoids."

With moving imagery that appeared to be integrated into the shirt's dynamic material, a ghostly-white flower with daisy-like petals began to blossom in a time-lapse fashion.

"You smell that?"

When the flower was fully opened, from it came a waft of a sweet fragrance.

"Uh-huh, it's like vanilla. That's cray," I replied with my eyes on the knife.

"It's a night-blooming Cereus that only opens once a year. But this one reopens. Very rare here, but the shirt is even rarer. Mister Zuffante would pay a fortune for it, but you can have it for the keys. And best of all, no water is needed," he said like the last ditch pitch of a used car salesman.

"The keys are in the kitchen drawer, Jack," Callie said. "With the forks and knives."

"Make sure they're for the commuter," the man stressed.

"And when we go down to the beach, there's no need for that," he added with an uneasy smile while gesturing to the folded black umbrella that was leaning against the wall in the corner by the front door.

"You saw the shark barometer," he said as the rumble of thunder got louder. "We're not in for a wet spell just yet," he chuckled awkwardly.

As we walked down some stone steps that led to the beach, I was in front of Callie, with the man holding the knife right behind her. Sea breezes ruffled the low shrubs, but despite the threatening sky there had been no rain. We were headed towards Zuffante's luxurious yacht tender, whose sleek dark grey frame was raised above the sand on smaller rubber caterpillar tracks.

When we reached it, the man used the remote to lower the auto-ladder from the angular transom. Since the amphibious vessel had been already rotated 180 degrees using the built-in all terrain landing gear, it would be easy to escape into the foamy billows that rolled towards the shore.

While facing us with his back against the twin Mercury engines, he pointed the knife at Callie.

"Again, I apologize for putting you both through this. They left me no choice after I delivered on my end of the bargain. But to me a deal's a deal so here's your shirt," he said while pulling it off with the slightest tug and dropping it in the sand.

When he stepped onto the ladder, there was a loud, sharp squawk. Thinking this was an alarm on the boat's electric door, I grabbed Callie by the arm and pulled her towards me. Seeing the look of sheer terror on the man's face, I turned to see what his gaze was riveted on. It was a bird with a large bill and glowing amber-yellow eyes that was perched on a nearby bush. Its intense glare was fixed on the man who stood frozen on the ladder.

"It's not an alarm," I said. "Just a bird. The X100's easy to operate. Use the land drive and go."

As the man continued to stare at the bird, its eyes flared while peering over its lengthy bill. That's when I noticed that they appeared to be strangely self-luminous as opposed to merely being reflected beams of light from the moon riding through the cloudy sky.

"It's a night heron," he informed me, "that's been extinct from the time of the first settlements. It used to be a delicacy here… that species of a night hunter. Take the shirt with the lunar flower," he said with a sense of despair in his voice, "and remember you don't need to water it."

Like a target in the crosshairs of a rifle, he slowly stepped down from the ladder and tossed the knife away before lying on the sand in a prone position. As he did so, his expression was one of utter hopelessness. He remained that way as a couple of uniformed figures approached. Both of them had broad, unfriendly faces.

After closing time, while in the confined storage space directly under the bar, I was repositioning a few sealed jars of loquat syrup (that I was planning to use for a cordial) when I noticed the knob of a sliding panel that was flush against the wall. When I pushed it along its squeaky track, a transparent pane appeared that offered a partial view of an adjoining spacious room that I didn't know existed. As I peered through the glass, I saw that something quite strange was happening in the dimly lit chamber.

Against a series of large canvas backdrops that contained colorful cartoonish imagery lifted right off the pages of Jeremy's vintage freak comix (panels depicting the adventures of the hippie armadillos on the Louisiana bayou), a couple of darkly robed figures were seated within the bluish circle of gelled alcohol lamps. Judging by the complex diagrams that had been painted onto the floor at the cardinal points, they were engaged in a magical working.

The gazes of their pale faces were focused intently on a large black mirror that was angled slightly upward. Suspended above this was an illustration of the sparkling 'party star' from the underground comix, whose title *JEET* was concealed (or revealed) by entoptic dots.

As I continued to observe whatever was happening, flurries of iridescent specks began to settle and accumulate on the mirror's polished surface. Like pieces of a jigsaw puzzle, gradually an image took shape from the glittering particles. When the mirror was completely coated by the variegated deposits, I was surprised to see that what had manifested as a result of the magical operation turned out to be a ridiculous-looking armadillo (the main character from the comix) whose features spiked in intensity as it scratched around its marshy surroundings with motions like a flash card animation effect. From a 'pocket' in its grey scutes, the critter pulled out a leather case with a tin star badge affixed to it.

When the robed figures stood up and slowly approached the vibrant activity in the mirror, baffled by what I had just seen, I quietly shut the panel of the hidden window.

There was only one table of people left in the bar after Jeremy finished another one of his of outsider jazz performances and they were having 'one for the road', which was fine by me as I was tired from diving all day. As I was hanging some clean glasses on the stemware rack, a man's voice startled me:

"Ahoy there, mind if I drop anchor here?"

When I turned around I saw the man who had interrogated me at Royalene's. He was wearing the same dark suit and black straw fedora.

"Look what the trade winds blew in," I said with a wary smile.

"Nice of you to relocate just so I could have a Gosling's Black. The dew of the still-vex'd Bermoothes as someone once said."

"I can pour that, but if you're planning on leaving a tip, I'd prefer a hog penny over the Monopoly twenty."

"Actually, make it a Brandy Old Fashioned. I hear there was some excitement the other night. So much for any delicate Ariel flitting about on this enchanted isle," he said with a short laugh. "I guess that bird had some Stymphalian in it. One peck from its beak and a person's kaput. Synthetic neutrality is fine until facial recognition enters into the equation."

"So, what do you want to know this time? I assure you I didn't see any dead mermaids."

"Who said she was dead?" he said while boring his eyes into me. "More than a few thinkabouts show up here, but you should probably return that shirt that you can't figure out how to button up. Better yet, wear it to the party you're working at Mister Zuffante's villa tonight."

"Tonight? That's news to me," I said with my back turned while shaking drops of bitters into a glass of brandy and club soda. "I'm about ready for bed."

When I turned to set the drink down, a different person reached for it. The man with the black straw fedora was gone, and in his place was the elderly spook with gold mirror shades. As before, his starched dark dress shirt exuded a subtle though distinctive aroma with aseptic vanilla tones.

Seeing frosted chandeliers hanging above a billiards table behind him, I was shocked to realize that I was no longer at the resort, but was standing behind a well-stocked residential bar in a spacious room with antique furniture and luxurious accents.

Italian prints in expensive frames that were similar to those at Felicity led me to believe that I had been taken to Zuffante's villa. As to how this seamless transition was achieved, my initial thought was that I had either been drugged or hypnotized, but with all the bizarro stuff I'd seen on the island, I couldn't rule out anything.

"I'm sure you can make a Stormy and Swizzle in your sleep, Jack, but let's see how you fared with my Old Fashioned?" the man said with an abrasive timbre but disarming smile. "Not bad, son," he nodded after taking a sip.

"How'd I get here?" I asked while checking to see if I had a bump on my head. Surprisingly, I felt extremely alert and focused. Also, there was a tingling sensation in my hands and feet.

"It's probably easier to just assume you're dreaming. You might recall the young Addison speaking through elderly Addison telling you at that country store that I was going to tell you something about the strange fish. I'm Kelby, the guy with the Cartier shades as you've referred to me in the past. Anyway, I like your shirt."

When I looked down, I saw that I was wearing the shirt with the greenish stem of the night-blooming flower (that evidently withered and became detached since it last blossomed).

"Seems you have a new friend that's trying to tell you something about itself that's of great interest to others," he said before taking another drink. "That's why you're here, but more about that later. I also know about the girl's precious family heirloom. The widget or *Anunna* device as it's called is a great documenter, maybe the source of the Akashic records, though sometimes things can get a little confusing, like when someone else's memories get mixed up with one's own recollections. We don't know why this happens – only that it does – and hope we might be able to use these shared experiences to our advantage. Did you ever have a questionable memory during your brief possession of the device after I assume you dug it up while detecting for coins? Callie was always hiding the thing from the searchers... as its possessors feel compelled to do."

The part about me finding Callie's doojigger was news to me, but what he said about shared memories was something I could relate to. In particular there was the stranger I had met when I was a little kid who was searching for traces of sunken Atlantis in the composition of the mortar applied to bricks used to build the town library. Recently I had begun to doubt this actually happened, even though my recollection of the event seemed perfectly clear.

"Speaking of these searchers, or collectors that the military calls Fast-walkers, evidently they were designed to gather up the few *Anunna* widgets that remained on the Earth and return them to their rightful owners... whoever that might be. They're essentially useless in that capacity, though, because the things were hacked millennia ago by those that managed to obtain the much sought after rarities. The chaser is right up your alley – a glorified detector platform with a high-sensitivity discrimination mode, though, like I said, programs in the devices they're after were breached by pre-deluge geeks. After making the jump from deep space, it rejects the fucking target due to manipulated code. Sort of like bit flip errors. My understanding is that the Air Force managed to capture one of the flying piggy banks and smash it open in the 1960s. Among the scraps of unusual alloys inside was a blank coin that they almost tossed in the trash along with the other bits and pieces. Other than being a historical treasure, the device was a real headache, until the twidges figured out some of its extraordinary features. I'll dilate on that later. As for the Fast-walker itself, last I heard they'd pretty much given up hope of reverse-engineering the damn thing, though they still fiddle with it every few years."

"Are you the only guest at this party?" I asked. "If so, how much longer do I have to stay here?"

"I'd imagine there are all kinds of things you'd like to ask me."

"Well, yeah, sure, but will I remember anything?"

"With perfect clarity, Jack."

"Bacon and the Shakespeare Group – it sounds cray, but did they speak with angels?"

"You mean like those depicted in Byzantine mosaics? Well, the images at least attempt to recall the aura of splendor of an extremely ancient super-advanced civilization whose toilets occasionally backed up. Have you heard about these new digital services that send pre-recorded messages to chosen family members after a loved one has died?"

"Yes, it's a smartphone app."

"In a similar manner, angelic technicians installed… divine anticipations. Left behind a virtual presence that has an uncanny ability to grasp and process questions from those who seek guidance. Equally impressive is how those summoned are able to instruct succeeding generations to translate the answers given in their native tongue into what were nonexistent languages at the time the responses were initiated. And, yes, the time capsule can still be accessed via a scrying zone. To give you an example, my occultist friends recently placed an Enochian Call via an obsidian sphere to order a pizza to be delivered to their home –"

"Oh, come on. That's cray."

"The ancients called this spirit they contacted Obelisong, meaning 'a pleasant deliverer.' For toppings they wanted sausage and olives, but no anchovies. The reply from Obelisong was to 'prepare a circle with a garment all bloody with the heads of scorpions', which it spoke to them in the angelic language. It then repeated the word, *fiteer*, which my friends found out wasn't Enochian, but referred to a layered flat bread pie that the Egyptians of the Old Kingdom enjoyed. Before fading away, the angel advised my friends to 'let them who understand serve you.' Pretty, good, right?"

"Okay."

"Had the maid of the person who found Dee's diaries inside a secret drawer in a chest many years after his death not used half of the pages as sheets to cool freshly-baked pies, they might have had better luck with their order. Anyway, as for Dee and others trafficking with spirits – those invoked being essentially a perplexing residuum – some were helpful, others not so much."

At that moment the Siamese cat jumped into a tufted velvet armchair with a gilded finish.

"This party's getting wild," I joked. "Look what just showed up."

"She was a stowaway in the hot rod when it was shipped here from the station in Mfkzt."

Once settled in, the cat's eyes twinkled in the glow of lamps with mauve lace shades.

"I've known Zuzulia for over fifty years," Kelby said matter-of-factly, "but she's probably much older than that. Obviously she wasn't fed the unhealthy shit in processed cat food."

"I heard she doesn't eat anything. Okay, here's another one. Is there anything to Bacon's items being stashed away in some secret vault?"

"I thought you might ask me that. The Shakespeare Group left clues of treasure placed in a secure vault in lots of places, including a book of emblems by one of the members of Bacon's secret society. A clue is given in one that was intentionally printed upside-down in a few copies only. This shows an equal-sided cube enveloped with radiant light shining from above" – he emphasized the word 'above' – "that's apparently suspended above the churchyard at Bruton Parish. Was it necessary to conceive of a city block in old Williamsburg and then construct it a century and a half later to draw attention to this? Apparently, someone thought it was. The emblem contains the location of a small-scale replica of a structure that's hidden a certain amount of fathoms below. Any valuables inside the Bruton vault – including a certain curiosity of seemingly no worth – disappeared after a tunnel was dug as part of the Underground Railroad for escaping slaves. It's used for a silly ghost tour now."

"So, how do the Beale Papers fit in?"

"Did you ever find the daleth hidden within the Gillogy Strings – the Phoenician letter shaped like a triangle?"

"Not yet, but there's –"

"Just as the Operative Masons of old left behind impressive monuments that attest to their building skills, a Speculative Mason devised a puzzle of similar complexity and magnificence. When solved, it reveals a Masonic allegory, as well as the location of an ancient structure whose unique physical properties render it just as invisible as the code concealed in *The Beale Papers*. Like the famous Temple of Solomon, the structure was prepared without the usual building tools. There was no noise of hammers as it was assembled by unseen hands."

"My friend Jeremy told me about the *Shamir* that was used."

"Keep in mind the Temple itself is an expression of human anatomy, with one of the chambers representing the brain."

At that moment a sweet fragrance filled the air.

"Don't look now," Kelby said, "but the night-blooming flower on that spiffy shirt just opened."

When I looked down, I saw that an array of white petals were clearly visible as the bloom had fully opened. Before I could say anything, a three-dimensional delicate female hand complete with a swirling nacreous lacquer on long fingernails appeared in the fabric's synthetic moonlight and reached down to pluck the flower, leaving behind broad leaves and a drooping stem.

"Not to worry," Kelby chuckled, "I've an even more interesting plant to show you — one not pollinated by a fucking moth. We'll take my golf cart."

The man with the fancy oxblood leather boots took me to a nearby greenhouse that contained a large hydroponic chamber in which an espaliered tree was bathed with a peculiar orange glow. On its trellised branches was an unrecognizable species of fruit that resembled a small apple with glossy bluish-purple skin.

"A similar piece of fruit contained the DNA that a team of geneticists used to create Ultra-1, whom we believe to be a link to the first wave of Earthly civilization — "

"How's that even possible?"

"It's possible to splice its junk sequences with different code, but that's another story. Your friend that showed you that navigable contrivance — one of its childhood toys — is more down-to-earth than you might think — "

"Friend that I've never met —"

"Try as we might, we are unable to grow additional fruit that contains the hyper-tellurian's stamp using the seeds from the original find. Even with water that contains special minerals transported from a certain region in the south of France. In case you're wondering, the original espalier fruit was found growing in an abandoned nursery module of unknown origin that was accessed by what we came to realize was a biometric key contained in an *Anunna* widget similar to the girl's."

"What's it called? The fruit?"

"A blurple. It doesn't have the heredity info we're after, but all's not lost. The damn thing tastes great. Better than anything you'll find in the local produce section. Here, take a bite."

When he pulled one of the espaliered fruits from a cluster of leaves, a vegetative perfume tickled my nose in the sterilized chamber. After he handed it to me, I stared at it for a while before hesitantly taking a small bite. The delicate texture of its cerulean flesh was odd, but quickly surges of intense, exotic flavors flooded my brain. It was strangely delicious, with surprising nuances that lingered on my tongue.

"Tasty, isn't it? Like something right out of Bacon's *New Atlantis.*"

"The juice would be great in a rum cocktail," I said while licking my tingling lips.

"I'm sure it would be."

"So what that girl in the video said was true," I said after swallowing the bite I took from the fruit.

"Zyla, being her real name, was also puzzled by the surviving fragments of the Babylonian historian, Berossus, where our cultural exemplars were depicted as being repulsive amphibious creatures. Maybe he saw images of the betweeners wearing some kind of aquatic suits. That or they presented themselves in an afflicted mirror scenario, meaning they disguised their true appearance by utilizing their uncanny mental powers. This is a form of cloaking that's far superior to our most advanced digies. They could look like anything I suppose, even the hideous Annedoti of Berossus' account. We only refer to Ultra-1 as a strange fish because of its current habitation module. She's on the island – Ultra-1's surrogate mother is. You've seen Zyla about. Okay, there's something else I want to show you, but it's back at the resort."

"Are you sure I'll remember this?"

"Every last detail, Jack."

"This is the lodge room of Adoniramite Freemasonry," Kelby said as we walked across a chequered floor that was surrounded by a tessellated border. We were in the spacious room that I had seen earlier through the hidden window in the storage area under the bar.

"Those who for countless generations preserved and nurtured the fruit containing the inserted code before the science was rediscovered."

We paused in front of a series of Masonic tracing boards on pedestals that contained painted illustrations of gardens surrounded by abstruse symbols. The one in the center showed an espaliered tree with blue apples that had a serpent coiled around its vertical trunk.

"We are temporarily borrowing the space with the Admiral's blessing. As you can see, most of the emblems are nautical, inspired by fanciful legends that included a voyage to Felicity," he said while pointing to decorative furnishings that included nautical-themed altar banners that were unique to the Adoniramite Rite. Seeing the horticultural motifs on ceremonial regalia draped over the back of chairs, I recalled the pendant of the golden trowel that Mogwan always wore on the lapel of his blue suits. He must be one of the members, I thought.

"The ceremonies held here are a curiosity to more orthodox systems – those that aren't spoken or written about, even in allegory," Kelby said.

As we proceeded into another section of the Lodge, all around us were large canvas backdrops that contained the cartoonish imagery taken from the panels of Jeremy's freak comix.

"Be careful not to contaminate anything that might still be charged," Kelby said as he stepped around a brightly painted protective circle and complex magical diagrams that were encircled by extinguished gelled alcohol lamps.

"Those engaged in an operation here are a valuable asset to the team. Highly qualified experimental magicians that were given a difficult assignment. There isn't a shadowy association – I've known the two for a long time and you've met one of them, albeit as a youngster captured by the widget. Few have the esoteric know-how for this, but they live in a world most people are completely unaware of. The techniques employed for the Working involve a dangerous species of Atlantean magic.

"What are they doing?"

"Attempting to affect a unique perichoresis. The idea is for the MagiZoths to enter a fictional work, in this case, an underground comix from the 1960s, so as to participate in the story with hopes of gaining intel – what I would call back-channel chatter... things that the creator of the work might have kept to himself. If I've lost you," he said after seeing my puzzled expression, "it's understandable. It's beyond rocket science, what they do. Essentially, they traverse through byways in the psychosphere that provide access to oblique neural regions. The *Shamir* they generate for this purpose is specially calibrated to penetrate what they call Nightside gates that are normally sealed–off, anatomically speaking, to prevent such trespassing in another's mind-stream. Along the way they have to deal with all kinds of phantasmata, and often there are no escape routes. It's about mental commos, Jack."

I'd heard some of this stuff before when Jeremy tried to explain the purpose of the *Shamir*, but his interpretation seemed so out there that I thought it was the lunacy of some obscure vodou cult. After hearing what Kebly just said, I couldn't help but wonder if he had actually tapped into the mind-stream of some archaic magical tradition. We've already learned that the principle character in the comix – "

"The armadillo?"

"Yes, Darby was a narc, which was probably only revealed on the last page that for some reason was removed from all copies –"

"What's that mean?"

"It means that it had a badge... that Darby was the fuzz, an undercover drug agent that was probably going to bust all the members of a hippy commune – the jumping Cajun frogs and flying silver carp – that planned to hang loose in a 60s stoner's paradise. It was going to be a bummer," he said while gesturing to the glittering "party star" that hung above the angled black mirror.

"So, it spoils the party. What's the big deal?"

"The big deal is with the comix's creator, Grumble's brother Grayson, and what he knew. We don't know why he removed the last page. Maybe he was going to do further issues... keep the comix going and didn't want to blow Darby's cover. Or, maybe the badge is a warning of sorts. Something to do with deceit. There's a parallel with the funny adventures of the goofy fucks that populate the cartoon strip world that's of greater significance in the world we humans populate. With this in mind, before proceeding with the plan, we're hoping that by using the same magical approach we can learn more about the subject at hand. Namely, is our gift of Ultra-1 really a gift? Okay, there's one more thing, though

I wasn't planning to show it to you just yet. It's what all of this is really about."

Behind one of the backdrops was a dimly lit slab of stone (stela) that bore variegated scenes of ancient Egyptian funerary customs in the gloomy, tenebrous shades of the underworld. Above the badly chipped hieroglyphic text, faded ochers on the buff-colored surface showed a jackal-headed deity overseeing the Judgment of the Soul by the weighing of a heart against an ostrich feather on balancing scales.

"This concerns a different kind of code," Kelby said. "A moral code. Cosmic harmony, Jack. After protracted study, we've concluded that the Rite of the Judgment of the Soul by the ancient Egyptians was a corruption of a more advanced process... a process for the benefit of the living, and not the dead. We know it wasn't the heart that recorded one's deeds and decided who was worthy of paradise."

"Why are you telling me this?"

"Ask the girl if there's anything she hasn't told you concerning Grumble's Star."

"Wake up, sleepy head. We get certified for open water today," Callie said as I blinked my eyes in the bright sunlight that poured through a window in my bungalow. She was holding a plate with a couple of scones while sitting on the edge of the bed. "A vegan scone with pepper jelly will get you going," she said while lighting a demi-slim.

"There's walnut bread when the scones are gone," I mumbled as a way of correcting her pronunciation like Mogwan had taught me.

"I was having a dream about your family," I said while rubbing the sleep out of my eyes. "How did your mother and Mister Zuffante meet?"

"At a charity event. Mom and her sisters – her other sisters – were members of a society. She was a female Mason."

"Did she wear a pin of a gardener's tool?"

"Yeah, on her gown. How'd you know?"

"Is there something you might have forgot to tell me about this star of Grumble's?"

"Did I tell you that after he died, some men from the government asked his brother about it? Grayson didn't have much to tell them. Only that it didn't look like a regular star in the night sky."

CHAPTER IX
PSYCHOSTASIA

"Behold, Behold Lo, behold,
my mighty power consisteth in this.
Learn wisdom by my words.
This is wrought for thy erudition,
what I instruct thee from God:
Lock unto thy charge truly.
Thou art yet dead: Thou shalt be revived."

Quartus Liber Mysteriorum (1582)

"We will not let thee enter in by us,"
say the bolts of this door,
unless thou speakest our Name.

Ritual of the Mystery of the Judgement of the Soul
From an ancient Egyptian papyrus
translated by Marcus W. Blackden

"You can go to heaven if you want.
I'd rather stay in Bermuda."

Mark Twain

A booming crash of thunder rattled the glasses and bottles behind the bar as I prepared Mogwan's noon tea. While doing so,
I couldn't help but listen to the raised voices of a couple of people
standing at the entrance to Punyaaloka. One was the attractive Bengali Indian lady owner of the restaurant, with the other

being a clean-shaven man with wireframe glasses that I hadn't seen before. He appeared to be in his late 60s and was wearing green cargo shorts and a purple tee shirt that read:

ALLOW ME TO REINTRODUCE MYSELF

"I liked you better when you peed your pants every time you thought a black umbrella was about to be opened," the woman in the floral-printed sari uttered.

That's because I've been in a fucking beyonder for who knows how long and know how to find the innershine. That's why I'm on the team. I can find innershine, even without my living eye tattoo, which is now blind because I allowed them to remove it. To cut it from my flesh with their scalpel, Aaloka!" he shouted while holding one of his palms up to her face. "Just like Addison's is now blind – "

"How could we know that would happen? Until we told you, you thought it was just a Cracker Jack prize."

"There are lots of things that happen in there that they don't know about, so I hope they're prepared for surprises like those unseeable doors popping open at any given time.

I'll bet those expanding black spots have your friends whizzing in their Bermuda shorts," he said before walking away from her and heading towards the patio.

"Those two are rumbling louder than the storm," Mogwan chuckled while lifting a starched white napkin as I filled his cup.

"Who is that guy?"

"He was the one who found that specimen of fruit you can't stop talking about, even though he wasn't looking for it. At the time he was skeptical of the whole business. That's because he had some issues with his memory – amnesia that was intentionally induced, I should add, by someone closer to the top of the hierarchy status than us. Someone who was obviously conflicted by the potential of modern biosciences as a means to discovering the ladder of divine ascent. Before this impenetrable haze caused by deep psychological manipulation, he was a genuine believer of 'ye are gods in potential.' Had an outstanding resume. Now, he's back in the loop for humanity-plus."

"You're talking about Ultra-1."

"Something right out of the genetic junkyard," he muttered after slurping his tea.

Just then a man that I recognized from the Pharos Club walked up. It was the film director with the landing-strip goatee and black circle glasses.

"Might you be Mogwan?" he asked.

"That's me."

"Ciao, I'm Julian, the director from Paragon Makings – here for the screening. I've been fascinated by the legend of the existence of the movie since first reading about it in a back issue of *Cinefantastique* magazine. That the government funded it just in case the footage they were trying to keep under wraps ever surfaced – to muddy the waters, as it were. I thought this was a clever gimmick by the producer. Per contra, why was it never released, even all these years later? Natch, I also can't wait to hear your famous whistling frogs."

"I'm not an aficionado of lost films," Mogwan said, "but Mister Zuffante has obtained a clip that's of suitable clarity to be included for the remake."

"If legit, it will make it." Julian said. "Send Tinseltown astir. You really are a bartender," he said to me. "Have you got a Pellegrino behind that stunning demilume?"

"I've got Vichy Catalan and WhiteHeaven from India. I steep Mogwan's Golden Tips in that."

"Let me have a Vichy. I'm trying to lower my triglyceride levels."

At that moment Jeremy walked in with the pretty girl with the stylish bob and pearl bangs. Zyla, being her real name, had on a sleeveless sparkly bodysuit that exposed to view her glowing tattoo.

Once she was seated at a table, Jeremy approached the bar.

"Jack, can I get a couple of Barritts, but first, if you have a second, can we talk?"

Because his tone sounded serious, after giving Julian his mineral water, I stepped away from the bar and motioned Jeremy to a corner in the room.

"What's up, bruh?" I asked.

"I had a lucid dream about the Willy-speak guy. We talked about Shakespeare's enchanting swansong, when Prospero spoke in *The Tempest* about all the actors melting away into thin air. How, instead of being a dramatic farewell to the theater stage by the playwright, he could have been alluding to a machine-system that dissolves people – "

"What?"

"I'm ready for a different kind of dream – one as substantial, or insubstantial, as this illusion. Want to experience something new – instead of the same old Farb Burger," he smiled. "I want to seize the moment, Jack – take a chance in the judgment seat and hope for a super ruling."

"Fuck are you talking about? Do you need a sugar fix?"

"I want out," I told Callie as she frantically opened kitchen drawers and cabinets inside her luxury treehouse. "I think we should both go back to Virginia. It's only 600 miles to North Carolina. Hell, I'd make the trip in a raft to get away from the cult on this isle. Maybe try to sell comet insurance when I get back."

"That's not what's going on here – Felicity isn't a cult."

"Jeremy's got ideas in his head that are even more cray than his Vodou stuff. Shit about getting beamed up to the world beyond or the Promised Land or whatever it is."

"Paradise."

I threw up my arms as if she had just made my point.

"Does that sound familiar to any cults you've heard about? I still haven't seen Zuffante. How do we know he even exists? What – is our leader supposed to be some god?"

The Siamese cat jumped up on the counter and went to see what Callie was looking for.

"And that cat gives me the creeps. Have you seen it eat yet?"

"It catches those lizards whose tails come off, but it doesn't want to eat them."

"What are you looking for?" I asked as she rifled through the contents in a drawer.

"A sucker."

"A sucker? Well, here I am – a sucker for coming here."

"A cherry one," she said softly while making a sad face. "Mister Zuffant and I have been working to get Grumble's Star to appear."

"Well, thanks for telling me that. What else don't I know?"

"His brother Grayson said it was exploded like he wrote in a letter that I read."

"Exploded?"

"Not like that. When he somehow brought it into better focus, it had different parts or sections like one of those diagrams that come with instructions for a gadget."

"You mean like an exploded view? Like a schematic diagram?"

"Yeah. Different parts."

After she told me this, I walked out onto the deck with the sweeping views of the beach and sat down in one of the rattan peacock chairs.

As I took in the seashore bouquet and incessant birdsong, something clicked. One of the more puzzling 'we haves' in the list of inventions in Bacon's *New Atlantis* was that they had the means of "seeing things that were near as being afar off." Was this a projection of imagery displayed against the 'screen' of the nighttime (or daytime) sky, and if so, was Grumble's Star a graphic representation of something beamed from the *Anunna* device? Along with Jeremy's line of thinking, perhaps it was a large mariner's chart that revealed the position of a secret location (that was only perceived by those tuned in to the thing). A point more specific to that concealed in the 'Locality Cipher' of *The Beale Papers*. Was the "party star" in Grayson's comix something that could be reached by using the instructions in the display? I now wanted to see that fucker for myself.

Those of us who were invited to view the footage were reclined in plush velvet seats in Felicity's private movie theater. The list included Callie, Jeremy and myself, along with Kelby, Zerrill (the guy who had the heated exchange with the Bengali lady) and Julian.

"This spool was found by a collector of vintage projectors in a shop full of optical junk called The Persistence of Vision," Mogwan said. "It was shot with an old Arriflex 16-millimeter camera."

When he switched on the projector, a grainy, scratchy underwater scene appeared on the screen. Swarms of colorful tropical fish were moving in a synchronized manner that when looked at more closely didn't seem natural. When the entire aggregation suddenly vanished, as if some high-resolution holographic display had been switched off, a large cube-shaped structure loomed in the nearby depths. Behind vertical viewing panes on its reflective surface, several indistinct figures could be seen for a few seconds before the schooling mass reappeared. The anomalous behavior of the vibrant cluster and mysterious edifice were just as Baldy had recently described to me.

"That's what I colored," Callie said.

"A drum heard from afar," Jeremy added.

The next shot was of one of the divers (who I assumed was Baldy) equipped with 1960s-era gear that included a bulky pistol-grip diving light. After this, the clip abruptly ended.

"We can reduce a lot of the distracting scratches with a noise filter," Julian said, "to enhance the glitchy holographic projection cloaking the alien super-structure."

"We don't want it to look like a mock-up when we're promoting the original ektachrome stock," Mogwan replied. "I'm afraid that's all there is, but the diver will share his impressions when he shows up as an adviser."

After Julian and Zerrill were ushered from the theater, Mogwan began setting up another film clip.

"Don't tell our director that I borrowed part of the plot from a rejected 1960s B-movie script," Kelby chuckled gruffly. "Okay, with apologies to Julian, whose unbridled exuberance will be the true distraction, this digital transfer from the same reel is for your eyes only. I hope I don't need to repeat that," he added while giving us a stern look. "Roll the film."

In the footage Baldy could be seen with much greater clarity (I also noticed that all of the scratches had been removed) while in close proximity to the coruscating assemblage. When he reached out to touch one of the life-like fish, amazingly, not only did it respond to his poking at it, he was actually able to grasp the agitated creature and pull it away from its complex virtual environment. While doing so, there was a series of freeze-frames that isolated his hand and zoomed in to such a degree that I could read the time on his vintage Zodiac SeaWolf watch.

"How about that. When in sharp focus you can see that the wiggly fella responds to touch within the lightfield. Not only does the holographic platform have polarizing properties – it's a physically interactive system. Now, if only one could fry the catch in canola oil. The reason for showing you this is that there is technology of a highly advanced nature inside the structure that the brain has trouble processing. At first I couldn't fathom certain things, but have since assimilated what I was witness to and come to appreciate such ingenuity."

"What he's saying is – prepare to be gob-smacked," Mogwan chimed in.

When the screen went black and the lights came on, Kelby looked each of us straight in the eye.

"You're all going to have strange dreams. There's a lot to absorb, but these classes should help once inside the beyonder, as I refer to the cuboid where your friend is being kept, and enable you to avoid any technical devilry."

Callie, Jeremy and I were seated in high-backed chairs in the library of the Masonic Lodge room in the converted basement of the resort. Along with a tingling sensation coursing through my body, I felt strangely weighed down, like I was sinking further into the red velvet cushion of the antique oak chair.

After taking a sip of his coffee, Kelby continued with his first lesson:

"As to who printed the structure using the exotic materials that account for its novel physical properties, we refer to this higher culture as humanity-plus. To explain their presence, let's consider the theory of panspermia siblings, in which microbes from the same stellar nursery were scattered like the florets of a dandelion and managed to survive their long journey through space. One of these hurtling rocks impacted with the Earth eons ago. If we can accept that this happened, further imagine that over time these migrating lifeforms evolved. Meanwhile, beings that had previously evolved from a spark in the same molecular cloud were intrigued enough by the spectrum of our parent sun to launch an expedition here. What they found were semi-humans with similar DNA, and they took the finest specimens of the most evolved of them back to their home world. While in captivity, over time, they made some tweaks, and at some point in the remote past, due to the result of their genetic manipulations, with or without assistance from something else, these improved upon beings that originated here returned, where they were worshipped as gods or intermediaries of the gods at the dawn of civilization. In this scenario the ancient astronaut theorists have it wrong. It wasn't aliens who gave us a nudge. Who or whatever *they* are – also our astro-biological cousins, I suppose – remain in the shadows, unseen. It was their tailor-made creations that we can thank for our elevated intelligence. While on the planet, these demi-gods with their boosted genetics had a tendency to get cranky with their recent creations – those of us still standing on a lower rung on the ladder of ascent. To get away from the terrestrial rabble – again, those who they, in turn, genetically tampered with – the demi-gods and their sidekicks – though the angels might not appreciate this term – escaped to restricted zones that we regular Earthfolk called paradise before withdrawing from the planet permanently. To date, we've discovered a few of these long-abandoned structures, some of a hyperstealth nature. Okay, one – we've evolving hominids spacenapped from the Earth and improved upon by their abductors. Two – they eventually returned to their place of origin, which was the Earth. Three – they did a few DNA edits of their own to us while here. Four – at some point they decided to vacate the Earth – maybe they didn't like the barbaric company – leaving behind traces of their mysterious presence, some more tangible than others, as you'll soon see."

As the pressed down feeling continued until I felt as if my weight had doubled, in glancing at the others for signs that they had been hypnotized or had their minds tampered with in some way, neither of their eyes were glazed over and the facial muscles of both appeared to be relaxed as they remained absorbed by what Kelby was saying.

On a large screen hanging above him there appeared a series of numbers that I immediately recognized as one of the cipher texts whose seemingly justified rows and columns filled a page from *The Beale Papers*.

"This isn't a test for corrective lenses," Kelby said, "but I want you to focus on the layout."

In the next projection the same numbers were placed on a grid. The peculiar line spacing between the original field of numbers – one of the odd features in the Beale cipher – had been darkened so that the 'blanks' formed a zigzag pattern that resembled a matrix barcode similar to one of those scannable digital menu cards one sees in restaurants.

"Now we'll shift the numbers onto a grid and shade in the blocks between them. The seemingly unnecessary spaces were part of the encryption mode and decoding process. This explains the odd typesetting painstakingly devised by the creator of the algorithm. The additional spaces were quite intentional and, as you can see, the resulting pattern looks like an optical label. Focus your gaze on the surrounding design… that arranged on the grid."

Were these slight adjustments part of another puzzle embedded into the original cryptogram? If so, the cipher (or sub-ciphers) in *The Beale Papers* were far more complex than I would have imagined.

"An optical label with stored data," Kelby added, "that's readable… by the human brain. Is this what was meant by 'a charm attended it'."

The pattern seen between the numbers on the grid he pointed to went fuzzy for a second. What appeared in its place was a remarkably vivid image of an ancient galley resting on the ocean floor. Other than a considerable gash in its long narrow hull, a twisted and splintered bank of oars and broken masthead, the warship from classical antiquity was intact. Even the elongated eye painted near a gleaming rostrum on the bow hadn't faded with time – the red and yellow pigments in a concentric design representing the iris still appearing vibrant in the limpid depths.

The complete lack of marine growth on its wooden shell was puzzling because the details were in high-definition. Being that the shipwreck was so well preserved, and with the various artifacts (such as amphorae) strewn on the seabed, why hadn't there been a salvage effort?

When I took my eyes off the screen, the colorful image persisted in my head. Only now, several tropical fish came into frame with rapid, darting motions. That's when I noticed that the backdrop to the Phoenician galley's watery grave was a large cube-like structure whose surface of glassy metallic tiles radiated a shimmering bluish energy.

"Is the hidden message coherent enough, Jack? Jeremy, is that clear to your eyes?" Kelby chuckled. "I guess we pesky humans were getting too close to one of their sanctuaries during our maritime activities of the time. This explains the artificial reef that cloaked one of their paradises. Those same fish have been there for a long time. Maybe that's why this Beale fellow, or whoever he was, never talked about his antecedents."

That what I was seeing in living color had been encoded on an old piece of paper and scanned by my eyes seemed impossible. Someone had to be monkeying with my brain.

"When we're taken inside and given a little tour of the place," Kelby said, "I want you to notice the black dots. Walk into one of these and you might not walk back. Zerrill can tell you about getting sucked into these fuckers."

"Let me know when you've had enough," I said to Callie as we walked down an empty hallway in the lower level of the resort.

"If my doojigger can do what it does, you should be able to believe what you've been seeing, no matter how cray it may seem," she said. "It's just more of the same angels' stuff. Now, I know I left my cigs in that room. When I locate them, we can go to the beach and chillax."

When Callie opened a door, we were both surprised to see Kelby standing behind a couple of figures seated in front of numerous video monitors.

"I thought we might have problems with the two of you opening doors that ought not to be." He shook his head with a faint trace of a smile.

"Sorry, Jack forgot something and thought this was the conference room," Callie said.

"Hello there, Callie!" one of the seated figures uttered after he turned his head.

"Hey, it's my favorite person from Pharos," Callie said excitedly. "Jack, this is Dal from ULTRAFX. Dal is responsible for the real-time CGI compositing you saw."

"I liked my render," I said while reaching out to shake the hand of her tech-savvy friend, "even though the beer I was drinking probably wasn't as good as the actual beer I was drinking."

"Who knows," Kelby said, "the render might have preferred its suds. And this is my partner from ex-Task Force Black," he added while pointing to the other guy.

As his partner nodded curtly, I recognized him as the man who was always dressed in black and was very selective about his potato crisps.

"Yeah, ahoy there," I said while nodding back somewhat reluctantly. "Prawn Cocktail Sauce. A new flavor?" I asked after noticing the open bag of crisps in front of him. "Are these guys with the military?" I asked Kelby while gesturing to the uniformed figures on the screens that were seated at control panels with their faces bathed in a cobalt-blue luminosity. "Like our Space Force?"

"There's not a lot of chest candy there. Mostly assets with science backgrounds carved out from an OUSDAT sub-set that doesn't have qualms about tinkering with ooparts. What's left from the original parent sponsor entity after the prochronism aspect upset many with orthodox religious beliefs. There were even suicides. My impression is that most of those involved wished the whole thing would just go away... that the antediluvian issue didn't exist. This room you see is tension charged because of its close proximity to the Leaper. They're worried about returning paradisers, even though none have come back since the cuboid was found. They're also on the watch for those with a terra-insecurity... adventurous types who are willing to have their flesh stripped from the bone," he said with a cryptic glance at his partner, "if there's anything to psychostasia as we understand the concept after finding something in the Oxyrhynchus garbage. Maybe the angels were charitable with their paradises. Anyone up for a game of leapfrog? But, things are being revamped now that we've been presented with your new friend. SAPCO is busy with a disinfo campaign in the event any of this tightly held stuff gets out. You've seen their handiwork. Ants building tiny pyramids, robotic deer zapping hunters and postcards sent from heaven − someone's inside joke about Ultra-1."

"But it's already out," I said, "in Siriana's... I mean, Zyla's video."

"They have to cover all the bases," Kelby shrugged.

"We've got a few tricks of our own," Dal said with a sly grin. "Testing face swaps with these fellows that exude a blue wetness. They've got to be convincing... perfect matches to our motion captures of you. Anything less would be a dead giveaway."

"So, then there's not really going to be free Fig Newtons when Jesus returns?" I joked.

""I could probably make that happen," Dal said, "using an old Sunday school picture. Have any of you read Francis Bacon's the *New Atlantis*? The part about false apparitions, impostors and illusions to make things seem miraculous."

While slipping through choppy waves in Zuffante's costly yacht tender, I noticed a dull greyish haze up ahead that had suddenly appeared out of nowhere. At first I didn't think much of this pop-up marine layer and continued full speed ahead towards the nearby island that I was headed to to pick up some equipment for Julian. It wasn't until the blue horizon disappeared into a milky white luminescence that I pushed back on the digital throttle of the twin V-8s in order to better assess the situation.

Leaning against the steering wheel, I could see that the ominous circular patch of what appeared to be a spiraling fog bank was rapidly expanding as it drew closer. As it continued to swiftly approach, some of the touch displays of the control panels started behaving erratically. Though I couldn't figure out what caused the instrument readouts to malfunction, knowing what stretch of the ocean I was in, I tried to laugh off thoughts about unexplained fogs and electronic drains.

As one by one the dash gauges winked out before both screens went black, I reached back to open the panel behind the seat cushions that contained the breaker switches. Behind me the sky was a postcard picturesque azure, though the water was unusually calm, almost deadly still. When I glanced back at the curved windshield I was shocked to see a sickly yellowish mist drifting over the carbon fiber hull before it rapidly enveloped the boat. When I couldn't see my legs in the thick, mustard-colored murk, the image of some grizzled angler finding a sumptuous ghost adrift flashed in my mind.

With both engines idling and poor visibility in all directions, I was startled as the hydraulic rubber tracks of the amphibious commuter automatically deployed seconds before I was shaken by a jarring thud. While bouncing in my seat, my first thought was that I had struck a sandbar. As I peered into the now stagnant calm of the eggnog funk that blotted out everything around me, inexplicably the hellish gloom quickly dissipated to reveal a long, narrow shoal that was surrounded by clear turquoise water.

When what at first appeared to be a discarded pile of clothing lying in the sand began to move, I realized a person was stirring on the exposed ridge where only a few hermit crabs scuttled about. As the square-set figure slowly stood up, he brushed the coarse sediment from the creases in his sunburnt forehead before scratching his balding pate. Despite the bronzed appearance of his haggard lineaments, his face looked vaguely familiar.

Dressed in a dark green waistcoat, a soiled linen collared shirt and baggy tan trousers that were rolled up to his knees, he hesitantly took a step forward with bulging eyes transfixed on the gleaming hull of the engineering marvel I was standing on.

"Blimey," he said with a croaky English accent, "I must 'ave had a good caulk, mustn't I, matey. What cunning tricks are these – a sloop lacking sails and cedar that when fast aground crawls upon the folde as able, allow one to presume, as she moves over water."

The peculiar vividity of this convincing pirate, along with the dreamlike aspect of the surroundings, was telling. Unlike previously, this time I understood what was happening.

"According to the sale brochure, the mobility system is powered by a lithium ion battery," I said. "What – no peg leg or eye patch? Not even an earring or parrot on the shoulder to maintain the illusion? You don't want to show yourself as you really are?"

"'Tis no conceit being marooned here," he said while fidgeting with a tin button on the dyed fustian cloth, "without even a tattered deck for solitaire. Aye, crimped for plunder by mine own comrades… hearties befitting as ruffians in any seamy punch-house."

"What do your comrades want from you?"

"Bethink oneself of the rhyme. Sing a Song of Sixpence, a bag full of rye, Four and Twenty Naughty Boys baked in a pye. And when the pye was opened... Savvy?"

"What do the others want – some who are my friends?"

"'Tis an appetency for Libertatia. Landlubbers be forewarned, portage to such a dreamt of colony shan't be coursed willy-nilly. Nay, heaven hardly falls without a faithful waggoner. Savvy?"

"You're saying such a place really exists?"

"Aye, tis an invented alternative engirded by prodigious means."

"How do you know this?"

"Perchance might ye have read Aristotle... how eels know where to make themselves? If fortune wishes it, one might make good with such brightwork," he said while gesturing to the shiny boat, "like eels that journey to the sea of floating weeds. Aye, fancy equipage to make fast from being harried by me vigilant guardians of this deep cerulean?"

"What can I do to help, my friend?"

"Speak narry a word, bucko... even to the likes of a bedazzled popinjay, Aye, matey, I like my chances... in good time... smartly from a quaggy trigon. Savvy?"

"Savvy," I said before poking the throttles until the engines roared. Cutting through the spectral display in the sun-flecked waves, I turned sharply and accelerated towards the island.

Late the following night I snuck into Zuffante's greenhouse to pick a few of those delicious pieces of fruit with the glossy bluish skin that were grown on espaliered trees. While heading back to my bungalow on the moonless night, I had some difficulty finding my way across the spacious lawn behind the darkened villa (maybe I should have worn my 'cereus' dress shirt) when I abruptly stepped into what might best be described as an enclosed zone of daylight.

In the direct sunlight of an ordinary day, I had wandered onto a putting green where Kelby was about to tap his ball into the hole. Wearing knee-length camo shorts and sporting two-tone golf shoes (instead of his trademark boots), he turned towards me with an annoyed look on his face.

Looking beyond the circumference of the green in all directions, I could only see an intense darkness. Somehow, none of the night passed through the plane of daylight, just as no trace of the 'sunshine' spilled outside the perimeter of the zone. Looking up towards the 'sky', from where I was standing, all I could see was a round expanse that was suffused with a 'daytime' bluish glimmer.

"No way, this is cray," I uttered. "I'm fucking wide awake."

"Affirmative, Jack, you're standing on a fast green on your way back from an all hours farmer's market. The separator is another invention smuggled out with the other thinkabouts. We just can't figure out how to filter out the nightly cacophony," he said with his scratchy voice raised over the nonstop shrill chirping of tree frogs.

"Since these Blurples don't contain Ultra-1-type DNA, I figured it wouldn't be a big whoop to see if I could use them for a specialty drink," I said with a sheepish grin.

"Just to be clear, I happen to know they check them all. But the ones from that yield are also duds, so any blended creation without genetic splicing will be our little secret."

"Did you ever consider what it knows – just knows like eels know where to go to spawn?"

"Ancestral memory – or nostophylia, a yearning for one's ancestral home? What it knows is what our occultist assets are trying to ascertain. It's their department," he said nonchalantly.

"The reason for asking is because you once said something about treachery."

"Subterfuge?"

"Yeah."

"There are two factions involved. One, I believe, is looking to use Ultra-1 as bait – a lure for a bigger catch. They want a reunion, so to speak, more so though with our loftier progenitors than humanity-plus. They hope to achieve this by returning certain personal belongings not meant to be tinkered with by meat vehicles. As I've said, the other side is disinclined to accept any pre-deluge remnants that aren't wattle and daub, and Ultra-1 is especially anathema. However, a deal has been struck. I've been hired to get Zuffante and company into the Leaper. To make this happen I need Callie's help, which reminds me, tomorrow you both have a lesson with the MagiZoths about the biometric iris lidded within the *Anunna* widget."

"I wonder what it looks like – Ultra-1's true form, don't you?"

"Because of its otherness, it presents a type of mirror, reflecting aspects of those around it. Whether celestial seraphic or grotesquely chthonic, the unfamiliarity will still be disturbing."

"And you really think we can pull this off?"

"I've a little device of theirs of my own that's literally a game changer. It might not turn one's adversary into a pillar of salt, but it works wonders when it comes to getting unfuckwithable types to reconsider their position."

"What type of Bermuda grass is that?" I asked to change the subject.

"Ultra-dwarf, of course."

When not garbed in their dark hooded robes, the couple that Kelby referred to as the MagiZoths looked like your average seniors. Casually dressed, both Addison and Patrice had pleasant faces with silver-grey hair – his thinning around bald spots and hers unwashed, long and straggly. I could easily picture them working in the garden, feeding bread crumbs to the birds or hunched over a crossword puzzle on a park bench – activities of the elderly that were far more typical than controlling phantasmal entities on spirit thrones or using magical techniques to explore uncharted regions of the human psyche. With rosy demeanors that were the direct opposite of the stereotypical (even cliché-ridden) image of hardcore occultists, I had to wonder if there was something more at play?

In contrast to their everyday looks, the furnishings in their cubbyhole beneath Felicity were reflective of their unconventional interests. A black glass electronic writing board mounted on the wall was filled with diagrams of cranial nerves that had zones extending from the human brain to illustrations of concepts involving a more subtle anatomy. Abstruse formulas scrawled with felt markers looked as challenging as advanced mathematical theorems or quantum physics equations. It was definitely the ponderings of a rarefied esoteric bent, and not those of an elderly pair feather-dusting one's Hummel figurines.

In a corner of the cluttered room there stood a battered antique Philco floor model tube radio.

"Does that thing work?" I asked.

"There was a time when we listened to Bach composing while testing a new organ," Addison replied. "That was just one of the layers of audio recovered from vibrations preserved in the surroundings. For some reason, while in the vicinity of the *Anunna* device, this floor model Philco plays back what's absorbed and extracted."

"You have the same device?" Callie asked.

"Used to," he said. "They might have been related to yours… or knew one another."

When he said this, I noticed a circular patch of skin on his left palm that didn't match the surrounding flesh, as if layers had been surgically removed and replaced by a graft.

"I'm getting woozy just looking at that stuff," Callie said while gesturing to the writing board as she slid a cherry sucker into her mouth.

"We've been eavesdropping on our whiz kid's thoughts. Patrice and I receive impressions from the unintelligible background noise that we're able to externalize. But we're not here to talk about the endogenous *Shamir* or pineal microcrystals."

As he spoke, once again I experienced a tingling sensation and feeling of being weighted down.

"There is no process we know of for organic release of the gift. No search algorithm or reasoning system that we understand."

"Not even vague hints," Patrice added, "from a lost source by some Ahmes scribe, but when the displays orbiting the device contain motifs that are predominately green, that's a good sign —"

"Just like a traffic light – where green signals go," Addison said.

"Gaze deeply into the liquidity of the un-lidded golden speckles," Patrice said with almost an incantatious tone. "With a focused projection of the sustained desire."

When she spoke in these simple terms, I also had a feeling that a more detailed set of instructions was being conveyed, with the more nebulous wording bypassing both Callie's and my waking consciousness and sinking like a weighted anchor into that which exists beyond some neurological veil.

"The process that facilitates the interface is self-activating once it gains your utmost trust. At which time the living eye will simply glide onto and into your palm as if by magic, resembling a tattoo, but one that's able to conceal itself subdermally at times."

At the same time as this suspected "double-talk", I could hear faint, tinny voices coming from the radio console that were the same as those I heard on a similar vintage model at the Sutton's estate sale.

"Grandpa, how come your star looked funny when it got bigger?" a squeaky little girl's voice asked over the crackling speakers.

"The doojiggy did that," was the nasally reply, "to show us something."

"Sometimes I don't like what it shows us," the girl said.

"Don't worry, sweetie, now it's back to just being a button."

"And the other stars will be back just like before?"

"Yes, want to see them?"

"If all else fails," I heard Patrice say, "try asking nicely."

Jeremy, Callie and I were seated in folding chairs around a cracking bonfire at our favorite hang. The water in the cove was glistening under a starry sky as I poured my latest work in progress cocktail from a thermos into a plastic cup that I handed to my friend.

"That slaps, Jack," he said after taking a gulp. "What are you going to call it?"

"Maybe Jack's Bermy Blurple."

"That's not a tongue twister," Callie laughed. "Either way people won't be able to order a second one."

"It tastes refreshing, but it's not perfected," I said. "Speaking of that, Jeremy, I hear you'll soon be on your way to the new Atlantis – the island hidden and unseen."

"If I'm admitted to the Stranger's House. You've heard what Kelby thinks – it's a simulated reality designed by humanity-plus."

"Only you can't just take it off like a VR-AR headset," I said. "You better hope there's also a Leaper on the other end so that your converted version – basic Atlantean model, or whatever semblance of Jeremy can push the panic button. Seriously, what if they stick regular people in a cage as an exhibit... like a zoo, like that empty-headed explorer did to that Congo Pygmy guy that's hanging on your wall?"

"It's my choice to go, Jack. That's the difference. I'm not being forced against my will. Kelby said that those people in the tanks – the paradisers – weren't left behind when humanity-plus bolted. They were their finely tuned representatives... go-betweens with the higher-ups, Jack. They still had enhanced genetics – were a notch higher than us ordinary folk, so there's no telling what they know... and could teach us."

"You better also hope they have simulated sugary pies, Pye."

"There's no biology involved. I'll be chilling in the fixtures... in a tank in the on-pause state."

"Yeah, hibernating," Callie said.

"You wouldn't go, would you?" I asked her.

"I don't know. Kicking back where angels breathe might be extra."

"Don't ask me to put a lit Vogue Perle Menthe in your mouth while you're in suspended animation."

"I mean is it really any different from a good dream?" she asked. "A long one, like binge-watching a good Netflix series?"

"Butterfly or Zhuangzi? Jeremy laughed.

"I'd swerve, bruh – there are no receipts."

"In the *New Atlantis* it said a few returned," Jeremy noted, "though their stories weren't believed. They were taken for a dream."

"Yeah, the baseless fabric of a vision," I responded, "like Willy or Bacon or some dude wearing a frilly lace bib once wrote."

"Just think what they might know," Jeremy repeated. "Answers to life's mysteries... There are all kinds of things they could pass on to those of us a little slower on the uptake."

"Like Kelby warned," I said, "what's to their liking could be a maximum sensory overload to us," I said. "Zuffante's bored, Zyla's part of the Ultra-1 package, but you don't need that kind of brain crush."

After saying this I saw an indistinct figure approaching silently through the seaside shrubs. I hoped it wasn't Kelby coming to reprimand us for discussing the plan, or, even worse, his ex-Task-Force Black associate, whatever the fuck his name was.

"Who's ready for an ice cold Beale's Gold lager direct from Bedford," a familiar voice rang out over the chorus of whistling frogs. To my relief, the shimmery copper hue of the face shining back the rippling flame patterns was that of my friend Baldy. Wearing beach shorts, he was carrying a portable cooler.

"I was told I'd find you here," he said. "They put me in a bungalow next to yours. So, what's this about you acting in our film?"

"It's just a bit part. We all play divers. You know how hard it is to find divers in Bermuda," I joked. "This is my friend Jeremy... and Callie."

"Hello, Jeremy. I've met the young lady – on a cabin cruiser when I was being questioned about the tech advisor gig. How are the finds on this isle? Anything unusual turn up?"

Zuffante's yacht *Azuria* was anchored in the slow rolling swells near the western fringes of the Sargasso Sea. As a small film crew set up equipment for a shot in which a nearby cabin cruiser was to be exploded by pyrotechnics specialists, Jeremy, Callie and I were watching the camera operators preparing to capture this from the afterdeck. Also eyeing them was Julian, wearing a bright cardigan sweater and purple chinos with kneepads.

"Rather than a gyro-stabilized steadycam with its two-axis mode, we've got two handheld Aaton 35's without splash deflectors," he said while cutting pieces of a chamois into small pieces and putting them into a ziplock bag. "Which is why the film's fucking director is busy making lens swabs. Let's hope one of them remembered to bring a polarizing filter to minimize the glare. This isn't exactly a shoestring budget," he shrugged. "A tough water shoot and we've got more Dramamine than camera equipment. I guess if the horizon goes all over the place without the hydro-gyro stabilizing gizmo, we rely on the model in the swimming pool. Maybe my smartphone wide angle will keep the SFX hotshot from tearing me a new one."

"I'm sure it will look great," Callie said, "once it's all put together."

"The gyre?" Julian asked while pulling out a bottle of imported sparkling lemonade from an ice chest. "Yeah, I can't wait too see what we've got once the algal mat and volumetric fog are implemented – our non-articulated mannequins staring at all the clumps of sargassum. I guess they're paralyzed with fear after finding themselves stuck in the Hoodoo Sea, which is why there's no specialized action from our silicon crew."

When I was shown images of the vast blanket of Sargassum seaweed that floated within the Bermuda Triangle area – the algal gyre that he was referring to – it brought to mind the invasive honeysuckle vines that haunted Grumble's sleep.

"What have you got there?" I asked.

"It's that *limonata* you picked up the other day. I heard about your razzmatastic drink, but this is made with Sicilian lemons. There's no alcohol in it, natch. Why don't you guys give it a taste," he said while fishing out three bottles from the ice.

"As long as it's not Peaden, I'll take one," Jeremy said while shooting me a quick smile.

As I continued to watch the activity of the various units, I noticed that Callie kept looking at her left palm. Even though she had been assured by the MagiZoths that the biometric eye 'tattoo' had made the transition from its housing (within the *Anunna* device) and was now concealed beneath her skin, she still had concerns due to it being totally invisible. I was also apprehensive about what was about to happen. Kelby had repeatedly warned us that the experience would be overwhelming, and each time he went through the list of dos and don'ts, I left the meeting with a tight feeling in my stomach. Of the three of us, only Jeremy didn't appear to be nervous after being drilled on these matters, which I thought was odd considering that he had the most to fear.

I still didn't get how things had gotten to this point. Why the three of us were chosen, presumably by Ultra-1, to be what Kelby called "ambassadors of humankind" (was he joking?). The best I could figure, Callie's connection was the *Anunna* device and

Jeremy might have inadvertently made contact with it through his "vudutronics" with its Afro-Atlantean roots.

But why had a hyper-tellurian being befriended me? Addison had recently told me he suspected that I had possessed the futuristic widget during a brief period when Callie had unknowingly hidden it somewhere after receiving a subconscious message to do so. If this actually happened, I had no memory of it.

Looking at the empty Iguana tender attached by towlines a couple of boats lengths from the *Azuria*, I wished the entire scheme would be called off and the three of us could just board the commuter and head full throttle back to the island.

Seeing Kelby making his way to the aft deck, I knew the time had finally come. When he reached us, after nodding hello to Julian (who was still cutting rags, oblivious to the ruse), he gathered us into a huddle.

"It's time to change into your costumes. And, Callie, keep in mind these people don't have a child's lollipop in their mouth while on duty. Ditch it."

A half-hour after we entered the spacious dining cabin, the four of us were dressed in crisp dark uniforms with the rank epaulets and unique insignias of what we referred to as the Silent Service.

"Where are the shoes that were issued with your service dress, Atkins?" Kelby bellowed after seeing the black penny loafers I was wearing.

"They were boats – way to big for my feet," I said. "Lucky I found these things or I'd be wearing my more comfy ones."

"Okay, Dal with ULTRAFX can take care of that detail. He has their issued steps in his render inventory… but it's still a snafu and I don't like – "

"Snafus," the three of us said in unison.

Once dressed to his satisfaction, Kelby handed each of us a Garmin inReach mini satellite communication device.

"This is your lifeline," he stressed. "You can use it to send text messages. Okay, folks, the submersible is in the exclusion zone and the NOAA forecast is favorable, meaning we're a go for this operation."

Shortly later there was a knock on the door. Opening it, Kelby let five figures into the room. All (including one female) were dressed in uniforms like those we had on. I recognized the highest ranked member as the guy who once gave me a stern warning after glimpsing something I wasn't supposed to see. As with the others, there was a serious expression on his face, though when he saw me, this time there was no menacing scowl.

"Lunch is served," Kelby said while gesturing to an eloquent dark wood table that was laden with food and drinks. As four of them walked over to the spread, we followed the commander out onto the deck.

As salty ocean breezes tingled our faces, we continued to one of the yacht's boarding areas where I could see a special-ops delivery vehicle pitching slightly in a the creamy wavelets below. Its overall shape and dark emerald color was similar to the mini-subs I'd seen beached at *Zirn*, though the frame was longer and wider to accommodate a larger crew. The name ATYAN-TICA was painted in white cursive script on the side. This was the dry combat submersible that would take us into the "belly of the whale", as some called the mysterious cuboid.

Using the *Azuria's* 'beach club' – a dropdown platform with a swim ladder – we carefully transitioned onto the sleek watercraft by grabbing hold of secure points.

On the way to our destination we listened to Beethoven's cantata, "Calm Sea and Prosperous Voyage." For reasons that weren't explained, all of the viewing ports had been covered, most likely to conceal something which I guessed was the whispered "Oceanus Trail", this being a code-word for an underwater tunnel that might explain the abrupt change in the sub's movements towards the end of the short journey.

Upon exiting the docked craft to the smell of diesel fumes, we found ourselves in a facility where more submersibles were tied to mooring pilings. In the dim glimmer of industrial lighting fixtures, I could make out launching bays for autonomous security shuttlecraft, pontoon boats for transferring cargo (how did they surface?), loading cranes and storage tanks. Nothing about the place seemed too far out of the ordinary, and we were told that it was constructed in more recent years as a protective structure. The one curiosity was a bulky shape under a canvas tarp on a ramp between the steel dolphins. When I got closer to it, I noticed green cloisonné hubcaps like those on the hot rod hearse. While running my fingers over the covered contours, it became obvious they had transported the meat wagon to the base from Zuffante's heliport on the island.

As the officer headed off somewhere, Kelby gathered us together and put his hands on Callie's shoulders:

"As I've said a dozen times, we'll be taking the back way where there's no security personnel... well, until we arrive, that is... granted your friend's shit works. Once inside, try not to gawk too much. The sedatives should help. The walls have ears, but you can talk. We're piping in our own audio. Remember the two-way texting. If things go according to plan, you'll both soon be back at the cove sipping those Blurmy Berples – damn, that's a mouthful, Jack. Now, straighten those lapel insignias and take a deep breath before we pass through our first black whoosh."

After taking a few steps forward, a luminous black dot appeared out of nowhere and, sensing our approach, rapidly expanded into an elliptical shape that we had been told was a door. Though I couldn't see anything on the other side, Kelby stepped into the darkness and disappeared from view. Having witnessed a similar effect at Zuffante's putting green, I followed him into the glossy void without the look of concern seen on Callie's face.

Once on the other side, my first instinct was to look back, but when I did there was only an oval of liquid blackness. Turning my head forward, I could see that I was standing firmly on an invisible surface inside an expansive chamber with a sloped, latticed metallic ceiling. The room was suffused with gorgeous cobalt-blue lighting that, while subdued, still radiated with a palpable intensity. The aseptic vanilla smell of the place called to mind the dress shirt that Kelby was wearing the first time I saw him.

Soon Callie and Jeremy emerged from the inky portal, both appearing to be in awe of the baffling lighting trick.

Glancing to my left and right, I saw several clear exosuits attached to 'something', though none of the contoured shells were equipped with instrument panels (and colorful readouts) like the one on the beach that the hibernating albino woman was encased in.

Without warning, our bodies began floating straight ahead. Seconds later we were gliding above the curved, silver-toned walls of a spacious lower level that was filled with perplexing machinery. While perfectly balanced, a powerful current inside an imperceptible sealed tube that was similar to a wind tunnel was propelling us forward at a non-alarming speed. At one point, Kelby pulled out a glowing green golf ball and tossed it to his right. Once in the air, it shot off at an incredible velocity before vanishing behind a sharp bend. A moment later, he repeated this with another high visibility ball whose flight path had a similar result. After seeing this little demonstration, I understood the reason for the protective sheathing.

As we continued to be impelled forward in the tingling zeph-yr, a luminous red dot dilated at eye-level, followed by a eupho-nious sub-vocal voice that I didn't understand. When our bodies gently braked to a complete stop, from the corner of my eye I caught sight of a variegated mass swiftly approaching to our right. As the confusing jumble decelerated, it turned out to be a bizarre assemblage that slowly floated by in single file.

The parade was led by a vintage Raggedy Ann doll in a red and white plaid dress with knickers. Close behind this was a dead (though well preserved) U-Boat officer wearing a fresh-ly laundered Kriegsmarine uniform and white visor cap. Next came a pudgy seaman in a leather jerkin and baggy breeches, who was closely followed (being chased?) by a slender Galapagos shark. Finally, sandwiched between a couple of Silent Service personnel, whose bloated profiles showed smudged blue streaks, was a Chief Steward in the Royal Navy dressed in a 1940s jack-et, though wearing boxer shorts instead of his uniform pants. Having crossed the intersection, the figures rapidly accelerated until their shapes became a varicolored blur that vanished from my sight.

"This is called Slocum's Carousel," Kelby said, "though I didn't see Joshua in that group. We don't know how they wound up in the hyperloop, but all – including the reef shark – missed their exit and died from lethal acceleration... so one hopes."

Once again there was a pulling sensation, and seconds later we were gliding in the invisible corridor, whose tubular shape periodically appeared to have a pellucid silvery sheen. After a minute or so we braked again. Without any effort on our part, our hovering bodies rotated as each of us was placed above a black circle. Before I could ask Kelby what was happening, I felt a prickly surge. I heard Callie shriek as we simultaneously shot upward with a rapidity that was lightning-fast, my body feeling as if it was tightly enclosed in some unseen casing.

When I popped out of an opening at the same instant as the others, I felt disoriented by the sudden transition onto an expanse of manicured greenery that seemed to be strangely aglow. Glancing about, we appeared to be inside a massive terrarium, whose sculpted vegetation glimmered with curious shades like some enchanted garden. Following a winding path of softly lit paving squares, we proceeded deeper into the virescent chimeras, breathing in the riotous delights.

As we continued through the maze of leafy wonders, trying not to be distracted by the faintly swirling patterns on the ornamental pavers, we paused at the sight of a bare-chested man with a sinewy frame in loud Bermuda shorts. He was drinking a can of Pabst Blue Ribbon while seated in a tattered lawn chair under a pedestalled globe teeming with lucent botanical enigmas.

"Howdy, folks," he said. "I don't see many people enjoying the park... if you can call it that. Those elevators are real doozies, aren't they?"

"We've just been assigned to the facility," Kelby said, remaining cautious despite the fellow's meek demeanor. "This is part of the tour we were told to take, but we don't have time to admire funny plants grown by some space-age gods."

"That's too bad," he said while running his finger through the sparse wisps of dark hair on his scalp. "If you could bottle the perfume from some you'd never go to the Macy's counter again, ma'am."

"See you around," Kelby said with a strained smile while motioning for us to move along.

"Pork chops tonight in the cafeteria," the man burped. "You'll get used to their blue tint."

When I glanced back at him, I saw that he was holding a small object that looked like a flat grey rod ringed with metal bands. Seeing my puzzled look, he nodded before taking another gulp of beer.

When we reached another mounted sphere filled with pulsing fluorescent growth, Kelby paused by the virid spectacle:

"Why do I feel like we just walked into a trap? That wasn't good. No chow hall and he didn't even salute."

He's probably just a maintenance guy," Jeremy said while making a dismissive gesture, "Like you told us, security personnel don't come to the boonies, even on time off."

As I was about to ask Kelby what we were waiting for, another black dot appeared near the path edging and quickly extended into an oval shape large enough for us to step into. When we passed through it, in a flash, we found ourselves in a stunning tubular corridor. The gently throbbing walls appeared as streams of eddying azure, and on either side of the rippling textures, puzzling furnishings continually shifted colors that blended together with an aesthetically pleasing conformity.

There was a melliferous drone in my ears as we proceeded along the metallic glass flooring. It wasn't long before I noticed Jeremy making what appeared to be discreet gestures with his fingers at the undulating abstract patterns on the walls. Thinking these might be coded signals of some type, I thought I should bring it to Kelby's attention.

"Don't get mad, but I need to take a leak."

"Okay, stay put," Kelby said to the others, "while I show Atkins a public convenience with a pisser that has a higher I.Q. than this little group does collectively."

With a swipe of his hand, he peeled back an invisibility cloak like flipping the page of a magazine.

"What – do you want me to take your hand?" he said with an irritated look on his face as I stared at the entrance to what I assumed was a high-tech lavatory.

"Okay, I'll show you, Jack."

The interior of the bathroom contained fixtures molded from some gleaming metallic material that radiated a soothing cobalt-blue glow. It was devoid of vanities or mirrors, at least any that I could perceive. As Kelby was about to leave, I grabbed his arm.

"I don't know – maybe he's having a low sugar attack – but Jeremy's acting funny. Been doing something with his fingers that might be Morse code or another sign system. Also, that guy back there had a weird device."

"Did it look like this?" Kelby asked while pulling out an object that resembled the grey rod striped with bands of metal. Only, this one had a curved handle with a postage stamp-sized touch-screen on the grip that displayed heliotrope fluctuations.

"Yeah, the part I could see."

"Damn, Jeremy might have been shot."

"What are you talking about? There's no blood."

"That's not how their weapons work. There's no physical trauma involved. They cause changes in the brain. Simply put – once shot, suddenly the enemy switches sides. See eye to eye with their adversary, meaning Jeremy might now be sympathetic to someone else's cause… hence, the finger dancing. That's how I got our friend who brought us here to cooperate. Shot him in the back of the head without a trace of pink mist. Thing adds a strange kink to committing suicide"

"So, what are we going to do?"

"I've only got one shot left, and I was saving it for an emergency, but maybe that's what we've got," he said as a photo of Jeremy appeared on the small visual display.

"Jeez, is there one of me in that thing?"

"Of course, with a stupid grin on your mug. Okay, I'll text my guy to see about any funny business. If he confirms, I'll take care of it. If not, I hope you brought some packaged sweets."

"Another thing I should tell you," I said, "if something bad goes down, know that I've got Callie's little friend in my pocket."

"If I get word of a problem with Jeremy, with my signal, distract him for a second and I'll engage. He'll never know what hit him... literally. We'll see if he comes back around to our side. Let's just hope the damage hasn't already been done and we have to abort."

When we returned to the hallway, after a minute or so, Kelby dropped back from his normal spot in the lead, which, I presumed, was to slip behind Jeremy in order to get off a shot with his device.

Moments later we reached the meeting place where the Silent Service officer from earlier was pacing in front of an ancient Greek fountain built of rough stones that had niches containing bronze statues of nymphs, Tritons, and heroes. The water was clear as glass and filled with thousands of coins from all over world. On the surface someone had placed a plastic toy dinghy with a decal at the rear that read:

SMALL CHANGE

"You're late," he said in a calm tone.

"Nature call," Kelby replied.

"Miss Cantrell and Mister Zuffante are inside getting ready with help from the violet-eyed things. He should be, too," the man said while glancing at Jeremy, "if he's still willing to take the place of our illustrious guest."

"Are we going to get to see it?" Callie asked.

"I'm afraid it has other ideas," the man replied, "though there are those who don't know this. This is our secret... for the time being."

"Maybe it doesn't like the idea of being used as a pawn," I said.

"That's quite possible," the man nodded. "Now, I must ask for the widget, which was our deal."

"Before we enter the room?" Kelby asked.

"Yes, I'd prefer it that way."

"Does he have to give it to you? Callie asked, almost pleadingly. "It's mine, and it won't do things with other people −"

"It belongs to someone else, miss. You were its temporary guardian. Mister Zuffante has signed papers and documents for you that are back at Zirn. You'll be quite comfortable. All you have to do is hold up your palm."

"What if I were to toss it into the fountain and make a wish?" I said with a serious look. "Talk about a needle in a haystack, and the needle is mimicking the hay −"

"That wouldn't be a good idea," the man said in a flat voice.

"Yeah, I can see why someone wants it so badly," I said. "Wants all of them to be confiscated. Who knows what their lenses captured over time. Things that might surprise people... even certain events in history that would come as a shock. Challenge their beliefs.... their faith. Best thing would be to bury it. Bury it deep. Take the fucker... here, take it," I uttered while pulling the disc out of my pocket and handing it to him.

"What's this − a trimmed bottle cap?" he laughed while examining the thing. "*Limonata*?"

"It's just playing possum − like the others did," Kelby said. "I hoped it would stop putting up a fight and come willingly, but the bond formed with the girl is strong. It's the real deal. My word's good."

"I'm sure it is," he said while placing it inside a miniature black safe that was no bigger than a wedding ring box. "After all, we're all on the same team. Okay, let's go."

After stepping into yet another ellipse that looked like lustrous pitch, we emerged into a cube-like room whose scintillating white floor, walls and ceiling were completely bare.

Feeling both claustrophobic and apprehensive, I shielded my eyes in the almost blinding whiteness.

Without warning the room became inundated with water to the extent that it was completely filled in an instant. As my body ascended in a stream of bubbles, I flayed my arms in a state of panic. Seeing Kelby's calm response, it took a moment before I figured out that what felt like cool water was actually a blue, fluid-like light. Once I adjusted to this (realizing I had no difficulty breathing), the medium was exhilarating to be afloat in.

Reaching for Callie's hand, I heard thrilling whispers that caused me to glance about. There was a flash of motion a second before I found myself face to face with a visage of mysterious beauty. Sprawling, dazzlingly white hair gloriously framed a pale countenance with delicate lineaments, the most striking of which were oddly slanted eyes like speckled golden jewels. The marvelous complexity of a silver-green skin-suit shone with myriads of tinted reflections that was befitting of the dulcet song-wail that issued from pouty, sirenic lips. As I raised my hand to touch the exotic physiognomy, in the blink of an eye, the beguiling presence and cerulean luminosity of the simulation went blank, leaving me standing on the floor in the stark white room along with the others.

"How about that," Kelby said. "A glitch during a preview. This place needs work."

"Any thoughts about turning back, bruh?" I asked Jeremy while touching my uniform to see if the material was dry.

"No, I'm ready for this, Jack. You have my letters and shit just in case."

When the cube disassembled itself in a most extraordinary way, we were standing in what Kelby called the preparation room for the transporter. With movements that were perfectly in sync, a couple of figures approached Jeremy. Both had faces like pliable alabaster, with sharply delineated features that included disturbing violet-colored eyes. Wearing rectilinear mauve suits that emitted a faint glow, the bendable robotic attendants dutifully led our friend away.

As I watched their keenly attentive actions, I saw rows of translucent hibernation tanks in which indistinct figures could be seen floating in an electric blue solution.

When another android with an inscrutable expression showed up in a similar boxy abstraction, I followed Kelby and Callie part of the way to the access point where she was to do her 'open sesame' bit with the biometric tattoo concealed in her palm.

On the way I noticed several objects strewn on the floor as a result of members of the Silent Service raiding the hyper-technical storage lockers of the paradisers. Though I couldn't tell an *orichalcum* gum wrapper from the fuel cell of a spaceliner, seeing these valuable leavings brought to mind the grave goods of the ancients – how everyday objects were placed in the tomb as provisions for the deceased in the afterlife. As was the process of mummification itself, this mimicking was most likely a corruption of a select few seeing (or hearing tales about) those personal belongings inside storage bins for the "leapers" upon their return from an extended simulated reality.

Among the scattered items were what appeared to be several identical 'rushing streams' about a foot in length and two inches wide. These made me think about a modern infinity pool whose water is pumped back, though I couldn't fathom the reason for this in a miniature version of a surging current.

There was also a spilled container with some sparkling bits that looked like lozenges of frozen fire. The most fascinating piece among some moving shapes was a silver necklace on which a realistic-looking (!) tiny, prismatic dolphin performed a series of acrobatic tricks. Though Callie would love to wear this, I didn't want to take any chances (besides, how often did it make those clicking sounds?).

When Callie returned, the officer indicated that we should follow him:

"The *Atyantica* is waiting to take us back to Zuffante's yacht."

"I said goodbye to Rex, and Zyla... and to Jeremy," Callie said while checking the skin on her palm to see if there was any trace of the glistening fixity of the subdermal iris.

As the swim platform was lowered for the officer, Callie and myself to board the *Azuria* from the delivery vehicle, Baldy was waiting for us in the salty gusts.

"I thought you guys were playing divers? Man, did you see the boat explode? Just before the pyrotechnics were set off, the film crew saw some strange being on board."

"It was probably just a dummy placed there for laughs," I said. "With a fish monster mask."

"No, this thing was moving. Julian has footage of it. There's lots of detail – enough to excite any monster junkie. Doesn't look like latex. Whatever it was, there's been no trace of it among the debris in the water."

"Julian's got receipts?" I asked.

"Yeah, he thinks it's going to make the film epic. Hey, where's your friend, Jeremy?"

Callie and I watched from the Commuter as the Silent Service officer and four uniformed figures transferred to the *Atyantica*. Having just released the tender from its secure mooring, I was about to head back to the island.

"You've got to give props to Kelby for pulling that off. If I had a Hog Penny, I'd bet Ultra-1 fooled them all, too."

"But, you *do* have one," Callie laughed while pointing to one of my borrowed loafers. "Look, it's right there in your shoe."

"Yeah, for all his attention to detail, I wonder if Kelby noticed it? He probably did, but didn't say anything because he appreciated the others being duped."

A confused look came over her face as she removed the cherry sucker from her mouth.

Her eyes widened.

"Is that what I think it is?"

"What do you think it is?" I asked with a devilish grin.

"You gave that man – a real bottle cap!"

"I wasn't worried, lad," Mogwan said while seated at the bar stirring his tea. "Not with the contingency plan involving the – what do they call them, oh, yes – renders of one of the pod-vehicles should a real one be needed for your safe return. As for Jeremy, everything seems in order, with those that monitor the area being under the impression he's a lady paradiser... though one that looks uncannily like the one that was secretly set-free into the wilds, one might say. Kelby, Addison and Patrice told me about this couple of betweeners that returned from their thousands of years of holiday in a simulation and found suitable innershine in a small town in the U.S.A. back in the 1950s, I believe it was. A certain Mister Schaufler and his partner whose name escapes me. If the Silent Service chaps can't find Ultra-1, and assume it fled, only to die tragically while boarding the wrong boat, well, there'll be no reason for them to pay the young lady a visit. Listen to me going on – I sound like one tying up loose ends to a work of fiction. The question is," he said after slurping his tea, "would the Good Pens deem such a tale probable to play on a stage?"

"They did... didn't they?" I replied.

While hanging out in Callie's treehouse condo, I watched intently as one of those large cockroaches crawled across a wooden shelf where I had recently placed an object that looked like a dark drink coaster. It was the first one to approach the thing, whose surface looked like a darkly glowing whirlpool that was fascinating to observe. When my relentless foe with its quivering antennas ventured onto this spiraling pattern, as if sucked into a vacuum, instantly it vanished without a trace. *Why didn't the lighthole swallow me?* I had touched the mystifying swirls numerous times to see what might happen. After witnessing the pest's startling departure, I had mixed feelings. However, unlike the copy of Bacon's *New Atlantis* that I purchased by deceptive means, I couldn't return this find.

When I returned to the kitchen table, where I had been flipping through the pages of emblems in Jeremy's old book, Callie walked out of the bedroom.

"Isn't that Jeremy's book with the spinner thingy?" she asked.

"Want to try your luck?"

"Really? I don't know? My mother used to play with it. It's a wonder it's not broken."

"Come on, close your eyes and turn the wheel. Stop when it feels right."

Rolling her eyes, she placed her finger on the paper spinner and rotated it for a few seconds.

"Let's read your fortune," I said.

"You read it – I'll listen."

"Great, so I have to read the funny words."

"It was your idea."

"Okay, here goes…

> Now, some good counsel, thou doft need;
> Of what we say, take, therefore heed:
> Beware, lest thou, too much, offend
> A meek, and, gentle-natured friend.
> Though power thou haft, be careful too,
> Thou vex not, long, thine able foe
> And e're thou love, be sure to find
> Thy match, in manner, and in mind.
> If thou demand a reason why,
> To thee, thine emblem will reply.

It tells us to see emblem thirty-four… and the key-phrase says…

When two agree in their desire,
One spark will set them both on fire.

"That's sweet, Jack," she said while ruffling my hair.

"That's bibliomancy."

"Hearing that makes me want some Isle of Pines time. But, what I came out to tell you is about tonight."

"Tonight?"

"Let's play my game."

"There it is," Callie uttered excitedly over the monotonous screeching of tree frogs. Jumping up from the beach blanket, she pointed to something in the starry night sky. "Do you see it, Jack? It doesn't look like the other blinkers, does it?"

"Keep concentrating," I said while scanning the glittering infinity until I found a point of light that was brighter than the others, but wasn't twinkling.

"That's weird," I mumbled while watching whatever it was quickly increase in size and intensity. It was as if we were somehow zooming into the thing. What did Francis Bacon say about making feigned distances?

"Yeah, but what's it doing?" Callie asked with a perplexed tone.

When I stood up I saw a lit cigarette fall from her dazed expression and land next to a sandy flip-flop.

"Jack," she whispered with a gaping stare, "what IS that?"

The piercing chirps of the frogs ceased.

"Should we wave at Jeremy?" she asked with a giddy nervousness while reaching for my hand.

Looking up, I was startled by the enormity of the thing. It appeared to be a sharply focused projection of a geometric design whose contours had a subdued glow. From a techno-centric prospective, it looked like a vectored futuristic logo – a lambent, steely blue symbol hanging silently over the gently swishing waves.

"I never would have imagined," I laughed, "that Grumble's Star would turn out to be a company logo… maybe, the trademark symbol for the *Anunna* device."

"That can't be true," Callie said.

"Like what first comes up when you reboot your phone. Hold on…now, it's doing something else – there's more to this thing."

As the silvery design began to fragment into various interlinked sections, each generating additional enigmatic symbols, the spherical object with the bio-florescent sheen and wing-like appendages we'd seen before passed silently beneath it, causing the reshaping configuration to wink out and the shrill chorus of frogs to resume.

"There's that flying Twizy again," Callie uttered. "What's it got to do with this?"

Shortly before dawn, unable to sleep due to racing thoughts, I climbed out of bed, being careful not to wake Callie.

Soon I was on an unmarked hiking trail, retracing my steps from the first time I saw the glowing orb floating majestically over a rock formation. Having made my way through dense vegetation and the mist-enshrouded inland salt marsh, upon reaching an overgrown field, I could make out the dark outlines of prefab storage sheds and Quonset huts with bluish undertones. I could also see the flashing lights of Zuffante's private helipad.

As I thought might be the case, parked within the spaced green beacons was the hot rod hearse.

Peering through the windows of the souped-up funeral coach, it wasn't until I pressed my face against the narrow pane in the side service door that I realized something was different. It was the wooden coffin that had been placed there for decorative purposes. Seeing that its lid was wide open added to my suspicion that the aquatic creature seen on the cabin cruiser was a ruse.

Tingles ran down my spine knowing *it* was somewhere on the island.

The sun was coming up as I headed back. On the way, every orange flicker seen through the silhouettes of foliage spray was unnerving, as was the flitting of plovers between the blurred shapes of spreading cedars and scurrying of Bermuda skinks across jagged rocks.

Fatigued from hiking, briny lashes from the shallow water beach didn't keep me from yawning as I walked across the damp pink sand.

While lying down on my blanket from last night, I gazed out at the clear turquoise water. In the sequined gleams someone was heading out on a dinghy. I didn't give it a thought until I noticed the name painted beneath the transom:

SMALL CHANGE

When I shouted out, the person wearing a casual bucket hat and colorful tee turned back.

There were no more hazy portrayals. No concealing of the disturbing reality behind the scenery. It took a second for my brain to assimilate features that extended beyond subtle distinctions, but once processed (as coherently as possible), in that instant I saw in shocking detail – as if viewed through an invisible magnifying circle – a transhuman possibility whose organic artistry was not yet meant to be absorbed by human eyes. Of the radiant pigment and peculiar fragility of its visage no description I could share would adequately convey the masterwork of nature (?) that peered back at me with an empathetic gaze. This, along with its intensely exquisite beauty made me feel dirty and ashamed, to such a degree that my curious response was to quickly suppress the glorious abstraction into a faint penciling before this, too, was mentally erased and substituted by a blank, detached oblivion lulled by the mewing of seabirds over the soothing rhythm of the tide.

My eyes twitched as the dark mask of our Siamese cat rubbed against my face.

ABOUT THE AUTHOR

Grumble's Star is the third novel in a trilogy by **Blair MacKenzie Blake**, with the first book entitled *The Othering* (2018), followed by *The Paragon Junk* (2020). Other works include *Ijynx* (a collection of occult prose-poems), *The Wickedest Books In The World – Confessions Of An Aleister Crowley Bibliophile* (issued in three impressions), *The Curious Diary Entries Of Verity Pennington* (a short story), and *Remember The Future* (of which he is the co-author). He has contributed essays to ten volumes of the anthology *Darklore* (Daily Grail Publishing), as well as to numerous esoteric-themed magazines, including *The CoSM Journal, Sub Rosa, Silkmilk* and *Dagobert's Revenge*. For over 22 years, BMB has been the writer/content manager for www.toolband.com and www.dannycarey.com. He currently resides in Las Vegas, NV.